The
END
of an
ERROR

Books by Mameve Medwed

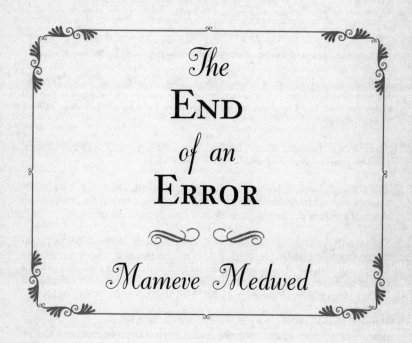

The
END
of an
ERROR

Mameve Medwed

AVON

An Imprint of HarperCollins*Publishers*

The Warner Books hardcover edition contains the following Library of Congress Cataloging-in-Publication Data

Medwed, Mameve.
   The end of an error / Mameve Medwed.
      p. cm.
   1. Women—Maine—Fiction. 2. Americans—England—Fiction. 3. Historians' spouses—Fiction. 4. Married women—Fiction. 5. First loves—Fiction. 6. England—Fiction. I. Title.
PS3563.E275 E53 2003
813'.54—dc21   2002033848

ISBN 978-0-06-133535-8

08 09 10 11 12 WBC/RRD 10 9 8 7 6 5 4 3 2

For John Aherne, *rara avis*

The
END
of an
ERROR

One

❧ ❧

Lee spots the package just as she turns into her driveway. She leaves the car running, the door open, the ignition pinging. She leaves the toilet paper and two percent milk, the previously frozen shrimp, the half gallon of Heath Bar Crunch, the mesclun mix, and four not-yet-ripe tomatoes imported from Holland on the baking vinyl seat. It's late March. After three weeks of rain and one freak snowstorm, the sun blazes. And there, slumping against her front step in its quilted manila sack, lies Lee's actual, palpable, three-dimensional book.

The first thing she notices: *Book Rate* Magic Markered all over it with a dollar's worth of last year's stamps patched along the top. And a postage-due Post-it, whose penciled-in four cents has been crossed out and signed *I paid, Pete Goodreau, mail carrier.* Shouldn't such a package have sped from the printer's in a brown UPS or white, orange, and purple FedEx chariot? Shouldn't it have flown in on the wings of a full-bodied jet? Not seven-days book rate with four cents owed. She shudders. What if Pete Goodreau hadn't anted up the pennies? What if the package had been tossed into the bushes? What if the cleaning lady had shoved it in the coal scuttle beneath four seasons of L. L. Bean catalogues? *What if, what if* could be the motto for her whole life. She stops herself.

She picks it up. It's the size of one of those journals of American history that Ben seems to receive on the hour. *Log a Rhythms: New England Lumber Industry Quarterly, The Thoreauvian Society Bulletin, Past Perfect Newsletter in Ethnography, Acadia Review* are all stacked on the table in the front hall. Hundreds of pages of dense print and inserted sheaves of maps. In contrast, her own package is light. But then again she didn't expect a *tome*.

She opens the door, kicks away the letters paving the floor behind it. She spies an envelope in Johnny's handwriting with *Photos: Don't Bend* and a margin of Japanese characters trellised up one side. Her heart lifts.

But first she goes back to the car, turns it off, unloads the groceries. In the kitchen she puts everything away. She runs water into the kettle, changes her mind and pours it out. Inside the refrigerator door stands a corked half-empty bottle of Vernaccia that she and Ben opened last night to mask the rubbery linguini. After a sip, Ben had set down his glass. "I'm pooped," he sighed. "I don't know when I've been so wiped out." And pleading an early class had gone to bed before nine. Lee had finished his wine and two more glasses, then stayed up until midnight flicking the remote between a panel of critics on Book TV and a rerun of *Brief Encounter* on the Movie Channel. When, at last, Celia Johnson forsook Trevor Howard to return to her husband, Lee staggered up the stairs, eyes filled, nose stuffed as if this had been the first time, not the thirty-first, in which she had witnessed these lovers part. In bed, Ben was snoring. He'd pulled all the covers over to his side; one hand was draped on her pillow; one foot stretched across her nightgown folded on the mattress's edge. His toenails needed clipping.

Now, upstairs she hears Ben pacing. His classes were over at noon today and he's back working on Nathaniel. Ever since he discovered, more than fifteen years ago, a few diary pages in the Hannibal Hamlin College Library written in Nathaniel Tarbell's idiosyncratic hand, this hitherto unknown chronicler of Maine's logging industry has become as much a part of the Emery household as the message board on the back door and the wind chimes on the front porch. Nathaniel, they all call him, as if in minutes he's going to show up to eat the meat loaf or take the garbage out. "So what's Nathaniel doing now, Dad?" Timmy might ask. His position is monitored the way you'd chart an invading army's progress across a mock-up battlefield. Is he on a boat, under a bridge, taking tea in Mrs. Higgins's front parlor? "Cut those bangs," she once ordered Maggie. "When Nathaniel trims his sideburns" was Maggie's reply. No wonder Ben's sermons on the evils of processed food yield no converts; the children are convinced that Cap'n Crunch is banned from their own table only because it has never filled Nathaniel's breakfast bowls.

In a month, Ben has to deliver a paper on Nathaniel's view of labor-management relations in the Allagash to the Organization of American Historians' annual conference. This year it's in Chicago. He doesn't want to go. He hates to travel; he's leaving home only for Nathaniel's sake. He could have walked to Chicago, the miles he's put in on her mother's Bokhara tribal rug. The pile is worn flat where he stalks the same twelve feet. Grooves like a two-lane highway run down the middle where he rides his desk chair's wheels up to his computer; she knows the exact spot in the wall where he lobs the crumpled balls of prose that fail to capture Nathaniel's Yankee eccentricity. Is he mimicking frustrated-writer scenes from Hollywood biopics? In her own literary struggles, she's never been tempted to pulverize a page of acid-free rag. But she supposes crunching typescript is physically more satisfying than blackening paragraphs and hitting *delete*.

Should she call him down to see her book, this fledgling whose birth took longer, was tougher than anything merely obstetrical? She can just picture his delight. The fuss he'll make. She starts for the staircase. She stops. Perhaps she'll wait. First, she might interrupt a brilliant sentence or dam a flowing paragraph. Second, well—she has no more excuses for forbidding him to read a not-there-yet draft; now it's a book, he'll read it—she wants him to—though some of it might be hard for him. Still, maybe she flatters herself, this was all so long ago. He won her; she chose him. Yet there's no harm in putting off even the mildest reckoning. This is a me-myself-and-I moment, she decides. She'll drink a ceremonial glass of wine; she'll open the package; there'll be plenty of time to celebrate with Ben. She clutches the mailer against her breast. She remembers holding Johnny, then two years later, Timmy, then three years after that, Maggie. Her first baby in her arms for the first time had the power of first love. She had worried about the second child. And the third. What could ever match that moment when Johnny wrapped his translucent fingers around hers? Wouldn't the strength of those initial feelings be diluted over time, by repetition? She knew the second-child syndrome: hand-me-down clothes and nary a photograph. But it hadn't been the case. Each new baby thrilled her as much as the one that preceded it.

And yet . . . She runs her thumb over a ridge of staples; she fingers the curled-up, perforated edge of a stamp. Can she really compare motherhood to that rush of light and sound and smell and taste, that thundering wonder of first love? Nothing, no one, has ever come close. None of the undergraduates bearing flowers and creased paperbacks of Hesse. None of the townies with pastry boxes and drugstore valentines. Not even her betrothed now pacing one floor above whom she's known almost her whole life and whose initials mark the band of Mexican silver she's worn since she was old enough to vote. Nothing, no one, was ever quite like Simon. "Simon," she hears herself say as if it's a word as ordinary as a brand of soap. She surprises herself. She who has tucked his name away all this time like the mothballed woolens stored in the attic cedar chest. It's the book, of course, that has brought these syllables to the front of her tongue.

She pours the wine into one of three surviving Waterford

goblets from a wedding gift of a dozen, twenty-five years ago. Then pulls the tab on the manila book mailer.

She fishes out an oblong of paper. It's a folder that looks like the menu from the single Chinese takeout that leaflets her neighborhood as if its stoops and porches were the lobbies of New York City apartment buildings. These pages, however, offer no Szechwan Spicy Shrimp or Buddha's Delight. *Pine Tree Press Catalogue, Summer, Fall, Winter, Spring* is printed across the top in letters that, if Lee hadn't known better, appear mimeographed. She smooths open the folder. Six blurry black and white badly reproduced book covers crisscross the creased page. Most of them involve snow, mountains, oceans, and the silhouettes of evergreens. All have Maine in their titles: *Maine Mountain Huts and Trails; Maine: Body, Mind, and Spirit; Maine Lore; The Lobsters and Blueberries of Maine; Upside Down East: Aerial Photos of the Rocky Coast of Maine.* In the lower left corner, Lee spies the sepia print of Marguerite. Her distinct features are indistinct on the cheap paper with its watered-down graphics. But Lee can make out the angle of the feather in her hat and the ruffles fluttering around her swan's neck. She can follow the trace of an imperious arch of a brow, the smudge of a kohl-applied beauty mark. And across a silky coat march the words: *Mainely Marguerite: Travels with My Grandmother; A Memoir* by Lee Emery.

Lee Emery! Of course she's seen her name before in twelve-point Centaur or ten-point Helvetica. In newspapers. College articles. Leaflets about the Junior Year Abroad program her office sends out every spring and fall. But never has a *by* held such significance.

"Lee Emery sounds bland, if not weak," Beatrice Burke Boardman, her editor, had complained. "If you look at it fast, it reads like *Lemery*." She'd frowned. "Can you add ballast—*gravitas*—by sticking in a middle name? To make it more memorable?"

"Just Lee," Lee insisted. "The way it is." Not even thumbscrews or electric shock would force her to cough up those words filling in the blanks on her birth certificate— Magnolia Lee Marguerite Chaplin.

"But why Magnolia?" she had beseeched her mother.

Her mother, who had adjusted to, if not embraced, her own designation as Violet Rose, sighed with inevitability. "When you were born your grandmother came to the hospital wearing a hat trimmed with pink and white silk magnolia blossoms of a size found in no garden I've ever seen. And carrying a matching bouquet. There's no saying no to your grandmother."

"Magnolia." Lee spit the word out like a sour lemon.

"Besides," her mother brightened, "you could have been Blossom. Nasturtium. Wisteria."

Lee Emery will do fine, thank you very much, Lee decides now. The name of an author. Plain and understated, like Maine, but on the page, transformed into something dazzling. And not just her name. What about this book it adorns? Its tattered envelope might as well be a silver box tied with silky ribbons. She thinks of *Brief Encounter:* the cinder in the eye that precedes the train-entering-the-tunnel love affair. Rather pedestrian analogies for one who's about to put her hand on her first published work, notwithstanding a spine that flaunts the logo of a Christmas cookie conifer.

If only her grandmother were still alive. How her grandmother would have loved this.

She sticks her hand back inside the bag and brings out another folded piece of paper. It's a note from Beatrice Burke Boardman, not only editor, but also publisher, designer, distributor, publicist, producer, marketer, CEO, and sandwich maker of Pine Tree Press. A woman of three names and many hats. And at twenty-four, only slightly older than Lee's daughter, Maggie. *Dear Lee*, is scrawled across a page torn from a yellow legal pad. *Here it is!!!!!!!!!!!!!!!!!!!!!!!!!!!!!!!!!! Isn't it a beauty? I'll give you your other three copies, per contract, in person. But meanwhile, enjoy. And call me the absolute minute you get this. Love, Beatrice.* Next to her name she has drawn an outline of a pine tree which encloses the eyes and the mouth of a happy face. An inch of Xs and Os underscores her signature.

"Triple B," Ben calls her. "Miz Over-the-Top." Beatrice, whose obvious job match might involve selling eye shadow and lip gloss from behind a cosmetics counter, was, because of her Seven Sisters degree and six-figure trust fund, destined for something that didn't suit her half so well. After fetching coffee in the publicity departments of two New York publishers, the accessories division of one women's magazine, and the garden ornaments section of an interior design monthly, she found herself unemployed. Until her multimarried, multiguilty father presented her with an infant half-brother and set her up back home in Homestead as a publisher. How to defend such largesse when her classmates were wondering if they could afford resoling their shoes at their entry-level salaries. "It's not that he's Condé

Nast," Beatrice would complain. "He keeps me on a very short string."

This Lee can attest to, at least as far as the press is concerned. Dealing with Beatrice's staff of volunteers from the college meant banging your head against a wall of incompetence. "But how could I possibly know the copy machine would print my whole hand?" a sweet young thing by the name of Isadora cried. "Gee," complained another, "Beatrice didn't tell me the pages had to have numbers on them!" The "office" could have been a dormitory closet. A phone and fax and e-mail all cluttered up one line; forty-watt bulbs cast the stingiest light on manuscripts; the file cabinets seemed salvaged from the merest wreck of their former selves put out for the trash; Lee'd had to supply her own paper and stamps for the letters she wrote under Beatrice's signature promoting her book.

Her own book!

She pulls it out. The best left for last. She looks at it. The photograph of Marguerite with the feather that bends in two directions. The copyright. The Library of Congress card catalogue number inside. The ISBN number on the back. The two blurbs from Hannibal Hamlin English Department stars: "An enchanting memoir of an enchanting grandmother and the in-her-shadow granddaughter who learns to accommodate her. I couldn't put this book down!"—Archer Huntington, *Shakespeare's Gamekeeper and the Origin of Mellors*. "A writer to send you traveling"— Elinor Edith Balfour, *Fly Imagery in Emily Dickinson* and *Licentiousness, Loss, and Literature*.

Lee had sent the manuscript to Stephen King, twenty-five

miles away in Bangor, reminding him that she had once spun him and Tabitha complimentary cones of cotton candy at the Bangor State Fair. Would he be so kind as to spin a few words of praise in return? she'd asked. When the manuscript came back in its self-addressed, stamped envelope, she had been inconsolable. Until Beatrice had implied that Stephen King lacked the *gravitas* for a back cover blurb.

Lee studies the quotes. "They're not exactly household names," she'd complained to Ben when they'd first been faxed to her.

"It depends on the household. They are here, in Homestead. For the people who'll know you best. For the people who'll buy your book."

"But I don't want to be read just by the people who pump my gas, who I played tag with when I was a kid," she'd said, feeling spoiled and petulant. "I want somebody to pick my book up in a library in Montana. To take it off the shelf of a bookstore on the New Jersey shore." She'd heard her voice rise into the whine of a two-year-old. "Is that what you want for Nathaniel? To stay within a ten-mile radius of the college grounds?"

"Of course not."

"See!"

"My work is different. Serious."

Her jaw tightened. "And mine isn't?"

"Not in *that* way."

"Which sounds dismissive, Ben. Considering you haven't read it yet."

He held up his hand. "You're jumping to conclusions,"

he'd rushed to add. "Would I have married someone who couldn't write a worthy book? All I intended to point out, believe me, is that there's some comfort in keeping one's little creations close to home."

"Meaning your children. Though it's not always so good for them."

And doesn't work anyhow, Lee thinks now. As demonstrated by Johnny in Asia, Timmy in Europe, and Maggie, who, though she's at the college, might as well be in Timbuktu given how much they hear from, how much they see of her. She studies the dedication: *To Ben, John, Timothy, and Maggie. With love.*

She feels love. For this book. For its dedicatees. For her grandmother.

For . . .

She climbs the stairs, clutching her book. She remembers the title of a story she once read, something like "His Child in His Arms Held Aloft." Could a more beautiful title ever exist? She pictures Johnny, home from school and running up the stairs with his cross-country trophy, banging into her study, the pewter bowl raised like an offering, his face lit, his eyes glistening. "It's got my name on it!" he'd shouted. "Look!" he'd cried.

Lee bangs into Ben's study. "Look!" she cries.

Ben is standing at the window staring out at the backyard and the roof of the garage. On its peak the old eagle weather vane has lost one of its posts and whirls crazily; its north tilts at south; its east, at west. Lee knows from the resolute angle of Ben's shoulders that he's thinking of getting a ladder out and fixing this; she knows how he likes his universe ordered, all roads that lead to Rome pointed in the right direction even though he's not going there. "Ben," she says.

He turns around. His eyes widen. His eyebrows rise in half-moon arcs. "Your book!" he says.

Lee studies him. He's tall, nice-looking in a flannel shirt with sleeves pushed up over substantial arms. He's wearing jeans, hiking boots; his face is wide; feelings flit across it like puffs of clouds across a brilliant sky. "He's got a face of the plains," announced a friend from Nebraska, and Lee knew what he meant even though she's never seen the plains and Ben, like her, was born and bred in Maine.

"Well, what do you know!" he exclaims, cradling her memoir as if he's been handed an egg of the most delicate shell. "Imagine!" He beams. He laughs. "It's a book, Lee. An actual book." He opens it and runs his fingers across a page as if he's smoothing fur.

Lee nods, then stops. Is his tone the lay-it-on-thick voice of a parent oohing and aahing over one of his kid's finger-painted masterpieces? To Ben, Marguerite must seem like a sugary, air-filled meringue compared to Nathaniel's foursquare meat-and-potatoes solidity. Lee's eyes move behind him to the shelf of *his* books. Official spines in a graduated row. Hard bindings in dignified crimson red, forest green, royal blue. His doctoral thesis brought out the year after he received it by the Yale University Press. The volume on Maine during the turn of the century. The one on Maine in the Industrial Revolution; the first families of Homestead. His name gracing a couple of anthologies, stamped in gold on a collection of papers on

New England history. And the OED-size space left for Nathaniel Tarbell, Ben's labor of love, his most important work.

Is this sibling rivalry? Lee wonders. Does nature—family life—so abhor a vacuum that lacking a sibling she must cast a spouse in his or her place?

Ben is flipping through the book. Smiling. Nodding. Then Ben's brows knit. He is stopped at a page that seems a quarter of the way through. He turns his face to her, a face that looks puzzled, perhaps even hurt. "But you've put in Simon," he says.

She was waiting for this. Knew it was coming. Not so soon, though. Not so fast. She slows her breath. Her voice is gentle. "Of course. This is a memoir. It's not fiction. I couldn't leave him out."

"I realize that. Still . . ."

"I figured this might be hard for you. One of the reasons I didn't show you any of the chapters earlier. I didn't want to upset you. Especially if nothing was going to come of it."

"I know. But . . ."

"Especially if it wasn't going to see the light of day." She ducks her chin, makes a little joke. "Or the dark of print."

He is not amused. His scowl deepens. "I'm not exactly upset." He shakes his head like a dog flicking water off its coat. "Why should I be? You're mine, after all." He pauses. "And it's been so many years."

"It has," she says. "It was a long time ago."

And yet, it hasn't. It wasn't. She understands when people

say, in wonder, it seems like only yesterday. She who can go to the market and forget the milk she came for, she who can lose her car in the parking lot, who can miss an appointment she's written on a note taped for days to her computer screen, who once went to a friend's house to pick up Maggie and was halfway back across the street before she heard the shouts of her indignant, left-behind child, who can mix up (only once, though) the history exchange student at Edinburgh with the French immersion candidate at the Sorbonne. She, who has such holes in her head, can remember Simon's smell, his touch, his words, his smile, the taste of his tongue. It seems like only yesterday. From the time with Marguerite, and later, that week in August when she and Ben had visited Netherend-on-Severn. When the children were all so small.

"You know, Nathaniel had some sort of romance when he was fifty. His wife was quite put out about it. In her letters to her sister, if you read between the lines, you can . . ." Ben's voice drifts off; his face turns dreamy, musing. His Nathaniel look, the kids call it, when he's back in the nineteenth century, in his parallel life, in a family they've all accused him of knowing better than his own.

"I was eighteen," Lee says.

"Of course you were," Ben says. "Who'd want to be *that* again." Unpleasantness dealt with, he claps his hands. "We'll have to open a bottle of Perrier-Jouët. Believe it or not, I was down in the basement the other day and spotted half a case from our New Year's party. Who'd have thought that rowdy crew would've left a drop."

She's about to tell him she's already had a glass of wine,

but stops. What will he make of her solitary celebration, of the fact that she didn't call him the moment she put her hands on her book, that she sat at her kitchen table by herself when he would have been so happy, so eager, and, unlike her, so generous to share a toast. She supposes that now she's a writer she might as well go whole hog and become an alcoholic in the classic pattern of literary cause and effect. She remembers the New Year's party. *What you're doing in the first hour of the new year you'll be doing for the next twelve months*, Gertie Mayberry of Gender Studies had announced. Ben and Lee had whispered about rushing upstairs and diving into bed, or at least hooking elbows and synchronizing sips. They had thought about adding words, side by side, to their work-in-progress manuscripts. But when the clock struck twelve, they couldn't have been more apart than the king in the counting room and the queen in the parlor. Ben was in the bathroom hunched over the toilet bowl and Lee was in the kitchen sweeping up the shards of a broken champagne flute. "Let's turn the clock back," he had said cursing the cheap gin.

"It's a silly superstition. It doesn't matter," Lee said.

What if it does? she had thought then.

What if it did, she thinks now.

"A glass before dinner," Ben is saying. He stops. "In fact, let me take you out to celebrate! We'll have a lobster!"

"At winter prices?"

"All the better." Ben hugs Lee's book against his chest. "We'll go to the Brass Rail. Champagne, lobster, and potato chips and cole slaw. To hell with Nathaniel. I'm going to start this."

"You're under no obligation. I mean, you've waited this long . . ."

"False modesty won't work with me. I know you. You'll be hovering until I reach the end. Don't forget how I volunteered—*eagerly* volunteered—to read the early draft."

For some reason Lee is annoyed by the word *volunteered*. It sounds like hardship duty. Like a mission impossible. Involving personal sacrifice. "I give you full credit," she says.

Ben moves closer, puts his hand on her chin, bends down to her. She smells mint toothpaste, pine-scented soap, lemon shampoo, freshly mown grass. "I didn't realize it was because of Simon," he says, "that you didn't want me to read this earlier."

"It's not because of Simon. Not *just* that." Lee feels her cheeks flush. "I wanted to wait until it was in print. It's more official, somehow. It makes it more real. And then I was superstitious. Never sure it would actually be a book."

Ben pats her back. He slings an arm around her and pulls her against his chest. Familiar. Safe. She looks over his shoulder. Her parents' Audubon prints hang on the wall. One of her father's binoculars rests on the window ledge. The red-covered notebooks have their own shallow shelf. This is her childhood home. She and Ben sleep in her parents' bed; her children stick their posters on the walls where her posters lodged.

Familiar.

Safe.

Until her parents took their binoculars, packed their bird books, and went on the trip of their life. And lost their lives when their little plane crashed into the Amazon before they could even spot the blue-faced, crested hoatzin.

A week later she was engaged to Ben.

Back in the kitchen, she swipes at the counters and puts away the recipe file, reprieved from turkey chili and Santa Fe rice and a mixed salad with balsamic vinaigrette. Perhaps she should go to her office at the college and organize the piles of brochures from study programs abroad tenting her desk. She can see the stacks of varied-colored envelopes stamped with so many heads of state they could be the Almanac de Gotha. But the day your book comes you get to eat dinner out and not go in to work.

Picturing her mail at the office leads her to the mail on her kitchen table. She snatches up Johnny's envelope. What's wrong with her that she didn't rip this open the minute she spotted the familiar and adored handwriting, the familiar but unknowable Japanese characters, the stamps of Buddha, the pagoda, the cherry blossom branch, the red-crowned crane. Shame on her that *Lee Emery* printed across the cover of an esoterically published paperback causes enough attention deficit disorder for her to choose author and forget about Mom.

Though not for long. She slits open the flap. Out spill a dozen photographs. She grabs the letter first; it's a serrated piece of lined paper torn from a notebook. *Dear 'rents*, it reads.

I like my school. The kids are cute and hardworking; the parents more hardworking. The opposite of you laid-back

Maine-iacs. The food is the best; no, don't worry, I haven't had blowfish yet. But Jeff (graduated college one year ahead of me) has gone to three fugu restaurants and insists that Dr. No stuff is hyper-dramatized. Okay. Okay. I know exactly what you're thinking now. Sushi worms are risky enough. No fugu for your firstborn. My romaji is passable but my kanji stinks. Enclosed are photos of me and Noriko when we climbed Mt. Fuji at the weekend. The sunrise is hardly done justice to by my photography skills. Tell Dad it's not the camera, thank you very much and did I get a deal on that, but the nut behind the shutter. Give Sis a high-five and tell her to plan on coming over this summer.

Lots of love,
Johnny-san

(PS I think Noriko is the one!!!)

Lee fans the photos across the table. At first she thinks the many images are all the same; her strapping son with Ben's broad shoulders and her reddish hair, with Ben's flat feet and her freckled nose, stands on a mountaintop. A bandanna wraps his head. He holds a kind of staff with writing on it and a banner flapping at its tip. Clutched to his side is a young woman wearing jeans and a Red Sox sweatshirt. Her hair is whipped around into half of her face; the rest of her face seems stuck into his ribs. Behind them a sunrise flames the morning sky.

As she studies the snapshots, Lee starts to make out the differences: a knee angled more acutely here, a smile more intense there, the banner blowing to the east, then to the west, the sun more orange or more yellow. On the whole, though, the gradations are so subtle this could be a series of time-lapse photographs. In each, hardly a sliver of light shines through to show whose shinbone is connected to whose knee-bone. The young woman clings to Johnny as if her jeans are Velcroed to his. Lee thinks of her firstborn, conscientious, worried, a perfectionist, anxious to do right, never exactly in the moment but always outside analyzing it. Am I having fun? his expression seemed to ask. Is this all there is to it? he seemed constantly to wonder. His smile always tentative.

But not here, not on top of Mt. Fuji poised like a bride and groom on a wedding cake with the sun haloing him and Noriko, who may be the one. Here his smile bears the private rapture of a beatified saint.

"Don't bring home a limey," her father had joked. They were at the Bangor airport where he was about to put his eighteen-year-old daughter on a plane to New York to meet Marguerite for their overnight flight. At Lee's feet stood a shiny set of luggage, a high school graduation gift, of a hard pebbly gray plastic lined with blue satin and which included a round hatbox and square cosmetic case; her patent leather pocketbook matched her patent leather shoes; she wore a necklace, bracelet, and earrings of tiny cultured pearls; a navy pleated skirt swirled over her hips; tucked into it was a shocking pink blouse almost the exact shade of her frosted lipstick labeled Blissful Blush. Though she weighed 105 pounds, a girdle squeezed her middle and held up stockings of Sun-washed Beige. Encased in this garment, obsolete everywhere it seemed except on the lingerie counters of Homestead, she still felt as chic as one of *Mademoiselle*'s college issue girls. "Don't take up with a foreigner," her father stressed.

She thinks now of the limey, the foreigner. She blames her book. She has been thinking more of him today than she has for years, she tells herself, though she would not be willing to put such statistics to the test.

Simon.

The foreigner.

His parents' house could have been her parents' house. The piano in the corner, the mahogany dining table, the grandfather clock on the landing, the Dickens volumes on the library shelf, the threadbare Persian rugs. Roses and peonies in the garden, bird books and binoculars at the kitchen window, overcooked roast beef and mushy Brussels sprouts. She and Simon were the same age with fathers who drove too slowly on opposite sides of the road and mothers whose identical mason jars held, on one continent, pennies; on the other, pence.

Unlike today, when going to London is called crossing the pond, the ocean had then seemed so vast, the differences so great, even between countries with the same language, families with the same books. How could a snowed-in, underpopulated Maine town compare to the foggy dense dazzle of city lights?

What would her father have thought of Johnny steeped and stopped in a culture with an impenetrable alphabet and a girlfriend named Noriko who eats raw fish and sleeps on a tatami mat? What would he have said to Johnny? Warned him away with euphemisms like Pearl of the Orient? Madame Butterfly?

"I don't know why you want to go jetting all over tarnation, traveling the globe," her father had said to her, "when everything you need, when your whole world is right here at home."

For them, everything *was* here; here in this town; here in this house. Home was their world. Hers was a happy childhood; her parents loved each other, loved her. And what was the lesson for their daughter that the only time they left the United States, the only time they flew far away to watch birds fly, they smashed into the wide blue horizon and flew straight into death?

And what does it mean that she married a reluctant traveler who once gave her a sampler stitched with *There's No Place Like Homestead, Maine.*

But times have changed. Johnny's teaching English in Japan; Timmy's at Oxford on his junior year abroad; and Lee has a book that, if she's lucky, will be read by people she's never seen, displayed in bookstores she's never visited. Even if she's grounded by a husband pacing the floor overhead, by the house on Evergreen Road, by the job on the campus that skirts it, anchored to the pine-needled ice-crusted landscape of Down East, her book can sprout its own wings, can take off anywhere. That is if Beatrice Burke Boardman and Pine Tree Press will know how to distribute it.

Speaking of which. Or, rather, of whom. Somehow the arrival of her book has put her day out of joint. She celebrated by herself, drank alone, opened Johnny's envelope last. She picks up the phone.

"Pine Tree Press. Mainly about Maine." Beatrice's voice is cheery if robotic.

"It's me."

"And who is that?" asks Beatrice in a tone Lee finds slightly arch.

"You know exactly who," says Lee. "The star in your stable of authors. Your only memoirist."

"At the present time," clarifies Beatrice. "Sorry, I've just found out my number is one digit from Domino's and I've already received two calls complaining about the pepperoni and another about the stinginess of the extra cheese. So, has it come?"

"It was sitting on the porch when I drove back from the store."

Lee hears a long whoosh of an exhale. Then a whoop of delight. "Fab-u-lous. Fab-u-lous. I suppose I could have brought it from Portland myself, then run it right over in the van, but I thought it would be more of a treat, not to mention more professional, coming in the mail. Vinnie at the Portland PO tried to get me to send it overnight. Frankly that seemed a little too New York. So it got there all right?"

"Perfectly," Lee says.

"And?"

"And?"

"You know, what do you think?"

"Beatrice, it's beautiful. Gorgeous." Oh, what the hell. "Fab-u-lous!" she adds.

"Didn't I tell you!"

"The last time I was so excited was when Johnny was born. And Timmy. And Maggie, of course, too."

"For me it would've been my first bra."

"Why am I not surprised?"

"Or maybe my first kiss." She gives a remembrance-of-times-past sigh. "I knew you'd love it!" she exclaims. She waits a beat. "And you didn't notice the little mistake?"

Lee's heart thumps, then sinks to her toes. Was her grandmother's name misspelled? Or even, more important, her own? Was somebody else's life story inserted between the sepia print of Marguerite on the cover and her own back flap saying-cheese author photograph? "Mistake?"

"It's not *that* big," says Beatrice, protesting so much it sounds gargantuan. "Just a nuisance, really. The printers put an extra zero on the price marked on the cover so it looks like it costs a hundred and twenty dollars instead of twelve."

"You're kidding!"

"If only. They said they'd print up some stickers so you'd never be able to tell. But they're insisting on charging me. Claim it's my fault since I didn't catch the boo-boo in the proof. I can hardly ask Daddy for another cent . . ."

Why not? wonders Lee.

". . . so I just hiked myself over to Woolworth's and got myself some of those thingamabobs you use for yard sales and an extra thick Bic. I thought you'd come by some afternoon and we can reprice the little buggers in no time. Thank God we have such a teeny press run."

"I guess that's one way to look at it."

"Not that we couldn't go back to press just like that." Lee hears a snap of fingers, a bang of knuckles against wood. "And I'm sure we will. I'm sure we'll have a runaway best-seller on our hands—as soon as I can slap on those stickers and put them in the trunk and start distributing them."

Lee sinks into a kitchen chair and is stabbed by a pasta fork. "Ouch," she cries.

"There's no reason to worry," says Beatrice, sounding worried. "Take it as an omen. Your book's worth a hundred and twenty."

"All very well and good. But the objective is, unless I'm mistaken, to sell the thing."

"*One* of the objectives. But remember, you've chosen a small select press . . ."

As if she had a choice, as if Alfred A. Knopf was knocking at her door. "Still . . ."

"You've written a book. You're a professional."

With a crudely lettered, tag-sale price tag stuck on the back. And a system of distribution relying on the cleaned-out trunk of somebody's Chevrolet. Rank amateur, thinks Lee. An amateur in everything she's done except motherhood where the only training is the doing and each time you start doing all over again. She's a phony, a fraud. Who am I? she asks herself. What am I getting away with here? How soon will everyone find out I'm not what I seem? Once a famous actress came to speak at the college, and Ben and Lee had dinner with her at the faculty club. She'd done *Hedda Gabler* on Broadway, three Woody Allen films, Letterman. Lee had sensed an instant bond. The actress talked about how her fame was hollow; how she felt like a fraud; how she was waiting to be found out. Every line written about her brilliance on the stage, her beauty, her charm she was sure was directed at somebody else. After dinner she had wrapped Lee in a perfumed, silky embrace. Lee had felt suffused with musk, velvet, fur, celebrity.

"We really connected," Lee boasted later to Ben.

He studied her. "She's quite an actress" was what he'd said.

"So has Ben read it?" Beatrice asks now.

"He's reading it even as we speak."

"Wow. And you're not hanging over him, watching his reaction to every word?"

"It didn't even occur to me," says Lee. Scenes from movies flash in front of her. Loved ones pacing, watching, wringing hands, tugging at earlobes and locks of hair as significant others—spouses, children, editors—riffle through their manuscripts. "Probably because it's already out in print. Because there's nothing I can do about it."

"Let me know what he says about the Simon section. If you ask me, that alone is worth more than a hundred twenty bucks. That part is really hot."

At the Brass Rail, Dotty Bouchard shows them to the best booth, the one with the protruding springs girdled by two layers of black electrical tape and the view of the activity going on at the five-and-ten across the square. She ties their lobster bibs with a tight little bow. "They-ah," she says. She'd been in Lee's high school class; they'd shared a locker junior year. That locker could have been a honey pot the way it attracted the irresistible bad guys of the school: those James Dean look-alikes whose Brylcreemed curls fell just so onto their sweetly devilish brows. Working on the combination (12–14–71, she can still remember it), Lee would watch them swarm around Dotty's swishy blond ponytail, her two perky breasts pyramided in her Cross Your Heart bra, ignoring Lee, even though Lee herself was so close she could sniff their Old Spice and count the cords in their ropy industrial-arts arms. It was no surprise that one of them got Dotty pregnant at the midterm. She didn't bother to clean her locker before she left, and for weeks Lee would find among her bags and notebooks pop beads, eyebrow pencils, Clearasil, bobby pins.

Now you can see Dotty's pink scalp through her mouse-colored hair, and she's missing teeth. She's raising three grandchildren all alone. It can be a hard life here, Lee knows, as it is for many of the people she's grown up with; people for whom the *Vacationland* across the bottom of their license plate is the cruelest of ironies. Their Maine is one of smoke-spewing factories, unemployment, downtowns ruined by gas stations and fast food joints, and empty, shuttered abandoned shops; parking lots towered with discarded tires, harsh winters, astronomical heating bills, humid summers fueling allergies, blackflies, mosquitoes; nothing for kids to do but drive the empty streets in rusted-out pickup trucks. More Beans of Egypt, Maine, than Bushes of Kennebunkport. "You come from Maine!" city folks will crow. Thinking it's a branch of Newport, Rhode Island, or one of the Hamptons gossip columnists always write about.

"I suppose you want a carafe of the house white?" Dotty asks as if the house red and white aren't the only two wines buried in the three-column list of beers on tap.

"Perfect," says Ben.

Only when they are cracking claws and sucking out meat

and squirting lemon and scraping tomalley and dunking forks in melted butter—and making the familiar joyful mess that is as much an accompaniment to the boiled lobster dinner as the side orders of cole slaw and steamed clams—does Ben finally say anything about her book other than the "to your masterpiece" with which he clinked her glass back in their living room.

"Would you care to elaborate?" she had felt herself compelled to ask.

"After dinner, when I'm sufficiently soused."

Oh, dear, she thinks now, as she picks up the carafe. It's a familiar shape. When she looks closely, she recognizes it in its recycled, recast form as the milk bottle from the old Hilltop Dairy that used to be delivered every morning as she set off for the Abraham Lincoln school. She pours him some wine. What does it mean that he has to be plied with booze to discuss her book?

"About your book," he starts now. Some of the liquid from his claw spurts across the table and into her eye.

She wipes it with the corner of her bib. Right at this moment, she'd just as soon the review were left at "your masterpiece." No need to explicate the text. Still, dutifully, she leans toward him. "Yes," she encourages.

"It's quite the portrait of Marguerite."

"You think?"

"You capture her, the way she talks, the way she looks. Talked. Looked. Considering you're not a professional. That this is your first . . ." He produces an insincere smile. "How you manage to show . . . I wouldn't have thought . . ."

"But?"

His eyes crinkle with professorial compromise. "No buts. A-plus."

"I'm not your student, Ben."

He hesitated. "Well, one. One *but*." He turns his lobster claw this way and that. He studies it. "You know, when Nathaniel's wife was worried about him, well, except for the hints to her sister, she kept it to herself. She never revealed a single thing to him. 'I shall forbear' is what she wrote."

"Ben!"

He shakes his head. His smile turns sheepish. "No forbearing for me, however. Frankly, you must have figured I would find the Simon section a little hard to take."

Here it is. "I can understand that . . ."

"And not just a little."

"I never . . ."

"It is so full of feeling." He picks up his cracker. He squeezes it. "I suppose it's a tribute to you as a writer, that the feelings are so real. If I'd read it in a novel, it would have been a fine and convincing love story. I would have thought, hey, what an inventive writer. What a tale she can spin. But . . ." He puts down the cracker. He twists off the lobster tail, then with the tines of his fork lifts out a pink slab of meat completely intact. He holds it up, poised on the tip. He waves it to make his point. "This is nonfiction. This is real. So fresh. So raw. So full of—well—love."

Is it? she wonders. How can she judge? Fresh? Raw? Love? After all this time?

"And after all this time," Ben says. His voice is sad. His eyes, bright copper pennies, look feverish.

"But it's set in time. Just that one trip. Limited. Circum-scribed. First love. A beginning, right, but also the end."

"I know about first love. You were my first love. My only love." He reaches across the table. His watch snags the bib, ripping the lobster sketch in half and separating, she can't help but notice, the *Br* from its *ass*.

She gives him her hand. Two moist hands, smelling of lobster and lemon wedges, sticky fingers clutched next to the salt and pepper and Tabasco sauce.

"You're wrong," she says. "For starters, what about Karen Stevens and Rebecca King?"

"Pit stops along the way to the final destination. Simple flings," he says. "The scales you practice for the Bach étude, the Tchaikovsky overture."

"I couldn't have said it better myself. Think of Simon as the stretching exercises for the marathon. As a signpost on the way to you." Is this true? she muses. Was Simon a fling? The practice? The trial run? First love as a concept with time limits built into it?

"But you didn't write it that way . . ."

"Even in a memoir, there's a certain amount of embel-lishment," she explains. "Poetic license, isn't that the term?"

"As a historian, I, for one, find any embellishment to be anathema."

"This isn't history. It's something more personal. More subject to interpretation, eye-of-the-beholder stuff."

"I suppose . . ." He frowns. "It's funny, but that summer we met him, that time in—what was it called?—Never. Neither . . ."

"Netherend-on-Severn," she supplies.

"Netherend-on-Severn. Well, this may sound childish, but I didn't think he was so great."

"He wasn't." She squeezes his fingers. "Not compared to you."

"You wouldn't have known it from the book," he sulks.

"But I wasn't writing about that time. I was only writing about the time with Marguerite. The first time . . ."

Dotty comes to clear the empty lobster shells. "Still holding hands," she says, "and after all these years." She slaps down new bowls for the rest of the shells. Lee and Ben are locals, she knows. Not the out-of-towner types, those couples who show up for Parents Weekend from Boston and New York, who gnaw on a tail and a couple of claws. Locals will chew and poke and prod until the carcass looks like one plucked by a flock of gulls.

"Just showing off, Dotty," says Ben.

"Who would've known. Little Lee Chaplin." She shakes her head and her hair flutters like streamers at a prom. "Back in high school you was such a quiet thing. Never would've given a guy—any guy—the time of day."

"Because all eyes were on you."

"Ah, shush now," Dotty says, looking pleased. "Get on with you. You were the quietest little thing . . ."

"Still waters run deep," grins Ben.

Dotty balances the tray against her jutting hip. "You never know. You never know about people. About how things turn out." She heads to a table in the back where somebody is shouting for extra tartar sauce.

"And look at how things turned out," Lee says. "You and

me and the kids. A long marriage. A good life. The memoir, it's filtered through the eyes of a *child*."

"I guess what counts is who you choose in the end. Who you pick for the long run."

"Exactly. That's all that matters."

He smiles. "And everything you write about Marguerite is wonderful."

"Which is not hard given how she sucked the oxygen out of every room. Even the dullest writer would have had trouble keeping her confined to the page."

"You can't go wrong with such a character. A force of nature in gravity-defying heels and a wide-brimmed chapeau."

"And then some."

Ben nods. "I remember the first time I met her. I brought her flowers."

"Carnations."

"Not the best choice. But I was florally illiterate. I hardly knew the difference between a daisy and a daffodil."

"She was thrilled," Lee says.

"She certainly was," Ben agrees. "She couldn't have been more pleased. If I do say so myself."

Lee remembers. "A nice solid, sturdy, dependable boy," Marguerite had pronounced. Her smile had been almost brilliant enough to mask the fact that it wasn't a compliment. "Now there's an interesting face," she had said of Simon. "I of all people can sense a soul full of poetry."

At night, in her parents' four-poster hewn from Maine lumber in 1864 by Elliott Arthur White, who carved his name on one of the maple slats, and under her parents' log cabin quilt stitched by the ladies' auxiliary of All Souls' Church, Ben pulls her to him. They come together with a choreography so fine-tuned in their quarter century of repetitive motion that there are no missteps or surprises, only the familiar comfort of rhythms long perfected and bodies accustomed to bend this way and that in an ongoing pas de deux.

Lee puts her finger against Ben's lips. She traces the full lower lip, the thinner upper one with only the slightest cleft at its center. She knows it as well as she knows her own mouth, the mouth she can slash lipstick across without the aid of a mirror, without going outside the lines. She knows his body the way she knows her own; she can read the slightest nuance of his voice, translate the tiniest twist of his brow. *You never know about people*, Dotty said, but Lee is pretty sure she can make a case for knowing everything about Ben.

Is this a good thing? she wonders. Is it better to have a face as open as the plains? Feelings lined up and accessible as cans of soup on a supermarket shelf? Or the unplumbable depths that must constitute a soul of poetry? "Oh, Lee," Ben sighs. Then laughs. "My wife. My little memoirist."

In the middle of the night, Lee wakes up and does something that so surprises her that later she will blame it on sleepwalking. On poltergeists. She tiptoes into the kitchen, grabs a glass, and takes it to the sink. Just as she's about to turn on the faucet, she sees her book glowing in a shaft of moonlight against the red-checked tablecloth. She puts down her glass. She picks up a Magic Marker and blacks out the *$120* on the back of the cover. In the cabinet, among the nest of pot holders and dish towels, she finds a mailer. She shoves the book inside. She staples it shut. Across the front she writes Simon's name and address without having to look up his postal code. She sticks on a half sheet's worth of stamps. Then scribbles at the bottom, *Priority.*

Two

It was the first day home from spring break, her freshman year at Hannibal Hamlin College. Lee's mother knocked on the door to her room.

The door was halfway open. The lights gleamed. Lee was dressed. Not on the phone. Not reading. Not tweezing eyebrows or curling her bangs. She had been doing nothing more lascivious than sorting the dirty clothes that had been accumulating like landfill between her and her roommate's twin beds. Carting home such a pile meant saving the quarters she'd hoarded for the unreliable machines in the laundry room of Hartley Hall. As a rule, even though her parents' extra-large Maytag washer-and-dryer stood side by side in burnt orange splendor in the basement of Evergreen Road less than a mile away, Lee was determined to erect a Berlin

Wall between her Homestead home in the east and the campus in the west.

"Pee—yew!" her roommate had exclaimed, holding her nose and pointing to the tumble of knee socks and leotards, half-slips, jeans, and turtlenecks. "Couldn't you just drop these off at your mom's?"

"Absolutely not," Lee said. "I'm setting boundaries." Boundaries exempt from spring break's forced march home.

Lee's mother, too, was setting boundaries, or at least obeying them—which was the reason she had knocked.

"Proceed at your own risk," ordered Lee.

Lee's mother stepped over the threshold. With the point of her toe, she kicked a flannel nightgown aside. She wore heels and stockings and an apron that was ironed into knife-edge pleats. She cleared her throat. "I've just heard from your grandmother, dear," she announced.

Lee looked up from her denim skirt, which had a wad of gum plastered to its hem. What did it mean, she wondered, that she was always the one who stepped in the dog doo along the campus's brick walks, that the plug of Juicy Fruit was always stuck under her desk in the lecture hall, that flour or ketchup or yogurt always frosted the seat of her chair in the school cafeteria? She'd once discovered her sleeve fringed with somebody else's masking-taped notes. *Call Marge about Deke*, one prompted. *George Santayana as opposed to Kierkegaard symbolizes that all meaning is but . . .* , the other trailed off. At the mention of her grandmother, however, the world became instantly more interesting than the mound of soiled clothes or her mother's immaculate apron strings.

"Another visit?" Lee asked. Excited for herself and sorry for her mother, who would be embarking on a round of enough scrubbing, scouring, polishing, rearranging to occupy a full Buckingham Palace below-stairs staff for a week.

Her mother had the pursed-lip look of someone about to break bad news. "She wants to take you to Europe for the summer."

Lee stopped. "Why does this sound like you're saying, 'She wants to walk you to the electric chair'?" she asked.

"You know your grandmother."

Lee nodded.

"Of course, you don't have to go," her mother added. "Nobody can make you." She hesitated. "Not even your grandmother."

"Don't be so sure."

"Extraordinary, isn't it, how she manages each and every time to get her way."

"But I want to go. Only a fool would turn down such an invitation."

"Italy. France. Belgium. England. Maybe Scandinavia." She rattled off these storybook places with as much passion as she might use to list Aroostook, Waldo, Piscataquis, Androscoggin, Sagadahoc, the counties of Maine every local schoolchild had to memorize.

"It's a dream come true."

"You know that adage: be careful what you wish for."

"Mom!" Lee leaned back against the bedpost. Eiffel Towers, Colosseums, castles, plum puddings, and *tartes tatins* scooted past her face in cartoon clouds. She looked at her denim skirt, its gummed hem, its puckered pockets. She'd need new clothes . . .

"Three whole months," pronounced her mother like a life sentence from a hanging judge.

"Three whole months! Yes!" Lee lobbed a sock into the air. The gesture of new graduates tossing their mortarboards out into the world. She paused. "But what about my job?" She'd been hired at the college library to file card catalogues.

"Precisely. You can't give it up. It's important."

"I *can* give it up. It's not at all important." It wasn't much better, in fact, than her high school summers spent scooping maple walnut into waffle cones at I Scream on Pleasant Street or grilling hot dogs at MacDoggit's on Post Office Square. Which at least had the advantage of free food. "I'm going," Lee said.

Her mother's hands fluttered. "You don't have to decide immediately. Why not give it more thought." She smoothed her smooth apron. "Besides, it will take you three months to get that laundry sorted out."

"Very funny."

"You know your grandmother," she repeated. "My mother," she sighed. "Just weigh the pros and cons before you make a commitment. One you might live to regret." Behind her, the door closed with the punch of a punctuation point.

Lee swung her arm and macheteed the laundry out of her path. On top of her bureau, dwarfing the snapshots of Girl Scout troops, long-buried pets, her parents' wedding portrait, high school best friends she'd already lost touch with,

stood the photograph of her grandmother in its silver curlicued frame. She picked it up. She studied it.

It was a formal portrait, sepia-tinted, taken when her
grandmother was close to her own age. Perhaps around the
time her grandfather visited Europe, spotted this vision in
taffeta and lace peering into the window of Liberty's on
Regent Street, and after a courtship of a week sailed her
across the sea to Homestead, Maine, as his bride.

Or maybe it was taken a little earlier, when Max Reinhardt, the famous director and theatrical producer, saw her
outside a café—in Berlin? in Vienna?—nibbling a Sacher
torte *mit schlag* and invited her to join his company. An invitation her father forced her to refuse: ladies of good family
did not go on the stage.

And yet, that same straitlaced, old-fashioned, waistcoated,
monocled father had allowed his youngest daughter to be
whisked away from the Old World by a stranger from the
New. Why? Because she was his fifth girl? Because he was
worn out? He had, of course, cabled the Western Union in
that ends-of-the-earth frontier town in the north woods. *To
Whom It May Concern: Would the family be acceptable?* he had
inquired.

More than acceptable came back by return wire. Since Aunt
Fan, working that day in the telegraph office next to the
train station, didn't feel the need to recuse herself from pronouncing sentence on her brother's worthiness to support a
wife.

Now Lee plucked a tissue and dusted off the photograph.
Her grandmother's dark eyes stared right into the camera.
The feather on her hat bent in two directions. The hat was

tied under her chin, which thrust out in a way the years hadn't changed, in a way that demanded attention must be paid. Ruffles cascaded over white-gloved wrists. More ruffles draped a perky chest. Something shiny sashed a Scarlett O'Hara waist. Against a backdrop of wispy clouds, of fading light, her grandmother's beauty was startling.

What must it have felt like, Lee wondered, to be the daughter of such a beauty? Someone who even at seventy could turn all heads in a room? Her mother wore not a lick of makeup to ameliorate the large nose and close-together eyes she had inherited from her gene pool's paternal half. Her fashion sense must have come from that short-end-of-the-stick side, too: plain turtlenecks and serviceable tweeds. Simple pumps in brown or black. Not a buckle, not a bow, not a flash of rhinestone or of brass. Her mother preferred evenings at home, sipping tea, poring through her bird books, the wind rattling the windowpanes. Her grandmother craved nights on the town, nights in assorted towns—New York, Rome, and Paris were a few of them—with champagne and music and laughter pealing from all corners of a jazz club or a restaurant. Never had Lee seen an apron gathered over her grandmother's hips, not even when she was dusting sugar on the raspberries of her heralded Linzer pastries. What a contrast between her grandmother, who spread her gilded wings and took off anywhere, and her mother, who studied the migrating patterns of birds from her backyard picnic bench. Lee was already into her second semester of Introduction to Psychology. She could recognize a reaction formation when she came up against it.

Still, she understood, could sympathize, with her mother's

reaction formation. This was a grandmother, after all, who had cut up the Persian rug in her parents' front hall to make a band for a hat, cuffs for a coat. Who would go through your bureau drawers, read your mail with a *droit deu seigneur* sense of entitlement. Whose bathrooms had no locks, nothing to stop her from marching in on you anywhere, in the middle of anything, to comment on your sprouting breasts and humiliating new-sprung body hair.

This was the grandmother who leased an elaborate *fin de siècle* apartment in a residential hotel a few blocks from Gramercy Park. Twice a year, a package would arrive in Homestead. Stuffed inside they'd find bars of ivory Hotel Canterbury soap, rolls of scratchy Hotel Canterbury toilet paper, and chamois shoe-polishing cloths. The bulk, however, comprised a stack of Hotel Canterbury sheets and towels. Which, though originally stitched *Hotel Canterbury* across their tops in red cursive script, now bore only an *H* and an off-center *C*. Painstakingly her grandmother would have unthreaded the *otel* and *anterbury*, thus producing a royal dowry embroidered not with the preferred VRC of her daughter but with the necessity-as-the-mother-of-invention initials of Henry Chaplin, her son-in-law.

"*Voilà!* A full set of linens completely monogrammed. And at no cost."

"This is stealing," Lee's mother would cry. "A misdemeanor. Maybe a felony."

"Nonsense. I pay an exorbitant rent."

"Which would no doubt increase if they found out you were raiding their stock to supply a second household. Sending contraband across state lines like a common crook!"

"Not common. Never common."

"*Common* crook," her mother stressed.

"Don't be absurd. The staff adore me. Bring me the left-over flowers from the suites of visiting dignitaries. Bring me *petits fours* from the dining room after hours. You know, there is a ton of stationery. Printed unfortunately with their address. Still, the envelopes might be useful for paying bills . . ."

"Mother!"

"I did my best, Violet, but sometimes, my dear, I think you suffer from a certain lack of imagination." She emitted a theatrical sigh. "No insult intended, *Liebchen*, but you are much too Maine."

Lee could see that from Marguerite's point of view, being much too Maine did not merit the grandmotherly seal of approval. As far as Lee's parents were concerned, however, one couldn't be much too Maine enough. While the standards and values of the rest of the world might be eroding, Maine grit and determination, plain old Yankee sensibility held as fast to the landscape as its pine trees and its rocky coast. You hid your wealth if you had any; you shielded your shining star if there was a gleam of it. Because you were surrounded by people less fortunate, it was your moral duty never to show off. You trusted the old, the worn, the used. You suspected anything bright and new. Though you rationed your words, when you gave your word you kept it. "Don't boast," her mother would instruct, "never stand out in a crowd." She was stingy with praise, worried about her daughter's getting a swelled head. Lee pictured a colossal case of the mumps caught from hearing too many *pretty*s or *nices.* As a child, she would keep running her hands over her skull. Was it getting bigger? Was the "good job" from her teacher going to result in a dire consequence?

"Plumage should be restricted to birds," her father would say, "for reasons scientific and evolutionary." The pale pink of her Tangee lipstick, he pronounced cheap.

Her mother bought Lee room-to-grow-in clothes from bargain racks. She sewed her rudimentary skirts gathered into uneven and unflattering clumps over her chubby hips and fastened with snaps that popped open every time she turned. As you got older, her mother instructed, you wore loose tops to hide your embarrassing breasts and a girdle to mask the embarrassing cleft in your buttocks. No matter that something had been invented called pantyhose. "It's a tough life for so many here," her mother explained, "with no room, no place, for frivolity."

Was wearing a girdle an act of anti-frivolity? Lee wondered. Certainly the tough-lived women in dungarees and lumber jackets, in overalls and Pendleton shirts, in flour-sack housedresses and lace-up shoes, the women with bulging stomachs and swollen thighs who crowded the benches at church suppers and the concession stands at state fairs, weren't wearing girdles to hide their buttock clefts.

How could a child make sense of this? Or even a teenager? Only later did she learn the term *mixed messages*.

"Be serious," her mother ordered.

"Scrape off that nail polish," her father commanded.

Things changed, however, when her grandmother came to visit. Into their serious, unfrivolous household, her grandmother in full plumage swooped, all color, light, movement, and noise. "My beautiful granddaughter," Marguerite exclaimed. "My pretty child."

Beautiful? Pretty? Lee looked into the mirror. She examined her pudgy, awkward-stage body, her in-between-stage dumpling face, her lank, poultry-sheared, *mother*-cut hair and felt transformed.

"My sturdy fireplug," her father called her.

"My enchanting gazelle," her grandmother now crooned. "Look what I have for you."

"Lee needs shoes," she had heard her mother tell Marguerite over the phone. "Something practical. With good support. Her toes turn in. I'm afraid she's inherited her father's feet." She paused. "Yes. Well. Where would she wear that? I suppose a warm cardigan," she conceded, "if you insist."

The day her grandmother arrived, she was bearing gifts wrapped in silver and gold. "Here are your shoes," she said, handing Lee fuchsia satin slippers from India, embroidered with tiny pearls, set with little mirrors. Bells dangled from the turned-up jester's toes.

Lee lit into the biggest box.

"Save the paper," cautioned her mother.

"Rip it to shreds," counseled her grandmother.

Lee ripped off the paper. She tore open the cardboard. From layers of tissue she pulled out a costume fit for a movie star. She gasped.

"Lounging pajamas," her grandmother explained.

Lee held them up. A mandarin collar topped the crimson brocade jacket. Silk roses looped through the buttonholes. Black satin trousers shimmered with light. Behind

Marguerite's back, Lee saw her parents raise their eyebrows and shake their heads. "Not exactly for Maine," her father said.

Her grandmother nodded; her earrings flashed. "Not for Maine, for *Lee*, for my princess," she said.

Every evening after school, Lee put on those lounging pajamas and became a princess. She lounged; she strutted; she slunk; she twirled. In front of the bureau mirror in her parents' bedroom, she stood on a chair to get the full effect. "Don't be vain," her mother warned.

"Like your grandmother," her father put his two cents in.

Lee knew her grandmother was vain. But she also had a smile that blazed, a laugh that chimed, a love of life, of adventure, a sense of endless curiosity. That she was not perfect made her both more human and more lovable. Her beauty was hardly her fault. Could anyone look like that and not be vain? Lee could understand. Even though she herself had more than once suffered from her grandmother's vanity, she could forgive. When she was ten, her teacher at the Abraham Lincoln elementary school had on the basis of her Dirigo project—a portfolio of Maine-related drawings—sent a note home to her parents suggesting art lessons, insisting she had a gift. Lee had produced a series of ballet dancers at their barre with cookie-cutter precision if not originality. These had been displayed at a Farm and Home Week exhibit in the college gymnasium on walls hung with seascapes and charcoal sketches of lobster claws. "*By Lee Chaplin, ten years old,*" proclaimed the card thumbtacked underneath her *oeuvre*, making her the only artist designated by age in the field of balding wood-carvers and blue-haired watercolorists. "You are the next Degas!" cried Marguerite. Who commissioned a portrait. And sent along a photograph she wanted copied in the alizarin crimsons and viridian greens and titanium whites of the new paint box that had been delivered from the best artists' supply store in all of Manhattan, the one where Jackson Pollock had been reputed to shop, where Marguerite herself once spotted a sketch pad in the hands of none other than Marisol.

Every afternoon, Lee had worked on the portrait, neglecting long division, giving short shrift to geography. When she finished, her parents shipped it off to New York, crated professionally by Jerry Newton, the eponymous owner of Jerry's Hardware Store.

Marguerite's excitement threatened to overpower the telephone. As the streams of German, French, English, Italian, and Polish *magnificents!!* came bursting through the wire, Lee had to hold the receiver a foot from her ear. Lee's own Rembrandt would take pride of place over the marble mantelpiece. Just as soon as it could be matted in linen, framed in gold leaf.

Was she destined for an artist's life in a Paris garret? Lee wondered. She imagined a studio where mustached men in berets played the accordion and sipped wine from silver goblets. *Chérie*, they'd croon as they lifted the draped velvet off her canvases and sighed *ooh la la*.

When Lee finally visited her grandmother's New York apartment, her painting indeed graced the mantelpiece. True to promise, it bore a wide creamy linen mat, set in the kind of carved wood frame burnished with gold you might find in the Renaissance painting galleries of the Metro-politan.

But something was wrong. Something more than the fancy frame, the expensive mat, accoutrements her mother would have dismissed as mutton dressed as lamb. Lee couldn't quite put her finger on it.

"You look puzzled, darling," her grandmother had said.

"It seems different. Not the way I remember it."

Her grandmother chuckled. "What a perceptive little imp you are," her grandmother trilled.

Lee's mouth opened. Where to begin . . .

"Which goes to prove your true artistic eye. I hired Sergei, he used to do set designs for the Ballet Russe—is out of work now, poor thing—to paint this over the teeniest bit. Which he did beautifully. Mere daubs, my sweet. The eyes here, the chin there"—her grandmother pointed a finger ablaze with two diamond cocktail rings—"notice the subtle brushwork around the neck."

"But why?" Lee could feel her chest tighten with affront. Even a ten-year-old could sense a threat to artistic integrity.

"Why?" her grandmother repeated. "Don't you see? It didn't do me justice, my darling. It wasn't flattering."

In Europe, flattery rained down on her grandmother with the force of a monsoon. Waiters, bellboys, concierges jumped to attention at the slightest crook of a pinkie or the arch of a Marlene Dietrich eyebrow. Museum guards and museum visitors appraised and approved. On the rue Cassette a young sailor saluted. On the Kärntner Strasse an elderly gentleman doffed his hat. An American tourist, lined up for a *bateau mouche*, pursed his lips to produce a wolf whistle that could have shattered a champagne flute. "You look beautiful, Grandmother," became Lee's daily refrain. "Your French is perfect. Those vendors over there are admiring you." She was glad to do it, assume her role as in-house yes-man, fan club, court sycophant. Still, by the time they arrived in London, after stops in Vienna and Paris, Lee was starting to have her own reaction formation. She understood the theory of ambivalence.

Was there a grandmotherly version, she wondered, of the word *matricide*?

Not that she didn't love her grandmother. Not that she wasn't the most beautiful, the most enchanting creature on the face of this earth. Not that she didn't deserve every morsel of attention as the world's most delightful companion in a first-class compartment or a rococo bedroom or a velvet banquette tasseled and fringed. Not that Lee wasn't grateful. Not that she wasn't having the time of her life.

Marguerite was wonderful.

Marguerite was impossible.

Wasn't it normal to want to murder someone who was getting away with murder, as long as you didn't act on it? Lee remembered the definition of *ambivalence* in her Introduction to Psychology textbook: *the coexistence within an individual of positive and negative feelings toward the same person, simultaneously drawing him or her in opposite directions.* She'd received an A in the course. *Consider this as a major, as a potential career,* the professor had written in red ink on the cover of her blue book. *Let's talk.* They hadn't. Lee had picked up her exam, checked out her grade on the department bulletin board, and hurried out to the waiting car, her parents impatient to drive her and her matching set of luggage to the airport with plenty of time to get her brand-new passport checked.

What she wanted to ask her psychology professor now was this: she understood ambivalent feelings toward a person. But what about the object of that ambivalence herself, who contained so many contradictions, so many positives and negatives, so much yin, so much yang, all within a five-foot-three, 110-pound grandmother? For instance, why was her grandmother so cheap about so many things? About stealing linens, to pick an example. Or saving string. Using up toothpick-thin slivers of soap before she'd peel the paper off a fresh cut-rate bar. And yet so extravagant. Only real butter. Only the heaviest of cream. Perfumes from France. Chocolates from Belgium and hotel rooms with marble tubs and heated towel racks. Lee had seen her dicker over a couple of centimes in a taxicab, then buy a single pink camellia for fifteen francs.

Her parents, on the other hand, were exactly what they seemed: kind, levelheaded, dependable citizens who voted, paid taxes, kept their house in good repair, respected nature, supported local charities, prized education. Their duty was to pass on these solid Yankee values to their only daughter. Perhaps they needed to work even harder to combat the Marguerite gene.

As for Lee herself . . . who was she anyway? Denim or silk? Home or abroad? Did personality mean compromise? Would a particular cluster of inherited traits turn out to be dominant? Maybe the self was simply cooked up like a stew—a pinch from this jar, a sprinkling from that bin. Right now she felt like an uncompleted portrait. The question was, Did she alone get to pick who'd fill in the defining strokes?

No such existential agonies plagued her grandmother. On the airplane over, Marguerite had tucked into her alligator pocketbook packets of mustard, ketchup, sugar, and salt, then ordered caviar. "Have some, darling," her grandmother commanded, holding out a tiny, translucent spoon.

Lee shook her head. She clutched the airsickness bag. The plane bumped through every cloud, bobbed up and down across miles of turbulence. Rain dashed the windows. Fog shuttered away any light. The steward brought Marguerite a complimentary glass of champagne. "Poor dear." Her grandmother had given Lee's heaving back a tender pat. "You'll be fine. I promise you, darling, we will have fun. Such magnificent fun."

As promised, they had fun. Magnificent fun. Opera, museums, theater, restaurants. Born in Alsace and at home in the great cities of Europe, her grandmother spoke every language like a native. And like a native, ate tongue and brains, sweetbreads and knuckles, snails and frog legs, pigeons and wild boar. Platters of strange-looking strange-smelling things Lee could hardly bear to gaze upon. They got up with the birds. Stayed out with the night owls. Went through all the starred sights in Lee's travel book. "Surprise, surprise," Lee wrote home on a postcard of the Arc de Triomphe, "Marguerite's the toast of the continent."

"How can you have a granddaughter, Madame?" asked a

man in Vienna with a curling mustache and a silver-tipped walking stick. "You can't possibly be old enough."

"What a lucky *jeune fille*," pronounced a man on a bench at the Louvre, "with a *maman* so completely *fantastique*."

She *was* lucky. Nevertheless, if she was having the time of her life, then why did Lee feel so often like a spear-carrier receding into the scenery away from the diva's spot-lit aria? "Our hearts are young and gay," she wrote home on a postcard of the Vienna Opera House, "especially Grandmother's."

"You're beautiful. Lovely," her grandmother said. "You remind me of myself."

"I adore you, Magnolia," her grandmother emphasized.

Lee understood she was adored. As practiced in the so-cial arts as her grandmother was, Lee realized Marguerite lacked the guile not to tell the truth. Lee knew she could do no wrong no matter what she did: her grandmother loved her because of the simple fact that she was hers. Even though Marguerite might be irritated, or disap-pointed, these feelings wouldn't last. Her love was pure and unconditional. Unlike Lee, whose protestations of gratitude and cries of admiration didn't always spring full-blown from the heart, her grandmother never offered what was expected or desired. Basking in being adored, Lee at the same time worried about not measuring up. If she was the apple of her grandmother's eye, she also felt like its worm. She was getting used to playing ingenue to her grandmother's star. She accepted her role as second ba-nana, second string, second-class citizen. What concerned her most, however, was to end up second-rate. Not that she'd have much chance to prove herself otherwise. "Be popular," her grandmother commanded one afternoon in Paris, pushing her toward a young man her age in the lobby of the hotel. But when they began to talk, when he bought her a *citron pressé*, and pulled out a chair for her at a table next to the bar, her grandmother, sitting alone by the potted palm, started to pout.

That night, Lee screwed up her courage. Her grandmother stood in front of the bathroom mirror. Her jewelry lay heaped in a discarded mound on the countertop. She slathered her face with cold cream, then wiped it off with cotton balls piled like meringues inside a silver-stoppered decanter of faceted glass. She unpinned her French twist. She removed the "rat," the gray net Tootsie Roll that she wrapped the front of her hair around. Unadorned, she looked older, like a grandmother. Unarmed, without makeup, and jewels, and clothes, and her rat, she looked approachable.

Lee approached. She picked her words. "What I don't understand," she began, "is that you want me to be popular, to meet people, to go out. And, yet, when I do . . ." her voice trailed off. She waved her hands in the air as if she were finishing the sentence in sign language.

One more language her grandmother seemed to grasp because—in quick succession—shock, anger, and acceptance moved across her naked face. Marguerite sank down onto the terry-cloth-padded stool. She grabbed Lee's hand. "I want everything for you. I want you to leave Maine. I want you to have a wonderful life. A great love. Travel. Excitement. Absolute happiness."

"I know that."

"But at the same time . . ." Marguerite stopped.

"Yes?"

Her grandmother reached up. She pulled Lee's face down to her own. Her grandmother's eyes were cloudy. The arch of her brows had been rubbed off. She cleared her throat. "This will shock you."

"I don't think so. I doubt anything will." *I am beyond shock*, Lee told herself.

Her grandmother looked away. Then gathered her resolve. "I'm jealous of you, darling. My own adored granddaughter. Your youth. Your beauty. You have your whole life in front of you. And I . . ."

So much for being beyond shock. *Jealous?* Impossible! Lee put her cheek against her grandmother's, which, in spite of the cream, felt thin and papery. Her grandmother's shoulders were bony knobs. Her hand trembled. Her breath came in quick hot rasps. Her perfume smelled off, like wine gone vinegary.

". . . and I am old. And afraid to be alone."

Lee's own fear rose to her throat. She slowed her own breath. "I'll never leave you," Lee swore. "You have my word."

"Of course you will. I want you to. I expect you to." Her grandmother stood up. She fluffed her hair with an ivory-backed brush. She smiled a big brave smile, put on for show. In seconds, however, she began to look more like her former self. She laughed with an undiminished peal. "Though not for a while." She swept her hair back and secured it with a clip. "Besides, *chérie*, before you try out your own little wings, I want to have a hand in picking out just the right prince for my princess."

It was a relief for them to land in London. A city where her grandmother had once lived. Where the telephone numbers of people she had known in her youth were tucked into the old Moroccan leather notebook she'd bought on the rue du Bac. Where these friends, and the sons and grandsons of these friends, might give them a break from their constant room-for-two, tea-for-two, table-for-two, two-on-the-aisle togetherness.

Bingo! They scored right away with the first family on her grandmother's list. Alistair and Hermione Abernathy couldn't have been more thrilled to hear from their dazzling friend whom they talked about so often and with such fondness. Yes, their daughter was away at university, but their son, Simon, was living at home and was about to start medical school. And wasn't it just amazing, the most uncanny of coincidences, that they had a son the exact age of Marguerite's lovely Magnolia? Of course they had begun their own family late, well after Sam Rybier had whisked Marguerite off to America (London was never the same after *that*), but still, how could it be possible, what kind of alchemy had occurred, that this beauty of Belgravia was—gasp—a grandmother? Wouldn't it be sweet if the children—dare one even hope?—took to each other. Though you couldn't count on such a thing these days. In fact, you'd probably have to expect the opposite.

But there was something to say, wasn't there, for old-fashioned arranged marriages.

The elevator descended, carrying Lee and her grand-mother down to the hotel lobby. Lee was wearing a green silk shirtdress her grandmother had bought her in Paris, matching shoes, and her suit-of-armor underwear—girdle, stockings, garter, a full slip over what salesladies called intimate apparel. Pearl-buttoned white kid gloves grazed the cuffs of her sleeves. "How sweet you look," her grand-mother cooed. Marguerite herself looked far from sweet, Lee noted, more like the actress her father had forbidden her to be. Cherries and grapes dotted her hat; diamond clasps glinted from her lapels. Jade and coral bracelets snaked up one arm. On the other, enough instruments to fill the string section of a middle-size orchestra hung in gold from a thick-linked chain. When she moved, her own brass section jangled and clanked. She was the only woman in the world, Lee thought, who could carry off—and overpower—such embellishment.

"Are you excited, darling?" her grandmother asked.

"Always. Everything's an adventure when you're around."

"You know what I mean."

"Not really."

"A young man your own age. You can't spend *every* eve-ning sticking to your grandmother." She lowered her voice. "Rest assured," she whispered, "I've quite gotten over my little *crise* in the Paris hotel."

Lee remembered the knobbed shoulder, the parchment

cheek. "But I want to stick to you. I can't imagine a better companion in the whole entire world."

Her grandmother rattled her bracelets. She made a few last adjustments to the cherries looping her Carmen Miranda brim. She nodded her head. The cherries bounced. "I can understand that. *Mais alors, ma chérie.* I have a good instinct about this."

When the elevator doors opened revealing the united front of Abernathy Mum and Dad—she in twinset, he in pin-stripes and a paisley pocket handkerchief—Lee wasn't so sure about the reliability of her grandmother's instinct. This yeomen-of-the-guard couple formed a solid, stolid barrier behind which their son seemed to lurk, all body language screaming *brought against my will, taken into captivity and forced to do slave labor by whip-wielding autocrats.*

This first impression was seconded the minute the Abernathys, releasing Marguerite from their jolly embrace, yanked Simon forward. Then gave him the shove of a piano teacher pushing a recital-averse student toward the Steinway to perform a few bars of *Für Elise.* Simon cowered. Was he trembling? Lee understood; she sympathized. Matchmaking by parents—or a grandmother—could only rend asunder. The same reason the children of your parents' nearest and dearest rarely turn out to be your friends.

"Alistair and I are spiriting Marguerite away for dinner," announced Hermione. "As Simon is just dying to take Magnolia out on his own."

I bet, thought Lee. "Actually, it's Lee," she explained.

Hermione flashed the smile of a fellow sufferer. "And I'm Hetty," she said.

"Shall we go, then?" asked Simon. He stepped forward and stumbled into a flowering orchid which he caught just before it slid off its marble shelf.

Lee nodded, a gesture of mutual recognition for their involuntary servitude. It was one thing in his favor, she had to cede, that he accepted his doom with the kind of let's-get-on-with-it grace the British displayed in the Blitz. She studied him. While hardly handsome, he had interesting looks. And not in the way her mother used the word—as a euphemism for ugly. He was slight and dark with a long, irregular, narrow face saved by the kind of cheekbones model agencies advertised for. She thought back to what she'd learned in art history class. Over the centuries, the ideal of Greek-god symmetry evolved into an appreciation for the textured, elongated Giacometti line. Perfect beauty was boring, anyway. Certainly Simon had the kind of eyes romance writers might refer to as deep soulful pools of pitch-black poetry.

Not that they had any effect on her. Not for a minute was she going to please her grandmother by falling for this awkward young man.

This isn't how I'd choose to spend my evening either, she wanted to say to him during their short, silent hardship-duty trudge to the obligatory meal.

In the pub, a block from the hotel, he ordered them the Scotch eggs and shepherd's pie scribbled across the sandwich board of daily specials that jammed the front door. He opened his mouth. "So," he began. He cracked his knuckles. Each in turn. On both hands.

She waited.

"Your grandmother's beautiful," he said.

Heat climbed from her collarbone and blasted her neck. She was aware of two circles the size of silver dollars flaming her cheeks.

So here it was. Would she have expected anything else? Marguerite could grab the spotlight in a room even when she wasn't in the room. Even when Lee might reasonably assume to have captured the sole attention of the single other occupant of their booth. Who would never see her without her grandmother's face superimposed on her own.

Irritation flattened into resignation. What was the point of getting upset? She might as well leave now. But where would she go? Back to the hotel to watch old movies about male camaraderie on battlefields? Or love in the drawing rooms of stately homes?

She shifted her gaze to the tables beyond their inglenook. In the dim and smoky pub, the beer was as black as Simon's eyes. Which were now so locked on his Guinness he might have been decoding the Rosetta Stone in its creamy froth. Peals of laughter rose from the bar. Balls knocked together on the pool table in the corner and dropped into side pockets with a thud. An old man was singing "Danny Boy" in the booth next to them. Crumbs from previous meals stuck to their scarred wooden tabletop where someone had carved *Rupert Loves Mavis* into the stained oak. An empty pack of Players Navy Cut lay crumpled into the ashtray on top of four ground-out cigarette stubs. The Birds of a Feather Public House was a far cry from the plush restaurants and hotel dining halls where Lee and Marguerite had been unpleating napkins as big as towels onto their full-finery laps.

What a dump.

Lee turned toward Simon. "People have been talking about my grandmother's beauty as long as I can remember," she explained, trying to keep the edge out of her voice. She looked down at her green silk skirt not surprised to see a snowfall of salt spilled onto her knees. She brushed it away. She peeled off her gloves. She was too dressed up. What must Simon think of her? she wondered.

Then again, why would she care?

A blush spread across Simon's cheekbones like the shadow moving across the map of Europe in newsreels about World War Two. "What must you think of me?" he asked.

"Nothing so far." She caught herself. "Since we just met."

"Not that. To give such a compliment to your grand-mother, to talk about your grandmother when you're . . ." He paused. He tugged his ear. He chewed his lip. His elbow grazed the Worcestershire. ". . . when such a vision of sub-lime loveliness is sitting in my direct line of view."

She smiled. She couldn't help herself. "That sounds lifted straight from a drawing room comedy," she pointed out.

Abashed, he ducked his head. "It probably is. I'm afraid my conversational models come either from heavy nineteenth-century novels or the kind of overly bright rep-artee you'd find in farce."

"Maybe, in this instance, the nineteenth century might be the better choice."

"I'm sure you're right." He kneaded his chin. "But all

suitable bearing-the-test-of-time phrases seem to have deserted me." He pummeled his napkin as if he hoped a thesaurus might emerge from its shreds.

Would she ever have imagined a city boy so physically country-bumpkinish? "It's okay," she soothed. "Don't feel you have to treat my grandmother and me the same. We're not siblings demanding equal time. Or equal compliments."

"Talk about getting off on the wrong foot. The one not permanently inserted into my mouth, that is. You look just like her. It's only . . ."

Lee held up a hand. "Don't worry. I'm used to it. I've been traveling one full month with my grandmother. I know how she draws every eye."

"You sound like one of those downtrodden governesses, those penniless paid companions in the novels my sister used to read."

"*Jane Eyre.*"

"*Jane Eyre.*"

"My favorite book," Lee confided. "I must have read it half a dozen times."

"Me, too," he said. "The sister remark is merely camouflage in case a passion for *Jane Eyre* is a trait you'd consider unseemly in a male."

"Not at all." Lee felt ice start to thaw, the weakening of steely resolve. "I'd say liking—loving—*Jane Eyre* is definitely in your favor."

"That's something then."

It was, she had to agree. A man who named *Jane Eyre* his favorite book must be the rarest of birds. If not almost extinct. "Isn't the ending wonderful?" she went on. "Though I can't tell you how many of my friends couldn't understand why Jane would go back to Mr. Rochester once she saw Thornfield in ruins and Mr. Rochester blind and crippled and in ruins, too."

"She loved him," Simon stated. Three words. A short declarative sentence. A simple fact.

"Yes, she loved him," repeated Lee.

"In this country, sadly enough," he added, "boys don't tend to read Brontë."

"In Maine, too," she said, "but then it's their loss." She remembered the first time she'd opened the covers of the book, how she'd carried the novel with her everywhere, its pages stained by tomato soup, by smudged fingers, by snow, by leaky fountain pens, by tears. "Still, my seventh-grade boyfriend did audition for—and get the part of—Mr. Rochester in our school play. He was, however, the only boy who tried out."

Simon's voice creaked up an octave. He frowned. "And because of the role, this particular Rochester stayed your boyfriend as a self-fulfilling prophecy?"

"At *thirteen*? Hardly. Especially since he hammed up the blind part, tripped over his cane, and tore my downtrodden-governess gown." She laughed. "I played Jane."

Simon leaned toward her. "That's what I'd call casting against type. Brontë makes it quite clear that Jane was—well—a plain Jane, and you . . ." He looked away.

Lee felt her head spring up in the preening manner of mating peacocks or vain grandmothers.

Simon cracked two more knuckles, then turned his palms

over like a supplicant. "I'm afraid I'm just hopeless at all this."

"You're doing fine."

"And *you're* amazingly polite. Considering." He ran a finger over *Rupert Loves Mavis*. He traced the letters as if he were reading Braille. He stopped on the *L*. "At the risk of mucking things up even more, I feel compelled to add . . ." He paused. ". . . I would have said it first—I wanted to—but a remark of this sort seems a bit forward for someone who imbibes British reserve with his tea. And yet . . ."

"Yes," she coaxed. *Pulling teeth*, her mother would have said. *Yanking weeds.*

"Your grandmother must be jealous of you."

She must have looked astonished, mouth agape, like that painting of *The Scream* her grandmother had been so excited about, because Simon went on, "I know this sounds like I'm trying to recoup lost ground, but believe me, I don't have the finesse to say something I don't mean. Let me put it this way. If you'll allow me to finish what I started earlier . . ." Once more, he ran a thumb over *Rupert Loves Mavis*. Once more he stopped on the *L*. "You are far more beautiful than she is, you know."

Beautiful? Lee's jaw dropped. Astonishment changed to a kind of joy.

Simon knocked over the bottle of Worcestershire sauce. Less an accident than a diversionary tactic, she intuited from the blush that was once again spreading across his exceptional cheeks. He daubed at a widening puddle of brown liquid like a desperate Dutch boy with his thumb in the dike.

Lee lifted the tankard of beer, which was as thick as sludge. And tasted like it. She supposed people could get used to anything. "I like the beer," she lied.

A change of subject, which seemed to bring Simon a measure of relief. He stopped blotting the sauce. He abandoned the napkin. He stretched his arms out to his sides. "Wait till you try the Scotch egg. We're proud of our best bitter—justifiably, I might add—but our food is truly terrible."

As if on cue, the barmaid slammed down their plates. "Bloody hell," she swore. Congealed into a drab indistinguishable mass, the pub specialties looked as appealing as the contents of the overflowing ashtray. She shoved silverware and more paper napkins into Simon's hand. Sweat beaded her upper lip. Half-moons of it curved under her arms. "Can you do the honors, duck? I can't be in twenty places all at once."

Simon folded the napkins into triangles. He set out the silverware with the meticulousness of a surgeon arranging instruments on a sterile cloth.

"I fear I'm the typical product of the English school system. All boys since the age of four. I'm hopeless with any girl who isn't my sister and who doesn't carry a field hockey stick."

"Especially when you're forced by your parents to take some friend's granddaughter out."

"Is it that obvious?"

"I'm afraid so. You have my sympathy."

"My mother quite despairs of me. The reason she was so eager to inflict her only son on you as guinea pig."

"Don't worry."

"That's all I'm doing. Have been doing. Not to mention acting like the dimmest, most pathetic twit. An absolute child."

Lee assumed her possible-psych-major stance. "It's common knowledge that girls mature earlier," she instructed.

"Even in America?"

"Even in America." She studied her Scotch egg in its dense, grease-saturated, breaded crust. What's Scotch about it? she wondered. Maybe because you can't tell what's inside the same way you can't see what lies underneath a kilt. "It is nice here that no one asks you to prove your age before they serve you alcohol."

"You can drink legally at sixteen. Probably a health measure to mask our social awkwardness."

Lee laughed.

Simon put a fork into his shepherd's pie. The potatoes were yellow and lumpy; the meat so gray and so stringy it could have been one of the unidentifiable organs her grandmother was always eager to devour. The whole thing looked dry as dust. Sawdust. "Actually, this isn't half bad," he said.

Lee picked up her own fork. It tasted awful. She was delighted. So much for those French chefs lording their toques in the English restaurants her grandmother chose, their Gallic touches complicating the roast beef and Yorkshire pudding, their unapologetic *sole à la meunière* or *boeuf bourguignon* served on china from Spode and Wedgwood and linens from Liberty. At last, an authentic experience. Real life.

"Actually," Simon said, "I'm having rather a marvelous time. I've quite surprised myself." A sense of wonder lit his face like a slowly rising sun. She'd have to admit there was something endearing about his odd looks, this terrible meal, this noisy, smoky dive, the off-putting barmaid, the off-tune *the pipes they are a calling*, this bitter dark beer, this awkward dark boy whose words came out the wrong way and made her laugh. All of a sudden the food tasted glorious.

"I'm having a good time, too," she said, surprising herself. She tried another sip of Guinness. Was it starting to grow on her?

Later, after dinner, Simon suggested a walk in the park. "Not my parents' idea," he added. "My own." He paused. "Unless you have to get back."

For some reason—the beer? the boy?—the offered straw of an excuse did not tempt her. "I'd like that," she said. "I mean I could certainly stand to walk off some of this food."

His eyes swept her waist. "I don't think you need to walk off anything."

They took the underpass at Hyde Park Corner. Simon gripped her elbow to steer her out of the path of three-abreast businessmen swinging briefcases and walking sticks. The minute they passed, he let go. Did he see her as some Boy Scout project? she wondered, unaccountably annoyed. Was she an act of mercy for which he could earn an extra merit badge?

Not that she wanted him to clutch her elbow anyway.

Her mood didn't improve when they came up the ramp to the sidewalk. Simon backed away from her. He stepped off the curb; he knelt down to scoop something up.

He held it out.

It was a child's airplane fashioned of cardboard and Popsicle sticks. Smudges of paste pocked the edge. One wing was bent. The other, torn. A piece of the tail was missing. Red crayon rectangles marked the windows. Mud streaked both sides and smeared the nose.

Lee turned around. "There's a trash bin just over there," she pointed. Who would pick something like this out of the gutter? she asked herself.

Simon shook off the dust. He smoothed the creased wing. He swooped the plane through the air in a figure-eight.

"This airplane has just crossed the sea and landed at my feet," he said. Gently he wedged it between two poles on the iron fence. He tapped and prodded, testing that it was secure. "I'd like to think," he said, "that whenever its owner comes back, he'll find it waiting there."

Lee's breath pounded in her ears like the ocean roar inside a shell. She touched the nose of the plane, its torn wing. She thought of Jane Eyre's long journey to find Mr. Rochester. She ran her fingers over the Popsicle stick stained strawberry at its tip. She pictured a sparrow that had flown into the window on her parents' garage door and stunned itself. Her mother had fed it water through an eyedropper; she had braced its wing with a Popsicle stick splint. They had all cheered from the back porch when it flapped its mended wing and soared up toward the highest branches of the trees.

"I'm awfully glad you came," Simon said.

"Me, too," she seconded. A small whorl of black hair peeked up though the top of his shirt just under his throat. She stared at it.

"I'm so happy you can say that, despite the difficulties of traveling with your grandmother," he added.

Lee stopped. "Does it show that much?" she asked.

He shook his head. "Not in the least." He took a step closer and Lee could see, under the hair, the small pulse throb in his throat like the ticking breast of a bird.

Lee felt a wave of dizziness. Was it something she ate? She forced her eyes away from his throat. She focused her attention on what he'd just said. "There are moments when my grandmother makes me feel like your downtrodden governess." She twisted a button on her cuff. "It's this trip. It's magical in so many ways, such a huge treat, that I despise myself when I dare to question . . ."

"Who wouldn't react like that? Under such a circumstance."

"But don't you think it's awful of me?"

His voice was quiet. Kind. "Not awful. Not awful at all."

And with those words, the kindness in them, yes, but also something else—interest? understanding?—words so soft Lee had to lean in to hear them, stones dislodged; floodgates opened. "Sometimes I hate my grandmother," she confessed.

She waited. No shock marked his face. No judgment flickered across his eyes.

Allowing a month's worth of injustices to come pouring out.

"I never told anyone that before," Lee said at last. "I didn't know I could ever say such things. This trip smacks of her personal propaganda. *Be like me*, is her message. *Want what I want*. As if all that glitters really *is* gold."

"I understand," said Simon. "How odd that what's supposed to be wonderful so often isn't. For instance, you've got your heart set on a Scotch egg." He stopped; he shook his head. "Not the best example. Let's say chocolate pudding. But once you have it, once you've gobbled it down, you're not sure. What about the lemon sponge? Or the raspberry cream?"

"Exactly," she agreed. "Human nature. Alas." Can it happen—is it possible—she wondered, that by the time your fair Prince Charming on his white steed crosses the moat to you, you might discover that the dark stranger on the other side of the elevator intrigues you more?

"And quite the reverse," Simon went on, "can come about, too. What you think you don't want. What you actually dread—a trip. A pub meal. An evening your mother's forced upon you—could turn out to be wonderful."

She stared at the little plane. At the hand adjusting it. At the whorl of hair against a throat. At the curve of a cheek. At the unvarnished, unglittering man.

Pure gold.

"Can I hold your hand?" Simon asked as they entered the gate.

"Lesson number one," Lee said. "Don't ask, just take."

Simon took. He had long thin fingers. She could feel his bones, his sharp knuckles, the bump of his wrist. The flesh was soft. Warm. His hand fit as snugly around hers as the kid gloves she had been wearing earlier. Is this what travel did? Broaden you enough to change your life?

"One thing you should know," he said. "I'm a good student. Give me a lesson and I grasp it immediately."

He squeezed. She squeezed.

She would never let go.

Hands fused, clenched, fingers laced, they wandered the paths. Everywhere she saw lovers. Among the pensioners, the families, and—because this was England—among enough dogs of enough varied breeds to form an international kennel club. She knew Paris, not London, was the place for lovers. How could you miss them along the Seine, in the Bois de Boulogne? But here?

Even here.

She wanted to stretch her arm across Simon's back, to place her fingers on the hard rise of his hip, to slide them lower the way the couple walking like conjoined twins in front of them cupped what Marguerite would call their *derrières*. What was wrong with her? She made herself stop. Perhaps, away from home, ready for an adventure, she would see any frog her own age as a prince just for a few hours out from under her grandmother. Perhaps she was so used to accommodating her grandmother that she'd accommodate any boy her grandmother picked out for her.

Not likely, she told herself, as Simon talked of Beethoven symphonies, of Shelley and of Keats. Of how he read poetry every night in bed. Of his evening treks on Hampstead Heath.

Each word entranced. The park shimmered with light. Babies, cream and pink, flapped their plump arms like Cupid's wings. Dogs wagged their tails and cocked their ears at her. The air floated with the scent of flowers. Even a bum snoozing on a bench seemed quaint.

They talked as if they'd been talking together from their

bassinets. His parents were worried that he had no social life, he confided. Maybe he'd turn out to be one of those crazy British eccentrics who harangued people at bus stops and coffee bars, who lived a hermit's life in a cabin in the forest with no electricity and no heat. He sounded as if this was something to aspire to, like choosing to major in psychology.

"But you're going to medical school," she countered. "At least that's what my grandmother said."

"One doesn't exclude the other. There's no telling what madmen lurk along the corridors of a hospital."

Simon dragged her out of the way of an oncoming perambulator, which, though right under her nose, she hadn't even seen. This time, he kept his arm around her. He held her tight. He pulled her against him; their hips touched; their thighs, knees, feet moved in step as if they were bound together for a three-legged race. Underneath silk and cotton and wool lay bones and skin and organs—certain organs in particular. Is this love? she wondered. Does it happen like that? On a path in the park at dusk with the whole city spread out? In a hotel lobby with your grandmother, elevator doors opening like curtains on a stage to reveal the one person who was meant for you?

Perhaps Simon was the romantic hero sprung to life in the novels she'd been reading for her English literature survey class. A Heathcliff brooding on the moor. A Mr. Rochester hiding his anguished heart. An artist, a European, an intellectual. He certainly *seemed* the opposite of those silly Homestead what-you-saw-was-what-you-got boys all wrapped up in fraternity parties, cars, and juvenile sports events. With their boringly perfect teeth, their dime-a-dozen wide shoulders, their unexceptional healthy glowing skin enriched by vitamins and homegrown vegetables. Imagine if, mad at her grandmother and mired in high school expectations of what constituted a dreamboat, she'd come close to missing the one person who was meant for her.

Lee slung her arm across Simon's back. Simon grabbed her hand. He guided it into the back pocket of his pants.

And held it there.

At Speakers' Corner, a small crowd had gathered. A man stood on an overturned box. He wore a top hat. His eyes were wild. "We are an insular race," he declaimed. "Provincial and closed off. Dark and difficult. Narrow in our thinking and our desires. Now how do we change all this? How do we go from the dark to the light?" He rotated his head with the evenly spaced nods you'd see in films of Queen Elizabeth acknowledging her subjects from her Cinderella chariot.

"Get out of here," somebody cried.

"Let's get out of here," Simon echoed.

"But I want to find out how to go from the dark to the light."

Simon pulled her across the grass. "And I want to go into the dark."

Which wasn't hard given how fast dusk changed to night. The fragment of her mind not focused on her hand tingling in the pocket over Simon's *derrière* sensed that people were leaving the park, streaming through assorted entrances. Somewhere in the outside world, along the curb, ice cream trucks were closing their windows, starting their engines, and steering into the glut of traffic. On the sidewalk, post-card vendors were boxing their scenes of Big Ben and the Tower of London and folding up their tables. Dogs, with their masters and mistresses in thrall, stopped sniffing tree trunks and pulled their weary walkers home.

Simon led Lee into the dark toward a cluster of gnarled and ancient chestnut trees. The sky was black. Wind whistled through the leaves. Lee heard the honk of a goose. The rustling of creatures that come out only when the sun goes down. She smelled damp earth and flowers, roses, jasmine, and a musky scent she couldn't recognize. If it hadn't been for the hum of traffic along Park Lane, she and Simon could have been two people alone on a heath or a moor.

Simon started to spread his sweater on the ground to make them a nest.

He froze, a sleeve held in midair as if he were about to swoop it into a waltz. "Listen," he whispered. "A nightingale."

He pulled her down next to him. It was all too much. The park. The bird. The tree.

The man.

Simon took her into his arms. He touched his thumb to the hollow of her throat.

An airplane flew overhead, churning its propellers and buzzing treetops. In the distance, Lee could hear a rumble of thunder.

"Rain?" she asked.

"Shhh." Simon put his finger on her lips. "It wouldn't dare."

If it did, it wouldn't matter, Lee knew. She was impervious. Oh, God, what was Simon doing with his hands?

Simon slid his mouth to her ear. "Since I'm going to see you tomorrow and the day after that and the day after that and every day until you leave—and no, not because my mother is standing there with a riding crop, and not because your grandmother is standing there with a cattle prod—don't you think we could skip some lessons in between?"

"Absolutely," she agreed. Beyond his shoulder stretched the sky, filled with stars and a gauze of fog.

"My darling," Simon whispered. His breath puffed warm and soft; his hair fell across her brow. He ran his fingers up and down her arm. He stroked her neck, her cheek.

She shivered.

"Cold?" he asked.

"No," she said. Just the opposite.

Overhead the trees whirled. Underneath them the hard ground teetered. She smelled licorice and cinnamon. She smelled roses, and wet grass. She looped her arms around his back. Through his shirt, heat rose from his skin.

She tightened her grasp. Thunder rumbled; lightning crackled; the tree shook.

He kissed her.

This is it, Lee knew. This is love.

For a long time they kissed. Rain spluttered, then stopped. The ripe tang of lanolin floated up from his damp sweater. His shirt was wet, her stockings drenched.

They didn't notice.

They kissed some more. All lips and tongues and fast hot breath.

"I'm pathetically Neanderthal," Simon whispered. "I never realized before what you can do with a tongue."

Lee pictured the orator at Speakers' Corner. What he had said about an "insular race. Closed off. Narrow in our desires." Hardly, she thought. She cursed the public park and the insurmountable obstacle of her girdle that began at her midriff and ended at her knee, her plain serviceable bra and unadorned slip, their puzzling straps and hooks, their confusing buttons and clasps, the elastic carapace that subdued her flesh.

Simon laid a hand on her tunneled-to-tautness hip. "Can you breathe in that?" he asked.

"Barely," she allowed. "Isn't it ridiculous?"

His fingers smoothed the green silk over her breast. He tugged at a silver button. "How dare I complain?"

Later, when at last the cold seeped into their equatorial body heat, they stopped. "You know I love you," Simon said.

Lee's heart opened; her throat closed up.

Then it was time to go. They wrenched themselves toward the exit. Arm in arm. Step to step.

This is love, said the Jane Eyre in her. Lightning struck. You've found him.

You've just met him, warned the Maine in her. Remember, lightning split the tree in half; rent it asunder.

I love you, Simon had said.

Yet in a few days she was going home. She must proceed with caution. To protect herself, she must put up barriers.

Though the barriers now in front of her were not the kind she meant. The gate they'd come in was locked. The gate nearest their cluster of trees, their trysting place, was locked. They rattled it. Lee pictured gorillas in captivity, frantic behind the bars of a zoo. She pictured Cathy and Heathcliff alone on a moor.

Terrifying.

Thrilling.

"Don't worry," Simon said, worried. "We'll circle the park. We'll try every gate. Surely there'll be one that's open."

"But the park is enormous," Lee protested. "Three hundred and forty acres. Miles and miles in circumference. It says so in my Baedeker."

"Then we'll have to spend the night." Simon grinned.

Yes. *Yes,* she thought.

"All night. Just the two of us," he emphasized.

Lee heard movement, the click of little hooves. There was more than just the two of them. Were there foxes in these woods? Rabid species native to these three hundred and forty acres of inky wilderness? What did a country girl understand about a city park? There was danger here. Not to mention the danger three blocks away in a five-star hotel. "What about my grandmother?" she cried.

Simon groaned. His getting-on-with-it-in-the-Blitz groan, one she was fast growing to recognize. "Alas. The world is too much with us. Namely, the senior Abernathys. Namely, the estimable Marguerite. Who in another hour will be calling Scotland Yard. There must be an exit." He tugged at the sleeve of his sweater now matted with mud. "What time is it anyway?"

Lee looked at the watch her grandmother had given her for her tenth birthday. It was platinum with diamonds marking the corners and a ruby on its stem. When she snapped open the red velvet box, her chest had heaved with disappointment. She'd been hoping for a Mickey Mouse. "My God, it's almost twelve!" she exclaimed.

"With thee conversing, I forget all time, all seasons and their change," quoted Simon. "Milton, *Paradise Lost.*"

"Paradise lost is right," said Lee yanking a padlocked gate. Next to it, she saw a sign chained to a metal post. *Caution*, it read. *The park closes at ten. All entrances and exits will be locked. Kindly evacuate with dispatch. No people are allowed on the premises after hours.*

"Simon," she pointed.

"Our only choice is to climb."

Lee examined the fence. Heavy iron painted black. Topped by the kind of spikes that must have speared freshly decapitated heads in the fourteenth century. She remembered once being locked inside the Homestead municipal track with a bunch of friends. She wore sneakers and jeans. Fifteen feet tall, the fence was chain, each chink big enough for the toe of a small-size foot. And somebody's mother had driven her station wagon right up against the other side to break the drop. She can still hear the hoots of laughter as, one by one, a whooping kid bounced onto the Oldsmobile's luggage rack.

No laughter now, she thought, more its opposite. She

held back tears. So this was the emotional roller coaster called love. Back then, she wasn't in the process of giving away her heart. A process that involved embarrassment at a lack of grace, humiliation at the prospect of someone peering up your skirt. *I see England, I see France. I see Magnolia's underpants* went the schoolyard chant. Speaking geographically, a self-fulfilling prophecy ten years after the fact.

Simon made a sling of his hands. "Let me give you a boost."

She lifted her foot. "Don't you dare look up my skirt."

"Scout's honor. As an English gentleman."

That she made it over was a miracle. Especially since she reached the summit and achieved the descent without drawing blood. Her clothes, however, didn't do half so well as her unpierced flesh. Her stockings were shredded. Her dress stained with rust. The heel to one patent leather shoe had disappeared. She thought of rock climbers, mountain climbers, those fools who scaled the sides of skyscrapers. Imagine calling such a thing a sport.

Simon hadn't managed any better. His sweater, which minutes before had lined their love nest, was now unraveling at the sleeve where a spike had skewered it. The cuffs of his trousers hung into a fringe, and a rather elegantly modeled knee with a sweet dimple on its tip now poked through a hole in the gray gabardine.

"I don't want to do *that* again," Lee declared.

Simon brushed away some leaves epauletting his shoulders. He pulled a twig from his hair. "It was worth it though." He rested against the gate to catch his breath. He flashed a cockeyed grin. "For the sight of those knickers."

He leaned forward. He tucked a lank of her hair behind her ear. He looked around with the staginess of a bad guy checking if the coast was clear. "This way," he whispered. He pulled her to the end of the gate. He steered her behind a post papered with flyers for concerts and restaurants. She could just make out, by the fogged light of a distant street lamp, a tattered, mimeographed notice: *For a good time, call Jane.* A ring of red hearts circled the telephone number. Under which somebody had penciled, *Hot. Hot. Hot.*

"What?" she asked Simon.

"This," Simon said. He reached up under her skirt. He found her garters.

Lee held her breath.

It took a couple of false starts, but, soon enough, with the kind of precision that validated a career choice in surgery, he unsnapped each one. Slowly, gently, as if he were handling delicate porcelain, fragile glass, he rolled her stockings down. He knelt on the hard dank pavement. "Lee," he whispered. His voice cracked. With cold? She wondered. Or—perhaps she might safely assume—desire.

She stepped out of her shoes. One intact; the other missing its heel.

He pulled the stockings off. He laid them on the patch of grass bordering the gate. He took her feet into his hands. He stroked her toes. He rubbed the bottom of each sole. He touched his lips to the inside of her wet and muddy and spike-abraded arch. Her whole leg sprang up as if he'd tapped her knee with the little hammer from a doctor's kit.

Then he slid her shoes back on.

She pointed to the stockings. A tattered, sodden tangled

mess. Fit only for the garbage bin. "They're ruined," she said. "We might as well abandon them."

"Never," he said. He picked them up. He wadded them. Lovingly, like clay in the hands of a master potter, he swiveled the coil of nylon between his palms.

And, to Lee's amazement, slid them into the pocket of his pants.

A man stumbled toward them. His jacket slung off one shoulder. He bumped a signpost. He lurched into a fire hydrant. *The summer's gone, and all the flowers are dying*, they heard him sing. Was it the same man from the Birds of a Feather Pub? Lee wondered. Or was there a whole army of Guinness drinkers out there wailing "Danny Boy"? *'Tis you, 'tis you must go and I must bide*, he warbled. His elbow brushed against Lee's arm, as he passed. "Sorry, miss," he said, which came out "thorry mish." He stopped. Rocking on the balls of his feet, he stared at them. "I know what you was doing," he accused. "You was canoodling in the park. Courting and cooing like two lovebirds."

He was right.

What's more, for the three remaining days of her London trip, they continued to canoodle, to court and coo like two lovebirds. And though Lee shed her girdle and Simon shed his embarrassment long enough to make a brave purchase of condoms at his local Boots, it was harder for them to shed the burden of their virginity. Simon thought his house might be empty for an afternoon, but his sister turned up from Sussex with four giggling friends. Lee suggested her hotel room while her grandmother was sipping tea and nibbling on cucumber sandwiches with one of the entries in her address book. But how to predict when she might return to change a dress or repair her painted-on beauty mark? Not to mention eluding the legion of devoted attendants—concierge, bellboy, room service waiter, the maid who fluffed up and turned down the duvet and placed an extra mint on the hemstitched pillowcase of her grandmother's bed. What tales might they tell of an ungrateful granddaughter who made hay—jumped in the hay—while the sun shined somewhere else? Still, she and Simon managed to touch, to stroke, to uncover an inch of thigh here, a nipple there. In the back row of the cinema, Simon placed Lee's hand inside his trousers, erasing the entire theater let alone the screen. In an empty gallery at the V&A—Islamic tapestries? Greek coins?—Simon slipped his fingers up her—girdleless—skirt. Though they returned to their haunt in the park, the ground was hard and damp. They were careful to leave at dusk.

And then they said good-bye.

"Unfinished business," Simon said.

"Unfinished business," repeated Lee.

They would see each other often. Simon would come over on his holidays from medical school. Maybe he could get a summer job in the Hannibal Hamlin biology lab. Lee would look into the Junior Year Abroad. They would get married. They would make love. Not necessarily in that order. So what if there was an ocean between them? Nothing would keep them apart. The cord connecting him to her stretched to infinity. Love conquered all. Lee gave him the rabbit's foot she had carried with her since she was six. "For luck," she said.

"For luck," he said. He ran his thumb over the white fur. He tapped the tiny slivered nails. "I'll keep this forever," he pledged.

Lee sobbed. A waterfall of tears drenched the front of her dress. She understood now the power of music. Of poetry. How a smoky, dirty pub and a rainy, crowded park could be lit up with stars. She understood how people could kill for love. Die from it. She brought new appreciation to Hero and Leander, Beatrice and Dante. Romeo and Juliet. Love translated literature better than any professorial dissection in a lecture hall. She knew why people spoke of broken hearts. Struck by lightning, she was a living illustration of the jagged fissure at the center of the soul.

Simon produced a pristine handkerchief. He daubed her eyes with such tenderness more tears spilled. "I admire you," he said. "So much feeling so easily shown." He pointed to the stoic set of his mouth. "We British," he explained. "Stiff upper lip."

Lee traced the line of those lips. Soft as velvet. And as pliable. "Baloney," she said.

He pulled her head against his chest. He stroked her hair. "Listen," he whispered.

She listened. His chest rose. His chest fell. His heart beat. She felt she'd been let inside. That he had opened himself up to her like the Visible Man she'd had as a kid. She smiled. Even if they had managed to find a bed to fall into, pull off their clothes, follow the instruction booklet for birth control, get to know each other in the most biblical, most earth-moving sense, she couldn't imagine anything more intimate than hearing the blood pumped through his body while the solid, thick, steady thump of his heart pounded into the cup of her ear. "This is yours," he promised. "It belongs to you."

In their bedroom, her grandmother was folding hotel towels into her Louis Vuitton case. "Darling, I can tell you've had a great romance," she said. She took Lee into her perfumed arms, held her against a quilted satin bed jacket that covered a nightgown paneled in Belgian lace. "I'm so happy."

"I'm so sad," Lee bawled.

"Of course you are."

Lee wept onto her grandmother's shoulder. One of her grandmother's earrings swung like a pendulum over her head. Could there be a better example of quintessential style—her grandmother in her nightgown with all her jewelry on? She sniffed her grandmother's heady scent. What was it? Shalimar? Maybe Je Reviens. Je Reviens, she hoped, an omen, with its promise of *I will return*. "There, there," Marguerite crooned, rocking her.

How could she have been so sore at her grandmother? Lee wondered now. Begrudging all the attention she demanded. Resenting the expected fealty. She was an ingrate. She should be kissing her grandmother's feet instead of soaking her bed jacket and flattening the marabou feathers that ringed its neck. Without her grandmother, she would never have met Simon, never have had a great romance. "And you didn't mind?" she asked.

"Mind what?"

"That I spent so much time with Simon? So much time away from you?"

"Never! Especially as he is a boy of such good family. Child of my dear and old friends. Especially since I recognize a soul of poetry." She smoothed Lee's hair. "Especially when I chose him for you myself."

For a long time, they sat like that. Lee thought she had never loved her grandmother so much. In the whole world—which thanks to her grandmother she was getting to see—only Simon held a larger claim to her heart.

And then her grandmother asked something in a voice so casual Lee was sure she hadn't heard it right. "*Alors*, did you lose your virginity, my little Magnolia?" her grandmother inquired.

Lee sat up; tears stanched like the sudden turning of a tide. "What did you say?"

"Your virginity, darling. Did you and sweet Simon make love?"

Lee's mouth opened. Of course. Since her grandmother's knowledge had to come from experience, her grandmother must have had lovers. The Puritan rules of New England would never apply to her. She was European. A beauty. A woman of the world. Why hadn't Lee thought of this before? Did she have lovers in America? While married to Sam Rybier of the large nose and close-together eyes. Did she scandalize their small town? Was this the reason she fled to New York? All of which would account for Lee's mother's reaction formation; the total embargo on any mention of sex. Evidenced by the booklet left on her desk called *An Introduction to Intimacy for Young Men and Women*. With

drawings of stamens and pistils and an alarming humming-
bird. By the flat rubber disk found in a bathroom drawer. A
filter from the old shower, her mother stammered, that she'd
meant to throw out. Add in the Greek chorus of her father,
who, when she announced her first period, pinned his eyes
to the ground. "This is more than I need to know," he
mumbled. Then he fled.

"We wanted to make love. We couldn't find a place."

"If only you'd consulted me. I would have arranged this
room for you." She sighed. "It makes it so much harder, you
know. When something's unfinished, you become obsessed
with it."

Three

Lee's in the bedroom changing the sheets when Ben calls up from the foot of the stairs. "I'm off," he cries. "Mail's here. It's on the hall table."

"Have a good class," Lee yells down. She freezes. She listens for the slam of the front door, the stomp of Ben's feet on the walk, the chug of the engine as his car starts up, the squeak of the tires as Ben backs out onto the street. All quiet. She throws aside a pillowcase and hurtles down the stairs. She's out of breath by the time she gets to the stack of letters, magazines, and catalogues. She sorts through them: bills, invitations, department notices, a postcard from a neighbor who is drinking piña coladas poolside on an island in the Caribbean. *Wish you were here*, she writes. *Really*, she underlines. So do I, Lee thinks, cocktails topped by parasols, sun and sand and for ten days not a care in the world.

Except she'd be away from the mail.

Which isn't promising. It's been three weeks. Even so, no thin blue envelope stamped with the profile of Queen Elizabeth. No thick black ink in such a familiar slant as to provoke a Pavlovian pang. She could be brain-dead and still recognize that robust *M*, that sperm-tailed *S*. Would Simon cry *Eureka!* over *her* handwriting? she wonders. Is he doing that right now? Lee sinks onto a bench. Its eighteenth-century legs creak. In protest, Lee's sure, to limbs heavy with disappointment and a leaden heart. She starts to calculate: three whole weeks since she mailed him her memoir. At the most, it should have taken five days to get to Netherend-on-Severn in Gloucestershire. A wide margin of generosity when you consider the excellence of the U.K. postal service. She's heard the boasts about how you could mail a love letter from Sloane Square in the morning which would set your honey aflutter in Notting Hill by three. Ben used to complain that it took longer for a document to reach Portland fifty miles away than to land on the desk of one of his colleagues at London University. Even if her package ended up on a slow boat to China, stuck on an around-the-world airline, stalled while striking workers threw themselves across the railroad tracks, it would be at Simon's now.

Unless Simon's wife intercepted it. Could she? Would she? Lee groans. She slaps her head with the back of her hand. It's too late, though, to knock any sense into her thick skull. Why hadn't she addressed her package to Mr. and Mrs. Simon Abernathy? Or the Abernathys? Or Caroline and Simon Abernathy? They shared a name; they shared a house; they shared a bed; they had two kids. They'd been married only one year less than she and Ben. Chalk up another Freudian slip to add to the trio of coin silver spoons she had chosen as a wedding gift. There were only three that matched, the antique dealer had pointed out. Buying just two seemed stingy. But when it finally dawned on her—that third spoon, eternal triangle testament to her inability to think before she acted—it was too late. She'd called the shop in Bangor. The parcel—packed for damage, insured for loss—had gone off in the morning's mail.

Why had she sent him her book anyway? Some middle-of-the-night, middle-aged madness? She was a happily married woman with three children. She and Ben slept so tangled together you couldn't tell where she started and he left off. "Mummy and Daddy are one great big hill," Timmy used to cry jumping on them in a Sunday morning ritual. She blames her book. It was the book that stirred up the sleeping dogs. The writing of it. The Pine Tree Press physical fact of it.

Her foot twitches with agitation. She considers the parts about Simon. The parts Beatrice pronounced hot. The sections Ben said were hard to take.

Come on, she tells herself. Get a grip. Ben read them. Had breakfast. Went to work. Resumed his life as a responsible adult. Why not Caroline?

Oh, please not Caroline, she prays. If there's a god of good sense, of second chances, she hopes he's listening. She remembers Caroline: wide hips, thick ankles, a pretty face. Good gardener, holier-than-thou cook, nice sense of humor

in that dry English way. Practical, sensible. A poor speller—
four words with reversed *Es* and *Is* in the thank-you note
for Ben and Lee's crock of Vermont maple syrup and jar of
macadamia nuts. Dyslexic? A school leaver? At the very
least no university. Could Lee dare to boast she was Caroline's opposite? "What do you think of her?" she'd asked
Ben.

"Pleasant," he said. "Nice."

"Pretty?" She couldn't help herself.

"Reasonably." He considered. "And intelligent."

"Really?"

"Practical wisdom. Sensible."

"The gene for which is missing in your wife?"

"Don't be ridiculous. There's no comparison."

Was that a compliment? she wondered then. Is it? she
wonders now. Are she and Caroline simply apples and oranges?

She'd been annoyed. That tendency of the professor to be
professorial. How many times had Ben, like his fellow historians, made pronouncements on things they knew nothing of, people they'd hardly met. She herself was proud she
wasn't always practical. Contrary to the way she had been
raised, she had become enough of her own person to accept
that not being sensible was not necessarily bad. Ben liked
that she was creative, an artist of a sort. So her checkbook
was a mess. So the cereals weren't always lined up in a row
in her kitchen cabinets. So she hammered in a nail before
checking for a stud. So not all her ideas worked. Her solutions were more intuitive, less thought out.

Or thought *through*, she concedes. Shouldn't she have

weighed the pros and cons, tested both sides of the debate before she stuck a bunch of stamps across her memoir and sent it off marked *Priority*?

But if you think too much before you act, you might not act at all. Ergo Hamlet paralyzed by his *to be or not to be*. Besides, if she'd given *to send or not to send* the Hamlet treatment, what would she have ultimately done? A compromise? Excised paragraphs? Blackened sentences? Never. She owed allegiance to her work. And, taking into account poetic license and a tendency toward hyperbole, what is still the most important feature of a memoir, after all? Something Ben would grant, Simon would understand, and Caroline with her dull-as-dishwater common sense would nevertheless recognize:

Honesty.

Lee gets up from the bench. She looks in the mirror. She runs her fingers through her hair. So much for her fifteen minutes as a writer. Now that she's produced the one book in her everyone is supposed to have, it's on to the next step. She needs to drop by Beatrice's office. Who has a new boyfriend and thus hasn't got around to attaching the price stickers yet. Lee left repeated and increasingly desperate messages on Beatrice's answering machine. She'd stopped by the office three times to find the door locked, the mail piled up. She sent two *friendly reminder* postcards to Beatrice's condominium. "But my book's been gathering dust, homeless, shelfless, all this time," Lee had moaned when Beatrice finally called her back.

"I know love's no excuse," Beatrice offered, "but I'm absolutely certain you of all people would understand."

"Couldn't you give the job to one of those interns?" Lee asked. "Like, what was her name, Isabel?"

"They're both on academic pro which bans outside activity. No great loss."

Lee can't help but agree. If you're failing English Comp or Intro to Biology, your ability to work the copier or stick stickers on the backs of books might be discredited. Never mind. She'll spend a few hours with Beatrice. Then go to her real job running the Junior Year Abroad. Where she can really put to use her major in psychology, her minor in romance languages. She needs to face facts: her Priority package—its handwriting unrecognized, its return address forgotten—is probably crushed under a heap of medical journals Simon plans to get to one of these days.

Lee rolls on some lipstick. She winds a scarf around her neck. Perhaps she can convince Maggie to meet her in the student union for a cappuccino and biscotti after she sorts through the mounds on her desk.

The Pine Tree Press occupies an office above the Awash And Adry Laundromat, owned by Ron Adry, who turned his name into a self-fulfilling prophecy. A tattoo parlor across the hall advertises not only run-of-the-mill *Moms*, but also "creative" piercings for rings in your nose and bells in your belly button. Next to the tattoo parlor stands the closet-size space of Hiram Cross, Watchmaker, who must be nearly one hundred, though Lee's mother used to say that Mr. Cross was nearly a hundred when she was a kid. All day, all night, Mr. Cross hunches over his workbench, a green visor shading his brow, working with tiny tweezers and wrenches and huge magnifying glasses while the walls and floor vibrate from the seismic washers and dryers one flight below.

Beatrice is on the phone when Lee opens the door. Awash And Adry appears to be doing a landmark business because the *Mainely Marguerite*s are rocking and rolling in a conga line across the tabletop. Beatrice holds up a finger, then places a hand over her heart. This she thumps twice. She narrows her eyes. "A client just stepped in. Gotta go. Talk later. Kiss. Kiss. Love ya." She puts down the phone. She gives a soap-opera sigh. "Kenny is just so hot," she swoons.

Lee, the client, pulls out the client's chair. Which is, besides Beatrice's, the only other chair in the room. Its sagging cane seat holds a spiral-bound notebook and a box of index cards. She sweeps them to the floor. She sits down. "Kenny?" she asks.

"Daddy would have an absolute cow. He—Kenny"—Beatrice pauses to savor the word—"pumps gas at the Citgo over on Broad Street. His day job. In real life, he's a poet and an artist."

"Oh?" inquires Lee with the tone of cautious encouragement long practiced as the mother of so-called young adults, the tone you might use to talk a sniper down from a dormitory roof.

"Free verse and mechanical genius. I'm thinking Pine Tree Press might be just the ticket to publish his most provocative, his most assured work."

Lee nods. She can only imagine Kenny's author photograph: His oil-stained overalls. The tire iron in his pocket.

The squeegee in his water pail. "So where did you meet him?" she asks.

"Not at the Citgo station like you'd expect. Daddy gave me a Gulf credit card." Beatrice leans closer. "But right in my own backyard."

"In the parking lot?" Beatrice lived in Lee's old high school, which had been turned into condominiums.

"No! Here. Across the hall. He was going for a tattoo. He intended to get a pair of intertwined hearts on his biceps. One with Kenny. The other with the name of his girlfriend—Sylvia."

"He has a girlfriend . . . ?"

"He did." She slams her fist on a *Mainely Marguerite*. "*Did* being the operative word. But when he met me, at that very minute our paths crossed on the peeling linoleum, that nanosecond in time and space, he decided his only choice was to leave the other heart blank!"

"So has it been filled in with Beatrice?"

"Not yet. It's way too early in our relationship." She shakes her head. "I'm sick of these captains of commerce, these investment bankers," she confides as if millionaire production makes up Homestead's main industry. "I want somebody who's authentic. Who's got roots."

Lee is starting to feel sympathy with the having-a-cow Boardman paterfamilias. But who is she to say that Noriko is no Kenny? Or Timmy's heartthrob from New Zealand? Or Maggie's flavor of the week? "I can understand the authentic part," placates Lee. Beatrice is after all her editor.

A role Beatrice suddenly resumes, for she says, "Enough about me. Let's do you." She picks up a sheet of yard-sale tags and two Bics. She hands one to Lee. "Sorry. I'm real behind on this. I hope you can understand how one can get *completely, totally, profoundly* waylaid by love."

Lee is surprised that it takes only an hour to write $12 on each sticker and cover the $120 on the back of each book. She'd prefer to give credit to Beatrice's and her efficiency rather than Pine Tree Press's Lilliputian print run. Ink stains her fingers. A tag marked $12 graces her knee. She stands up.

Beatrice stands up. She peels a few stickers off her jeans. She walks Lee the two steps to the door. "I'll start distributing them this afternoon," she says. "Maybe Kenny will help when he gets off work."

"That'll be nice," lies Lee. Through the heating registers, steam wafts up from the dryers downstairs, and she can smell the moist warm cotton of tumbling sheets.

"And I'll set up your publicity tour." Beatrice stops, her hand on the knob. "Not quite tour. Local appearances. There's the Friday night poetry slam at Charlene's Golden Comb. I know you're memoir, but they're pretty loose about letting almost anyone who wants to, read and sign a book. I've already talked to the College Co-Op. When I explained you were Professor Emery's wife, they definitely promised to fit you into their slot."

"Great," Lee says. Right now she'll try not to worry about taking advantage of a system so patently unfair that college politics extend to the college bookstore and the hierarchical value of college professors extends to their wives. She steps over the threshold. She steps back. "I nearly forgot. I'm meeting Maggie after work. I haven't seen her in an age. I think I'll bring her one of my books." She turns toward the table holding her freshly stickered, soon-to-be-distributed first editions.

"Just one minute." Beatrice blocks her path. "I already sent you your four author copies specified in our contract."

"For which I'm truly grateful. However, I need another. Since I . . ." She thinks fast. ". . . I brought one to an elderly aunt in the hospital."

Beatrice says nothing.

"An unexpected emergency."

Beatrice holds her ground.

"Who is very sick. *Very.* Heart. Maybe some involvement in the lungs. It's serious."

Not serious enough, however, to provoke a milk-of-human-kindness, there-but-for-the-grace-of-God response. Beatrice is unmoved. She doesn't move.

"Which leaves only three copies for one husband and three kids. You do the math. Then add in an extended family. Close friends . . ."

Beatrice's mouth stays cemented into a stubborn line. She plants her feet a yard apart; she crosses her arms over her chest. It's the block of Hannibal Hamlin's MVP football guard.

"You mean I have to buy my own book?" asks Lee.

Beatrice nods.

"The book I wrote?"

"Yes."

Lee points. "The one you wouldn't have over there if it weren't for me?"

"Yes."

Lee fishes two tens out of her pocketbook.

"Twelve will do," Beatrice says in a Lady Bountiful voice. "I won't charge you tax."

The Junior Year Abroad office seems a haven when Lee gets to it. A clean well-lighted place with fresh coffee perking away in the hall outside and enough sharpened number two pencils to supply the most addicted crossword puzzle fiend. Hers is the last in a string of offices that form the Department of Modern Languages. Though better than the broom closet she was first assigned, Lee's home away from home is the runt of the litter, a cubbyhole with a door and four warped walls just short of the ceiling. She can still smell the cloying cologne of Pierre Marelli, Beginning French and Intermediate Italian, who resigned under threat of a sexual harassment suit. Assessing the space, Lee figures there wasn't enough room to swing a *gatta* or a *chat*, let alone sexually harass. At least horizontally. But maybe, in Professor Marelli's case, that was what the language lab was for. Along with the office—whose Eiffel Tower and Colosseum posters she replaced with the dreamy spires and Gothic towers of study-abroad universities—she inherited the department's secretary. Miss—no Miz for her—Peavey was beloved, befuddled, and incompetent. Miss Peavey just hated these newfangled computers; she just couldn't get the hang of these multibuttoned phones. She recorded appointments in a Mr. Micawber ledger that would stymie the code breakers of the Enigma machine.

Now Lee arranges a few dozen brochures on the table along the wall so they look inviting. They do look inviting.

Airbrushed to a fare-thee-well. Green lawns stretching down to rivers on which smiling students punt and row. Gargoyles and stained glass windows. Modern Scandinavian high-rises of pale wood and bright blocks of Mondrian color. Low-slung gingerbread houses hung with wisteria. In these ivory towers, the sun always shines, the sky's clear; it's an eternal spring or autumn. The Rainbow Coalition of students are all beautiful. They carry pristine books while raising frosted steins in picturesque Old World taverns with half-timbered walls and quaintly thatched roofs.

False advertising, accuse some parents whose kids complain about tiny rooms, lumpy beds, cold water, chipped tubs without showers, inedible food, no on-the-premises psychologist, no professional facilitator. And let's not even get started on the infirmary. Is this what we're paying all these thousands of dollars for? Besides, in my kid's dorm, everyone's from Long Island. Who can they practice their foreign language on?

But others send in letters of gratitude. The experience is building character for their portfolio-craving, want-to-be-a-millionaire kids. Let them rough it. Let them spend an underprivileged term. Let them see the world. And by the way, what's the best plan over there for a cellular phone?

Lee tackles the mess on her desk. Sorts the brochures by country, by language. Files memos from deans and administrators. Checks the letters of recommendation from faculty, the application forms. She digs out the chart of credit exchanges and conversions for satisfying prerequisites. She studies the lists of inoculations needed for the Third World. She notes the State Department warnings of political unrest.

She's doing pretty well, she tells herself. Burying yourself in your work helps you forget your fluctuating coping skills in your non-day job life. At least if you try to keep your eyes away from a photo of the London School of Economics at dawn or the sun setting over Imperial College of London University. The whole word is these kids' oyster. She pictures them backpacking, hiking, dancing, carousing, having love affairs in student hostels around the globe. Not at all like what she's come to view as her own personal Victorian era, the time when she accompanied her grandmother to Europe wearing a girdle and a chastity belt.

She is just about to get up and fill her Hannibal Hamlin mug when she hears a scratch at her door like the pecking of a small bird.

"Mrs. Emery?" a voice chirps.

"Come in, Miss Peavey," Lee says. *Call me Lee*, she had begged. A plea Miss Peavey ignored, to Lee's relief, who would never have been able to address her as the Edna listed on the department's manifest.

"Well, dear . . ." Miss Peavey begins. She is all in lavender to match the rinse in her hair. A piece of pink paper flutters in her outstretched hand.

Lee takes it. A series of shaky numbers marches across it followed by *first name B*. "What's this?" she asks.

"Well, dear, it's the telephone number of the parents of one of our students. Let's see, dear. Is it Betsy? Beverly, maybe? Bill?" Miss Peavey's hands fly up and down like two white doves. "There seems to be a problem . . ."

Lee waits. "The problem," she prompts.

"Oh, my. The problem." Miss Peavey sighs. "You know, I

just can't be in several places at once. With all my duties . . . These parents have been calling all morning looking for you. Five times. Ten times. Where were you, dear? I have been searching frantically."

"At my publisher's," Lee states. Then adds, "My book's just come out."

Miss Peavey is not impressed. "Which shouldn't excuse you from not calling these people back."

Who I didn't know called in the first place, Lee wants to protest. But you can't pick on an institution however crumbling, whatever its state of disrepair. She sweetens her tone. "If you tell me their names, I'll phone them immediately."

"That's just the problem, dear . . ."

"I see," says Lee.

Miss Peavey brightens. "But I wrote down their number."

"For which I couldn't be more grateful. Thank you, Miss Peavey."

"You're welcome, Mrs. Emery." She looks around as if this is the first time she's seen these walls. "Such lovely pictures. Though I quite miss Professor Marelli's Eiffel Tower. *Tour Eiffel.* I visited it with my dear mother many years ago. We were too wicked, really. Had a whole bottle of the most delicious wine."

"When in Rome . . ."

"Quite. Though in this case, Paris, dear," Miss Peavey corrects. "However," she goes on, "just between us, I can't say I miss Professor Marelli. That terrible, rather cheap cologne. Not at all good for my allergies. Frankly, I don't approve of men wearing perfume. Do you, dear?"

She thinks of Ben's healthy mix of sweat and soap and freshly cut grass. Of Simon's smell. Licorice. An overlay of cinnamon. "Not in the least."

Miss Peavey frowns. She looks around. Her face is puzzled. "I know I came in here for something . . ."

Lee takes her elbow, which feels so brittle it could snap with the slightest pressure of her fingertips. She holds open the door. "Thank you so much. You've been extremely helpful, Miss Peavey. No doubt you want to get back to your many duties."

Miss Peavey nods, lavender curls bobbing, lavender shoes squeaking. "They do tend to accumulate, don't they?"

Lee smiles. "I can't imagine what we'd do without you," she grants. Maybe when she gets to be Miss Peavey's age, she'll find it a real accomplishment to write a number on a note, to amass a wardrobe and a hairdo all within the same pastel color range, let alone come to work each day.

She picks up the telephone. She studies the number. Should she go through the Bs in her list of the one hundred and fifty students overseas for this term? Which might not even fit into B if you sorted Bill under William; Betsy under Elizabeth. She checks the area code: 617, Massachusetts. Since a good chunk of the students hail from Boston, this hardly narrows the playing field. She'll have to wing it. Not that she hasn't before. She deals with international educators. She'll use her well-practiced international diplomacy skills.

"This is Lee Emery, director of Hannibal Hamlin College's Junior Year Abroad," she announces to the exasperated voice, female, which answers on the first ring.

"And this is Hilda Teagarten, mother of Judy on the Junior Year Abroad. And it's about time you called," the voice declares. She takes a breath. "Phil," she yells. "Pick up the other line. It's from Judy's school."

Judy. Teagarten. So much for the B.

"It's about time you called," echoes a man—presumably Phil—whose vibrato thrums over the extension like a tuning fork.

"About Judy?" Lee begins.

She might as well have yelled *Fire!* in a crowded theater. One with state-of-the-art Dolby surround sound stereo considering the panic that ensues. Lee holds the receiver away from her ear. Hilda cries. Phil shouts. They interrupt each other. They clip the tails off each other's sentences. *Overprotective*, accuses one. *Total denial*, insists the other. She realizes that in the middle of this family feud she is pretty much irrelevant. How to unravel this tangle of blaring words? Lee strains her ears as if she's trying to extract the *Paul is dead* from the background of drums and bass and keyboard on the Beatles' *White Album*.

This is the gist as far as she can tell: Judy has not been attending classes. Not that anyone gives a damn in these inferior foreign universities. She has not shown up for her monthly tutorial. Not that any *in loco parentis* has reported this. And where are their tuition dollars going anyway? On the watery gruel and beer served to minors in unheated baronial dining halls? This winter—can you believe it? Have you ever heard of such a thing in the good old U S of A?—Judy got chilblains. Something out of *Oliver Twist*. To add insult to injury—to chilblains!—her roommate hasn't seen her for two weeks. Check with Julian, or Colin, or Mohammed, the ditz suggests. Whose last names she either forgot or never knew. Mohammed! Maybe their Judy's been kidnapped, disguised under a chador, and shipped to a harem in Saudi Arabia. They hold Hannibal Hamlin responsible. Their lawyer—white-shoe New York firm, a *shark*—is a phone call away.

Time out, Lee yearns to cry. She wants to blow a whistle. Pound a gavel. Scream *Shut up!* But then there's the annual fund to consider. Not that Hilda and Phil Teagarten are poised to write a check to support scholarships or a wing for the new gym or a second science lab.

"Listen," she says. "Please calm down. Let me get to the bottom of this."

Miraculously, there seems to be a cease-fire in the war between the Teagartens. Or maybe the lull can be laid to battle fatigue. "You must understand," Lee explains, "it's not unusual that a couple of weeks might pass when you don't hear from your child. Independent study means just that. For the student on the Junior Year Abroad, not all learning takes place within the confines of the classroom or on the college grounds. There's a whole world out there to explore."

"You've nailed that baby on the head. Just what we're worrying about."

Lee ignores him. She's on a roll. "Foreign study means immersing yourself in another culture. The student is spreading his or her wings. Is letting go of the umbilical cord—"

"You have exactly twenty-four hours, Miz Emery, to find our girl."

"Phil," sobs Hilda, "where did you hide the Librium?"

Lee puts down the phone. She picks up her coffee mug. The coffee is cold. Just as well. She's more than wired. She checks the clock. Even with the time difference, she's pretty sure she'll find Dr. Iris Kidney in her office in St. Stephen's Hall.

"Lee, how lovely." Iris answers her own phone. Through the years of dealing with her, Lee has come to view herself and Iris as mirror images divided into identical cubbyhole pods that have attached themselves, if not to parallel universes, then to parallel universities. She knows they're the same age, that they each have three children and husbands who are historians. She's pleased to imagine that English irises and American magnolias can thrive in the same garden patch. "Great minds must think alike because I was just about to ring you up."

"Judy Teagarten!" Lee groans.

"A wild one," Iris admits.

"Is she in trouble?"

"No more than anyone else." In the background Lee hears a drawer slam and a warbly voice. Iris turns away from the phone. "Just file that, Miss Tucker. Thank you very much. Sorry," she says to Lee. "I need your advice. Because of our success with Hannibal Hamlin, we are planning to run a weekend in early June to attract new foreign studies departments across the U.S. to our program." She lowers her voice. "Speaking confidentially, in addition to the obvious benefits, I can't begin to tell you how profitable this is. And I was wondering if you might suggest possible colleges?"

"My Rolodex is your Rolodex," Lee says. Lee thinks of the university in Wyechester. The school that she's grown to know but has never seen. She's memorized photos of the manicured lawns, the architecturally important chapel, the library's collection of Bloomsbury manuscripts. She's located Wyechester on the map. With her finger, she's measured the from-the-knuckle-to-first-joint distance to London, the from-first-joint-to-second-joint distance to Bristol, the thumb tip's thirty-three kilometers to Netherend-on-Severn. She holds her breath. Can she even dare to dream of it? To suggest such a thing? "Why don't I come over myself?" she says.

"This is strictly for people unfamiliar with our program. Though it's very kind of you to offer."

Kind has nothing to do with it. "Just a fleeting thought," Lee excuses.

"On the other hand . . ." Iris pauses. She considers. Politeness turns to enthusiasm. "You really should see where so many of your students end up. You could talk about your success with our program. How your students thrive. How pleased their parents are. What a broadening experience. I can't think of a better advertisement. On top of, naturally, my own selfish desire to put a face to a voice. Why, you and Ben could make a trip of it."

"And visit Timmy at Oxford," adds Lee with such fine family feeling she almost fools herself.

"Let me talk it over with the committee. I'll get back to you. But, you know, Lee, I have rather a good instinct about this." She rustles some papers. "Is there anything else?"

Lee gets down to business. She explains about Judy

Teagarten. Her irate parents. Their Saudi Arabia phobias. Their legal action threats.

Iris's voice soothes like a Caswell-Massey bubble bath. "Don't worry. I'm sure there's no problem. Give me a day to sort everything out." She laughs. "Not to belittle the Teagartens' concerns, but there is something to say, I expect, for the repressed good manners of the Englishman."

Reassured, Lee hangs up. But before she can sit back and contemplate her shocking, self-serving behavior, the possible weekend in June, the distance of the tip of her thumb, the *will she or won't she* Hamlet obsessions lying in wait, the phone starts to ring.

With no preliminaries, no English good manners requiring at least a hello, no diplomatic calm before the shoe-pounding storm, a voice ruptures her ear. "She's in a place called Gretna Green. She's just eloped. With Mohammed Al fucking something or other. We're taking the next plane out. We hold you responsible. You'll hear from us."

Surprise. Surprise. Maggie the unpunctual is already seated at a corner table in the student union when Lee arrives. For a few minutes, Lee stands behind a stack of discarded trays and watches her. If your heart can lift and sink at the same time, then Lee's does. Lifts at the sight of her, the *fact* of her, sinks at the sight of her, the rags she wears, the Cleopatra curtain of blue/black hair dyed the color of widow's weeds that covers her glorious natural red. Why was everything so much simpler with her sons? Lee wonders. Those darling boys who thought she was just fine. Who loved her chocolate chip cookies and, by extension, her. Who might start sentences to their friends with the thrilling words *My mom*. Who, towering over her, patted her head on the way to the refrigerator. Who consulted her on the color of a corsage to match a prom date's dress. With Maggie, it was all push and pull, mostly push. She was a Daddy's girl. *He* could do no wrong; *she* could do no right. "To her, we're opposites," Lee had complained to Ben, "like Jack Sprat and his wife."

"Don't worry," Ben said. "She'll come around." He'd paused. He'd laughed. "Besides, Jack Sprat isn't such an unflattering analogy. Between the two of them, remember, they licked that plate clean."

A small consolation, which she tried to hold on to, especially during Maggie's adolescence, with limited success.

"You smile too much," Maggie once complained. "Your clothes are bor-ring." "Get off my case," she'd shout when Lee was simply passing in the hall. At a parent-teacher conference in Maggie's sixth-grade classroom, Lee sat on a Goldilocks chair, knees tucked under her chin, to listen to Mrs. Archibald who had been her teacher and was now Maggie's. "She's nothing like you, Magnolia," Mrs. Archibald said. "She seizes life."

Yet Lee hadn't been like her own mother either, who was quiet, and sweet, and proper under her starched apron and coiffed curls. Or her wonderful and difficult and glamorous grandmother. For so many years, she'd felt herself whirling in a high wind like the pointers on Ben's weathervane. I've had my feather boa moments, she wants to tell her daughter. I've danced a tango with a rose between my teeth.

What would Maggie have remembered of the visit to

Netherend-on-Severn the time, that second time, Lee had seen Simon? The farm perhaps. Probably the goats. She would have noticed nothing special about her mother, Lee was sure. Nothing out of the ordinary. Maggie had been a toddler. And Lee, pretty much a child herself.

Though no longer. All too soon, her family's skip-a-generation chain of who gets to show the plumage reasserted itself. Now Maggie's got the rose clamped between her teeth, and Lee's the mother hen clucking over her brood. Not that she'd have it any other way. She loves Maggie with a passion that often frightens her.

"Mom!" Maggie waves her arms. She wraps them around her mother's neck. She's already ordered two cappuccinos; their peaks of steamed milk dusted with chocolate look like snowcapped mountains. Two biscotti studded with slivered almonds sit on a tray amid a clutter of napkins and spoons. Lee recalls her own student union days. When you were more than satisfied with a Coke and a Devil Dog. "I can't stay long," Maggie says. "I've got class. And then I'm meeting Paul."

"Paul?" asks Lee. "What about Brett?"

"History."

"Really?" Lee frowns. She quite liked Brett, a standout in the paper doll garland of blue-jeaned, guitar-strumming, haiku-writing youth. Her office had sent him to Oxford. His tutor had raved about his way with words and his way with an oar. He had won first prize for an essay on Marlowe. He had rowed single sculls at Henley and come in second.

"He's such a nerd."

"He is?" She couldn't conceive of anyone less of a nerd than Brett. Blond and strapping. A scholar athlete in the classic sense.

"For instance . . ." Maggie leans over. Her eyes are blood-shot. Either she's lost an earring or has chosen to wear just a single silver hoop. "Last week he was mugged."

Lee sits up, back rigid with the alertness to danger of a lioness protecting her cubs. "A mugging? On campus?" In *Maine?* she wants to add. On this idyllic greensward where the usual crime meant a shoplifted pack of nacho chips, a hijacked truck, a graffiti assault by town upon gown, an ob-fuscated tax return. "I haven't heard anything."

You wouldn't, implies Maggie's look intended for the out-of-it. "Both Jenny and Sarah have had their purses snatched."

"Weapons?"

"No gun or knife or anything. A bat, maybe, or a stick. No one's seen him. He comes up from behind and surprises them." Maggie dips the biscotti in the coffee, which splashes over the rim. She tilts the saucer into her mouth.

"Rape? Sexual assault?" Wouldn't an all-campus notice be circulated? Ah, yes. Ending up decorating the no-exit inbox on Miss Peavey's desk.

"Uh uh. Ordinary mugging. Run-of-the-mill." She takes a bite of the cookie. A mustache of milk foams her upper lip. Lee smiles, heartened to see that underneath the Halloween wig, the too-little-sleep, not-enough-fruits-and-vegetables face, the baby Maggie exists. "But as I was saying . . ."

"Go on."

"The guy comes up behind Brett. Puts his arm around his neck. Pokes whatever into his back. 'Your wallet. Pass it over your shoulder,' the mugger hisses." She bangs the side of the table with the side of her hand. More coffee spills. "You're not going to believe what Brett does."

"I hope, not resist."

"That would be better. He hands over his wallet. Then asks, 'Would you please give me back my library card?'"

Which seems eminently sensible considering the hoops you have to jump through to get into the Hamlin stacks. But Lee, sensitive to being out of it, chooses her words. "Imagine," she says. She waits. Then adds, "Did he get it back?" She can't help herself.

"Yes. Isn't that the worst?"

Far from it, she knows but only nods. A plane roars overhead on its descent to the Bangor International Airport to the east. For some reason, she fixes on all the articles about air rage flooding the local press. Bangor's become the landing place for out-of-control passengers. The freshly scrubbed Penobscot county jail sits waiting to lock them up. Unplanned stops mean big bucks, explain Bangor's two FBI agents, who boast of their ability to remove a peace-disturber and calm the flight attendants holding him. She pictures Hilda and Phil Teagarten, fists clenched, sleepless over the Atlantic, on their kamikaze mission to rescue Judy from Mohammed Al something or other. "Which reminds me," she says in the kind of maternal non sequitur Maggie detests. From her bag, she pulls out her book.

"Oh, Mom," Maggie cries. She flings an arm across Lee's shoulder. "It's your book!"

"For you. My one-fourth dedicatee. It's already inscribed."

Maggie opens to the page marked *To my darling daughter* with its columns of kisses and hearts. "I can't wait to read it!" she exclaims. An unfamiliar glow of admiration lights her red-rimmed eyes.

Which Lee feels compelled to dim. "I'd better warn you, darling, there might be passages that make you uncomfortable."

Maggie stares at her.

"My first boyfriend. My first love when I traveled with my grandmother."

Maggie's eyebrows shoot up. "Daddy was your first love. Your only love."

"It's entirely natural that you'd think that. And so sweet. But there was someone else."

"Mom!"

"A long time ago."

"*You?*"

"Believe it or not, Maggie, I was once your age."

"When you married Daddy. You've known each other forever. Since Adam and Eve. Didn't you meet him in first grade?"

"Yes, though I hardly remember him. Don't forget he went away to high school. It wasn't until college . . ." Lee pictures the lecture hall for Art History 101. Some semi-alphabetical seating chart put her next to Ben. They shared one arm of two chairs. "Pardon," he'd said each time their elbows knocked. When class was over, when she got up, her skirt was stuck with the previous occupant's gum. Ben had grinned.

He raised two fingers in a Boy Scout salute. "Always prepared," he'd laughed. He opened a Swiss Army knife and
scaled away the gunky, filthy mess. Then asked her out.

Mysteriously, Maggie's face shifts from shock back to
admiration. She checks her watch. She jumps up. "Thanks
for the book. I'm late for Buddhists and Hindus." She grins
Ben's grin. "What do you know," she exclaims, "who would
ever have believed my own mother has a past!"

On the way home, Lee takes a detour to avoid construction
along her usual route. She winds through small residential
streets lined with ancient elms and spreading chestnut trees.
She admires Victorian porches, tall shuttered windows,
generous silken lawns. This is the fancy part of town, not
far from the college but far from the vinyl-sided two- and
three-deckers and tiny ranches the size of diners that make
up the mostly working-class community. At the corner, two
little girls sit out on milk crates. Lee sees a table. A cage. A
handmade sign. She stops. What mom isn't a sucker for a
lemonade stand?

This isn't a lemonade stand, however. There's not a
pitcher. Not a glass. When she gets out of her car and comes
closer, she realizes the little girls are cuddling two rabbits.
The sign, scrawled in orange crayon, reads *Petting Zoo, 25
cents for one hold of Mopsy or Topsy, 50 cents for two turns.* Lee
takes out fifty cents. She drops it in the small sadly empty
plate set out on the tabletop. "May I?" she asks.

One of the little blond-haired girls nods. She is wearing
Peter Rabbit overalls. She places a small brown bunny in
Lee's open arms. "Mopsy?" Lee asks.

The little girl shakes her head. "Topsy."

Lee sits on the grass between the two little girls, who must be sisters with their matching perky ponytails and round hazel eyes. The other, smaller girl wears a white tulle ballerina's skirt. Lee holds the rabbit. Its pink nose twitches. Its ears point like Bugs Bunny's in Saturday morning cartoons.

In Hyde Park that summer, she gave Simon her rabbit's foot. "For luck," she had said.

"I'll keep it forever," he had promised.

She strokes the soft fur.

"Did you ever hold a rabbit before?" the girl in the overalls asks.

Under her hand, Lee feels the quick, sharp beat of the rabbit's heart. "Once," she says. "A long, long time ago."

Four

〰〰

There were rabbits in Netherend-on-Severn. A multicolored, multicultured Beatrix Potter hutch of them. Wandering nearby, goats butted the children. Fat sheep dotted the fields like upholstered sofas in a furniture store. A woebegone pony named Swifty lumbered through the grass at a tortoise pace. Still, it was the rabbits the children loved most. "Toys," exclaimed Maggie, "but *real*!" How old was Maggie then? Three? Johnny was seven; Timmy, five.

But Lee is getting ahead of herself. She needs to turn back to that August in London fifteen years ago, to Ben intent upon his research, to an exhausted wife with three young kids in a two-room flat.

When Ben found out the Hamlin History Department would give him a grant to track down Nathaniel Tarbell's early years and family origins in England, he decided he didn't want to go. He'd been carried on the wave of excitement over Nathaniel's diary to write the proposal, which, once accepted, sowed the seeds of doubt. "You know how I hate to travel," he'd said to Lee.

"But this is your *work*," she pointed out. It was a covenant between them. Between many couples she knew. That a wife and children danced around the man's work like planets around the sun. Especially when she herself held no outside job. It was different in the cities. There, women were demanding equality in any number of astonishing ways, for any number of mind-boggling things. Fashion in politics, art, manners, and just plain fashion itself, took longer to make the trek up north. A circumstance that made the phrase *As Maine goes so goes the nation* more than a little presumptuous.

"I think I can really do something with this Nathaniel material," Ben said, "and make a lasting contribution to the historical archive. It's just that I can't stand leaving home."

"In that case we'll go with you," sprang full blown from Lee's mouth like an inflated cartoon cloud. Surprising herself.

And surprising Ben. Whose face lit up with a sudden spark of delight. Then he assumed his responsible-father-of-a-growing-family look. "With the kids . . . It will be hard. It will be expensive. We'll have to find a place."

"Not necessarily. We can exchange houses. There must be a nice British faculty family who'd like to spend an August in Maine, who might want to study England's emigrants—Pilgrims, colonists—from the New England point of view."

"Maybe . . ."

Lee played her advantage. "And it will be great for the kids. As my grandmother always said, 'Travel is so broadening.' Besides," she added with a flourish, "the dollar is strong."

Not that she knew this, not that she was a reader of the *Wall Street Journal* or even the *Homestead Herald*'s one quarter of a financial page, but why couldn't a strong dollar be as possible as a weak one.

"Well, it's worth considering," allowed Ben.

Lee was on a roll now. "The plane fare for the four of us will be paid by what we save on the kids' day camp."

When it was a done deal, Lee had to admit to a few stabs of guilt. Did her eagerness to get her family across the pond have anything to do with an old love on its other side? With unfinished business and the obsessions that went along with it?

If so, then she was punished in a way: the dollar wasn't strong. No British academics occupying a stately manor or charming cottage wanted to spend a month in a college/factory town more than an hour from the sea. She and Ben had to settle for the flat of Merrion Sackville, who taught water sanitation engineering at Basil Street Polytechnic and would love a holiday in Maine near Skowhegan where his brother had moved in with his wife's parents and sister-in-law. Admittedly the flat was small—Professor Sackville was a bachelor sad to say—but it faced Kensington Park and abutted the Mongolian embassy. And although at first glance the exchange might not seem equable—a whole house swapped for a mere two rooms—*his* digs were in London, and theirs were, well, not to put too fine a point on it . . .

Did London make up, Lee wondered, for a flat not much bigger than her front hall in Homestead, three kids in one room, she and Ben on the sprung spring pull-out couch, and a kitchenette whose size someone in a trailer park might scorn? Not to mention the under-the-counter half-refrigerator that could barely contain their supply of apple juice. Upstairs, the smells of cardamom and coriander, of turmeric, of simmering curries and baking parathas, of slow-burning incense and fast-cooked garlic cloves filtered down from the large extended family—ten, twelve—jammed into the same stingy square footage as theirs. She passed them in the corridor, women in saris, men in Nehru jackets or white jodhpur-ish pants with turbans on their heads, and Keene-eyed children whom her kids beseeched to play, but whose parents and grandparents, uncle and aunts, hustled out of the Americans' path.

Downstairs, an Israeli couple yelled at each other in a language Lee assumed to be Old Testament. Funny how you knew obscenities even when you couldn't translate them. Doors slammed; crockery shattered; once three suitcases with El Al luggage tags sat outside their entrance for two days.

In the mornings, Ben left for the British Museum or Somerset House, his briefcase in one hand, his London Underground map in the other. Libraries abroad, he was starting to realize, weren't that different from libraries at home; one lamp shade was green; the other brass; one place served coffee; the other tea; one provided card catalogues Dewey Decimalized; the other, large leather folios in the middle of the reading room. What was most the same, however, was the universal scholarly hush that signified important work being done.

On the other hand, not much important work was being accomplished at 11 Prince of Wales Terrace. Lee felt herself turning into a domestic slouch; maybe it was the exotic smells from upstairs; the all-too-recognizable drama underneath. Maybe it was the two burners, the teeny refrigerator, the fact that you could stretch your arms to the side, your toes front and back and hit all four walls of the kitchenette. Maybe it was the constant companionship of children under three feet and under seven years, their constant demands. She hardly cooked. Never sewed. Rarely cleaned. Almost every night they ordered the take-away Third World cuisine unimaginable in the restaurants of Maine. The variety astonished them: Indian (which never smelled so delicious as the twenty-four-hour boiling, baking, broiling going on one flight up), Turkish kabobs, Persian rice, Middle Eastern falafel, Moroccan couscous with shredded lamb, Korean bulgoki and kimchee, Brazilian black beans. To salve culinary homesickness, they tried deconstructing the burgers at Frenchy's Diner back home. Was it the pickles? The special grill? The sesame seed rolls that made them so good? "I'm flabbergasted that all I miss—and not that often—is the food," Ben had exclaimed. "What a good idea this was."

Her idea. This August. One she was starting to regret. Ben's absorption in Nathaniel seemed to make him lose his fear of foreignness; so much did Nathaniel Tarbell signify home to him, he must have felt he'd never left. He came back to the flat every night full of him, pregnant with him.

"Nathaniel descended from solid yeoman stock," Ben would say, sipping a Guinness and putting his feet upon Merrion Sackville's ratty, tartan-covered settee, "who lived right near the Forest of Dean. Perhaps," he guffawed, "that's why he liked lumber so much."

"Perhaps," Lee said, one ear pinned to the shouts and scrapes of chairs down below. She heard something thrown against a wall, then drop.

Ben didn't notice, lately didn't notice anything. She was dying for grown-up companionship, an intelligent adult conversation to fill her turning-to-mush mind, a responsive adult male body to fill her heat-seeking adult female one. Not so easy on a roll-out bed three feet from the flimsy folding door closing off your three kids. Not so easy when you're in your husband's arms and he's in the Forest of Dean charting the Tarbell family tree, its cadet branch and the oaks and elms that inspired its most successful sapling. Not so easy when your husband's in your arms and you're in Hyde Park a mile away and fifteen years ago.

"Sorry I'm so preoccupied," Ben said. "Let's hear about you. How was your day?"

"Well," she began.

He cut in. "And by the way, another fascinating tidbit: I found an aunt of Nathaniel's who was quite mad. Barked like a dog. Pecked like a bird. According to her doctor, she chewed the leaves of stately oaks but wouldn't touch a maple or a beech. Tree fetishes must have run in the family. Finished her days in Broadmoor, poor thing."

Lee could sympathize. Was that any better, she wondered, than living out your days—August days, the dog days of summer—at 11 Prince of Wales Terrace next to the hostile Mongolian embassy? "Poor thing," she repeated.

"So what did *you* do?"

She told him. Madame Tussaud's. The Tower. A zillion tourists in Bermuda shorts. Five visits to the bathroom. Ten unbearable thirsts. Three tacky souvenirs. *And a partridge in a pear tree.*

And that was the good news. The bad news: the group of ruffians who were picking on children in the park. One stole Timmy's chocolate cornet. The ice cream vendor gave chase until they jumped on the back of a double-decker bus and made their escape. "Are they underprivileged?" Johnny had asked.

"Just rotten little criminals," said Lee and hated herself.

She told Ben how the kids' ball had flown over the fence of the Mongolian embassy; how they'd had to ring the bell and present themselves, this motley crew of four. How uniformed armed guards had glared at them as if they were spies who deserved to be flattened against a wall, how after interminable negotiations—where was the UN when they needed it?—a servant was sent to fetch the offending weapon, which he placed, like an unexploded missile, into Timmy's sticky five-year-old hands.

"Well, you've certainly had an interesting day," said Ben. "Speaking of servants," he added, "I found a rather intriguing document which listed a significantly substantial belowstairs staff in the Tarbell household—now this was a middle-class family, no blue blood at all, and still . . ."

And still, the things she could do with a staff—both kinds, but especially, a stick to stick him with. Remember me, she'd prod. I'm here. Your wife. The mother of your children. The invisible woman. Could a marriage transplanted to foreign soil survive let alone thrive? Maybe there should be more changes than simple geography. We need to do something, she thought.

She'd start small. That night she pulled out the sofa bed, switched his alarm clock with her radio, his *Maine in the Revolution* with her *Things to Do with Children in London*; she even swapped their pillows, both supplied by Merrion Sackville no doubt from the same scrawny goose, whose feathers nevertheless bunched in different but equally unpleasant lumps. While Ben was flossing and brushing in the bathroom, she turned off the lights and arranged herself Maja fashion on his side of the bed. The same side he staked in their Homestead four-poster, on the mattresses of lakefront cabins, in the guest rooms of their friends, on the futons unrolled along the floorboards of cousins' living rooms.

Now Ben reached for the blanket and found her hip. Patting it, he took its measure as if it were some undiscovered land mass rather than the contours he'd been mapping all his adult life. "What's this?" he asked.

"Me," Lee replied.

"I know that."

"Which comes as a relief . . ."

"I mean, why are you in this particular spot?"

"Because I'm your wife. Because as such I share your bed. Because—"

"But you're on my side . . ."

"An arbitrary designation."

". . . where I always sleep. For our whole married life." He paused. "And even before."

"I thought a change was in order."

"If it ain't broke . . ."

"Who says it isn't?"

Ben sighed his woman-is-a-mystery sigh. With gallantry that was heroic, Lee noted, considering this was a planned attack, he felt his way along the bed frame in the dark and stubbed his toe on a corner that had never marked his regular route. He dropped onto alien springs. He reached for her breast, which was encased in a few flimsy inches of purple lace she'd bought that morning from a stall in Camden Lock. "And what's this?" he asked. "Another change?" He rolled on top of her.

"Change is good."

He laughed. "Some. An improvement on my old T-shirts at any rate." He tugged at a silky strap.

Three feet away, a child sneezed. Something fell to the floor. "Mummy," another child called out.

"Don't you move," Lee said.

"Not on a dime," Ben groaned. "I swear."

And when she came back from tucking in Timmy, filling Johnny's glass, showing Maggie that the shadows on the windows were only branches, smoothing brows and adjusting stuffed animals, Ben had reclaimed his side, annexing whole new inches with his splayed arms and legs. His blissful dead-to-the-world snores made her blood boil. She shook him awake. "You *swore*," she accused.

"War?" he grunted. "Sore?"

"Swore," she repeated. She nuzzled her head into the side of his neck. "Let's take up where we left off."

His voice was thick. "I'm beat. Need my sleep." He launched an arm over her which dropped onto her shoulder with the force of a felled tree. He put his lips against her ear. His breath was hot. "Nathaniel . . ." he crooned.

Lee slipped off the seductive purple silk. She should have asked for a money-back guarantee from the vendor who'd wrapped her purchase in a layer of tissue, then rolled it, like a cone of fish and chips, in a sheath of pages from the *Daily Mail*. "This will make 'im sit up, it will," the salesman had leered.

Now Lee turned her back on her lying-down husband. Fish and chips might have been the more seductive choice. She grabbed her Babe the Blue Ox T-shirt from the floor. They'd get through this, she knew. The demanding children, the tiny flat. A preoccupied husband and the lack of privacy was an equation that was not about to add up to great sex. She understood that peaks and valleys marked every marriage. Was there a single magazine in any dentist's office that didn't deal with this? Welcome to the human race, Lee Emery. Still, exactly how *was* she going to get through this blip in the long smooth line of what she counted on as, if not always wedded bliss, then wedded comfort? What was she going to do?

What she did was find the library. Not Ben's kind, to which you had to submit your first-rate CV and three references attesting to your first-rate character to get a pass. But rather, the local, public one, behind the High Street, a block away. With a sunny children's room. "They have a story hour," said the woman at the greengrocer's who was pushing a sleek new pram cradling a spotless rosy-cheeked child inside. Who must have taken pity on her, three tattered kids hanging off her like the sons of Laocoön, while tucked under her arm, teetered against a hip, leaked an overstuffed grocery bag.

So while a cheerful young woman named Miss Priscilla read a story about pelicans and magic elves; and while her children sat rapt with other children their age whose welcoming parents promised play dates and nature walks, Lee wandered the reference section. Here is the church. Here is the steeple. Look inside. Here are the people. Ahh, here was a physicians' guide. Hmmm, look inside. Surprise! Surprise! There was Simon Abernathy. She copied out his address on a yellow, blue-lined book request.

That night, as the children slept, as Ben slept, as she couldn't sleep, she shut herself in the bathroom and wrote. *We are in London for the month of August, husband, three children, and myself. This is the number of the telephone.*

One day after she pushed the note into the red postal box, the phone rang. Ben picked it up. Unexpectedly, he had come back for lunch; he needed some papers, he explained, bearing chicken kabobs and basmati rice and whole wheat nan, and decided he'd sit down to eat with his family, he saw them so rarely during the day.

Just her luck it was this particular day he chose, thought Lee, feeling cross at him, feeling guilty for feeling cross at him, his burnt—or rather barbecued—offering sticking in her throat. When the phone rang, she'd jumped. "Let me," she'd said, trying to tamp down her eagerness. "Probably a play date for one of the kids."

"I'll get it." Ben reached for the receiver next to his chair. He stopped. "Simon?" he said.

Lee's throat closed up. Of course Ben wouldn't even remember the name. *I had a boyfriend named Simon*, she'd told him once in the college cafeteria. *He was English*. She'd stopped, then added, *A long time before you*.

Ben had barely blinked, and went on to tell her about— who was it?—Stacy? Meredith? The way people who have a future together reveal and then dismiss their in-the-light-of-new-love suddenly inconsequential past.

"*Lee* wrote you?" he asked now. His voice was puzzled. His eyebrows knit together over his nose. He glanced at her: who is this person I think I know? "This weekend?"

Lee forced her hands behind her back. She studied the pattern of crumbs on the tabletop, a spattering of rice. In Asia rice was lucky, she'd heard, as long as you finished every grain of it.

All at once, Ben's forehead smoothed. "Ah," he sighed in a voice that conveyed that at last everything was clear. "I see. You live near the *Forest of Dean*." He smiled. "I suppose we could rent a car. Yes. Yes." He picked up a pencil. He scribbled on the side of an envelope. "M4. Then. Yes, a church. Hedges. Eagle Nook Pub. Two rights and a left. Easy."

Two rights and a left. Easy. Two wrongs don't make a right. Not so easy. She knew one wrong. What was the next? Lee dug her nails into her palms.

"And you have kids," Ben said.

So he has kids. She *knew* he had a wife. On a postcard of Hyde Park the year after she'd married Ben, he'd scribbled, "I've followed your example. My wife is called Caroline"—the only time she'd heard from him after she'd written, two years before, that she'd become engaged. It was Caroline who'd penned the note thanking her for the wedding gift of three, *oh horrifying numeral*, antique spoons.

"Great," Ben declared now with the kind of enthusiasm he usually reserved for all things Nathaniel. "Let me hand you over to Lee."

"Simon?" Lee said. "Simon." The word tasted on her tongue like forbidden fruit, as though the very act of pronouncing it would result in a biblical punishment.

But no lightning struck. No locusts swarmed. No skies lashed out forty days and nights of rain. Only a soft clearing of Simon's throat. Then:

"I recognized your handwriting."

What to say, while Ben was clanging about sorting through papers, scraping leftover rice into the trash, looking for his keys. While Johnny and Timmy were fighting over a truck. While Maggie was crying to be taken to the park.

What to say?

The usual banalities. The polite inquiries about wife and children. The state of everyone's health. Jobs. Meteorology. How nice it will be for the families to get together; for Lee's family to escape the city, to enjoy some of England's famed countryside. He's looking forward to meeting Ben. She's looking forward to meeting Caroline. "And I can't wait to see you, Lee," Simon said.

But there was no time to savor this. Or to analyze the various ways the sentence might be parsed depending on where the accent fell. The minute she hung up, Ben grabbed her in a hug. "You sweetheart, you," he crowed. "You perfect wife." He danced her around the table. "Imagine your arranging this visit. So close to the Forest of Dean, so close to the home of Nathaniel's ancestors. I can't even begin to thank you for planning something that would please me so much."

The rental car was tiny. In the back seat, the children fought. Ben's knee hit a button and the windshield wipers went on. They were almost out of the city, the sun shining, the blades squeaking against dry glass, fellow drivers honking and pointing until Lee found the right page in the manual. "Stay left. Stay left," Lee kept screaming at Ben as the car wandered to the right. Getting on the roundabouts was easy. Getting off, as they circled endlessly like a demonstration of centripetal force, was impossible. Lee imagined their little family wiped out in a head-on collision or bearing in the wrong direction, tumbling over a cliff. It would serve her right. And she would take them down with her, her innocent lambs.

After a couple of bumper-car hours, Maggie claimed she was about to throw up. Timmy had to pee. Hedges scratched both sides of the windows; witches' hands, Maggie cried. "We should've stayed put," Ben said.

We should've stayed put, Lee thought.

"I don't mean that," Ben said. "It will be worth it to see the Forest of Dean. Driving on the wrong side of the street is the price you pay."

"But they think *we* drive on the wrong side of the street," Johnny pointed out. Her child the peacemaker, the concili- ator, who could project himself into another's point of view, see the opposite side of any argument.

Am I on the wrong side of the pond? Lee asked herself.

"Ah, there's the Eagle Nook Pub." Ben stuck a finger out the window at a half-timbered lopsided building. A wooden eagle needing a paint job hung over the door. A couple of picnic tables bore the sticky remains of a dozen abandoned glasses of ale. A dog dozing in the driveway raised its head and gave their car a lackluster bark.

Lee fished in her pocketbook for her lipstick and comb. If she's on the wrong side of the pond, she'll find out all too soon.

They parked by the rabbit hutch. The children tumbled from the car like a string of circus clowns and swarmed toward the rabbits, the goats in the field beyond, and the picture-book pony poking its head over a picture-book stile.

The house itself could have come out of a picture book, too. It was long and low with rectangles of different-colored stone, added higgledy-piggledy, Lee supposed, in different centuries. Pansies poked over the top of green window boxes, cockeyed shutters framed windows patched like a crazy quilt into the jagged facade. Flanking the front door stood two red phone booths, the kind you'd find gracing half the postcards in the racks outside news kiosks and tour- ist shops. These seemed to be filled with rakes and hoes. A tubby marmalade cat—the Cheshire Cat minus the smile— sunned itself on a scooped-out step.

And then the door opened.

First came Caroline.

Followed by two blond boys with Buster Brown haircuts and falling-down socks and Simon's eyes.

And then there was Simon.

Simon.

The ghost of Marguerite—the hostess with the mostest, the queen of social skills—must have been propelling Lee because she felt herself move forward, hand outstretched, smile clothespinned to her ears, mellifluent tones ringing from her lips forming the words "How lovely, Simon," as her real self froze, feet rooted to the paving stones of Simon's front walk.

But in seconds, Simon's hand was taking her hand. Simon's eyes were looking into her eyes. She could smell his lunch—cheese, pickle, onion, ale?—on the rush of his breath. He smiled. Between his teeth, she could see his glistening tongue. "Lee," he whispered. "Lee."

After dinner, Sebastian and Dombey, Simon's to-the-manor-born mannered sons, picked up cricket bats and balls and took their three rowdy American contemporaries outdoors. It stayed light these evenings until well after nine, Caroline explained. The children could even lie down in the middle of the street—not that they would of course—Lee and Ben's car had been the only vehicle to motor by their lane that day. It was different in America, Caroline had read, even in towns far away from New York. After all, didn't everyone in America carry a gun?

Ben explained that nobody they knew had guns, that

people got a Wild West impression of the States from the media, that he and Lee kept their door on Evergreen Road unlatched, that children in Maine were safe.

Lee tried not to think of pickup trucks sliding down their street after the bars on Hancock had closed. She tried not to picture the stop sign two blocks away riddled with bullet holes. Homestead seemed a less placid place than Netherend. Bigger. Grittier. Could this be explained by the meaning inside their names? One depicting both a frontier town and deep roots—a contradiction in terms? The other linking the lowest to the last—an intrinsic redundancy? She shuddered. Still, there were other dangers besides guns, and doors you had to lock and streets you couldn't lie down in. There were doors you shouldn't open, beds you shouldn't lie down in. She glanced at Simon. Her cheeks flamed. What was the matter with her?

"Let's move into the sitting room," Caroline announced.

"Can I help you clear?" asked Ben.

Caroline awarded him a star-on-the-forehead smile. "A little later," she said.

Simon brought out a decanter of port and a bowler-hat-shaped crock of Stilton cheese. Next to her on the sofa, upholstered in a faded chintz of cabbage roses and crawling vines, Ben stretched out his legs. He patted his stomach. "What a wonderful meal," he said.

"Yes, lovely," seconded Lee. Plain English food. Roast chicken, roast potatoes, overboiled Brussels sprouts, vanilla pudding dolloped with whipped cream. Nursery food, one of her guidebooks had informed, is what the English do best.

"This is by far the most satisfying meal I've had in this country since we touched down at Heathrow," Ben went on.

Lee gave him a sharp look. Was he out-Englishing the English in obsequious good manners? Or was it nursery food that was hitherto missing from his life? She pictured the parathas and tagines and pickled cabbage leaving their stains on Merrion Sackville's yellowed plastic tablecloth. Perhaps their culinary adventures in unfamiliar tastes were as unsettling to Ben as the unfamiliar side of a bed. She studied Caroline's wide haunches and dewy English rose skin, the luck of the climate and not superior genes. With her apple cheeks and ample bottom, she could have been the nanny illustration in an old-fashioned children's book. Who better, after all, to rule the nursery and spoon the Marmite out? Caroline had the kind of no-nonsense demeanor that would keep a house running smoothly, that would keep children—and a husband?—in tow. Her blouse was white with a lace collar. The buttons pulled apart over pillowy breasts. Lee gazed down at her own narrow hips and small breasts. Accentuated by her snuggest jeans, her most flattering black ribbed scoop-necked shirt. She raised a hand to the sharp angles of her face. "Good bones," her grandmother had said. "In a certain light," her grandmother had added, "you and Simon could pass for brother and sister. The point of the nose. The slant of the chin . . ."

Lee stared at the point of the nose, the slant of the chin she'd been struggling to ignore. Impossible. Every minute she meant to move, his eyes held hers. How has she endured these hours, nerve ends inflamed and exposed, buried feelings thrusting up like raw green shoots out of hard, cold soil—all the time talking and laughing and passing plates and eating. While two feet away she can hear Simon breathe and swallow. While two feet away, she can sense the warmth of his body filling the distance between them. Now Simon handed her a goblet of port, a rich ruby liquid sloshing in a thin, etched glass. His fingers brushed hers.

"What did you do to the chicken?" Ben was asking Caroline. "I never had a breast so soft and moist."

Caroline beamed. "Just a few sprigs of rosemary from the garden. You mix it with a little oil—I infuse it myself—and rub it in all the cavities."

"That's all?"

"That's all. As with most things, proper preparation determines the desired result." She smiled, schoolmarmishly, Lee thought. "You just need the patience and effort to make sure each nook and cranny is sufficiently attended to."

"I see."

"Which keeps it tender. So it never dries out."

"Lee's . . ." He stopped. "*Ours*," he corrected, "are always too dry."

"Not always." Lee rushed to defend herself. She felt betrayed. As though he were giving away secrets meant to be kept between husband and wife. She cast him a sidelong glance. He had sunk so far down on the sofa he was practically parallel to it. *Sit up straight*, her grandmother would have ordered, *the way we comport ourselves affects our stature in the world*. Lee squared her shoulders and stuck an imaginary dictionary on her head. What's wrong with him? He's never complained about her chickens before. He adores her coq au vin. Her arroz con pollo. Her mole poblano. Her chicken tetrazzini. Her chicken with forty cloves of garlic. The Cornish game hens she stuffs with mushrooms and covers with a complicated lemon sauce. Even though she's forced to invent substitutions for the foreign ingredients unavailable at her local A&P. A simple roast chicken anyone can cook in her sleep.

"The point is to keep it simple. Not to do too much," Caroline lectured.

"Ahh," said Ben, who was nodding like one of those toy dogs with a disjointed neck and continually bobbing head. "The English understatement we've been hearing so much about."

"Entirely apocryphal," Simon said.

"There are virtues in simplicity," Caroline continued. "But the most important thing is the bird itself. You need a plump, healthy one. From good stock. With plenty of meat on its bones. We get ours from a farm nearby. We know what they've been fed, how they've been treated, that they're not around chemicals or pesticides."

"How comforting it must be," Lee said, "to be so sure of what you put in your mouth."

"Indeed." Simon grinned.

Caroline nodded. "Which is possible only if you insist on getting what nature intended." She stopped. She tsk-ed. "I understand in America they inject dye into their birds, paint them with food coloring, wax them to an artificial shine."

Lee brought a hand up to her artificially shined face—lipstick, blush, gloss, mascara. She stared hard at Caroline. Was it possible that those pink lips and luminescent skin were entirely natural?

Ben lifted his head from the antimacassar. "So natural's the key," he deduced with the kind of *quod erat demonstrandum* he'd use to fill in a piece of Nathaniel history. "Unfortunately, ours come from the A&P—the *supermarket*." He was preaching to the choir. Whose chickens were passed to them flapping from the hands of farmers, who dug their parsnips from the ground and plucked their plums from the tree, whose milk squirted from the udders—the nether ends?—of cows straight into their pails, and who never ordered a take-away lamb tikka or even a vegetarian thali in their life.

"That's too bad." Caroline shook her head at the deprivations Americans had to endure.

"Maine is well known for its poultry industry," Lee felt the need to point out. "*Famous* for it," she added. "I'm sure you can get any kind of chicken that you might want. And more varieties than you ever dreamed about."

"O brave new world that has such chickens in it," sang Simon.

Caroline ignored him. "All well and good," she said, "but sometimes you can venture too far. I do feel that when you find something that satisfies you, you should stick with it."

"That's a lesson for life," Ben conceded, "not just for cooking."

"Hear! Hear!" Simon cheered.

"Though there hasn't been a whole lot of cooking going on in our flat these days," Ben continued, bent on not just airing but flaunting the family linen.

And thus infuriating his wife. "Because we've been so

excited about all the Third World cuisine in our neighborhood. Because it's so good for the children to taste new things," Lee protested.

"Well, I'm sure Lee's a fine cook," Caroline said.

"Believe me, I'm not complaining," complained Ben.

"It's probably because you don't have the right equipment to do it properly," Caroline sympathized. "I know those London flats." She waved a dismissive hand. "No room for an Aga. Simon and I were so happy to flee the city, all that noise and dirt." She frowned. "All those distractions."

Distractions from what? Lee wondered. She looked at Simon, who was staring into his glass as if the sediment of the port were tea leaves to be read. He swirled the liquid. He sniffed the rim. Lee thought of the Magic 8-Ball she'd had as a child. What questions would she ask? What answers would float up?

Caroline brushed invisible crumbs from her skirt. For the first time, Lee realized how clean she was, all white and plump and soft as a crumpet. "Speaking of which," Caroline continued.

"The city?" Simon prompted.

"Only by way of contrast. I thought Ben—and Lee— might like a quick trip to the Forest of Dean. There'll be tomorrow of course, but . . ."

Ben popped up, his whole body alert and throbbing with Nathaniel arousal. "Do you think . . . ? So late . . . ?"

Caroline turned to Simon. "Shall we take two cars? The children . . ."

"I'll stay with the children," Lee said.

"That's too much to ask."

"Not at all. Why take two cars, since tomorrow we'll have another chance."

"But you're our guest."

"Who couldn't be happier staying put"—Lee pointed toward the window—"in such a lovely spot."

"And I'll do the washing up," Simon volunteered.

"Of course, the children can be left alone. Dombey can watch Maggie. It's perfectly safe," Caroline considered, "for an hour or so."

"I'm sure it is," Lee said, "but I think my three—well, it's the first time they've . . . I know it's silly, but mothers . . ."

"I understand. They've just come from the *city*," said Caroline. "There'll be plenty of time tomorrow. Simon, be very careful with the glasses. Wash each separately. Set them on the linen tea towels. Double thick."

What did Lee expect when Ben got his maps and camera and notebook, when Caroline fetched her extra cardigan against the evening chill, when the car sped away with a chug and two honks—for the goat in the road—and a spray of gravel in its wake? Lee could see this scene of departure from the kitchen window where she stood over the sink rinsing the plates Simon handed her. Did she expect that the minute her husband and his wife peeled off in a storm of pebbles and trailed by two goats, she and Simon would fall into each other's arms? That he would shove her against the refrigerator and lift up her skirt? That she would slide her fingers down toward the buckle on his belt? That she would get as dewy and moist as one of Caroline's prize chickens? And Simon? Did she expect his rod and his staff to comfort her? That he would rub it into all her lubricious cavities?

Did she hope for this?

Did she want this?

Of course not. A mere fantasy. The stuff of movies, of cheap novels, not real life, she reminded herself. Doing dishes was real life. Sleeping on the same side of the bed for the eternity of your marriage was real life. Unfinished business was meant to be unfinished. Or finished by somebody else. She put the dish on the draining rack, and took the fragile, etched glass from Simon's hand.

"Look," he said, "I have something to show you." He reached into his pocket and brought out an object small enough to close his fingers around. He held out his fist. "Guess," he said.

"I'm not good at this."

"Try."

"Is it a magic trick?"

"Depends on what you mean by magic," he said. "Have a go."

"I haven't the slightest idea."

"But you do."

"I do?"

He nodded. His eyes were dark. His brows raised into expectant arcs. His smile, lips slightly turned up, mysterious.

But not mischievous. Not the smile of her snips-and-snails-and-puppy-dogs'-tails boys whose grubby fists might reveal spiders and beetles and worms. *Look, Mom*, they might say. *This is really cool. Don't be scared.*

"Come on," Simon coached. His hand stretched out an inch from her chin. He turned his wrist from side to side. She smelled the lemon of the dishwashing soap. She saw nails cut straight across the sinuous fingers whose long-ago touch was still imprinted on her skin. She saw he didn't wear a wedding ring.

"Is this twenty questions?" she asked.

He shook his head.

"How about a hint?"

"Hyde Park," he said.

Lee's breath stopped, then came out in a ragged gasp. So he hadn't forgotten—the trees, the grass, the fence. Her goddamn girdle. They missed the sexual revolution by a minute. Missed birth control pills and hotel rooms with no questions asked. Missed places to pass a night where the gates were never locked. And yet fifteen years ago these fingers in front of her had cupped her breast, these lips now forming this odd half smile took her nipple into his mouth. Fifteen years ago, her own hands had traced the ridge of his penis, tested the sweet soft weight of his testicles.

He smiled. How could such an angular face hold such appeal? Such *sex* appeal?

"I don't mean to torment you," he said.

"But you are," she said, "tormenting me."

"In that case . . ."

"Yes . . ."

"Look," he said. One by one, he uncurled his fingers.

And revealed a rabbit's foot.

Her own fingers tightened.

And shattered the glass in her hand.

"Oh!" she cried.

"Oh," he cried. He put the rabbit's foot back in his pocket, and grabbed her wrist. "You're bleeding," he exclaimed.

She looked down and saw bubbles of blood. Saw her hand in his. Felt the warmth of his flesh as he picked out slivers of glass. "I hadn't even noticed . . ."

"I'm no surgeon," he said, "but I think I can manage this."

"Please," Lee said.

His dark eyes met hers. He brought her hand up to his lips. Then he grabbed a linen tea towel from the counter, wrapped her hand in it, and pulled her to him. "My darling, Lee," he sighed. She smelled licorice and cinnamon. She smelled roses and damp earth. She was eighteen again. In the park. Under the trees. An airplane buzzing through the night sky. Across Park Lane, in a bright, mirrored, chandeliered hotel room, her grandmother waited. "My darling Magnolia," she was saying, "I want you to have a great love."

But she wasn't eighteen. And neither was he. And she was married. And so was he. And outside the kitchen window danced the voices of their children. His. Hers. Louder and louder as they came closer to the door. He pulled his tongue from her tongue. He pulled his lips from her lips. He sat her at the kitchen table, and spread out the linen cloth—lettered *Tudor Kings of Olde England* in Gothic script across the border and stamped with Holbein's head of Henry the Eighth. Whose forehead was now polka-dotted with her blood. Simon removed the last splinter of glass from her hand.

"Androcles . . ." she whispered.

He painted her cut with Mercurochrome, bound it with a length of gauze, and taped the ends. "Pretty good for a pathologist," he said.

"Pathology? Hadn't you planned on something else?"

"Yes. However, I discovered I wasn't terribly good with people."

"I don't believe it."

"My bedside manner was sorely lacking."

"Not in my book," she said.

"Depends on the patient," he said. "I'm afraid I'm one of those unreliable chaps who play favorites."

Favorites. Her cheeks burned. She turned her head away.

"So what do you think of my surprise?" he asked.

"I hardly have the words."

"I would have saved the stockings, too," he added, "but my mother found them and, not recognizing a treasure, threw them out."

"No wonder." She waited. "*My* rabbit's foot," she said. "Better than a rabbit pulled from a hat," she added. "And not much the worse for wear."

"Because it's been cherished. I keep it with me always." He patted his pocket. "I shall never part with it."

"Simon . . ." she began.

He put a finger against her lips. "Shhh," he whispered.

The children were at the door now. There was a clang of bats, the thump of balls. "Great!" she heard Timmy cry. "We can play rounders," suggested Sebastian or Dombey. "I wish you had a sister," whined Maggie.

"We'll have tomorrow," Simon said.

Simon touched her lips again. "Tomorrow," he said.

But before tomorrow there was that night.

That night, in the Abernathys' guest room, up under the eaves, purple delphiniums stuck out of a Wedgwood pitcher; white periwinkles festooned old crocks; in a Toby jug pink phlox crowned Churchill's head. Every bureau, table, windowsill held a bouquet. Did such decor represent VIP treatment or the standard welcome of a nation of obsessive gardeners? Lee wondered. On one nightstand lay a well-thumbed guide to the birds of Wales. On the other, an Ordnance Survey map of the Wye Valley and the Forest of Dean, a big glossy book of photographs of the Gloucester Cathedral, and a small worn leather volume of *Paradise Lost*. Lee picked up the Milton. Was this, too, part of the permanent guest room collection or a changing one depending on who was sleeping in the bed?

Secretly—with not a little guilt—Lee had pulled open drawers, searched the corners of the wardrobe, the cubbyholes of the writing desk. Would she stumble on Caroline's diaphragm the way she had once found her mother's beneath a pile of underwear? Would she discover a locket clasping a silky curl? Or an old wish-you-were-here postcard missing a signature? But she unearthed not the slightest clue either to Simon and Caroline's marriage or to their separate lives. All she turned up was a dusty 5p and a small red rubber ball.

In bed, Ben shook out the map until it covered them like another sheet. "I'm so glad we came," he said. He traced a finger over a swath of green somewhere in the vicinity of his belly button. "The Forest of Dean is unbelievable. The river valley is exquisite. No wonder the place was a royal hunting ground. At one time, Nathaniel's ancestors supplied timber from it for warships. The rail lines from the nineteenth century have been turned into a network of paths and tracks. There are quarries, and woods, trails, and walks, a nature reserve, a Roman temple, and an arboretum. I can't wait to explore further. It's the most fantastic place imaginable."

"You sound so happy."

"I am." He slid a finger to just under his collarbone. "Here's the dismantled railway. And, here, a bridge . . ." He rustled the map. "Caroline is remarkable. She knows every nook and cranny . . ."

"But she would. Isn't she after all the master—the mistress—of cavities?"

"Come on, Lee."

"Sorry." She vowed to behave. "Didn't she grow up around here?"

"Yes. As a child she used to ride her pony in the forest." He chuckled. "She named him Sir Pony."

"Clever."

"For a nine-year-old, yes." He turned to her. "You know what?"

"What?"

"You're not going to believe this, Lee, but . . ." He stopped. "I know it will sound silly, but . . ."

"But . . . ?"

"But, well . . ."

"Ben!"

"Well, I felt so close to Nathaniel today. I sensed his presence everywhere." He held his hand in front of his face. He spread his fingers. "Almost as if he were leading me by the hand. *My* hand. It was—the only word I can come up with is—spiritual."

Lee leaned against a flower-sprigged pillow and stared up at the pitched ceiling of Simon's house. She let Ben's words flow over her. *Woods* and *horses* and *brooks* and *Nathaniel* this, *Nathaniel* that, *Nathaniel*, *Nathaniel*. She nodded encouragement with a polite *oh*, or a lackluster *ah*. *How nice*, she answered. *Yes, lovely*, she added. And all the while, underneath, she was aware of some other noise, an echo, a murmuring. Footsteps. Muffled words. She heard a door slam. A drawer slide open. Voices stop and start. Then it came to her. Of course. Where they lay now was directly on top of Simon and Caroline's room. Caroline had led them up a twisted narrow stair. The window overlooked the herb garden and an old stone wall. "*Our* view," Caroline had said, setting out towels and filling a water carafe. *Acorn patch*, Ben was saying now. *Blackpennywall Green*. "Simon," a voice rose in anger. And Lee could just make out the word "broke" followed by the word "glass."

When Ben had folded up the map, turned off the lamp, straightened the covers, he turned to her. The bed was old and high, its corners marked by fat columns and spindly legs. Even the gentlest roll onto a hip or back caused the springs to squeak while the whole bed seemed to slide another inch along the varnished floorboards. "How about it?" Ben asked. "All those dark woods and fresh air—no wonder Nathaniel was so lusty—the Forest of Dean is a perfect aphrodisiac."

Lee thought of the noise they would make no matter how quiet they'd try to be. Simon and Caroline would *know*. Besides, how could she commit this act of infidelity—correction, *fidelity*—after that kiss, and that kiss's promise of tomorrow? What is wrong with this picture, she wondered, that having sex with her own husband made her feel disloyal to somebody else's mate?

Ben sat up. He started to pull off his corner of the covers. "In fact, you're not going to believe this, but I'm feeling so adventurous, I just might switch sides."

Lee put her hand on his shoulder. Gently she pushed him back down. "No need for such extreme measures," she said. "Though I appreciate the heroic gesture. Besides, I'm so exhausted all I want to do is conk right out."

"Sure?"

"Sure."

"Tomorrow, then," Ben said.

"Tomorrow."

She awoke to the rain pounding overhead and three distinct *pings*—one on the bureau top, one on the windowsill, one on the glass lamp shade—where the roof leaked. Behind the starched organdy curtains, the sky filled the window with a square of solid gray. She felt sweat pool between her breasts and under her arms. She'd had wild dreams: gnarled branches hung with chandeliers, logs floating down the Thames, birds with her parents' faces on them, lobsters riding ponies, and days and nights of sex with a faceless man each of whose arms and legs ended in a rabbit's foot. She needed a shower.

Which meant in old English—*Olde English*—houses, a bath. The bath was downstairs, along the hall and around the corner from the door to Caroline and Simon's room. She heard rustling below. Footsteps. Whispering. Would Simon have turned to Caroline in the night, or the morning, and asked, *Shall we? Your side or mine?* While Caroline, pointing her hand to the ceiling, would shake her head and say, *The guests* . . . Beside her, Ben stirred. "What time is it?" he groaned.

"Early," she whispered. "Go back to sleep."

She listened to a toilet flush, the clanging of old pipes. More footsteps. More doors open and shut. When the footsteps had receded, when the pipes had grown silent, when she thought she could smell coffee brewing and oatmeal—porridge?—cooking, she slipped on her robe—a silky kimono patterned with chrysanthemums and cranes that had been her grandmother's—and tiptoed down the stairs.

At the bottom step, she stopped. She heard the soft pad of a bare foot. Simon, his back to her, a towel around his hips, was walking down the hall. She studied the sharp shoulder bones, the rosy flesh, the tapered waist. Once the heat of that back had almost singed her fingertips. She noted the hard high curve of his buttocks, the muscled calves of his legs; how his wet hair stuck up like a little boy's. When he turned the corner, she slipped into the bathroom, which was moist and steamy from his bath. On a shelf stood his shaving brush and soapy mug. His washcloth, wrung out on a towel rack, was still warm. She touched her cheek to it. She filled the tub. She understood what Ben felt trampling the woods that Nathaniel had trampled. His exultation. Was it any less spiritual to sit in a tub that Simon had just left, to soap her own body with the bar of Yardley's English Lavender still slippery from its lathering slide across Simon's just-glimpsed flesh? She forced herself to picture Ben's wide back, strong shoulders, long enveloping arms. His solid chin and straight white American teeth. She tried to feel guilty for a stolen kiss, for lust outside of her matrimonial bond. But you couldn't wedge the hearth-bound scenes from a marriage into the diorama of dreamy landscapes from your past. In Simon's bathroom, Simon's house, Simon's village, Simon's country, there didn't seem a place for Ben.

At breakfast, everybody grumbled about the rain. Except Caroline with her *April showers bring May flowers* English getting-on-with-it. "There's no reason on earth why the weather should hold us back," she declared.

Lee looked toward the window. The panes rattled. Shutters flapped. Sheets of water curtained the outside world. In a corner of the kitchen, a quartet of metal pails caught the drops plunking into them like cascading marbles. Lee stirred her oatmeal, which inspired no talk of juiciness this morning. She remembered the child's rhyme *Pease Porridge Hot*. What was pease, anyway? This cereal was more like peat. Thick, dry, slightly burnt. With a funny smell.

Though not to Ben, who was wolfing it down with an enthusiasm that was as patently false as it was irritating. "So this is the full English breakfast," he said. He helped himself to bangers and mash, to the platter of tomatoes and mushrooms as waterlogged as the sodden fields beyond the kitchen door. "Delicious," he pronounced.

Lee turned her head toward Simon, who was spreading jam on toast. "Ginger for Maggie, lemon curd for Dombey. Timmy, do you want to try the gooseberry?" he asked. How amazing to realize these hands now wielding knife and fork, pouring tea, passing plates of bread and jam, smoothing napkins, slicing oranges, performing such quotidian tasks had sopped her blood, picked glass from her flesh, bound her wound, laced his fingers through hers, held her against his chest. And these lips . . . She forced herself to stop. What a difference a few hours and a few more people made. To-morrow was now today. In the gray light of this morning, a kiss, a touch seemed like a delusion of midsummer, mid-afternoon madness. Eclipsed by the ordinariness of jam and toast, of slickers and boots. Here at this table, she was part of somebody else's domestic interior, like a person painted in as an afterthought. Had she imagined everything?

"We've got enough Macs and Wellies for the whole lot," Caroline announced.

"Though not everybody may be quite so intrepid as you," Simon warned.

"Nonsense," stated Caroline's no-nonsense voice.

"You know," Ben said, "this weather may be a blessing. A blessing in disguise." He jumped up from the table. "I'll just be a minute," he said. "I want to read you something from Nathaniel's diary." He stomped up the stairs.

In the kitchen Lee could discern every step, every turn of his foot. She could hear him make his way across the guest room two floors above. She could hear the protest of springs as he put something—his suitcase?—onto the bed. Thank goodness Ben hadn't had his way. Hadn't had his way with her. How embarrassing to face the Abernathys over the silver toast rack and jars of homemade marmalade.

Now Caroline passed the sugar to Lee. The front of the bowl bore a likeness of Princess Margaret and Antony Armstrong-Jones. Tiaraed and top-hatted, they flashed false smiles opening on tombstone teeth. *Married 1960* stated the caption plastered across her white and his black chest. Poor soul, who could be Lee's soul sister with her similar name and similar enough predicament. Was Princess Margaret pining for Group Captain Peter Townsend even as she took her vows? Even as she posed for the commemorative portrait that would mark tea towels and serving trays? The marriage was in trouble, the tabloids at Kensington tube station blazed. Photos pictured the Princess Margaret Rose on a dock in the Caribbean spilling out of a bikini and drinking gin with a scoundrel half her age. Lee traced a finger over Princess Margaret's face. Does such passion ever die? she wondered. Do you ever get over your first, true love?

Caroline poured herself more tea. "You know, I find it extraordinary and quite touching, really, how devoted Ben is to Nathaniel Tarbell," she said.

You're telling *me?* Lee marveled. "It is," she agreed. "Of course we've all lived with him so long he's like a member of our family."

"Nathaniel's dog was named Prince," Johnny supplied.

"Cute doggie," put in Maggie.

"He was a lumberman," stated Johnny.

"In Maine," Timmy added. He turned to Dombey. "Where we come from."

Caroline nodded. "So I've been told. Ben gave me a brief biography in the car yesterday. Your husband has such a way with words, he must be a wonderful writer."

"He is," seconded his loyal wife.

"It must be so rewarding to be an academic. To teach young people. To lead the life of the mind." Caroline looked at Simon. "Sometimes, I worry about Simon, that he's so closed up in that lab of his."

"No need, my dear. Since this was my choice."

"Still, it must be wonderful to feel so passionate about something," Caroline said.

Simon gave a vigorous shake of his head. "It must be," he repeated, "to feel so passionate."

Just at that moment, preceded by a couple of bangs and a few thumps, the man of passion—*Nathaniel* passion—rushed back into the kitchen, waving a sheaf of paper. His face was flushed, his eyes bright, almost feverish.

Lee considered: might the madness in Nathaniel's family tree rub off on one so closely working on it? If a couple of hours in the Forest of Dean could foster such exhilaration what would a whole afternoon do? Ben shoved plates and mugs out of the way and spread his papers on the tabletop. "Listen to this," he said. He began to read in a tone so reverent even the children were hushed. *I have never loved my Forest of Dean so much as in the middle of a great and powerful rainstorm. The sound of the wind and the rain and the trembling branches of the majestic trees is nothing less than a chorus raised to God. The river runs swift, the greens and browns and blacks and yellows—all the colors of nature are deepened and polished; every-where one looks lie shadows and mystery. One senses one's ances-tors. One feels all the ancient rituals. The oaks and beeches of centuries are as thick silent sentinels, witnesses to God's power. Stand in the Forest of Dean in the rain and you will feel the blood of your ancestors course through your veins and the power of God in your heart.* Ben's voice cracked. "Imagine," he gasped.

"I know precisely what he means," Caroline said. "I've experienced those feelings myself."

"Ah. Now I see that the rain is a bonus for you," Simon said.

"For me," Caroline agreed.

"Me, also," Ben underlined.

Not to mention me, Lee thought. Had the gods of weather conspired to give her and Simon a chance to finish what they'd started? Dare she hope? And yet what had they started? Perhaps the kiss, *that* kiss, was less the overture and more the finale. "I'm afraid I'm not much of a foul-weather friend," she confessed to Caroline.

Caroline cast her a look of pity, a city slicker on whom the natural wonders of the world were lost. If you only knew, Lee wanted to protest. I'm from Maine. I'm no stranger to the power of pine trees and snow to make me feel the blood of my ancestors—certain ancestors—course through my veins. Only the lure of your husband keeps me from strut-ting my open-air skills and inbred hardiness.

"I want to go in the rain," cried Maggie.

"Me, too! Me, too!" chimed the other children with the fervor of the born-again. Not a surprising response to the gospel pitch of Ben's delivery.

"We'll *all* go," declared Caroline.

"I don't think Lee's too keen," Simon ventured.

"I never meant Lee." Caroline brushed crumbs into a napkin. "Simon, you should stay and keep her company."

"I don't need—" Lee started to say.

"I'd be glad," Simon said.

"I've brought books to read."

"And I can stand in the Forest of Dean in the rain any-time," explained Simon. "My keeping you company is hardly a sacrifice."

"That's settled, then. Now we can fit everybody into one car," said Caroline, the enabler.

And in a flurry of green rubber boots, and shiny yellow raincoats, and crackled Barbours, and black umbrellas, and knobby walking sticks, they were gone.

Simon took her hand. He led her up the stairs. "Simon . . ." Lee began.

His fingers tightened around hers. "I know," he said.

They walked from room to room, two eighteen-year-olds looking to open a gate; two thirty-three-year-olds hoping to close a door. Like Goldilocks and the three bears, they considered and eliminated each bed. Not Simon and Caro-line's. Not the guest double assigned to Lee and Ben. Were the children's too small?

"Nothing is too small," said Simon.

But even so, said Lee, they'd be surrounded by Snoopy backpacks, and Paddington Bears, and toy trains and trucks. A child's world to remind them of adult responsibilities.

Not exactly the background for grown-ups doing things that grown-ups desire.

In the living room, Simon lit a fire. He spread a blanket on the floor.

Lee put on her wisps of purple silk. She adjusted a strap. She smoothed an edge of lace. She stopped. Her hand froze in midair like a mime's. She had bought these in Camden Lock. For Ben. To seduce him out of his rut and from his side of the bed. To stir merriment into the sour and ancient springs of Merrion Sackville's lumpy divan. It was a costume an actor might wear to play a part. Something Marguerite might choose for a role as odalisque in a *tableau vivant*. Or even, Lee supposed, in real life. Lee pulled off the silly bits of silk. She threw them on the floor.

With Simon she would be herself.

"At last," he sighed. He stroked her cheek, the hollow of her neck. She curled her arms around his back.

The fire roared. The rain lashed. The ancient floorboards creaked. And together Lee and Simon found what they had lost fifteen years ago.

Later, Simon rolled up the blanket. He set it back on his and Caroline's bed. They got dressed. Simon made tea. Lee filled the sugar bowl. She poured milk into the matching Princess Margaret/Antony Armstrong-Jones creamer. Was she projecting, or did the couple look a little happier? Maybe such gritting-their-teeth expressions were the fault of the artist and not the relationship. Everyone knew you couldn't trust what you read in the British press. Simon cut up lemon wedges. Lee studied the photograph over the mantelpiece of Caroline in her wedding dress. She wore a simple country frock of dotted Swiss with an uneven hem. No doubt she had made it herself. And roasted the chicken for the wedding feast. She was standing in an arbor of beech trees. The Forest of Dean? She held a bouquet of wildflowers. Circling her head was a wreath of primroses and buttercups. She had a wistful smile and startled eyes. "What a pretty bride," Lee said.

Simon got up from the sofa. He filled his mug. Then came to stand by her.

He touched Lee's shoulder. He swept his fingers along her arm. He tucked a lock of her hair behind her ear. He looked so sad, Lee thought. She felt it, too, this sadness. In spite of their great joy. In spite of fifteen years of anticipation and its sublime result. Which was not at all the anticlimax one might prepare oneself for after so much hope. Perhaps the sadness could be chalked up to the postcoital *tristesse* the French are always talking about.

Still, there was more reason to be sad than the usual, universal one of after-the-fact. What lay between them was the truth, unstated but acknowledged, that this act of love would be both the first and the last. They had been making up for a loss. Filling in the missing chapter in their mutual history. Now they would go on with their separate lives.

"My darling," Simon said. And put into words what Lee felt. "I was always certain," he sighed in a voice so low she had to tilt her ear to his mouth, "that the person waiting for me at the end of the aisle—the bride, *my* bride—would be you."

Five

*B*efore the wedding came the funeral.

Or, rather, the memorial service. There were no bodies to set into caskets. No ashes to fill an urn. Lee's parents' plane had gone down over the Amazon. A Cessna Cardinal whose flimsy frame belied its hardiness, it had flown endless missions without a mishap, she'd been told. Painted across its side were red block letters, *Ave do Paraiso*, spelling out *Bird of Paradise* in Portuguese. Lee had seen such Fisher-Price toys at the air show at the local air force base. Years ago, to inaugurate her father's new camera, she'd posed in front of one. When she leaned an elbow against the wing, the whole plane had so trembled and lurched, it could have been constructed out of a *Homestead Herald*'s folded comics page. The *Bird of Paradise* had been a four-seater, holding Lee's parents, their two traveling-light rucksacks, their bird books and binoculars, her father's silly hat with fishing flies and a lucky shamrock pinned to it, her mother's out-of-style harlequin sunglasses, and the extra roll of toilet paper she'd been advised to carry by the Audubon Society ombudsman. And the pilot, Inocencio dos Santos, who had left seven children under ten. "At least you are grown," consoled both the Brazilian consul and the State Department liaison. "Think of Señor dos Santos's seven fatherless sons."

It was no consolation. The starving children in India did nothing to stanch a privileged American's hunger pangs. Seven grieving young sons was no more a tragedy than one grieving near-adult daughter. Who, at twenty, still believed in fairy tales.

It was all a mistake, she comforted herself. A story with the wrong ending tacked on. For weeks, for months, after the memorial service, after the condolence notes, after phone calls and casseroles, after the dinner invitations and penetrating looks and the *if there's anything you need, any time of day or night*, after the Audubon Society's memorial fund had raised enough for a full ecological scholarship, after the rest of the world had got on with it, after Marguerite had gone back to New York and packed away her somber *peau de soie* dressmaker suit and black mantilla, after wills were read and estate taxes paid, Lee waited for the happily-ever-after to be revealed. At any moment, her parents would once again take up their rightful places on Evergreen Road.

You couldn't ignore the signs: look at the name of the pilot, for example—Inocencio dos Santos. *Innocent. Saint.* How could harm come to anyone christened with such a prescription for evil's antidote? Today, tomorrow, by the weekend, the phone would ring, static bouncing across a line that spanned continents; or a letter would arrive with foreign stamps and fading ink on watermarked waterlogged stationery. Or a yellow telegram delivered by somebody in a snappy Western Union uniform. STOP. MISTAKE. STOP. Her parents had been found. Cast away on an island. Clinging to a raft. Sighting exotic species off a cliff in the Andes. Living with a native family inside a mud-baked jungle hut. Or in a nomad's tent subsisting on the eyeballs of sheep and the larvae of butterflies. *We wrote you*, they'd say. *We'd tried to call. We sent a messenger. What a lot of needless fuss.* Of course they would come back.

"You are an orphan," sobbed Marguerite. "And I have lost my only child."

Mourning became Marguerite. In her grief she was magnificent. A whole Greek chorus evoked in one small black-shrouded body keening on stiletto slingbacks that exposed pumiced heels and crimson-lacquered toes. Her wrath was biblical. Her tears rivaled Noah's flood. She rose to the occasion the way a kneaded and pounded slab of dough rises into a yeasty, thick dense loaf.

Lee, on the other hand, felt diminished by her tragedy. She disappeared into corners, flattened herself behind furniture, clung to the periphery.

The words of the Brazilian consul kept coming back to her. *At least you are grown.*

Never.

Who is ever old enough for this? If it were simply a matter of years, then her seventy-five-year-old grandmother should have been the essence of maturity. And here she was, weeping and wailing like a full-tantrum toddler.

The service had been held in the college chapel. The altar was so bedecked with flowers it looked like a homecoming float. And the whole town had turned out, too—standing room only—as though for a homecoming.

Without, however, the homecoming cheers and campus razzmatazz. Heads lowered, handkerchiefs clutched against the sturdy worsteds and tweeds of solemn Sunday best, they whispered, *Poor Marguerite*. In hushed tones they asked each other, *Have you ever seen somebody so bereft?* They daubed at their eyes. *The unfortunate daughter*, they added as an afterthought.

From the pulpit, the chaplain, who had graduated two months earlier from the Harvard Divinity School, talked intimately of people he'd never known. "In spite of everything, they died fulfilling a lifelong dream, on a quest to see something they had never before seen," he intoned. "The *hoatzin*," he emphasized. He pronounced it Watson. He cleared his throat. "And though we don't know this, can never know this, we should have the faith to believe, we should take comfort in the thought, that they did see this magnificent bird, that they did fulfill their dream, before they met their final destiny."

Next to Lee, Marguerite was nodding her head with the vigor of a Holy Roller. "Yes! Yes!" she chanted, her jet earrings clanging a jingled amen.

The chaplain wasn't much older than Lee. He had pimples on his forehead, and a shiny baby face. *What if it was your parents?* she wanted to ask him. *Take comfort, my ass.*

And as for this magnificent bird. She had looked up the hoatzin in one of the guides left behind in her parents' room. She had studied the photograph. It was a funny-looking thing. Ugly, like a turkey. Helter-skelter feathers poked out from the top of its head like a cartoon character whose beak had been stuck in an electric socket. Captioning the picture were lines of description that Lee could quote from memory: *A South American bird that molecular studies indicate may be most closely related to the cuckoo, even though the foot structure of the hoatzin is different. The adult gives off a musky, offensive odor causing the natives to call it stinkbird.*

Lee smelled her grandmother's scent. Expensive. French. Which was it today? Chanel? Arpège? Shocking? Scandal? Tabu? Marguerite decanted each newly bought brand into filigreed perfume bottles stoppered with crystal knobs. These she displayed on her vanity table among silver-backed brushes and silken powder puffs and jars and vials of mysterious emollients. Lee remembered, as a child, holding out her scrawny, sticklike arms while Marguerite daubed a trail of different samples along what she called Lee's "pulse points." "You smell like magnolia blossoms, Magnolia. Delicious. Good enough to eat." And her grandmother had made little smacking noises with her Kewpie bow lips.

Stinkbird, Lee thought now. Cuckoo. Hoatzin. Fancy spelling for a plain name. What could be sillier? More insignificant? This smelly modest bird, this *turkey* of a bird, was hardly the prize to justify a quest.

What the chaplain didn't know was that her parents were

modest people. Their desires and ambitions were small. Not like the flamboyant Marguerite whose cosmically heaving breast was now shaking their whole pew. No lowly hoatzin for her. A peacock at the very least. Or a gorgeous, deliciously scented creature not yet dreamed of in any birder's philosophy. Marguerite squeezed Lee's hand. Her big square emerald dug into Lee's palm. Lee looked down. She blinked away a blur of tears. What had happened to the perfect ovals lacquered scarlet? These nails were naked, waxy, yellow, ridged. The cuticles torn, the tips nibbled to a sawtooth edge. Lee studied her own shredded fingernails. The ladder in her stockings. *Déshabillé,* her grandmother would have scorned. Lint stuck to Lee's skirt. One sleeve was unraveling. She was unraveling. "Help me, help me," her grandmother cried. How could she help her grandmother? She had no reserves. She was a fast-sinking vessel. How could she bear Marguerite's grief on top of her own?

"Alas, there is nothing so awful as the death of a child," the minister was saying now. "Nothing more terrible to try the soul."

"And all for a *bird,*" Marguerite wailed.

Lee turned to her other side where her father's two brothers, George from Cleveland, Martin from Skaneateles, were lined up in a row with their wives, a stoic foursome, eyes straight ahead, hands folded on squared-off knees. "You must be strong," Ernestine, George's wife, had said. "We must trust in God's wisdom. He's always here with us."

Ben was supposed to be here with her. In this very space now occupied by Uncle George. He had, in fact, been already seated when the family filed into the front row after the chapel had been filled. "He'll have to leave, darling," Marguerite had whispered, "this is the family pew."

"I asked him to sit with us."

"It wasn't your place to decide."

"But I want him here. *Need* him."

"All you need right now is me, darling . . . your grand-mother, who loves you more than anyone."

"For which I couldn't be more grateful. What would I do without you? Especially now. Still . . ."

"He's not a relative."

"He might as well be. He's certainly closer to me than Uncle Martin and Uncle George."

"That is beside the point."

Lee was incredulous. "You want me to ask him to get up and move? Now? Here? In the middle of everything?"

"This is the *family* pew," issued forth like the Eleventh Commandment from a mountaintop.

"But he's my *boyfriend*," Lee had pleaded. The word, once out of her mouth, sounded paltry and inadequate.

And fell on the deaf ears of her grandmother.

"What about Simon?" Marguerite had asked earlier. "When I feel stronger, I'll write Alistair and Hermione. But shouldn't you call and tell him this terrible news?"

Lee thought about Simon. About the thin blue letters that had been crossing the Atlantic twice a month for the last three years. They wrote about school and friends and poems and concerts. About their desperation to see each other. And the thwarting of their deepest desire. They cursed geography. They begrudged their youth, which left them without funds and subject to their parents' rules. They pledged eternal love. Meanwhile, Ben was scraping gum from her hem, carrying her books, helping her with statistics assignments, and—oh guilty unfaithful wanton woman that she was—sometimes sharing a narrow dormitory bed. "I like Ben," her mother had said. "He's a sensible, realistic choice."

"But Simon and I pledged eternal love," she told her mother.

Her mother had smiled. "At your age, a summer is eternity enough."

Had she ever given her mother enough credit for being wise? She remembered the Mark Twain quote. How did it go? Something like: *When I was young I thought my parents so ignorant. When I grew up I was amazed at how much they'd learned.*

Her mother understood. Her mother knew. She would have counseled Lee. It was only human nature, she would have explained in her gentle, modest, understated voice, that if you don't see someone you stop *seeing* him.

In the here and now, in her hour of need, was Ben. Clear eyes and strong jaw. Who should have his hand on her hand. His thigh wedged against her thigh. Except for Marguerite. Who always got her way. Never more than when she had suffered that most terrible of tragedies, the loss of a child. Because of this. Because of Marguerite, Ben had to climb over a tangle of knees and feet incurring irritated sighs. Because of this. Because of Marguerite, Ben had been forced to the standing-room-only at the back. There he remained jammed up against the stained glass window donated by Elihu Cuttlethwaite, Hannibal Hamlin College,

B.A. 1928, captain of the Lumberjacks' all-state champion-
ship football squad.

Covering every kitchen counter on Evergreen Road sat casseroles in Pyrex or earthenware pots wrapped in foil. Lee
counted meat loaves and spiral-sliced hams, tubs of coleslaw, potato salads, breads and cakes, boxes of chocolates,
crocks of franks and beans, home-baked brownies and
store-bought ginger snaps. Neighbors and friends had
slipped in through the unlatched back door and left them
there. With little notes: *In time of need, During this terrible
tragedy, With deepest sympathy, You are in our hearts, You are in
our prayers, The ways of God are mysterious* . . . The refrigerator wasn't big enough. Food would have to be stored at the
Wilburs' next door, the Goodwins' across the street. Yet
this overflowing larder was intended only for them. The
family. Four rotisserie chickens for her and Marguerite.
Five quarts of coleslaw. Two dozen caramel squares. Uncle
George and Aunt Ernestine and Uncle Martin and Aunt
Lillian were taking the evening flight out.

In the dining room, the table had been extended with the
two extra leaves her parents had never used. On a linen
cloth were crowded platters of roast beef and turkey, bowls
of salads, pickles, radish roses, trays of sliced cucumbers
and tomatoes, dinner rolls and cornbread squares. Hors
d'oeuvres and desserts claimed separate corners and different ends. A groaning board's worth, along with a waitress
and bartender her grandmother had ordered from the Brass
Rail. Bottles of scotch and gin, brandy and vodka graced
the sideboard. Bucky's liquor store had made two deliveries

since her parents' "bar" had yielded only a bottle of Harvey's Bristol Cream. "We can have the reception in the anteroom of the chapel," Lee had suggested. She pictured the room, the Ritz crackers spattered with cheddar cheese, the centerpiece of potted chrysanthemums left over from Sunday's service, the watery punch of Kool-Aid and ginger ale. People would pay their respects and get out fast. How long could you linger over a cracker and a grape? "That's what most people in Homestead do," she'd said.

A red flag to Marguerite. "But not Marguerite Chaplin," informed her grandmother. "How could I arrange anything for my daughter that was less than gracious, less than dignified?"

Now Lee sat next to Ben on a bench in the corner of the living room. Ben held her hand. He stroked her fingers. He wrapped an arm around her shoulder. He searched her face. He touched her cheek. Which was dry. She had no tears. She had no words. All the tears, all the words were coming from Marguerite. A vale of them. A spewing. As if she had stolen Lee's words and tears and made them her own. Lee felt robbed of her own sorrow. Upstaged once again. It was Marguerite who played the central role in Lee's own tragedy.

Not that this should surprise her. Not that she'd expect any less. One thing about her grandmother was her consistency. In a screwy way, you could always count on her. Besides, it wasn't as if Marguerite weren't suffering. There were black mascara tracks down her cheeks. Blotches along her neck. Her nose shone raw and red. Ruined beauty, Lee thought. Which could nevertheless be restored with the flick of a powder puff.

"Let's get married," Ben whispered.

Lee surveyed her parents' once orderly rooms. Now swimming with a sea of people. Around the table. In the hall, the kitchen, sitting on the stairs, leaning against the windowsills. Chairs had been dragged away from the walls. Sofas reangled. Furniture removed and rearranged like transplanted begonias. On the mantel someone had placed her father's extra set of reading glasses, which, for as long as she could remember, had been jammed into the pencil jar next to the telephone. Three people were clutching Marguerite's two hands. A man was patting her knee. Uncle George held a shoulder. Aunt Lillian, an elbow. A blue-cuffed, gray-suited arm extended a snowy handkerchief. "Where's Lee?" she heard her grandmother ask. Her grandmother's eyes traced a quick circuit, found Lee and blinked and brimmed with eloquent tragedy. She blew her a sorrowful kiss, then reached for a held-out glass of Armagnac.

By tonight these rooms would be empty. In a week, Marguerite would return to New York. She thought of Simon on the other side of the world. Of Ben right here in her world. What was left of it. She was as much of an orphan as Jane Eyre. Ben pulled her close. "Let's get married," Ben said again.

"Yes," said Lee. "As soon as possible."

"Oh, no!" Marguerite exclaimed when Lee told her. "It's the trauma. The shock. You can't possibly be thinking straight."

At last, everybody had cleared out. Ben, assigned airport duty—the aunts and uncles on the eight o'clock, her mother's childhood playmate on the ten—was forbidden to come back. "I need to handle Marguerite on my own," she'd explained.

"No argument from this quarter," he'd agreed. "I wouldn't even try."

Within an hour, the Brass Rail barman and waitress had cleared the dining table, wrapped the leftovers and stored them in the freezer, though not before marking them *hors d'oeuvres, turkey, smoked salmon, miscellaneous desserts.* "Let me," Lee said, starting to sort china and put away silverware.

"Absolutely not." Her grandmother grabbed the plates. She slapped them down on the countertop so hard that a bowl of salad greens slid to the floor. She kicked lettuce leaves and parsley sprigs to the side. Then left them there. "Mourners don't clean up," she announced. "Not the bereaved."

When the house was silent, when once again you could hear the hall clock tick and the refrigerator hum and the buzz of the streetlight and the bark of the Goodwins' dog, Lee took her grandmother's hand. "And I said yes," she announced.

"No!"

Her grandmother sank into a kitchen chair. Lee pulled out the seat across from her. A pyramid of fruit swaddled in cellophane rose from a basket that could have served as a bed for a full-grown Labrador. A black-bordered card was attached with a black satin bow. *With our deepest sympathy to the family of our faithful customer,* it read, *from the staff of the Moose Lake Bank and Trust.*

"I thought you'd be glad. That in the middle of such a tragedy . . ."

". . . comes such a mistake?"

"Grandmother!"

"Am I to believe you love this perfectly ordinary young man?"

"I do. You are."

"Alas," sighed her grandmother.

"However one defines love," Lee felt compelled to add.

"Aha!" her grandmother nearly shouted. She bent forward and knocked over the salt. "And what about Simon?"

"What about him?"

Her grandmother raised her arm. She pounded three swift knocks to the back of her French twist. "Now let me see, if I can rack my poor depleted brain to the summer only three summers ago when you fell in love. Pledged eternal love."

"At eighteen. My mother—*your* daughter—told me that, at such an age, *eighteen*, a summer was an eternity."

"So you want a life like your mother's. *My* daughter's?"

Lee nodded. "She was content."

"*Content!*"

"What's wrong with content?"

"Nothing, if you're content to settle for a life like your mother's. If you want to settle for a man like your father."

"My father. My father." Lee felt her throat tighten. Her eyes filled. "My father, who was just killed . . ."

Marguerite reached for her. "Darling, I don't mean that the way it sounds. Your father was a lovely man. He and your mother had a fine life. Exactly what she wanted. He was her ideal husband. It's just . . ."

"Just . . . ?"

"Just that I want more for you. More than your mother's life. More than your being stuck in Homestead with a steadfast Homestead man." Marguerite shook her head. Her earrings jangled. Her ruffles fluttered. Her pearls slid around her throat. Her bracelets clanged. She could have been a kinetic sculpture, thought Lee, a Calder mobile in full wind. Except for her not-a-hair-out-of-place hair, molded and sprayed into its usual immutable roll. As iron as her will. "Violet lacked imagination. A sense of adventure," she went on.

"She had enough sense of adventure to get herself killed seeking it."

"The most cruel of ironies." Marguerite stopped. She pulled a pear out from behind its curtain of crackling cellophane. She stabbed it with a knife. "Believe me, I know."

"Know what?"

The skin of the pear slid off in the unbroken spiral of a double helix. Was there anything her grandmother couldn't do with grace?

Presumably not. She sliced the pear into perfect translucent little disks. She passed one to Lee.

Who shook her head. "No thanks. I couldn't possibly."

Her grandmother took a bite. "It's important to keep up your strength." She blotted her mouth with the corner of a napkin that advertised *Brass Rail Catering. No Job Too Small.* "Let me tell you something, *ma petite*," Marguerite said.

Lee crossed her arms over her chest. She had inherited her mother's breasts. The kind of breasts that didn't pass the pencil test—the pencil fell!—and thus required a padded bra, advised the pages of *Seventeen* and *Junior Miss*. But if she'd inherited her mother's breasts, why not her mother's life?

As long as it didn't include the end of it.

She hugged herself. When she had children, *Ben's* children, contours would change . . .

Now her grandmother clamped her hand on Lee's elbow. "You noticed all those people today?"

Lee nodded.

"Your parents' neighbors and friends?"

"Yes."

"How attentive they were? How they flocked around me? Fetched and carried. Hovered and fussed."

"Like bees around honey. The way it always is when you're in the room."

"But not the way it always *was*."

Lee leaned forward. Marguerite leaned forward. She shoved the fruit basket to one corner. She looked from side to side. She tented her hands over her mouth. "*Entrenous . . .*" she began. Her voice was hushed.

"You don't have to whisper, Grandmother. There's just the two of us."

Marguerite put down the pear. She picked up an apple. Without bothering to peel it, she took a sharp bite.

"So . . . ?" Lee encouraged.

Her grandmother took another bite. She chewed with a slowness that was both glacial and delicate. She swallowed with a soft rise of her throat. "They say that knowledge is a dangerous thing," she began.

"A *little* knowledge," Lee corrected.

"I didn't figure you needed to hear this." She lowered her

head. "Perhaps because I didn't want to color what you felt about where you were born. Where you grew up. Perhaps I was concerned that you might think less of me."

"Never," Lee pledged, thumping a splayed hand of allegiance against her chest.

"I realize that now, darling. That trip we took convinced me of your complete devotion." She smiled. "Your love."

Almost complete devotion, Lee thought, and very good acting skills. But yes, love. Of course, love.

"Which gives me the courage to tell you this." Her grandmother tilted back in her chair. Her shoulders were tense. Her chin jutted out over the tight cord of her neck.

Lee felt her own jaw tighten. *Brace yourself,* she thought. *Be prepared for anything.*

Marguerite blew her nose on a lace-edged handkerchief. "When your grandfather brought me to America," she started conversationally, "the steamship was named *The Old World*. What a glorious passage. We dressed for dinner every night. The champagne flowed." She poked the cellophaned tower of fruit. "Oysters were piled this high in silver bowls of shaved ice. A full orchestra played in tails and white gloves. And such flowers. Glorious and in full bloom. Your grandfather, he was so happy. *We* were so happy. He wouldn't let me out of his sight."

"He worshipped you. My mother always told me that."

"She did? Your mother . . ." Her voice trailed off. She turned her head away.

Lee waited.

Marguerite folded her handkerchief. She twisted her ring. "Where was I?" she asked.

"The steamship."

"Ah, yes." She nodded. "In due course," she continued. "*The Old World* came to the New World. First New York. Followed by Boston. Then . . ." She stopped.

"*Then* we sailed to the Gulf of Maine. Homestead," she spat out, "but hardly home. I confess that I smoked, when women in this country, women of a certain class, wouldn't even dare. Not to mention my black Polish cigarettes the likes of which they'd never seen before." She clicked her tongue. "I had the most enchanting holder. Onyx set with diamonds and mother-of-pearl. Your grandfather actually suggested I smoke behind closed draperies. Of course, my clothes were from Europe. My trousseau was divine. Stitched by hand. Beige satin with Alençon lace."

"You must have made quite a stir."

"Not in the way you'd think. I was a foreigner. The natives were not exactly welcoming."

"No?" Lee was surprised. Granted, you could count on a certain New England reserve. Yankees didn't draw attention to themselves, didn't like to stand out. And didn't like others to, either. Even as a young bride, maybe *especially* as a young bride, Marguerite would have been formidable. Yet basically, and not to put too much of a Pollyanna spin on it, people here were nice once they warmed to you.

"They weren't nice," Marguerite was complaining now. "Surprisingly enough, they had a social life. More class-conscious than the British. Where I have always been well received. Small towns are like that. Full of clubs and lunch parties and teas and hospital boards. They shut me out."

"Are you sure? You mean, intentionally?"

"I gave a little musicale. I ordered *petits fours* from Boston. I bought imported sherry from Jerez. The cook made dozens of watercress and cucumber sandwiches with the crusts cut off. I sent out two dozen invitations. Engraved. On the thickest English stock. Nobody RSVP'd. Only one person showed up."

"You're kidding."

"Mrs. Ellsworth Arsenault. Whose husband had been your grandfather's bookkeeper. Whose son he'd helped out with the tuition to veterinary school."

"Perhaps everyone else got the day or time wrong. Perhaps you hadn't put enough stamps on the envelope?"

"I checked."

Lee thought of her mother. Getting her hair done for this luncheon, that tea. Readying a treasurer's report for the Historical Society board. Putting on her plaid suit and her single strand of tiny pearls. *Dinner's in the oven*, she'd write on the kitchen memo board, *preheat to 350 and cook for one-half hour.* "But my mother belonged to those clubs."

"Of course. She was one of them."

She *was* one of them, Lee realized. And clearly her grandmother was not. She could see her grandmother, dressed like a Sargent portrait, waiting at the door before her musicale. Had she hired a singer of lieder? A pianist from the college or the Portland Symphony Orchestra? She pictured the cucumber sandwiches on their doilies, the sherry on its silver tray. The ormolu box that would have held her grandmother's black cigarettes. She imagined her grandmother's expectant look. Her dashed hopes. The humiliation. And the fury that would grow out of it.

"So what did you do?"

"Lived my own life."

"Meaning?"

"Your grandfather was often away. On business. He was always traveling. He had this charming alligator briefcase which he'd bought in Cuba. He went there from Miami, when he was buying the land that turned out to be nothing but a big black swamp." She picked up the apple. "The briefcase clasped with the head of the alligator. You could see—could feel—every one of its sharp little teeth. Curling around the back was the tail. I used to joke with your grandfather that he was hardly in the front door displaying the head of the alligator before he was turning right around, marching right out and showing me its tail. I couldn't travel with him. Violet was so young. And so colicky."

"You must have missed him."

"Indeed. Furthermore, thanks to the snobbery of the citizens of Homestead, I was very much alone."

"How did you manage?"

"I took a lover," said her grandmother, as casually as if she were saying *I took two aspirins*. In a tone that implied *isn't it obvious?*

Though not obvious to Lee. Had she heard her grandmother right? "What?" she exclaimed. "You did *what*?"

"William Hitchinson, president of Moose Lake Bank and Trust. His wife—no waist and three chins, an unfortunate permanent—ran every single one of those terrible clubs."

"But," Lee sputtered. "But. But . . ."

"Your grandfather understood. I told him everything. He

was surprisingly sophisticated considering where he was born. And we loved each other."

"My God!" Lee's mouth fell open. Though Lee had had her suspicions, she still felt stunned. Her surmises had all been in the abstract: a lover. Lovers. Hotel rooms with tapestries. Assignations in the Bois de Boulogne or the Borghese Gardens. Not a name or a face or a job or an address. True, she couldn't see her grandmother settling in Homestead without ruffling feathers. Without spreading her wings. But to sully her own nest? To pick a lover in her own backyard? A backyard she never would have picked in the first place if she'd known beforehand its stingy parameters. Then, compounding the indignity, to tell her granddaughter this fact in a tone so matter-of-fact. As if it wouldn't have, *hadn't had* any effect.

It had no effect on my marriage," Marguerite said now. "In actuality, your grandfather and I were even happier." She held up her emerald ring. "He bought this for me the day after he learned of my adultery. 'The rules of ordinary people don't apply to you, Marguerite,' he said. But I was snubbed in the aisles of the grocery store. There were whispers behind my back. I received heavy-breathing telephone calls. And anonymous notes that began with the word *Repent*." She shook her head. "They might as well have thrown stones."

Or more likely pinned a scarlet A on her lapel. "What happened to Mr. Hitchinson?"

"Nothing. That's the point. He continued to be a pillar of the community. His wife continued to chair meetings and pour tea. He'd done nothing wrong. He was one of them, you see, who had been tempted and seduced by a foreigner."

Lee folded her arms on the table. She laid down her head. "I'm so sorry, Grandmother."

"Not I. Not for a minute. *Je ne regrette rien.* I have no regrets. But they are. They have. Flying around me like, as you so aptly noted, bees around honey. Because they're sorry and guilty. And because their lives have changed. They're alcoholics and wife beaters and petty embezzlers. And adulterers. Their children have let them down; they've lost their promise and their looks. Their small, narrow-minded town is full of scandals and inequities." She stopped. She caught her breath. "I don't want this for you. This place. This life. Your mother's life." Her eyes flashed. She turned her head. She sobbed. "Do you think my daughter was killed as a punishment?"

Lee reached for her. "Of course not! Don't even say that. Don't even think that. It was an accident. A stupid, silly accident."

"You're sure?"

"Never surer."

Marguerite stroked Lee's hair. "I know, darling. I know." She kissed her forehead. Lee smelled vanilla and oranges. "Do you love this Ben?"

"Yes."

"You're sure?"

Lee nodded. "Never surer." At least right now, right here, in this kitchen, at this table, with Marguerite and a pyramid of fruit, she told herself.

"And Simon?"

"Irrelevant."

Marguerite got up. She swiped at a counter with a squeezed-out sponge. She straightened the canisters. Rinsed a glass and left it in the sink. *Mourners don't clean up*, Lee wanted to say. But this was stage business. She wasn't exactly cleaning anything. Marguerite picked up a cloth to wipe off the memo board. Then froze. HAIR APPT. 2 P.M. was printed in neat capitals. She put down the cloth. When had her mother written this? Lee wondered. How many weeks ago? Was she getting her hair done before her trip? Preparing her face to meet the hoatzin's face? She heard Marguerite's sharp intake of breath. The long low whistle when she let it out.

"Well, darling, if things get stale with Ben, a love affair will shake things up."

After the funeral came the wedding.

Following swift upon it—the *discussion* of it—came fights and arguments. "Why not New York?" Marguerite contended. Her building had a lovely reception hall. With the right flowers it would be sublime. And the restaurant, the prophetically named Les Pommes d'Amour, down the street did the most exquisite canapés.

"We don't know anyone in New York," declared Lee.

"*I* do," boasted Marguerite.

"But it's not *your* wedding," Lee pointed out.

"I realize that," stated Marguerite, who sounded unconvinced. "I want to do this for you."

Ben took Lee aside. "Let her have her way," he advised.

"She always has her way," Lee answered. "Not this time," she warned.

Her grandmother conceded if not with grace, then with resignation. "The chapel. And after, the faculty club."

"No!" Lee was both stunned and adamant. "Not the place where the memorial service for my parents was held!"

"You don't have to rush," said Marguerite. "Take your time to decide."

I do have to rush, thought Lee. To fill the hole in my heart. To fill the hole in my life. There's no time to take, my time. I have to hurry and decide.

First the books appeared. On coffee tables and nightstands. Propped against the stairs. In the basket that held old magazines. *How to Plan the Perfect Wedding. Emily Post. Amy Vanderbilt. Beautiful Brides of the Last Century. Champagne to Mark the Occasion. Floral Bouquets.*

Then the packages piled up on the front porch. From New York department stores along Fifth Avenue. Bergdorf Goodman, Saks. A going-away outfit in pale blue shantung. A matching rolled-brim hat. A bridal gown of white silk gossamer, its train wide enough to carpet a cathedral's nave. A tiara fit for a princess. And for her grandmother? No mother-of-the-bride pink faille or lilac lace. Rather, a grand, grandmother-of-the-bride slinky column woven of silver and gold. "We're sending these right back," Lee shouted.

"To deprive me of giving a wedding for my only child's only child?" Marguerite's hand fluttered at her throat. "Your parents eloped. It was after the war. A big wedding was unseemly, they thought. I couldn't convince them how wrong they were. 'The war is over,' I pleaded. 'People want to celebrate.' 'In the light of so much suffering,' your mother said and denied me my heart's desire." Marguerite shook her head. "You know what your mother was like . . ."

"Like mother, like daughter."

"Not if I can help it. Such traits are supposed to skip a generation. By rights you should want the extravaganza I want for you."

"The theory of skipping a generation is an old wives' tale."

Marguerite gasped as if she'd been stabbed. "So you'll be a wife and not a bride." She wiped her eyes. She scooped up the silvery gold dress. She danced it around the room. It rippled. It glowed. "You win. I'll send everything back." She stopped. She held the gown in front of her. "Except this dress."

Lee called Homestead Town Hall. She and Ben picked up the forms and copies of their birth certificates. They filled them out. The license would be issued after three full business days. They could be married in town hall by a clerk of court. No, they didn't have to supply their own witnesses. Betty, the receptionist, and Evelyn, the secretary, were available as long as it wasn't their lunch hour. Betty, in fact, was their most enthusiastic and most popular witness. She could produce sobs at the drop of an *I do*.

"Lee, I'm afraid that, at this point, I must draw the line," warned Ben in his gentlest voice. He cleared his throat. He chose his words. "So far I haven't wanted to interfere. I prefer to give you my full vote of confidence."

He'll make a wonderful teacher, Lee thought, so patient and so calm.

"You know I've been patient with you," he went on, "completely willing to go along with anything. You have my utmost support. And you understand that I am in total agreement with you about getting married as soon as we can with the least amount of fuss. Even if your parents hadn't died, I'd still want the simplest ceremony possible."

"I do know this. Which is why we're so compatible. And you've been wonderful . . ."

"But face facts. There's not a chance in hell that you're going to keep Marguerite away from the office of the clerk of court on our wedding day."

"*Your* parents aren't coming. Or your brother. We've forbidden our own friends."

"They understand the circumstances. They respect our wishes. They're normal people. Sensitive. And sensible."

"And Marguerite isn't?" Lee paused. She laughed. "Of course she isn't. To her, normal counts as a pejorative." She took Ben's hand. "Yes, she'll be there. What could I have been thinking of?"

On the morning of the wedding—a Tuesday—which was scheduled for three that afternoon, Lee heard the mail come through the slot, then, seconds later heard the doorbell ring.

Cappy Kellogg, a year ahead of her at Homestead High, stood on the welcome mat holding a large box. Behind him, on the street, she could see his father's florist van garlanded with daisy decals. "Hey, Lee," he said. "How's it going?" His eyes took in her T-shirt and jeans, and stopped at her bare feet. "So, this your wedding day?"

She pointed. "What's that?" she asked.

"Your grandmother ordered you a bouquet. The Victorian special. You know, the one copied from that portrait of the mayor and his wife hanging up at town hall. From back in the old days." He placed the box in her hands. "I tied the knot two years ago. Remember Rita Edgers? Lived over on Exchange?"

Lee nodded. Pretty. Petite. Red-haired. A dancer. A cheerleader.

"Got two kids now. Boys." He reached into his shirt pocket and pulled out a photograph.

Lee tried to keep the shock from her face. Was *that* Rita Edgers? If Cappy hadn't told her, she'd never have known. Fat with a scowl and her flyaway hair tucked up under a kerchief—the exact image of a babushka from Siberia. And in her enormous, Michelin-man lap, two cute kids.

"Cute kids," Lee said.

"Aren't they though?" Cappy beamed. "Me and Rita are real happy."

Lee looked at the photo again. Not an ounce of pleasure lit up Rita Edgers's moon-shaped face and turned-down mouth. "That's good," she said.

Cappy nodded. "There's nothing like marriage," Cappy said, "to change your life."

No sooner had she shut the door than Marguerite skipped down the hall stairs. "So they came," Marguerite marveled. "I ordered the Victorian special. An exact copy of the one held by Mayor Bushwell's wife."

Lee turned to her. Her grandmother's face was slathered with white cream that had hardened at the edges like a plaster-of-Paris mold. She could have been an actor in a

Noh play. A troupe from Osaka had put on a performance at the college once. At intermission, the theater had emptied with the speed of prisoners on death row granted an unexpected reprieve. "An acquired taste," Ben had pronounced. "Hard to bridge the cultural gap."

Or the generation gap, Lee thought now, opening the box that held Mrs. Bushwell's white lilies, blowzy cabbage roses, snapdragons, peonies, parrot tulips, and delicate baby's breath. The stems, pushed through a lace frill, were bound with white satin streamers like the ribbons on a ballerina's shoes. What could Lee say? Today was her wedding, to be held in town hall, not in the gilded rococo ballroom of a Manhattan hotel. She was to wear her mother's plain white linen suit, not a pricy powder puff from a Fifth Avenue bridal salon. Her grandmother's cast-of-thousands invitation list had been pared to the bride and groom, her grandmother, the clerk of court, Betty the receptionist, and Evelyn the secretary. For the most part—amazing!—Lee'd got her way. How to answer? "Thank you" were the only words conceivable.

A concession her grandmother barely acknowledged, all her attention now centering on the hall floor, on a pale blue envelope stamped with the profiles of Queen Elizabeth the Second and King George the Sixth.

"What's this?" asked Lee. Her breath stopped.

"You know exactly what *this* is," said her grandmother. She waved the letter. *Catch it if you can*, she seemed to tantalize.

Lee snatched it from her.

Her grandmother groaned. "I can't think of worse—or better—timing, depending how you look at it."

Lee ran up the stairs and into her room. She slammed the door. She collapsed onto the bed. The envelope was so thin she could hardly feel it against her fingertips. It had so little weight it might have been air. She wished it were air. She wished it would disappear into thin air. She looked around the room. This was her childhood room—which she was leaving to become a bride. This was her single bed—which she was leaving for a double one. This was her separate life—which was going to be joined to somebody else's.

She tore open the envelope. *Good news*, Simon wrote.

> *I've delayed so long in writing you in the hopes that I would be able to send you this good news. There's a summer exchange program with a lab at the Massachusetts Institute of Technology for which I've been told I qualify. Room and board, and even a stipend. Eight whole weeks only 175 miles from you. I know the distance, I looked it up and drew a line the way the crow flies. Soon I will fly to you. What can I say, my darling, only that at long last we can be together. At long last our dreams are about to come true. I'll write you soon with details. But, as always, I pledge to you my dearest and beloved Lee, eternal love.*
>
> *Simon*

Lee sank her head onto her pillow. She stared up at the ceiling. Her father had pasted stars there when she was— how old?—ten? twelve? Little gleaming stars that he'd arranged like the constellations, checking in his celestial atlas for authenticity. At that age, she'd been besieged by nightmares: monsters at her window, bogeymen on the roof, bats and vultures flying over her bed. Her father had given her a flashlight to shine on the stars. "When you wake up, turn this on and you'll feel safe," he'd promised.

A knock struck her door. A formality, since Marguerite walked right in without waiting to be asked. She plopped down beside her. In addition to the mask, she had slathered gunk all over her hands. She stroked Lee's arm, leaving on it a thin slick of oil. "It's not too late, darling," she said, and her voice had a catch in it that Lee had never heard before. "You can change your mind. You can call the whole thing off."

Again, Lee stared up at the stars. Above her ceiling, under the attic's eaves, she heard the cooing of pigeons. Maybe doves. Unlike her parents, she couldn't tell the difference. Doves were snowy white. Always shown in pairs to symbolize weddings. In contrast to those plain old pigeons. Dirty, gray. With ragged feathers and crooked beaks. Her parents would know which sounds belonged to which. One kind, welcome. The other kind, not. Unless pigeons and doves were variations on a single theme. Like this husband or that, depending upon how you placed the word on your tongue, the person in your heart.

Once, searching for a bicycle pump in the cellar, she'd found a spray can shoved to the back of a storage shelf. *Roost No More* was this product's name. *A nontoxic bird repellent that prevents pigeons from nesting*, the manufacturer assured. You sprayed it on the targeted area, and—poof!—your bird problems were solved.

If only that would work on her heart. Remove the wrong species and keep the right. If only she could figure out where to roost no more and where to make her nest. It was dangerous to leave home. To take a risk was to venture into the unknown; not to run that risk meant you'd be doomed to live forever with what if. She looked up again at her father's pasted-on stars. *Star-crossed lovers*, she thought. But which combination was the ill-fated one? She considered Jane Eyre, an orphan like herself, who ended up with dark and brooding Mr. Rochester. Would Jane Eyre have picked such a man if she'd been able to sail into the safe harbor of home with someone like Ben? This is a time for joy, not anguish, Lee decided. She turned over Simon's letter. She slammed it facedown. Her choice, she realized, was irrevocable.

"There are no right and wrong solutions, darling, only what you want. When you figure out what you want," her grandmother said.

In the clerk of court's office, flags flanked either side of a metal desk. The Stars and Stripes on the right, the state flag, with its seal of *Dirigo* (I lead), on the left. Lined up along the walls were photographs of Homestead's former mayors going back to the Civil War. Stern fellows with mustaches and wing collars, their civic duties lying heavy on their broad shoulders, their responsibilities wrinkling their high foreheads and setting their mouths in a serious line. Lee recognized Jacob Bushwell. When she'd first arrived, she checked out the bouquet in Mrs. Bushwell's wedding portrait. Cappy's father had done a fine job. Down to the exact lilt of the lilies and the precise breadth of the baby's breath. The new bride didn't look happy, though. So grim was her expression she might have fit right into the gallery of mayors. Maybe that was the cause of her distress: she had wanted to be the mayor, not the wife.

"This serious state of marriage," the clerk of court was saying now. His voice was solemn. His suit was solemn. Though Lee and Ben were standing right in front of him, his eyes flew over their heads and alit, unsolemnly, on Marguerite.

No wonder. Marguerite was wearing her silver and gold dress and every diamond that Sam Rybier had ever given her. In shooting beams, she radiated light. Her dress rustled like candy being unwrapped in a darkened theater. Against the hard oak floors, her shoes sounded as if they had taps attached to the heels and to the toes. Any second she might break into a dance like a character in a musical. She was carrying the kind of large cloth-covered basket that might belong to Little Red Riding Hood.

"What's this?" Lee had asked earlier.

"You'll find out soon enough," Marguerite had replied. Then added, "Should I take off some of this jewelry? Is it a bit too much? I wouldn't ever want to outshine the bride."

This bride didn't mind being outshone. She was used to it. Glad for attention deflected somewhere else. Let Marguerite milk as much enjoyment as possible out of an occasion that, if her grandmother had had her druthers, wouldn't be an occasion like this. Even if Lee could claim a father to walk her down the aisle, she'd never want the kind of aisle to satisfy Marguerite. She was grateful for the small gathering and the steadying daguerreotyped gaze of Homestead's mayors. She was grateful for Ben, tall and handsome

and solid by her side, and Betty and Evelyn in their comforting denim A-lines and navy blue polo shirts.

Ben slipped a thin silver ring on her finger. She rolled its
mate onto his. They had bought them from a booth at the
Bangor State Fair. "Made in Mexico," the salesman had
said. "Nine hundred part silver. Not quite as pure, as solid,
as the sterling you get in the States."

"If it's good enough for the Mexicans," claimed Lee.

Now Lee twisted the 900 part silver ring around her finger. It felt strange, unfamiliar, like a cinder in the eye, a tiny
splinter in the foot. A foreign body. But she supposed she'd
get used to it. She thought of her mother's wedding band,
now in foreign soil or water somewhere near the Amazon.
By the time Lee was in her teens, her mother's ring had
worn thin as a wire. Lee remembered the touch of it, the
delicate metal, the etched design, the initials inside, the
tops and bottoms all rubbed off. "I'd love you to have this
for your own wedding," her mother once told her, "but by
then it will probably have turned almost invisible."

"And I now pronounce you man and wife," the clerk pronounced. He winked at Marguerite. He flashed her a large
smile of two gold teeth and several silver-filled cavities.
Betty sobbed and snuffled on cue and with a satisfying intensity. Evelyn adjusted the earpiece of her eyeglasses. Lee
and Ben waited for *you may now kiss the bride*. Futilely, it
turned out. The vision of Marguerite seemed to have made
the clerk lose his lines along with his head. Unprompted,
Ben leaned over and found Lee's lips. "We did it," he said.
Then whispered, "Mrs. Emery."

The audience of three broke into applause. Betty tucked

her handkerchief into her waistband. She pushed a stray hair back into her tidy bun. "Well, weddings or not, the city's work must go on," she said.

"One second," commanded Marguerite. She ripped off the Red Riding Hood cloth. *"Voilà!"* she said. And revealed a bottle of champagne, six flutes, and a plate of hors d'oeuvres.

Lee noticed the napkins first. *Brass Rail Catering. No Job Too Small.* Next, she recognized the pigs in the blanket, the mushrooms in puff pastry, the cheese straws, and the bacon-wrapped water chestnuts. "The funeral baked meats," she hissed to her grandmother.

"Waste not. Want not," answered Marguerite. Then uncorked the Bollinger.

Two couples were waiting on the bench outside when they left. Brides in veils, grooms with boutonnieres. "But no champagne. No hors d'oeuvres," her grandmother crowed.

She followed Lee into the ladies' room. She put something into Lee's hand. Hard. Cold. Square.

Her emerald ring.

"Oh, no!" Lee cried.

"But yes."

"I couldn't."

"You must. I want you to have this," ordered Marguerite.

"I can't," Lee said. She knew Marguerite was disappointed that no diamond solitaire sticking up from its Tiffany prongs now gleamed from her third finger left hand. She realized her grandmother might be upset about the thin

184 • *Mameve Medwed*

silver band of a metal neither solid nor pure. Did Marguerite need to make it up to Lee for this lack? For her own loss and for her granddaughter's?

"I insist," Marguerite insisted.

Lee pressed the ring back into Marguerite's palm. "When I picture your hand, I always see this ring on your finger. I count on that constancy."

"I want to give it to you."

"And I want you to wear it the way you always have." Lee paused. "Please," she begged. "There have been too many changes in my life."

Marguerite sighed. "I understand," she whispered. She slid the emerald back on her finger. "For now, my darling Magnolia . . . Remember, though," she brightened, "it will be yours when I'm gone."

"You'll never be gone." Lee grabbed her grandmother's shoulder. "Never!" She kissed her grandmother's face. She wiped her own eyes. She forced a smile. "Besides, what does it mean," she asked, "that you're offering me the ring Grandpa gave you after your adultery?"

Six

~⚬~

This morning Ben is getting ready to leave for Chicago, for the meeting of the Organization of American Historians. Lee offers to drive him to the Bangor airport. "I don't have to be at the college until noon," she says.

"Don't bother," he says. "I'll take the car and park it there. Airport good-byes always remind me of *Casablanca*."

Lee is about to say, Bangor, alas, is not Casablanca. You and I, alas, are not Humphrey Bogart and Ingrid Bergman, but changes her mind. "You'll be great," she encourages.

"You think?" he asks.

"Not think. *Know*."

He smiles. He checks his briefcase for the paper on Nathaniel's view of labor relations along the Allagash. He runs his hand over the bright blue binding in its plastic sheath. Lee remembers the book covers they used to make out of wax paper when she was in grammar school. "So if you dribble jam on *Treasure Island*, you will avert a disaster," her teacher pointed out. A contingency that made sense, Lee had realized, only if the book was closed, only if you weren't reading it.

Ben snaps the two briefcase clips shut, then spins the dial on its center lock. Its combination, like their bank IDs, credit card PINs, telephone passwords, Internet access codes, marks the day, month, and year of their first date.

"Where could your paper have disappeared to," Lee asks, "between now and breakfast when you last confirmed it was there?" Tucked into his pocket is the backup disk containing not only his paper but his whole Nathaniel Tarbell *oeuvre*. At the bottom of his garment bag lies an extra printout, in the event of an emergency.

"I have seen more than one briefcase the spitting image of mine."

"With your name on it?"

"Anything's possible."

"Locked with the precise combination of numbers as our first date?"

"Why not? 'Caution is its own reward,' Nathaniel always said." He pats his bag. "The quote is right in here." He frowns. "You know where my extra copies are? On the top of the file cabinet. The one behind the closet door next to my desk."

"Ben!" Lee laughs.

"Some things aren't funny. If I lost—"

"Impossible!"

He holds up his hands. "I'm acting silly."

"I'll say."

"Still, even taking into account paranoia, bad things can happen once you step out of your own backyard."

"As if disasters can't occur right *in* your own backyard. Within a foot of your kitchen sink."

He shrugs. "I guess it's the prospect of leaving home . . ."

"Not that you haven't done it before."

"But I'm getting older. More stuck in my ways. And in the past, you've usually been at my side."

That's true, she agrees. She's spent more hours than she'd care to count sitting on the folding chairs and bar stools supplied by Westins and Marriotts and Holiday Inns; she's filled whole days as a glazed-eyed attendant at panels on hay threshing methods or colonial courtship rituals; she's been trapped in corridors as an unwitting witness to dueling theorists and plagiarism accusations—all courtesy of the Organization of American Historians. Except for the time of her grandmother's death, she can name hardly a night when she and Ben didn't share a bed.

"It's only a few days," she soothes. Could there ever be a worse case of homesickness before-the-fact? She remembers the children's first summer away at overnight camp. *I'll write every morning*, Maggie had pledged. In six weeks there had been only one card: *The counselors are making me write you before I go to the marshmallow roast.* "And *you* are a grown-up," Lee adds.

Ben grins. "But I hate missing you read."

"There'll be plenty of chances," she says. Though she doubts this, given the level of response to Beatrice's press release. She's scheduled to read this afternoon at the College Co-Op. Beatrice had tried to find a date when Ben was available to fill a seat; the schedule was already packed, informed the bookstore manager, the author should feel grateful to be furnished a slot. Especially since she wasn't a household name and, considering her publisher, wasn't about to become one. As it was, they would have to double her up with a woman who had just brought out a watershed book on how to teach your child to train your dog.

"I sent an e-mail around the department. Some of my colleagues ought to put in an appearance," Ben says. "Namely the tenure-track young Turks. That is, if they know what's good for them."

"All warm bodies are welcome. Though I'd hate for people to come because you'd twisted their arms." Lee hands him a packet of dental floss and the travel-size tin of aspirin. "Maggie said she'd bring friends." Or was it *a* friend? "And Beatrice will be doing her my-client-the-writer thing. Who knows, maybe a huge audience of dog lovers will stampede the doors." She stops. "And their kids."

"I pity that writer, having to be paired with you."

Lee smiles. A statement of true loyalty if she's ever heard one.

Now Ben tucks the dental floss and aspirin into his toilet kit. He picks up his suitcase. He puts it down.

"So, what are you going to read?" he asks with a tone of studied casualness. He examines his flight information. "Not that section about Simon," he adds.

"Marguerite in the airplane. I've marked it up."

A barely audible "Phew" escapes between his lips. He

gives a vigorous nod. "Good idea. It will make them laugh. It's always best to start with a laugh."

"My feeling, too."

"In fact, I've taken my own advice. I'm beginning with the anecdote from Nathaniel's diary. You know, that entry about how he was in the Forest of Dean and it was raining so hard and he didn't notice until he came home and took off his clothes and saw he was soaked to the skin?"

"That'll grab them."

He touches Lee's shoulder. Tilts her chin up to him. His eyes looked worried. "I'll call you every night," he promises.

In the kitchen, Lee boils water. She stirs tea leaves into the pot and lets them steep. She sits at the table. She opens the newspaper. Why did Ben have to mention Simon and the Forest of Dean when she has been trying so hard to cast these words from her head? She would never have read the Simon part of the memoir anyway. Such a tiny fraction of the whole. Unlike her descriptions of Marguerite, detailed from the spring of the curl on her brow to the tapered grace of her toe, Simon's portrait is painted with a broad and impressionistic brush and seen through the hazy pink filter of first love.

First love. In front of her, filling two columns of the *Homestead Herald*'s society section, is a list of aphorisms from Tina Andrews, the paper's "Breakfast Chat" editor and the intimate friend of two past governors. First love is the most powerful, Tina holds forth, because nobody's yet been hurt. As for marriage, she goes on to write, the longer you're with the same person, the more annoying he or she becomes.

Lee looks out the window. It's the end of April. The last frozen islands of dirty snow have melted. The trees are in bud. The birds are singing in the branches and dive-bombing her parents' feeder for the seed she's never forgotten to put out since their death. The stems of early spring flowers are thrusting up. On a day like this, all's right with the world.

Or at least all would be right if she could stop thinking about things she shouldn't think about. She hasn't heard from Simon since she sent him the memoir more than a month ago. Maybe he and Caroline have moved to a far-away place—Africa, Bangladesh, Bosnia—with no forwarding address. Or are in the middle of an around-the-world cruise. Just because she and Ben have stayed in the same town, in the same house, all this time doesn't mean other people don't see the Pyramids along the Nile. You have only to check the class notes in the alumni magazine to realize that she and Ben are the exception compared to the peripatetic lives of everyone they went to college with. She sighs. Maybe the package never arrived. Or—even worse—maybe it did and Simon threw it away. Or maybe . . . She stops. She thinks of the gray hairs she can't snip out fast enough, of the Clairol Warm Brown on the shower ledge. She thinks of her stiff right knee when she gets out of bed, of calcium supplements and a scheduled bone density test. Or maybe he died.

Could he have died?

Could he have died and she not have found out?

When her parents died, she'd received a condolence card bordered by lilies and a white dove, and, inside, a poem that couldn't have been more lugubrious with its angels and rest-in-peace metaphors. "The end of an era," penned her father's secretary.

They shouldn't have died, she felt the need to protest. "The end of an *error*," she had wanted to write back.

And Simon's death would mean what? The end of her youth? The end of youthful fantasies?

She clears the breakfast dishes. She rinses the plates. She holds an emptied orange juice glass under the faucet. Her fingers tighten around it. She sees a tea towel, her blood dotting its Holbein Henry the Eighth. She puts the glass upside down on the draining rack. Are her obsessions about having lost Simon any worse, any more pathetic, than Ben's over losing his Nathaniel pages? The difference, though, is that she did lose something and he did not. How can she worry about not hearing from Simon when she was the one who sent him away? You can't lose something you never really—*really*—had.

Of course, in the literal sense—the *biblical* sense—she had had him. They had each other. With all the intensity and passion of Ingrid Bergman and Humphrey Bogart. And with all the sadness in their parting. "We'll always have Paris," Bogart told Bergman. What would Simon have said to her? "We'll always have Netherend-on-Severn" couldn't sound more ridiculous.

On the plane home from their August in London, from their Netherend-on-Severn interval, she had stared out at the clouds and pondered what she was leaving behind. Ben and the children had been cataloguing all the things they had missed, all the things they were returning to: chunky peanut butter, Welch's grape jelly, Marshmallow Fluff, backyards, rooms of their own, studies and telephone extensions, baseball cards, strong coffee, real showers, cars with steering wheels on the left and driving lanes on the right. "And my own bed!" Ben exclaimed.

"And my own blanket," added Maggie.

Lee thought of Merrion Sackville's roll-out sofa, of the high old bed under the eaves in the guest room of Netherend.

And the blanket Simon had spread on the floor . . .

Through the smeared glass of the airplane window, a cloud scudded by, its edges crimped purple by the setting sun. Lacy. Wispy.

She cast her mind back to the lacy underwear she had bought from the vendor at Camden Lock. She remembered how Simon had rolled up the blanket when they were done. The blanket was camel-colored. Of a soft wool worn thin at the corners. With whipstitched edges and two small moth holes puncturing one side. She pictured her purple underpants. The minute she'd realized she'd acquired those bits of silk to entice Ben, she'd pulled them off. Now she saw them: a garish purple blot against a sedate camel-colored field. Then—poof!—they disappeared. Into the blanket from Simon and Caroline's bed. The blanket that was placed back at the end of it.

She groaned.

Ben turned to her. "Are you okay?" Alarm sped across his face. The alarm of a fearful flier, a reluctant traveler. "Did you see something? The propeller? The wing?"

Nothing, she reassured him. She'd just thought of something she'd forgotten, something she might have mislaid.

"Serious?"

Serious? Ha! On a scale of one to ten, a twenty she wanted to claim, a *serious* twenty. "Not serious," she said.

"Well, then." With a toe he nudged the briefcase under the seat in front of him. "Make fun of me if you will, but at least I have all my Nathaniel research. I *triple*-checked." He pressed the recliner button. He leaned back. Worry-free, he went to sleep.

Worrying, Lee lay against the headrest. She shut her eyes. She knew she couldn't sleep. Never mind the terry cloth eyeshade and earplugs in the complimentary travel kit. Never mind that across the aisle her kids were busy with the coloring books and crayons and toy planes and headphones supplied by British Air. Never mind that at the push of the steward's signal would appear Cokes and crisps with no parental intervention required. The flight attendant had passed out pillows and blankets. She'd winked. "Shall we let Mummy and Daddy have a bit of a nap?" she'd asked the three happily occupied young Emerys.

No, Lee would probably never sleep again. She had left her underpants in Simon's house. An error. A terrible accident, even though, according to Freud, there are no accidents. Caroline would find the underpants. "What's this?" she'd ask, holding them at arm's length because they were flimsy and unserviceable, because they weren't hers, because—oh, God!—they reeked of sex.

No sooner had she stepped inside the door on Evergreen Road than she'd started—furiously—to unpack.

"Let's leave this for later," Ben yawned, "and go straight to bed."

Ignoring him, she'd emptied the children's suitcases, their duffel bags. She searched through all her clothes, even shook out her shoes and her extra pocketbook.

In the midst of such a frenzy of activity, Ben turned into a still, silent center of resignation. He unzipped his own luggage. "What's the rush? What's the problem?" he asked. He shot her a look of Jobian suffering embellished by a man's compassion for a woman's lot. "Is it PMS?"

At last, when he'd unfolded his pajama top. At last, when her purple underpants had tumbled out from his blue cotton, red-piped sleeve, she had felt not relief but a disappointment so sharp, so bitter, tears sprang to her eyes and her throat constricted as if she'd been stung.

Yet she's a different person now, she tells herself. No matter. The kids thrive; the marriage endures. She's got a job; she's published a memoir. Add in the maturity, the wisdom, the *ripeness* that come with the years. What does she care that Simon doesn't write her back? She probably doesn't even want him to.

And because she's told herself this. And because she's putting this out of her mind. And because she's thinking about Ben's Nathaniel paper and his work on Nathaniel which is soon to become a book. And because she's thinking about her children's lives and loves. And because she's told them that things happen when you least expect them to, that the watched pot doesn't boil, that, as Marguerite used to say, waiting results only in waiting, look at Godot. And because she's thinking about her reading this afternoon, and about what to wear. Because of all these distractions, today, just now, the letter comes.

One page.

Three sentences:

Dear Lee, The memoir arrived. I read it right away. I was touched. As ever, Simon.

Over and over she studies it. One page. Three sentences. Nothing between the lines. No invisible ink turned suddenly visible. She checks the envelope. The postmarked date registers three days ago. He's had the book for a month. She doesn't understand. If he read the memoir right away, why didn't he answer right away? She looks inside. No supplement is sealed underneath the flap. Again, she scrutinizes the sentences. What does *as ever* mean? And *touched*?

She notes that the letterhead bears the familiar address. And the same telephone number, numerals she's memorized but has never dialed. Why hasn't she ever called him?

When she could have, would have, wanted to, such things weren't done. You wrote letters. You tried to cram as much onto a page as possible to save on stamps. You used the flimsiest paper possible to save on weight. Who in Maine would ever think of calling England or France or Italy? She remembers her father phoning Waterville, the next town, seven miles away. "No idle chitchat," he'd ordered, "this *is* a long distance call."

If the mentality hasn't changed, however, the rates have. And the technology. No international operator. No terrible connection with tinny voices or the rumble of other conversations patched in, no ham radio hobbyists saying *Roger and out.* She stares at the hall telephone. It's red with an illuminated dial. It beckons like the light at the end of Daisy Buchanan's dock. A light for summoning old loves. In less than a minute she could be talking to Simon. *About the memoir,* she might begin. *What touched you? Where? And how much?*

She stares at the phone. Her eyes move to the memo pad next to it. The basket of bills. Bills! If she calls now, Simon's phone number will show up on next month's account. "You called Simon?" she can just hear Ben exclaim. Will she feel compelled to confess that she sent Simon the memoir? Even if she keeps her mouth shut, Ben will make the connection: her memoir. Its cause and effect. Either way, Ben's feelings will be hurt.

So she'll telephone from her office. Where she's going anyway. Where international code numbers are punched in as often and as easily as the Dial-a-Pizza run by the campus student agency. To spare Ben's feelings.

And to salve her own.

At noon, the hall of the Department of Modern Languages is hushed. Dark. It's an interior corridor which, because all the windows are apportioned to the offices lined up on either side of it, is usually flooded from the checkerboard of buzzing fluorescent bulbs. Not this morning, however. Lee heads for the coffee urn. The metal is cold. When she lifts the lid, she finds the basket sludged with yesterday's dregs. Lee is surprised to see Miss Peavey isn't at her desk. No neatly folded lunch bag centers the squared-off blotter. No crocheted incase-of-chill cardigan hangs from the back of her chair. Her lamp is off. A tarp of plastic covers her ancient Olivetti; her bud vase sports brackish water and a single dying rose flopped over on its spindly stem. Where could she be? She's ageless in her age. Indomitable in her frailty. This is the Miss Peavey who won an award for forty years of never having missed a day of work.

Lee opens the door to the office of the Junior Year Abroad. From somewhere along the corridor she hears the click of a keyboard. Through an open window she can make out the swish of Frisbees sailing through the air. Students are wearing sandals and shorts. A few hardy seminars are already meeting under trees on the rolling lawn of the quad. Every year, spring comes to Maine despite February doubts.

On Lee's desk accumulate the usual letters and brochures, which she pushes to one side. From her pocketbook, Lee pulls out Simon's letter. She reads it again. As if she hasn't memorized it. As if the short journey from home to college might have scrambled these sentences and let loose a rearrangement of new Boggle-game words. *Dear Lee, The memoir arrived. I read it right away. I was touched. As ever, Simon* hasn't changed from twenty minutes ago.

She checks the clock on her desk, the watch on her wrist, the hours and minutes stamping the tool bar on the computer monitor. Greenwich Mean Time is five hours ahead. Simon should just be getting home from work.

Her hands tremble like a teenager's when she lifts the receiver.

She bangs it down.

She steps away. How could she?

She steps forward. How could she not?

Then picks it up again.

She dials.

He answers on the first ring. "Simon Abernathy here."

"Simon?" she asks.

"Is this who I think it is?"

"Lee."

"Lee?" A question. Followed by, "Lee." An answer, a statement of fact. "Your voice," he says. "Never, ever, could I not have recognized it."

Lee tries to calculate how many negatives make a positive. What has Simon just said? She waits a beat. "Because it's an American accent," she replies. "A Maine one."

"Not that," he says.

"No?"

"Because it's you."

"Yes. Well."

"Even after all this time," he adds.

"It has been a while."

"From when our children were young. My boys are all grown up and on their own."

"My kids, too. Practically."

"So much time has passed." He sighs.

She sighs. "Hasn't it, though?"

"Fifteen years. It's been too long."

Too long to take up where they left off. Too long to have sent a book. What has she done? "I got your letter," she says. "Your *note*," she corrects.

"Yes," he says. A silence stretches into a void. The clock ticks. Footsteps pound down the hall. *Hey, dude, wait up,* somebody calls outside.

What to say? How to reply? Once she had no trouble. Once the words came unbidden, in a continuous flow like water poured from a glass. Once she couldn't stop the words.

Which now stumble and halt. From both of them.

"Your memoir," Simon says at last.

"Yes?"

"I can't find the words to tell you what it meant to me."

"Those are words enough," she says.

"Especially now," he says.

Especially now? "I was worried," she admits. "Afraid you'd mind."

"Mind?"

"That you'd think it was an act of—I don't know—hubris on my part. That I was stirring up dead ashes, not letting sleeping dogs lie, that—"

He groans. "You don't know how dead those ashes are. How sleeping those dogs . . ." he says. "Yet how easily stirred . . ."

"Simon," she says.

"Lee," he says. "I read it right away. I found—find—it a masterpiece."

"Oh, Simon, it's hardly—"

"And I'm so awfully sorry, so terribly remorseful I waited so long to reply."

"That's all right."

"No it isn't." He stops. She hears paper rustle. The clank of silverware.

"I've interrupted your dinner," she says.

"You haven't interrupted anything." He waits. "You see . . ." he begins. "You see," he continues. He lowers his voice to a whisper. "I'm afraid I've been ill."

"*Ill?*" Lee sinks into her chair. Her ear throbs from where she's been jamming the phone into it. A lump swells in her throat.

"With what?" she demands. She knows it's not polite to ask details of a person who confesses he's been ill. Especially a native of the stand-on-ceremony British Isles where politeness and discretion are virtues bred in the Anglo-Saxon bone. *He's got C. She had P*, her grandmother would whisper as if cancer and polio were obscenities so bad you couldn't even sound them out. "What's wrong?" she asks.

"Heart," he says.

She freezes. Heart! Oh, darling, there is nothing wrong with your heart, she wants to cry.

"I have a damaged heart."

"Oh, Simon."

"A hole. A hole in the heart."

She places her hand on her own heart. Which is beating wildly. She remembers the thump of his heart under her fingers, the steady pounding against her breast.

"For a while I was very sick," he confides. "But they patched things up."

Tell me everything, she wants to yell. Draw me diagrams. Show me X-rays, CAT scans, MRIs. Chart me a map of valves and veins and muscles and chambers and walls. Auricles and ventricles. Supply a list of doctors, evaluations of their training, their bedside manner and the deftness of their fingertips. Provide an inventory of the equipment, its degree of cutting-edge modernity.

But these aren't questions that she can ask, demands that she can make. Not Lee Emery. Not someone who spent a night in a park and an hour on a blanket carpeting the floor of a sitting room. This is information available only to a wife. She slows her breath. "I hope Caroline's taking good care of you," she says.

"Actually," he says. He stops.

"Actually?" she repeats. She waits.

"Not that I'm complaining, mind you."

"You have every right . . ."

"But, in fact, I'm quite alone. Caroline left me six months ago."

A bomb dropped. A stone thrown. Endless ripples, Marguerite would say.

Before she can form a response, her other phone rings. A student knocks on the door. "Oh, Simon," Lee says. She spins her Rolodex to *Iris Kidney, Wyechester.* "But I'm coming over," she cries. "In June. I'm crossing the pond. I'll be near Netherend. Where I can see you if you'd like."

"If I'd like? Lee!" Simon's voice cracks.

After she deals with the phone (*Yes, there is a program in Switzerland; yes, skiing counts as extracurricular*) and the student (*No, organic chemistry credits are not transferable*), she calls Iris Kidney.

"I'm glad you got me, Lee," Iris says. "I was just going out the door. Another endless meeting in an endless round of them."

"I won't keep you long. I wanted to check about the foreign studies weekend," Lee begins.

"Perfect timing. Our committee's just agreed. We'd be delighted to have you here to speak to us. And I, for one, am thrilled."

"Not half so much as I am," Lee says.

"Though, unfortunately, we can't underwrite the whole fare. I tried. But the bursar will only allow a third. If that's acceptable."

"That's fine." More than fine, for someone traveling under the auspices of the Junior Year Abroad who has something entirely different planned.

"And naturally we'll house you and supply all your meals. Both yours and Ben's, of course."

Ben! She hadn't even thought . . . "I'm afraid it'll just be me," she says. "Ben's swamped. It's so much harder for him to get away."

"Too bad. Nigel is particularly anxious to meet him. He admires his work."

Dr. Kidney, Lee hears somebody call.

One minute, Iris says. "I'll fax you details, schedules, and the like." Iris pauses. She chuckles. "You'll never guess who's slated to share the podium."

"I give up."

"Judy Teagarten."

"Judy Teagarten!"

"None other. Our program's worst nightmare."

"Whom I seem to have put clear out of my mind. Or more likely repressed. I'm afraid I passed that hot potato on to you. Since we last talked, I haven't heard a word from the senior Teagartens. I expected a slew of calls, letters. Or at the very least, a sheriff to show up at my door with a subpoena for my arrest. What about the elopement to Gretna Green? And Mohammed Al . . . ?"

Iris laughs. "A nightmare transformed into a dream. Mohammed Al et cetera turns out to be Kuwaiti royalty. His family owns chichi hotels and wine bars and boutiques and restaurants all over Knightsbridge and Holland Park. Right now Phil and Hilda are living it up in a suite at the Dorchester. And studying Arabic on the Open University."

"Will wonders never cease?"

Iris laughs again. "I'm afraid I have to tootle off. But, Lee, I can't tell you how much I'm looking forward to your visit here."

In her bedroom, Lee changes her clothes twice. She's dismissed a black pantsuit as too New York, chinos and a plaid shirt as too Homestead. She wants to look writerly but approachable, East Coast intellectual but Down East down-to-earth. She chooses gray pants and a navy jacket. She clips on earrings made of old typewriter keys, two keys apiece, each set in silver. Off one lobe dangle *delete* and *backspace*; off the other, *shift* and *return*. Ben had bought them at a craft booth at the Bangor State Fair. "Where we got our wedding rings," he reminded her. "Of which Marguerite didn't approve." She'd looked down at her finger, the thin silver band completely obscured by the emerald she'd inherited from her grandmother.

Now she combs her hair. She slides on lipstick. She brushes pink blush onto her cheeks. She opens her book. For the fourth time, she makes sure the Post-its are still marking the paragraphs she's chosen to read. She's getting to be as bad as Ben. If she'd only known she would be joining the ranks of the making-a-list-and-checking-it-twice, she wouldn't have poked so much fun at him. She picks up the book. In spite of the sticker covering the $120 on the back, the sticker whose edges are turning brown and starting to curl, in spite of the cheap paper and skimpy cost-cutting page layout, *Mainely Marguerite* has a heft that pleases her. She puts it in the leather tote especially bought for carrying it. She adds the fountain pen especially designated for signing it. Green enamel trimmed in gold with a thick nib. Tools of her trade. The writer's trade.

She is just grabbing her car keys when the phone rings.

Ben's voice bursts over the line. "Lee, you're not going to believe this."

"Aren't you supposed to be in a seminar? Weren't you planning to call me tonight?"

"I couldn't wait. I'm playing hooky. My paper. My book is causing quite a stir."

"Really?" She catches herself. "I mean, I'm not surprised . . ."

"So far I've been approached by French, Italian, English, and German university publishers. Not to mention the Japanese. Who have lined up two potential translators. The

British are practically sticking a contract under my nose. They offered to send me a ticket whenever I want to come over and talk to them."

"Ben!"

"I figure maybe sometime in June. After commencement. Before summer school. Isn't that when you're hoping to attend that conference on the Junior Year Abroad?"

Don't panic, she tells herself. Stay calm. "In fact, I've just heard from Iris that the invitation's official. I'm forced to go for my job. But you hate to travel. Let alone the interruption to your work. I can't believe, these days, the details can't be arranged by e-mail and fax." She's a looking-out-for-his-best-interest wife. Whose every breath now surges and ebbs on a mounting of guilt and a sinking of hope.

While he's riding a crest. "We'll see," he says. "They promised a first-class seat and a five-star hotel."

Punishment enough for someone jammed into steerage and billeted in a dormitory. Still, she reminds herself, even if he goes, even if they overlap, London is miles from Wyechester.

And from other places that border it.

"What's more," Ben goes on, "I've been advised— Haddad, you know at Texas, wrote that huge biography of Sam Houston. It's already won the Bancroft Prize. There's talk of a National Book Award. He advises me to hold out for a big commercial publisher. Says it's got best-seller all over it. His agent has already left three messages at my hotel."

Lee gasps. *Agent. Commercial publisher. Best-seller.* All for Nathaniel Tarbell who sent logs down the Allagash and got soaked traipsing around the Forest of Dean? She can hardly take it in. "But that's wonderful," she manages.

"Isn't it? Who would have predicted," he marvels. "Imagine. I've spent almost my whole academic life on Nathaniel. I've been working on him for a huge chunk of our marriage." He sighs. "I feel as close to him as I do to you."

"Well, thanks a lot."

"You know what I mean."

"Just joking." She lifts the tote that holds her book. "I don't mind sharing you with Nathaniel," she says in her most gracious, grown-up tone. "Our ménage à trois has been my great privilege."

"Which is going to become a great big benefit. Which could turn our life around."

"You sound so happy. So excited."

"Why not? I'm the toast of the town. Or at least the Organization of American Historians. Aherne sent up a bottle of champagne. And you know how cheap he is."

She does. John Aherne, an expert on the Irish potato famine, who has an office across from Ben's, was once detained in the A&P for taking the stems off cherries before they were weighed. "Imported?"

He laughs. "Domestic. Some spots won't change."

"I wish I were there to celebrate."

"Me, too." He stops. Lee hears something poured into a glass. She checks her watch. Almost two, his time. It must be quite the occasion for Ben to drink before six.

"I'll take you out for a lobster when you get back." She buttons her jacket. "Like you did for me."

"Did for you?" His voice is puzzled.

"When *my* book came out."

"Ah, yes. Of course." She hears a sip and a slurp. The clink of ice cubes. The creak of a chair. "So what are *you* up to?" he asks. "You know," he continues, "I think in another week I could have a perfectly finished, fine-tuned manuscript."

"Well, as a matter of fact. *Since you asked.* My reading's this afternoon."

"God, Lee, I almost forgot! Guess that's what heady success will do to you." He chuckles. "Go straight to your head. I'll call you tonight. Knock their socks off." He pauses. "Isn't it amazing that my book is garnering so much attention, so much interest?"

Heady success and knocking their socks off don't seem like realistic possibilities when Lee arrives at the nearly empty College Co-Op. A cashier is filing her nails. A lone customer puzzles over a shelf of Hannibal Hamlin coffee mugs. Lee takes a deep breath. As long as she doesn't make a fool of herself. As long as she gets to use her special pen to sign a couple of books and hold a listener's ear—she's honed her reading down to fifteen minutes max. It's only right that Ben's book gets the attention, creates the stir. She's happy for him. She really is. Though the timing could be better. His large success coming on the heels of her small hope just to muddle through. She's big enough to acknowledge the tiny green worm of jealousy, of Nathaniel envy, of competition between husband and wife. And then dismiss it, thanks to psychological insight and the maturity of an adult. After all, while he's been buried in Nathaniel, she's been just as absorbed with Marguerite. Still, why does her little moment in the sun, her little book, have to be eclipsed by his bigger moment, his bigger book? Even though the supporting player is a role she's trained for her whole life as the granddaughter peeking out from behind the spotlit skirts of her grandmother.

A position, she soon realizes, she's not about to relinquish this afternoon at the College Co-Op. On the second floor, between *Children* and *Travel* and *Gerontology* and *Gay and Lesbian*, a few folding chairs are set up. In the back stands a long table with two equal piles of books balancing each end. Sandwiched between them are two chairs, two Perrier bottles, and two black pens. A young man wearing the name tag Jonathan above the Hannibal Hamlin college seal (*Domi lux veritasque*—at home, light and truth) is adjusting a lamp on the podium. A poster is taped to the front of it: *Reading Today!!* Under a photograph of Lassie is printed: *Nationally acclaimed dog trainer and prolific author Hannah Harriman Weatherbee-Ross with local writer Leemery*. Lee squints. No, it's not her imagination; her name is missing an *e* and a space.

Jonathan turns to her. He's tall with big brown eyes and a lot of brown curls and a sweet face. She thinks of the sweet faces of her own tall, brown-eyed, brown-curled boys and feels the familiar mother-of-absent-sons tug of acute longing. "Are you here for the reading?" he asks.

"In a sense. I *am* the reading. One half of it."

"You're Miz Emery?"

"How did you guess?"

"No guess. I must have seen Miz Weatherbee-Ross on

Today, Good Morning America, CNN like, oh, six or seven times." He points in the direction of *Gay and Lesbian*. "The extra chairs are back there. Would you mind helping me put out more?"

Lee looks at the clock above the *Your Place for College Textbooks* sign. "Do you think anybody is going to come?"

"It's early yet. Most people figure it's way too uncool to show up so far ahead." He reddens. "Not that . . ."

"Never mind." She waves a hand. "I'll get it right with the next book."

"Hey," he says. "You bet."

At precisely five past three, a few dozen people arrive in a pack. And, to Lee's astonishment, take up almost every seat that has been set out for them. Toward the middle of the fourth row, she spots Maggie in patched denim frayed at the knees. Her hair seems to consist of a series of cowlicks wrapped in rubber bands. Next to her sits a tall black man with a shaved head. He wears a robe whose lapels and sleeves are trimmed with orange and purple Kente cloth. Lee's heart soars. What better proof that a college plunked in the middle of a small town in a remote and lily-white state can broaden horizons and bring to an insular place the fresh air of a multicultural world. Has he been pulled here by the magnet of her grandmother's life? Unless . . . her heart sinks . . . he has a dog.

Maggie waves, then signals a beringed thumbs-up. Leaning against *Gerontology* slouches a doctoral student of Ben's, who nods at her with the Brownie-point-collecting, notice-me eagerness of a mongrel pup. Lee scans the others. Where's Beatrice? she wonders.

No sooner has she asked this than Beatrice arrives, yanking the arm of a man who drags his feet like a second-grader marched off to the principal. He's ponytailed and wearing a stained Citgo uniform with *Kenny* embroidered on its pocket flap. A State of Maine-shaped yellow bruise marks his sullen jaw. His left arm lies oddly pitched into a none-too-clean sling.

"Lee," Beatrice stage-whispers. She and Kenny take seats near the aisle. Kenny slumps; Beatrice perches. "I'm her editor," she announces to the room at large and no one in particular.

Sixty seconds later, a great commotion flares. Every head turns. "It's Hannah Harriman Weatherbee-Ross!" someone exclaims. Lee remembers the A. A. Milne poem her mother used to recite to her. The one she used to recite to her own children: James James Morrison Morrison Weatherby George Dupree. All those syllables, all those words to add the weight, the ballast, the gravitas to make a name memorable.

"She's so much prettier than her photograph," a woman in the front row declares. Down the aisle, sprinting like an Olympian, rushes a tall, blond, strapping goddess, in purple silk and stiletto heels, holding the hand of an adorable child, and with the other, tugging the leash of an equally adorable dog.

Both are straight out of central casting. The child, a boy of about five, has a tousled mop of golden hair, cornflower eyes, and dimpled cheeks and chin and knees (exposed by Little Lord Fauntleroy short pants). The dog is a honey-colored cocker spaniel with flopping ears and bobbing tail and a mouth turned up into a lopsided grin.

"Ooh. Aahh" erupts from the audience.

Lee's shoulders sag. She projects herself to the signing table after the reading. At one end will loll the multisyllabled author, the adorable child, and the grinning cocker spaniel. In front of them a line of dog lovers will snake around counters and shelves, down the stairs and out the door. A fast-depleting pile of books will empty like an hourglass with too big a hole.

On the other end will sit plain ordinary Lee Emery. *Leemery*. Attended by the paltry trio of Beatrice, Maggie, and Ben's favor-currying advisee. Her skyscraper of *Mainely Marguerite*s will never shrink, will never leave this store.

She prepares herself.

After a brief introduction by Jonathan—"Hannah Harriman Weatherbee-Ross needs no introduction"—Miz Weatherbee-Ross explains that she will read a few short passages from her book and then demonstrate certain commands with Casey the child and Woodles the dog.

Dozens of pens fly out of pockets and purses and backpacks and totes and hover over notebooks and yellow legal pads.

Under half-closed lids, Lee rolls her eyes.

"Let's look at the power issues between dog and owner," Miz Weatherbee-Ross begins. "Just as cultural gaps exist between people, there are strong cultural differences between dogs and human beings which can lead to serious misunderstandings."

Pencils scratch across paper.

"The salient points are as follows," Miz Weatherbee-Ross

goes on. "Your view of your behavior toward your dog does not equal the dog's view of the same behavior. You pet your dog because you love him and want him to feel good. He, or she, on the other hand, may see the attention as proof that you rank lower than he does in the family structure. Lower-ranking animals, to elicit attention from superiors, give appeasement behaviors such as groveling, licking, and panting to the higher-ranking animal. The disease to please. Petting your dog without asking for anything in return may result in your dog believing he ranks higher than you."

"Why, yes," a murmuring chorus chimes.

"To resolve any behavior problem, you will need to change your own behavior. All family members should agree on the following program or you doom your dog to failure."

In fast sequence Miz Weatherbee-Ross ticks these off like the plagues visited on the Egyptians.

"Self-control.

"Training.

"Limit play.

"Anticipate problems.

"Regular exercise.

"And finally." She waits. Woodles the dog sniffs the floor. Casey the child chews on his sleeve. "When in doubt, walk out."

A deafening round of applause issues forth. Two faculty wives on the side rise to a standing O. Miz Weatherbee-Ross holds up her hand. "Now I'm going to have Casey and Woodles demonstrate our basic training techniques." She glances at the clock. "If I haven't used up too much of your time."

"Oh, no," whirls from the audience in a mighty roar.

Lee follows the speaker's eyes to the clock. Miz Weatherbee-Ross has gone eighteen minutes beyond her allotted twenty. Lee looks out at the audience. Maybe not *their* time, Lee wants to protest, but what about *mine*?

Miz Weatherbee-Ross leads Casey and the dog to the front of the room. "Remember, training is a lifetime process, not a quick fix. The sooner you begin, the more years you will have together to love and enjoy each other." She places Casey at her left knee; Woodles, at her right ankle.

Before Casey can order Woodles to roll over, however, something happens. It comes so fast, in such a swirl of color and light and noise, that Lee gets dizzy trying to follow the action and for a couple of minutes has to drop her head to her knees. The scenario plays like this:

Suddenly, out from behind *Travel* rush two Hannibal Hamlin campus police. Nightsticks in their pockets. Handcuffs hanging off their belts. Trailed by a Homestead cop— Billy Fosse, Lee went to school with him—dangling a holster and a gun. The three of them grab Kenny's one good arm and two legs, handcuff a wrist to his waistband, and heave him toward the back. Kenny struggles. "You've got the wrong man," he yells. "I'm innocent." All four lurch into the table. Which falls over in a loud crash. The books shudder to the floor. And mix together like flour and sugar sifted through a sieve.

Beatrice screams. A lady in a red dress cries. Casey sobs. Woodles barks. Woodles jumps. Woodles rips Billy Fosse's uniform. "Sit. Sit," Miz Weatherbee-Ross orders. Her voice grows frantic. "Down. Down. Stay. Stay."

Finally, Jonathan grabs the microphone from the podium. "The reading is canceled until further notice," he declares.

Half an hour later, order is restored. Kenny has been hauled off to jail. Miz Weatherbee-Ross carts Casey and Woodles away. Beatrice heads for Portland to ask her father to raise bail. Maggie flings her arms around Lee's shoulders. "Poor Mom," she says. She introduces her mother to her new boyfriend, Scott, the black man in tribal robes with the shaved head. *Scott?* Lee thinks. They shake hands. And he and Maggie both set out toward the library. Ben's advisee is late for a class; he'll buy her book another time, he promises. Those in the audience who haven't fled sort out Miz Hannah Harriman Weatherbee-Ross's *How to Teach Your Child to Train Your Dog* from Lee Emery's *Mainely Marguerite: Travels with My Grandmother; A Memoir*, scoop it up and take it to the downstairs cashier.

Before Billy Fosse leaves, Lee claims old-school ties to elicit this information: Kenny is the campus mugger. He had the bad sense to attempt to mug Miss Peavey. Who attacked him with her pocketbook. Hence the bruised jaw and the broken arm.

"And Miss Peavey?"

"Nary a hair out of place." Billy stops. He guffaws. "Actually that's why she took the morning off. That and the lineup at police HQ. Had to repair the damage at the hairdresser." He shakes his head. "Quite a gal. With an amazing right hook. Hate to run into her in the dead of night. That pocketbook's the kind of weapon of destruction you ought to register."

On her way to the parking lot, Lee passes the drama building. She turns back. She halts in front of it. The door is open. She can hear voices. Music. The funereal beat of a drum. Carved into the stone over the door are the masks of comedy and tragedy. She studies them.

She considers her *Mainely Marguerite* never taken out of its bag; the fountain pen never uncapped. This is her life. Its present, a farce if not a comedy; its past, a drama if not a tragedy. She scrolls through the absurd events of the day: Her book. Ben's book. Hannah Harriman Weatherbee-Ross's book. Kenny. Beatrice. Kids and dogs. Judy Teagarten. Hilda and Phil. Miss Peavey. A series of comic turns. A barrel of laughs.

If she looks back to the past, however, she can find very little to laugh about. Only the births of her children represent pure bliss. It's hard to hold on to the kindness of her parents, the enchantments of her grandmother, when they ended in such tragic deaths. She thinks of Marguerite's death. Her parents'. The lowly hoatzin. The little plane. *Ave do Paraiso*. She thinks of a hole in the heart. Even the joys of first love, of married love, contain so much sadness.

How do you fill a hole in a life to make it whole? Knit together a divided heart? Connect the past with the present? How do you reconcile those qualities of her mother in her with those qualities of her grandmother? How do you reconcile Simon and Ben? Home and away? Comedy and tragedy?

Sometimes what's funny can make you cry.

She walks up the stairs. Two students pass her arm in arm. They're of indeterminate sex. All in black. Not the usual Hannibal Hamlin khaki and Pendleton wool. She remembers when she was a student here. Even then, art majors dressed with drama, with art.

A pink notice is stapled to the rehearsal room door. Lee moves closer. *Quiet, please,* she reads. *Rehearsal in progress for the theatrical adaptation of The Death of Ivan Ilyich.*

She opens the door a crack. She sees a bare stage. A bed. A man in it. A woman at his side.

"Life was here and now it is going," the man says. "When I am not, what will there be?"

"It's very sad," the woman sighs.

"Show more resignation," orders the director standing at the back of the room. "Bend slightly. Lower the register."

The woman bends. She softens her voice. "Sad," she whispers.

"Better," the director says. "Remember, you can't save him."

Quietly Lee shuts the door.

Can she save Simon?

She couldn't save her parents.

Could she have saved Marguerite if she'd got there earlier?

Seven

❧ ❧

Four years after Ben and Lee's town hall wedding, Marguerite started to fail. First came a series of small strokes. "Not surprising," Marguerite's New York doctor had told Lee when he phoned her in Maine, "for someone in her eighties. A smoker, a drinker, who's kicked up her heels her whole life. Who's never bothered to take much care of herself."

"She wouldn't listen to us," Lee protested. "We told her to watch what she ate, get more rest, use moderation . . ."

The doctor offered a few soothing *now nows*, the practiced response for patients on the verge of hysteria. "Believe me, Mrs. Emery, I'm not blaming you. I know how impossible it is to get your grandmother to listen to anyone." He paused. "Still, it's not such a good idea to let her continue living alone."

"Don't even suggest it," Marguerite had exclaimed when Lee first broached the subject. "Return to Homestead? Never!"

"You could bring all your things. We'll fix up the room with your own antiques, paintings, and tapestries. Your *bibelots*. It'll look like you never left the Canterbury. You'd have your own bath. You'd be with *us*."

"Not that I don't appreciate the thought, my darling Magnolia, not that I'm not grateful. But there's nothing wrong with me. Dr. Stern is aptly named. Entirely lacking in *joie de vivre*. A complete alarmist. Between you and me, I think he's getting along in years; I think he should retire."

"Grandmother! He's half your age."

"Age is all in the mind, *ma petite*. I refuse to grow old." A statement punctuated by an explosion and the sound of clanking metal and hissing steam. "One minute, *Liebchen*," said her grandmother. Lee listened to rustling and banging. Should she notify the concierge? The maintenance men?

When her grandmother came back to the phone, she was slightly out of breath. "Now where were we? I'm afraid I forgot all about the tea and started the slightest little fire . . ."

The concierge called the next day. "I realize Madame has been living here for forty years," he began.

"I'm going to New York," she told Ben.

"Good idea," he agreed. "Shall I come with you? I'll try to get someone to cover my class . . ."

"I think I'd better handle this on my own."

"I understand," he said. "Absolutely," he added, barely able to hide his relief.

At ten in the morning, Marguerite opened the door to her apartment wearing all her diamonds and a black evening dress. A ruffle of crimson lipstick fluttered outside the lines of her lips and onto her chin. Her nose was floured with powder. She'd raccoon-ringed her eyes with kohl. Accentuating their filminess. Cataracts? Lee wondered. Underneath the overpowering perfume—a dressing table's worth of garden flowers and fruity oils, of sandalwood and patchouli and bergamot—arose the smell of somebody who hadn't bathed. Lee tried to keep the alarm off her face and out of her voice. "Grandmother," she exclaimed. She took her grandmother into her arms. "How beautiful you look."

"And no wonder," Marguerite beamed, "since I dressed especially for you. I suppose my ensemble is the teeniest bit outré for before noon, but it's such a festive occasion. I wanted to show you how happy I am about your visit." She made the moue of a coquette. "Now that you so rarely come to New York. Now that you're so settled in Maine. With . . ." She shook her head. The "rat" came loose from its pins and flopped over one ear like the tail on a Davy Crockett hat. ". . . that exemplary husband of yours."

"Ben," Lee supplied.

"Ben," she repeated. She pursed her lips. "But don't just stand there. Come in."

One step into the tiny front hall and Lee felt she was being ushered into Miss Havisham's house by Miss Havisham herself. Dust covered the tables; papers carpeted the floor; clothes draped the chairs; unread *New York Times*es leaned against the wall in a precarious pillar. Lee spotted a gold-covered box of Marguerite's black cigarettes and thought of fire. She smelled food gone bad and thought of bugs. "What about the maid?" she asked.

Marguerite waved a dismissive hand. Her emerald flashed, then slid around her finger. For the first time, Lee noticed how thin she'd become. "Oh, her," said Marguerite.

"*Her?*" said Lee. "*Clara.* You've had her for years." One thing about her grandmother's residential hotel, one comforting thing, Lee thought, was that the staff never changed. The bell*boys* she'd known as a child: Jimmy, Mickey, Louie, were still there huddling as always around the reception desk. Now white-haired, with arthritic knees and swollen knuckles, they wheezed so loudly when they grabbed her suitcase it was all she could do not to wrestle it back from them. And Clara, who'd been a girl when she'd first worked for Marguerite, who had sneaked Lee cream puffs from the hotel dining room, who had taken home Marguerite's mending on her Sundays off, now had three grandchildren of her own and one great-grandson. "And Clara?" Lee asked again.

"I discharged her. She steals from me."

"I don't believe it."

"Lee!" Marguerite's penciled-in eyebrows shot up. "Are you doubting my word?"

Lee extended her stay for a week. She hired a cleaning service. She stuffed the refrigerator with fruits and vegetables.

She filled the medicine cabinet with vitamins. She bought bath salts and shower gel and a dozen hand-milled French soaps. She bought fat sponges and loofah brushes. And when she wrung washcloths over her grandmother's back, helped her in and out of the tub, she averted her eyes from mottled flesh hanging off bones and shriveled flattened breasts. Just the sight of Marguerite's feet, blue-veined, gnarled with defiant scarlet tips at the end of her vulnerable, misshapen toes, could provoke a sob.

She took her to the doctor. She has glaucoma, he whispered to Lee, and can't be relied upon to put in the drops.

She called three agencies. And set up interviews with nurses and companions and housekeepers.

"No!" Marguerite shouted. "No!"

"You have two choices," Lee said trying for firmness to disguise her jellied knees and liquefying heart. "You can either come home with me. Or consent to have someone here to live with you."

"I won't have a stranger in my house," insisted Marguerite. "A nurse. As if I'm infirm."

Lee studied her grandmother, all five feet three inches of her, whose erect spine and spindly heels and held-high head with its foot of hair rolled on top had once made her seem the tallest person in a room. "*Trompe l'oeil*," her grandmother would mumble, hairpins stuck between her lips, "a trick of the eye." Now her shoulders curved. Her neck had lost its swan's length. "Not infirm," Lee said. "But who can't use a little help? Frankly, I wouldn't mind some myself."

"No wonder with that rambling house in that godforsaken place. Where you couldn't find a marzipan bonbon or a *Paris Match* throughout the whole state." She shuddered. "It's you who needs the help. Not me."

"If you come to Homestead you'll be with your family."

"And if I stay in New York, I'll be with my friends."

What friends? Lee wanted to ask. So many had died. Or moved to the suburbs to be closer to their relatives. Or gone off to retirement facilities or nursing homes. As a child, she used to be taken to luncheons at Schrafft's with ladies whose shoulders were draped in foxes' tails clasped between the sharp little teeth of glassy-eyed foxes' heads. They wore gloves and brooches and ate ice cream with long-handled spoons saying all the while *we really shouldn't but just this once* . . . What had happened to these women?

Her grandmother's best friend, Manizucka, who used to sing at Marguerite's Gramercy Park musicales, had left years ago. Lee could picture the rise and fall of her pigeon breast and the handkerchief clutched right where the cleavage came together in a V. Manizucka had moved to Hollywood, to a residence for retired performers. *The man who composed the score for Marlene's last film is in the room next door,* she'd written. *We play canasta in the evenings. You'd love this place. If only you'd had a professional musical career to qualify.*

"I can't stay with you," her grandmother repeated. "Besides," she added, "you know what they say about fish. After three days it starts to stink."

"You wouldn't be a *guest!*"

She interviewed dozens of women. Women in starched white nurses' uniforms and good tweed suits, women from the country and women from the city, women with brogues and French *u*'s and German *w*'s and the flat vowels of the Midwest.

She picked a woman from Boston with good schools, good clothes, a plummy accent who'd been married to a Lowell twice and a Cabot once. A woman of enlightened views if reduced circumstances. A woman who loved music and poetry. And if she didn't know how to draw blood or take a pulse or concoct a blancmange, she knew what glass to pour the sherry in.

"Not a nurse or a paid companion, but a friend," Lee told her grandmother. "Just the kind of person you'll like. Who'll adore you. Who needs a place to stay."

She got a power of attorney. She ordered checks. She set up a grocery tab. She bought a subscription for two to the opera. She made doctor and dentist appointments. She contacted a taxi service. She arranged for the florist to deliver roses once a week. For the candy store to send marzipan cherries and chocolate-covered hazelnuts.

"We'll be just fine," said Mrs. Cabot at the door. "We are going to have a marvelous visit."

Jimmy the bellboy, panting and rasping, lifted Lee's suitcase onto a trolley with two hands and an alarming lurch. He pressed the button for the elevator.

"Don't worry, my darling. Everything's going to be wonderful," Marguerite said. She was wearing a red dress. Bracelets circled her arms like rings on a curtain rod. Limbs which had once been willowy and sleek now looked as brittle as sticks. Under the flesh Lee could see the outline of her skeleton, the shape of her skull. How can I leave her? Lee thought.

"Leave," Marguerite commanded. "Go. You'll miss your flight." And the wave of her hand was so gay. Her smile was so brave that it broke Lee's heart.

This is the beginning of the end, Lee told herself, the beginning of the end. On the plane home, she cried so hard that the man on the aisle next to her moved his seat.

Yet if there was a beginning of the end, there was also a beginning. A week after she came home, she discovered she was pregnant.

When she told Ben, he shouted out his delight, then went to throw up.

She felt great. He felt rotten. She ate bacon and eggs, pancakes and waffles, hot dogs and sauerkraut.

He munched Saltines.

He bought insurance. He picked out a movie camera. He ordered an up-to-date set of encyclopedias. She treated herself to earrings of silver and lapis lazuli. Because she couldn't drink wine, he stopped. Because he was off anchovies, she threw them out.

In bed at night, she read Jane Austen and he read Dr. Spock. He slept with his body curled around hers, his hands on her stomach. "My baby. My baby," he whispered.

"Which one do you mean?" she asked.

"Both of you."

"We're Jack Sprat and his wife," she said.

He nodded. "The ideal marriage, separate but equal. Complementary." He patted her belly. "With a pea in our pod."

Despite her worries about Marguerite, a gnawing dread

of the inevitable, she was a happy pea in her marriage pod.
A baby was growing inside her; a devoted husband lay beside her. For the time being, at least, things seemed stable
with her grandmother.

"We are managing," reported Mrs. Cabot.

"My new friend is a woman of good taste and refined
manners," informed Marguerite. "Isn't she lucky I invited
her to live with me."

So Ben and Lee steamed the wallpaper off the room Lee
had offered Marguerite. They painted it a sunny-side-up
yellow. Where the wall met the ceiling they stenciled a border of white rabbits and ruby-throated hummingbirds. In
the attic they found Lee's old bassinet, which they stripped
and sanded and varnished. Lee sewed an organdy ruffle.
Ben made a bentwood canopy.

Everything was fitting into place, Lee thought. The four
years after their wedding, the four years they waited for Ben
to get his doctorate, had sped by in a comforting flurry of
work, hers and mostly (as it should be) his. Not to mention
fixing up her parents' house, which they'd moved into right
after their honeymoon, and the round of dinner parties
where the sport was to outmaster each other's mastering of
Mastering the Art of French Cooking. She'd made the right
decision. She and Ben were compatible and companionable
both at the kitchen table and in bed. Confirmed by the fact
that when they were ready to have kids, she'd become pregnant the instant they'd stopped using birth control.

Amid such domestic bliss and blessed-event anticipation,
Lee was pleased to notice that thoughts of Simon were rare
and fleeting. She felt as if she'd been successfully eased off a

drug. Her cravings for him lessened; their former intensity diluted. No longer did these memories come unprovoked. Something might stir them: An article about Hyde Park. A recipe for Scotch eggs. The accent of a visiting professor from London University. But then she'd pat her stomach; Ben would massage her feet, and they'd start choosing names from their Name-Your-Baby book.

Until one morning, when she picked up the *Homestead Herald*'s Sunday supplement and saw two photographs: dark-haired young lovers cuddling in a park. Gray-haired senior citizens embracing in a backyard. "It Was the Saddest, Most Difficult Choice of My Life," announced the title. Printed just above it was this paragraph: *Simon Caldwell was her first passionate love, the man with whom she'd promised to share her future. When she learned he'd been killed, Elisabeth Kraus agreed to marry another man who adored her. Then one day she met Simon again.*

Lee gasped.

Ben looked up from his tea and toast. "Morning sickness?"

"Maybe," Lee said. She *did* feel sick.

"Here." Ben slid away her plate of eggs scrambled with peppers and onions and replaced it with two triangles of dry whole wheat. "Phew," he sighed. "It's a relief to know I'm not the only pregnant person in this room."

She managed the wan and grateful smile of a queasily expectant Renaissance Madonna, then went back to the article: Elisabeth met Simon during the war when she was eighteen. It was love at first sight. They made plans to wed at the Hotel Lutèce in Paris. But Elisabeth and her family were rounded up by the Nazis and sent to concentration camps. When the camps were liberated by the Americans, she searched and searched for Simon. Eventually she found his name on the list of dead. Heartsick, she left for America. Where she met Ed Horowitz, who pursued her relentlessly. *I don't love you*, she told him, *I left my heart in Europe. No matter. I love you*, he replied. *I want to marry you*. They married; had three children. Two decades went by. She took her own daughter to Paris. In the lobby of the Hotel Lutèce, she looked across the tuberoses and lilies and saw Simon. Their eyes met. *When he hugged me, time stood still*, she wrote. He—married and with children, too—wanted her to run off with him immediately. She promised she'd give him her decision the next day. She agonized. She tortured herself. Then she thought of her husband, of his devotion and love for her and their children. Of how he'd worked so hard for them. She thought of the life she had made for herself. She realized that, though she'd had a first love with Simon, her love with Ed was a grown-up, enduring love. She took her daughter and went home to America. *Young love and mature love, I've experienced both*, she explained. *Over the years, I've had second thoughts*, Elisabeth admitted, *but nevertheless I know I was completely sensible. I know I made the right decision.*

Now Lee looked at her own right decision and felt enormous relief. *See*, she told herself, *first love and grown-up love. Young love and mature love. I've been completely sensible.* She studied the photo of Elisabeth and Ed, their broad smiles and gleaming bifocals, their matching forest green jogging suits. They looked so content in their grown-up love. She should take this as a sign. Accept this as a blueprint for her own life.

"Are you feeling better?" Ben asked.

"Much."

But if, like Elisabeth, she was at peace with her choice, she feared the peace, the moratorium with Marguerite would not last.

It didn't.

"There are difficulties," Mrs. Cabot cautioned.

"She's stealing from me," Marguerite complained. "I no longer want her as my guest."

"Shall I come?" Lee asked.

"Wait till after the baby," Marguerite said. She giggled. "Could you ever imagine me with a great-grandchild?"

"I don't want you to travel," Ben ordered.

She was six months pregnant. With a belly like a fish-bowl and a baby swimming inside like a fish. "Feel this. A somersault. A kick. A dive," she'd announce to Ben, who would lay his ear on her stomach and run his hands along her stretched-out bulk so tenderly you'd have thought she was an archived Nathaniel manuscript. "Don't worry. I'm fine. Dr. Solomon says I can fly through the seventh month."

Ben worried. He catalogued disasters. "Lousy weather. Bumpy planes. Delayed flights. Wind shear. Ice on the wing. Bad air. Other people's germs. Not to mention leg cramps and seat belts not big enough."

"Let's wait a little while," Mrs. Cabot soothed. "I'll see how long I—and your grandmother—can hold out."

Within a week, however, Marguerite was in the hospital and Lee was on the plane.

It was snowing when she landed. What would have been considered a mere sugar dusting in Maine had New Yorkers bundling up and worrying about delayed flights, canceled schools, and storm-snarled trains and buses for the nightly commute. Lee wanted to take a taxi right to the hospital, but Mrs. Cabot demanded to see her first. She had keys and papers to turn over, things to explain. Lee agreed with an alacrity that surprised herself. Besides, she might as well dump her luggage, have a shower, try to look presentable. Petty justifications, she knew, for putting off the painful reckoning.

Mrs. Cabot was waiting in her grandmother's apartment when Lee arrived. Her suitcases were lined up in a neat row inside the door. She had found new employment, she informed Lee, Palm Beach. A distinguished name which a confidentiality agreement forbade her to reveal. She'd have her own suite of rooms including the services of a live-in maid. And a bit of a vacation first, considering—ahem—the job stress she'd lately been suffering from.

Jimmy rolled Lee's bags into the opposite corner from Mrs. Cabot's matched set of American Tourister. Mrs. Cabot buttoned up her coat. Lee unbuttoned hers. They might have been handing off a baton, Lee thought. Mrs. Cabot might as well have been saying, *I've run this leg of the race—the final sprint is yours.*

"Has it been that terrible?" Lee asked.

"Not at first. But lately." Her face shifted into incredulity. "The things she accused me of."

"You mean stealing? I never for one moment . . ."

"Not that. Other things."

"Such as?"

Mrs. Cabot shuddered. "Seducing her husband. Enticing lovers. Hiding suitors. What is that term? Lewd and lascivious acts. I couldn't even bring myself to repeat some of the things she said."

"I'm so sorry."

"I do realize that certain aberrations were due to hardening of the arteries, to her various illnesses. Still, with no family here . . ."

Lee looked down at her stomach, which obscured her toes and was straining the guaranteed-to-stretch fabric of her most voluminous maternity blouse.

Mrs. Cabot looked, too. "Not that I don't understand. But it was hard deciding when to call the ambulance. Your grandmother was so adamant. She didn't want to be moved. She refused to accept the limits of her age. She refused to acknowledge anything could be wrong." She sighed. "I should have insisted she go to the hospital a week ago."

"It's not your fault. I should have been here."

"You know what they say about hindsight. What's important is that you're here now." She pulled on her gloves. She pointed to a stack of files on the hall table. The labels were neatly typed: *Household. Medical. Entertainment. Miscellaneous.* "I think you'll find everything in order," Mrs. Cabot said.

Lee glanced beyond her trim no-hair-out-of-place silhouette at the neat-as-a-pin apartment with its uncustomary you-could-hear-a-pin-drop hush. The books were squared off on the coffee table. The chairs were at right angles to the sofa. Shawls and throws were folded into neat little packets like the American flags presented to the widows of war heroes. Even though you could no longer trace your initials on the tabletops or trip over a pom-pommed satin mule in front of a chair, she missed the luscious *déshabillé* of her grandmother's rooms.

"Your grandmother's a bowerbird," Lee's mother had once explained. She had pulled down her Peterson's guide and opened it to a page showing a small, golden bird with a white orchid clutched in its beak. Underneath was a photograph of its bower, an intricate maze of towers and branches ribboned like a maypole with flowers and grasses and seedpods. "Its decorating skills are so prized," her mother went on, "that other birds try to steal the bower's ornaments."

Now Mrs. Cabot cleared her throat. "As for her jewelry. It's in the safety deposit box. Her lawyer has the key. There's an inventory. You should find everything . . ."

"I never had a single doubt."

"Except for her emerald ring. She insisted on wearing it. She screamed when anyone tried to take it off. She actually knocked over an orderly. The hospital said they wouldn't be responsible. Made her sign a release. Imagine. She's nearly blind and hardly able to hold a pen, let alone write her name. 'A scribble will suffice,' they said. I did try to talk sense into her."

"My grandmother was never one for sense."

Mrs. Cabot nodded. She permitted the hint of a wintry smile. She extended her hand. She gave Lee's fingers a firm, capable, well-bred clasp. Halfway out the door, she turned around. "You will of course notify me when . . ." She stopped.

Lee froze.

"When it's over," she said.

First Lee went into the guest room, Mrs. Cabot's just abandoned quarters, where she had slept on childhood visits, her parents having been booked into one of the Canterbury's mid-priced doubles on a lower floor. Stripped of its froufrou—bed skirt and needlepoint pillows and tassels and embroidered Chinese spread—it had the appearance of a monastic cell. A blanket was pulled taut over the bed. A single water glass stood on the night table. The parquet tiles were bare, the rugs rolled up in the closet along with the Staffordshire dogs that had graced each side of the bureau for as long as Lee could remember. The lace bureau scarf was gone. In a drawer lay the photographs of Marguerite: with Manizucka; at a fund-raiser with Eleanor Roosevelt; with Lee herself—the spillover from other rooms' tables and mantelpieces, which Marguerite had once crowded onto the now bare windowsills. Boston understatement had replaced Marguerite's European excess. New England chill had blown away New York warmth.

Never mind. She'd sleep in her grandmother's room. She'd be closer to her there. Surrounded by her photographs and paintings and books. Lee put her suitcase on the bench at the end of her grandmother's bed. She looked around. *Inviting* was the word she'd use to describe her grandmother's opulently feathered nest. Her *bower*. The mattress was thick enough to offset the princess's pea, the pillows were goose down, the sheets silk, the covers velvet and satin and finely spun wool. She thought of the bright spare rooms of her parents' house. Now her house. Along with beauty, her grandmother loved comfort. She luxuriated in every inch of it.

There was no comfort in her grandmother's hospital room. Only utilitarian plastic and steel and harsh fluorescent light. A green curtain was draped around her grandmother's bed. Another bed, empty and covered with a rubberized pad, stood near the window, which looked onto rooftops and air-conditioning stacks and a toothpick's sliver of sky. Lee waited on the threshold of her grandmother's room. She willed herself to go in. She couldn't move. She clutched the potted azalea she'd bought from the lobby shop. "Don't you have an orchid?" she asked.

The candy striper shook her head. "We get no requests for them."

Not a sound came from behind the green curtain. It was an island of stillness in a cacophony of bells and buzzers, of metal carts and loudspeaker announcements, of footsteps and squawking television sets. Somewhere behind her Lee heard hoots of laughter and the cry of a child.

She rested the flowerpot against the ledge of her stomach. The baby kicked.

She stayed motionless.

"Her sight's nearly gone," the nurse had warned her. "She's very frail."

Just step through this doorway, Lee told herself. One step. Two. Three. Stick one foot in front of the other.

The baby turned.

Take baby steps, she ordered herself. One little inch at a time.

What was wrong with her? She'd traveled from Homestead to New York. She'd traveled from La Guardia to the Hotel Canterbury. She'd got another taxi from Gramercy Park to Lenox Hill. She'd walked a tangle of corridors and ridden two elevators. Unwieldy and pregnant, she'd crossed vast distances. She'd come all this way to be at her grandmother's side.

But.

Yet.

Now that she was here, she couldn't navigate these final few feet.

The green curtain rustled. She heard a voice call out. Faint. Cracked. Plaintive. "Sam? Violet?"

Her grandfather's name. Her mother's name.

These two words worked like a miracle drug she'd once read about, a drug that had thawed the frozen limbs of people paralyzed with a rare disease. Lee sprang to life. Her knees unlocked. She rushed to the bed. She pulled open the curtain. "Grandmother, it's Lee," she said.

Her grandmother lay on her back in the hospital bed; the headboard had been so angled up, she'd slipped down to the middle where the mattress bent. The blankets were tucked under her chin. Her skin, as bleached as the sheets, was tented on the sharp frame of her cheekbones. Her lips were as pale as her skin. Her eyes were dull and filmed. Her mouth sagged open. Her breath rasped. Her hair was coming in white at the scalp. The lobes of her ears seemed huge and flat from the heavy earrings she'd always worn. Lee felt as if she were looking at a photograph, blurry and faded, of some ancient ancestor who bore only the faintest family resemblance to her grandmother. *Yes, well, I see a bit of a likeness there in the chin*, someone might say. Lee swallowed hard. She was sure she was going to be sick. She expelled a few Lamaze-school puffs. She put down the plant. She pulled up a chair.

"It's Magnolia Lee," she said.

"Where's Sam?" Marguerite asked. Her voice sounded tinny, as if it were coming from cheap speakers, broadcast across a piazza paved with flat, echoing stones.

"Actually . . ." Lee hesitated. *But, of course*, she decided. "Actually, he's on another trip," she said.

"Ah, I'd forgotten."

"He'll be back soon," she added.

"And Violet?"

"At a meeting."

"Yes," said her grandmother. "She told me that." She moved her head from side to side. Under the blanket, Lee could see her fingers open and close. "It's very dark in here. Can you turn up the lights?"

Lee averted her eyes from the blaze of fluorescent bulbs that crisscrossed the ceiling, the naked tube that glared across the head of her grandmother's bed. On the other side of the room, one light flickered and buzzed. "They're not working. Electrical problems. Don't you think it's more restful, more romantic, to keep them off?"

"You have a point. Not to mention much more flattering to the complexion." She frowned and a shadow of the old, familiar imperiousness passed over her face. "What do those doctors know? The lies they tell about my sight." She rolled her head again. Back and forth. "And where am I?" she asked.

Lee gazed through the window at the stingy bit of sky, the gray clouds, the jutting roofs. Smoke poured from chimney stacks on some of them. An eyesore of scaffolding crowned others. She could see a yellow hard hat and a bucket of what could have been cement. Even this high, patches of snow had turned to soot. A line of crows perched on a steel beam. "You're in Paris," she said. "In the Hotel Lutèce."

Did her grandmother smile?

"We're traveling. You and I," Lee said. "We have the most beautiful rooms. We'd only reserved a double, but when they saw you, when they realized who you were, they moved us into the royal suite . . ."

Did her grandmother nod?

". . . where there's an Aubusson rug on the floor. And this huge Gobelin tapestry. Cherubs and flowers and unicorns. The fixtures in the bathroom are all gold. The tub's marble. There's a heated towel rack. Your bed has a silk canopy. And the view. We can see all of Paris. Notre-Dame. The Eiffel Tower. Montmartre . . ."

Her grandmother turned her unseeing eyes to the wall. "Yes, I can see it," her grandmother said.

"And there are orchids on every surface," Lee continued. "The rarest species. Purple and pink and an astonishing white."

Faintly, Marguerite's nostrils flared. "I can smell them. Lovely. I adore orchids. I used to like the Bird of Paradise." She stopped. She trembled. The blankets rippled. She slid another inch into the valley of the bed. "Will I see Violet soon? My daughter?"

Lee took a long deep breath. She measured her words. "Of course," she said. "And later, we have tickets for the opera. A box. You will wear your gold silk."

"Have the maid press it," her grandmother said.

"She's already taken it away. Naturally, they sent up a bottle of champagne."

"Bollinger?"

Lee remembered the champagne her grandmother had uncorked at her wedding. The gay basket of hors d'oeuvres. Funeral baked meats. *I am too young for this*, she wanted to shout, *too young for so much loss*. "Yes. Your favorite. In a silver bucket. Filled with shaved ice."

"A five-star hotel always remembers what I like best." She shifted her head toward Lee. She lowered her voice to a whisper.

Lee bent forward.

"And where am I going next?"

Lee pushed her fist to her mouth. She turned her head away.

"Where am I going next?" Marguerite repeated.

"Where are *we* going next," Lee corrected. "To London," Lee said.

"Alistair and Hermione Abernathy," her grandmother said.

Lee's heart thumped. "In fact, they're picking us up at the airport."

"Simon?" her grandmother said.

Lee's throat closed. The baby somersaulted. A hard ball

was forming in the muscle of her calf and climbing to her thigh.

"Did you marry him?" her grandmother asked. "Simon. Did you marry Simon?"

She put a hand on her stomach. Forgive me, Father. Forgive me, father of this child. Forgive me, Ben. "Yes, I married him."

"I am so glad. It's what I wanted for you." She paused. "Baby?"

"Soon," Lee said. "It will be a girl. We're calling her Marguerite."

"I was sure you would."

Lee took her grandmother's hand. Her grandmother's fingers twisted and tightened around Lee's wedding ring.

"My emerald. I want you to have it. Take it off my finger."

"There's plenty of time . . ."

"No!" her grandmother ordered. "Take it now. Now!"

Lee slid the ring off her grandmother's finger. She slid it onto her own. Cinderella's slipper. "It fits," she said.

Her grandmother nodded. "For you and Simon. For your happy marriage," she said.

Then, for a short time her grandmother slept. Lee held her hand. Her grandmother's breath rattled and hissed. Lee watched her chest rise and fall. If she kept her eyes fixed on her grandmother, if she didn't move them, she could force the chest to keep going up and down. Her will was as strong as the moon which controlled the ebb and flow of the tide. Surely she could will her grandmother to breathe. Her desperate wanting would be enough to keep her grandmother alive.

Her grandmother woke up. "Did the maid press my dress?" she asked.

"Perfectly," Lee said. "Beautifully."

"In London. In Paris, when I appear childish, jealous . . ."

"Never!"

"When I act as though I fear you might steal the spotlight, take attention away from me . . ." She plucked at Lee's hand. She tapped the emerald. ". . . I want you to know it is only because I realize you really can. That you have the capacity."

"Nobody can . . ."

"Sometimes my behavior shames me. I want to say this. To tell you how like me you are. How proud I am."

"Oh, Grandmother," Lee cried. "Oh, Grandmother."

An orderly appeared at the door pushing a metal cart. Lee could smell chicken and cabbage and bleach.

"Room service," Lee said to her grandmother. And to the orderly, whispered, "Leave it. Let me."

"I'm not hungry," said her grandmother.

Lee lifted up plastic covers on thin soup flecked with scraps of chicken, canned peas, and dots of fat, on watery yogurt and quivering lipstick-red Jell-O and tapioca pudding the color of dirty snow. A separate plate held a sponge of white bread bordered in an orange crust. Her stomach turned. *Gruel.*

Next to these, on the brown melamine tray stood a small Dixie cup of vanilla ice cream with its tongue depressor wooden spoon. "But wait till you see what we've got," Lee said. "Sweetbreads. Oysters. Brains. All your favorites. And for dessert." She stopped. "Mousse *à la crème* and Grand Marnier."

"*A la crème*," her grandmother said. "The Hotel Lutèce knows how to do it right."

Lee thought of her baby about to be born. Of her swollen heavy breasts. Of their network of veins and capillaries and ducts primed for the milk to rush in. She thought of mother birds. Of fat little worms. Of baby birds in their nest, their expectant beaks agape and reaching out.

"Open wide," she said.

Tenderly she spooned ice cream into her grandmother's open, waiting mouth.

"Shall I spend the night?" she asked the nurses. The doctor. She pointed to the empty bed.

The doctor and the nurses pointed to her stomach. "You'll be more comfortable at home. Besides, we may have to use the other bed."

"But when she wakes up?"

"We'll give her something to help her sleep. If there's a change, if we need you, leave us the number of your telephone."

Back in Marguerite's apartment, Lee lay down on Marguerite's bed and tried to sleep. Her head swam. Her baby swam. She wrapped her arms around the mound of her stomach. My life raft, she thought, without this I would surely drown. "There. There," she said to her baby. Her little Marguerite. *It'll be a girl*, she told her grandmother. *We'll name her after you*. How could it be otherwise? After all, she'd promised her grandmother. "Marguerite Emery. Marguerite Emery," she practiced over and over, until, like scales, like French verbs, like Latin declensions, she had mastered it.

But little Marguerite Emery would not be the only one, she vowed. Just the first of many. The beginning of a long line. She catalogued the books of her childhood: *The Five Little Peppers; Little Women; Life with Father; The Boxcar Children; The Lion, the Witch, and the Wardrobe; Little House on the Prairie.* Families awash in brothers and sisters. Even the Hardy Boys and the Bobbsey Twins came in pairs. It was terrible to be an only child. To be the only child of parents. Of grandparents. To be left alone to go through their underwear. To sift through their books and their clothes. Sort through their papers and their letters. Handle their toothbrushes and combs and perfume bottles and razor blades. Read their grocery lists, their memo pads. To run your hands over everything they had touched. And would touch no longer. So that everything you touch burns into your fingertips the brand of a searing memory.

To be left alone to do this alone.

To be left alone.

In time, though, the memory of Marguerite, as with her parents, would bring comfort, not just terrible pain, Lee hoped. When she'd tell stories about them, show her parents' bird books, their binoculars, Marguerite's photographs, this ring now on her finger, they would come to life. *This was theirs, they wore this, held this, they live on.*

She was not alone, she told herself, even if right now she felt more alone than she had ever felt in her whole life. She had Homestead, her community, her friends. She had little Marguerite. She had Ben.

Ben. She reached for her grandmother's phone. It was a copy of a French antique. Ivory colored with gilt trim. A rotary dial topping gold Roman numerals. A high neck on which the receiver lay suspended as on a pedestal. When she lifted the receiver, she could smell her grandmother's perfume. And there, on the bottom against the enamel, she spotted a slash of her grandmother's crimson lipstick, a kiss of it.

How could Marguerite die!

"We're having a terrible storm," announced Ben. "They're predicting four feet. What's it doing there?"

Lee looked between Marguerite's red velvet draperies into a black night. She stared at the glowing rectangles cut into the building across the way. In one window, a family sat around a table. In another, three heads topped a sofa in front of a TV. The next window over, two lovers seemed to embrace. Beneath them, four ladies were playing cards. She thought of *Rear Window*. Where, framed inside these panes, one man would be murdering his wife and, on the floor below, a woman would be sobbing over a solitary glass of wine. Lee peered toward the haze of a street lamp. "It was snowing earlier. A dusting. But it's doing nothing now," she said.

"And you? How are you? How's Marguerite?"

"Oh, Ben," Lee sobbed. She cried. She wept. The baby kicked. Lee's nose ran. Her eyes overflowed. And when she daubed at the tear-drenched phone, she saw she'd wiped away Marguerite's lipstick trace.

"Honey. Honey," Ben said. "I could kick myself. You

shouldn't have to go through this alone. And now, with this weather, I'll never get out."

Lee had a sudden vision of herself stranded here for weeks on end shuttling between hospital and hotel. Her belly swelling. Her grandmother shrinking. And Ben snowbound in Maine. The two of them separated by a wall of snow. An ocean of snow. An ocean which had once, when it mattered, divided Simon from her. Yet, even something so vast as an ocean was nothing compared to what will separate her and her grandmother. She held out her hand. Light from the lamp bounced off the ring. She studied the stone. It had been faceted to look bottomless. On certain days, at certain hours, she had seen the ocean turn this very green.

Ben lowered his voice. "How long?" he whispered.

"A week. Weeks. She has such an astonishing will." She started to cry again. "What am I going to do?"

Ever practical, Ben suggested, "You can start by packing up. Not the big stuff. We'll hire someone to do that. But the papers, photographs. You can decide what you want to keep and what to throw away."

Not that, that's not what I meant, Lee wanted to scream, can't you see? She took some breaths. Though perhaps Ben was right: a small discrete task might distract her, might take away her sense of helplessness.

"It sounds like you'll be there for a while. Marguerite will not go gently. As soon as the weather clears, I'll take the first plane out. I don't want you to lift anything. I don't want you to tackle anything the least bit heavy."

"Heavy like death?"

"That's not . . ."

"I know."

"Oh, Lee," he said.

"I know."

"Take good care of my baby."

"Which one?"

Lee slipped on her grandmother's cashmere robe. She knotted two sashes together to make a tie even though the satin-bound edges still gaped a good two feet. She slid her toes into a pair of her grandmother's backless satin mules.

In the living room, she reached into the big crystal vase of matchbooks on her grandmother's mantelpiece: The Stork Club, Copacabana, The Latin Quarter, The Dubonnet, El Morocco, Toots Shor, Café Society Uptown, Café Society Downtown. All in Manhattan. All long gone. Did she keep another collection of European bistro souvenirs? Lee picked up the matchbook from the Dubonnet. She lit a fire. She put a Cole Porter album on her grandmother's turntable. *Ev'ry time we say goodbye I die a little. Ev'ry time we say goodbye I wonder why a little. Why the gods above me, who must be in the know, think so little of me, they allow you to go.*

She decided to start with the drawers in her grandmother's desk. *When you're near there's such an air of Spring about it. I can hear a lark somewhere begin to sing about it.*

Lee began to sift through old newspaper clippings. She made two piles. One to save. One to discard. She mounded recipes. Theater reviews. Wedding notices. Obituaries. All yellowing, and ripped at the folds. Names and faces she'd never heard of, didn't recognize. She tossed out old bills and receipts. *Milliner's, twenty dollars, French bonnet with ermine trim*, one read. She threw away *Playbills* and concert pro-grams. A Things-to-Do pad: *restring pearls, repair clock, shoes resoled, Sam's pants cuffed, chestnut puree* was scribbled across the first page. Is this what a life comes down to, she won-dered, bits of paper?

And yet biographers construct whole lives from bits of paper. For example, Ben's Nathaniel treasure hunts where he'd unearthed not only the diary, but also letters, bills of lading, receipts, old wills and tax records, entries in household and church registers. With these, along with charts and family trees and maps, he'd drawn a timeline of Nathaniel's life, which marched around his study wall like the border they'd painted on the baby's room. "My object is to know the man and his era completely. To know him as well as I know you, my own wife," he'd told Lee.

"How can anyone know anybody?" Lee had asked.

A silly question, Ben's look had implied. "It's the work of the biographer. And of course," he instructed, "it's the work of a husband to know his own wife."

Now Lee divided her grandmother's papers into what was important and what was not. How could she tell? How could anyone know what was important to somebody else? She'd kept things from Ben. Hidden away parts of herself. And not just the obvious things that would trouble him. But bits of herself kept just for herself, kept *to* herself. My life's an open book, people will say. Yet what mere book can con-tain a life? Even with Ben's methodical historian's approach—erecting the structure brick by brick, scaling the peak foot over foot—there will be holes. Who can read what's between the lines or hear what's left unsaid? Who can parse the undocumented, unmapped heart? *Especially* the person whose heart it is.

Lee picked up one of her grandmother's old visiting cards. Under Marguerite's engraved name, her grandmother had written *I wish* in her curlicued Old World script. At the deckled edge of the card, the *h* trailed off. What did her grandmother wish?

What secrets might Ben uncover about his utterly known, utterly knowable wife?

And . . .

She stopped.

What secrets might she uncover about the husband she had practically grown up with?

From the back of the drawer, buried under an avalanche of canceled checks and bank statements, Lee pulled out two fat packets of letters, each tied with a fraying blue satin ribbon. Love letters. How many times had she seen this old saw of a stage prop at the opera or the theater or on a movie screen? Here they were: love letters found under a pillow or in a drawer, found in the second act only to cause havoc in the third.

She placed the two packets onto her lap. One pile contained letters from her grandfather to her grandmother. *Samuel Rybier* in bold cursive topped the upper-left-hand corner of every envelope. Underneath were printed the names and addresses of hotels all over the United States, all over the world. These were the letters he had written to her grandmother while traveling. To the house on Evergreen Road. To the Hotel Canterbury. A few to European cities care of American Express. Had he tucked them away in his briefcase, the one that clasped with the alligator's head, until he'd found a convenient postal box?

She picked up the other packet. She untied the ribbon. She fanned out the letters. The envelopes were both thin and thick. Blue and ivory. Gray and white. Different handwriting. Different postmarks. But no return address. Several postmarks were stamped Maine. From that pillar of the Homestead community, the banker Hitchinson? Others came from France, England, Switzerland, and Austria. Traveling men like her grandfather? Or had her grandmother a chicken in every pot and a lover in every port?

She could open all these letters and learn about her grandparents' marriage, about her grandmother's lovers. There might be cautionary lessons here for how Lee should live her life. It would be so easy to pull out these folded pages. Right there on the desktop she saw her grandmother's letter opener. A sharp blade glinted from its handle of silver and malachite. Ben would have grabbed it. He would have speared such grist for the biographer's mill the way he'd extract a lobster's meat from a lobster's claw.

Lee lifted an envelope up to the lamp. She could make out the word *darling*. She could make out the word *love*. She held up another, a white business-size envelope from her grandfather's pile. She turned it around. *My most adored wife* was the salutation. *Your loving husband* was the close. Had her grandmother reached the same conclusion as Elisabeth Kraus about grown-up, enduring love? Would her grandmother have run off with her first *amour* if she'd spotted him two decades later at the Hotel Lutèce? Probably not, since she had stayed with Samuel Rybier until the moment he died. And never married after that. Would these letters explain why?

Someday Lee might want to write her own book about her grandmother. Their trips together. Their special relationship. She remembered what Ben had said about the biographer's need to know absolutely everything. In such a case, you could defend prying as scholarship. Lee pulled out a bunch of letters postmarked London. Carefully, she withdrew one of them. She cast her eyes to the bottom of the page.

Oh, no.

Could it be?

It couldn't.

She read through to the end.

But it was.

The letter was short. One page. In a scrawling hand, splattered with ink the writer hadn't stopped to blot, were these words:

My dearest Marguerite,

I think there is no choice but for you to leave Sam and me to leave Hermione. It is to our credit that we are both fond of our spouses and would never wish to cause them harm. Furthermore, not only do we both adore our children, your Violet, my Simon and Fiona, but also we take our responsibilities to them seriously indeed. Leaving wrecked lives behind in the wake of our selfishness would be beyond comprehension to either of us. In the ordinary scheme of things such actions would be unthinkable. But our love is not ordinary and thus compels extraordinary measures. It

*will take only one word from you, my darling, to give us
world enough and time.*

> *While I await your answer,
> I pledge, as ever, eternal love,
> Alistair*

Lee dropped the letter. She lowered her head to her hands. She felt dizzy. Reeling from a blow. So her grandmother had been having an affair with Simon's father. Had they had their own tryst while she and Simon were locked inside the gates of Hyde Park? This would explain so many things: especially her grandmother's promotion of Simon as suitor. Lee summoned up Alistair Abernathy. His dapper mustache. His English pinstripes. His paisley pocket handkerchief. The disparity in age hadn't been that great if you considered Marguerite as a young grandmother, Alistair as an old father.

I married him. I married Simon, she had lied to her grandmother. Hoping to please her. Knowing this was what Marguerite had wanted for Lee.

But now, taking into account Alistair's letter, Lee wondered if marrying Simon to her granddaughter was only what Marguerite had wanted for herself.

She picked the letter up. She read it again.

The possibility that her grandmother was advocating Simon out of self-interest seemed almost comforting. Had she wanted Lee to marry Simon to maintain her own tie to his father? Or to marry Simon to clinch a decision she had regretted not making herself?

She didn't want to know any more. She wanted to discard

the troubling evidence and keep the pretty truth. If she wrote about her grandmother, she'd write with imperfect knowledge from her own selective point of view. She put the letters back into their separate stacks. She tied the ribbons back into tight little bows. She added her grandfather's packet to the pile to be saved.

And threw the letters from her grandmother's lovers into the fire.

She watched the logs crackle and burn. She watched other men's words crumple into ash. She watched the men from her grandmother's past, the man from her own, flame and fade away.

The phone rang just before six. "It's about your grandmother. You'd better come to the hospital."

She threw clothes on top of her Hannibal Hamlin T-shirt. She didn't comb her hair. She didn't brush her teeth.

The taxi slid and skidded over a fresh layer of heavy wet snow. Lee clutched her stomach. The baby dived and kicked. She can sense my fear, she thought, and willed herself to be calm.

It didn't work. "Can't you go faster?" she implored the cabdriver, Vishnu Kapoor, Hackney No. 111468121472. A plastic Ganeesh hung from the mirror along with some silver bells. She could smell fresh sandalwood and stale pizza. "Can't you step on it?"

"For this weather, hurrying is not being safe." In the rearview mirror she saw a gold tooth glint through a drooping black mustache. "You are wanting maternity?" Vishnu Kapoor asked.

"Not yet." Lee thought of her wedding which had followed so closely on the funeral of her parents. She pictured the maternity ward at the Homestead hospital she and Ben had visited. The smiling nurses. The proud new parents. The balloons and flowers and colored Polaroids. Rainbows arced along the hospital walls. Happy faces grinned out from the Formica of the nurses' station. The nurses' uniforms were pink and blue, polka-dotted and plaid. The birthing rooms sported wallpaper and flowered bedspreads and framed prints of pastoral landscapes and ecstatic children building sand castles and jumping rope.

Lee summoned up the marble and gilt of a grand hotel suite. The festooned nest of a bowerbird. A hall of sunny, cheerful maternity rooms. She thought of her grandmother's green-curtained bed in the geriatric wing. The dun-colored walls and scrubbed linoleum tiles. Could there be a more unlikely, more unsuitable place for her grandmother?

By the time she arrived, her grandmother wasn't where she was supposed to be. The green curtain was drawn open. The bed was stripped. In the other bed near the window lay a woman watching *Good Morning America*. Filling the TV screen stood a man with a parrot on his arm. "Polly want a cracker," the parrot squawked. "Welcome to New York." With a great flap of feathers, the parrot flew into the air and settled on the anchorman's stylishly side-parted head. "I love New York," the parrot croaked.

"Look at dat boid," marveled the woman from the bed.

In the visitors' lounge, the nurse held Lee's hand. Old *Good Housekeeping*s crowded the tables. Children's drawings covered the wall: Lee studied a stick figure family by Marnie, age 6; a Wonder Woman, by Alexandra R., age 12; three big butterflies circling a robin digging a worm, by Bugs Jones, age 5½. On a bookcase lay two Styrofoam coffee cups rimmed with lipstick blots. Through the long windows Lee could see the East River roll vast and gray. A tanker passed. Then a rusted-out tug.

"It was peaceful. There wasn't any pain," the nurse said. "I sat with her. I held her hand."

"I should have been here," Lee said. "*I* should have been holding her hand."

"We didn't think it would happen this soon."

"I should have been here," Lee repeated. "Should have . . ."

"At the end, she wouldn't have wanted it."

Lee sat up. "What do you mean? I'm her granddaughter."

The nurse stroked Lee's fingers. Her hand was soft and white. She had a motherly shelf of a chest and high Irish color in her cheeks. Her name was Greta. Her kind blue eyes must have seen everything.

"I've seen everything," Greta said. "And sat with many patients when they passed. If you'd been there with her, your grandmother wouldn't have been able to let go."

"And that's a good thing? She would have lived longer if I'd been at her side."

"No. She was ready. 'I've said my good-byes,' she declared. 'I want my granddaughter to remember me the way I was.'"

"She said that?"

"She said that."

They sat for a while. Lee looked out at the river. She watched the water ripple. She watched the snow fall. It was falling onto the dark waves. Falling onto the window ledge. If it was falling here, it must be falling in Maine. Burying the Homestead house. She felt like a figure trapped in a snow dome, rattled, shaken, turned upside down. She thought of the letters she had burned in Marguerite's fireplace. She thought of the bowerbird in its orchid-decorated nest. The last night of Marguerite's life she had spent in Marguerite's bed.

"When's the baby due?" Greta asked.

"A couple of months."

"Excuse me." A woman poked her head into the lounge. She was wearing a comical knitted wool hat with a yellow pom-pom. The pom-pom bounced. "My husband misplaced his glasses. Where can I find Lost and Found?"

Greta pointed. "On the left. Next to the vending machines." She turned to Lee. "Funny, isn't it?"

"Funny?"

Greta nodded. "Life." She placed her hand on Lee's stomach. "Something's lost. And something's found." She paused. "Your grandmother was quite a dame."

"You're telling me?"

Greta smiled. Her voice was gentle. "Guess what her last words were?"

"Oh, God. I couldn't even begin . . ." Lee rubbed at her eyes.

Greta fished a piece of paper out of the pocket of her nylon uniform. "I wrote it down." She held the paper up to the window. Behind it, the East River churned. The snow fell. The paper looked like a prescription form bearing two crooked penciled lines. Greta smoothed it out. She chuckled. Then she read: "Dying's so boring. Frankly, I've never been so bored in my whole, entire life."

Eight

"Where will the funeral be?" the social worker on the geriatric wing had asked. "Where is her home?"

"I'm not sure," Lee had said. "She was a citizen of the world."

The social worker had not been impressed. She had forms to fill out. She poised a ballpoint pen over a sheaf of them. In the waiting room other families sat with paid-for cemetery plots and the names of funeral directors in their neighborhoods. "Where are her loved ones buried?"

Lee stared at the giant economy box of tissues on the social worker's desk. At dusty silk flowers. At a brass clip in the shape of a hand with a rhinestone missing from its ring. "She hated Maine," she said.

"My favorite place on earth," the social worker gushed. "We rent a cabin every summer on Sebago Lake. Oh, those blueberries. That corn. The lobsters. The crunch of pine needles underfoot. Let alone the natives with their a-yahs and he-ahs and they-ahs."

Lee looked out at the East River. On a file cabinet stood a coffee mug lettered with the slogan *I Love New York*. "It might as well be New York," she said.

On the day of her grandmother's funeral, it had snowed and snowed. *Storm of the Century* shouted the tabloids with expected hyperbole that nevertheless contained a shred of truth.

"Don't even bother," Lee had said to Ben. The airports were shut down. Even the once-a-day Greyhound—ten hours to the city—was indefinitely postponed. *Thank God Marguerite didn't live to see her funeral* kept running through Lee's head.

In the small side chapel of the funeral home, the black-suited professionals outnumbered the mourners: Lee, two Hotel Canterbury bellboys (the third, Louie, lived in Yonkers outside the subway's reach), and a distinguished man with a cane and fur-collared coat. No crowd, no food, no drink, no music. *Marguerite would have died if she already hadn't*, thought Lee. The minister, whom the funeral home supplied for the unaffiliated, recited the Lord's Prayer. He pronounced Marguerite's name as Marjy-right. Though Lee wanted to cry, it was all she could do not to laugh. She felt ridiculous in her navy maternity dress with its pilgrim collar. She felt knocked off balance by this pared-down good-bye to a baroque life. When she stood at the lectern, her stomach pushed against the wobbly three-footed stand.

She opened her grandmother's copy of Edna St. Vincent Millay. *For my darling Marguerite from your Sammy* scrawled across the frontispiece. Lee cleared her throat. Then read:

"My candle burns at both ends;

It will not last the night;

But ah, my foes, and oh, my friends—

It gives a lovely light!"

Just as she took her seat again, the man in the fur-collared coat slipped out the door. He hadn't signed the register.

In the office, furnished in low, soothingly shaded lamps, ebonized mahogany, neutral carpets, and sailing prints, she wrote out a check and accepted the small black urn. The funeral director handed her a plastic bag from Bloomingdale's. "To protect your loved one," he explained, "from the inclement weather." He shook his head. He pointed his hand toward the darkened, draped window. "Though our clients often prefer it, a sunny day can seem, under the circumstances, a bit of a slap in the face."

By the time she'd accepted yet more professional condolences and buttoned herself into her winter layers, everyone had left. Two Charles Addams–faced men opened the heavy oak doors and offered to hail her a cab. "I'll walk. It's just a few blocks," she said.

Four eyes fixed on her stomach. "Are you sure?" one man asked.

Only three-quarters of the way down the first block, however, she was exhausted from sloshing through unshoveled snow, from pitching into the wind like a figurehead on a ship's prow. Along the avenue, little Hondas and Toyotas and Subarus—brands her grandmother wouldn't

258 • *Mameve Medwed*

recognize—without snow tires, without chains, were spinning and slipping like bumper cars. Infuriated drivers kept
their hands on the horn. Where were the snowplows?
Where was there room for snowplows? Suddenly she was
filled with warm thoughts for cold Maine. For its compe-
tence. She remembered snug nights of being lulled to sleep
by the rhythmic march of snowplows clearing the roads,
their lights sliding along her bedroom walls as they attended to the community's needs. She thought of her always
prepared neighbors with their shovels and picks, and planks,
and buckets of sand, and four-wheel drive.

In front of her, a woman teetered on high heels. She
leaned over to scoop up a yippy mop of a dog in a leopard-
spotted coat. A drift of snow covered her ankle and sank
into her shoe.

Lee ducked into a coffee shop. She slid into a booth a
young couple were just vacating. Their arms crossed their
backs and settled into the pockets of each other's coats. The
girl wore big red mittens that looked like something a
mother had knit.

Lee placed the Bloomingdale's bag with Marguerite
across from her. "Are you alone?" the waitress asked. "Are
you expecting somebody?"

Not alone. Not expecting anyone, Lee wanted to say. She
ordered a hot chocolate. Then called the waitress back to
add an éclair.

"Normally we wouldn't let one person take a whole
booth," the waitress smiled, "but I see there are two of
you."

Lee sat up, startled. She stared across the salt and pepper, the Sweet'N Lows, at the bag. She looked at its handle, which clipped together with an arc of plastic knobs set into little holes. How could the waitress know?

"When's it due?" asked the waitress.

Of course. Lee leaned back. The room was crowded. It hummed with talk. With laughter. It smelled of wet wool. Of strong coffee. "Bridge Over Troubled Water" wailed from the loudspeakers set into the ceiling. A Christmas wreath hung in the window even though it was the end of February. Umbrellas, hopeless against snow, dripped puddles onto the buckling floor.

"I've got two little ones at home myself," the waitress confided. "I miss them like the dickens when I'm away from them." She walked toward the kitchen.

"I'll miss you like the dickens," Lee whispered to Marguerite.

The hot chocolate arrived with a Taj Mahal dome of whipped cream. A wreath of it surrounded the éclair. "I brought you extra." The waitress winked. "I know what it's like to eat for two."

Lee spooned a cloud of cream into her mouth. *Sail on silver girl. Sail on by. Your time has come to shine. All your dreams are on their way*, sang Paul Simon. Or was it Garfunkel? She sloshed the cream on her tongue and felt oddly comforted.

In the middle of the night she woke up in Marguerite's bed. She'd been dreaming of snow, and yellow hats, and an office of Lost and Found down a long corridor next to a vending machine. She checked her watch. It was three in the morning.

She clutched Marguerite's horseshoe-shaped neck pillow to her chest. She smelled her grandmother's perfume.

What was the matter?

What was wrong?

It came to her.

She had left Marguerite in a small black urn in a large plastic bag on a red vinyl seat in a Formica booth in a Manhattan coffee shop.

Where the coffee was strong.

The chocolate rich.

The éclairs fresh,

And served with extra cream.

Sail on silver girl . . .

She never went back for her. She could have called the restaurant. Could have asked for Lost and Found. But what would she say? She practiced several versions of *I lost my grandmother. I misplaced her. I left her ashes in the third booth from the door.* Then gave up. It was as good a place as any, she told herself. A lively coffee shop in a highfalutin neighborhood near Gramercy Park. Near the private garden to which only the abutters held keys. Near the Greek Revival building that housed the Arts Club where Marguerite had once heard Edna St. Vincent Millay read. And who had asked for the name of the milliner responsible for Marguerite's hat trimmed with ostrich feathers and marcasite stars.

Three months to the day Marguerite died, Marguerite's great-grandchild was born. The baby Lee was convinced would come screaming and kicking into this world as Little

Marguerite Rybier Emery turned out to be John Henry Emery.

Who arrived fast requiring no forceps and no drugs. Who departed the womb at the considerate and convenient hour of six in the evening on a clear and balmy day in May. Who announced his entry into Homestead, Maine, with a modest hiccup and a bawdy squeal.

"It's a boy," declared Dr. Solomon.

"We have a son!" exclaimed Ben.

"I don't believe it," cried Lee. And it was only when she inspected the acorn of a penis from all possible angles that she began to realize the limits of her grandmother's power.

She looked around the birthing room at the sunny wall-paper, the bright potted plants. Calico curtains framed the windows. A graduated row of wooden duck decoys rested on a shelf. She and Ben had stayed in a room like this once. In a shingled country inn along the coast where wicker rockers lined the porch and birdbaths marked the graveled paths. All that was missing here was the sampler stitched *Home Sweet Home.*

At the foot of her bed, after a Polaroid pause to capture the miracle of birth, Dr. Solomon was now going about his business sewing her up. For him, it was a day like any other, all in a day's work.

Not for Lee. The new mother.

Not for the new father. Ben's grin stretched so far across his face it looked as if the ends were stitched to his ears. Like the obstetrician, Ben had donned a green surgical uni-form. But unlike Dr. Solomon, whose scrubs covered a striped turtleneck and jeans, Ben seemed to be wearing nothing underneath. His curly chest hair filled the deep V of the neck. His arms were bare; his legs stuck out like an adolescent's below the too-short cuffs; his feet slapped around in paper slippers. He had on no socks. "Where are your clothes?" Lee whispered.

Ben kneaded her shoulders with the technique he'd perfected in Lamaze. "I was worried about germs; didn't want to contaminate the OR," he confided.

A concern that seemed to have eluded her doctor, who was now plunging his hands into places no man had gone before.

Lee looked at the lollipops Ben had brought and the bowl of shaved ice, neither of which they'd needed to use. She felt a sharp tugging between her legs. "Ouch," she yelled.

Dr. Solomon poked his head over the top of the draped sheets. With his Julius Caesar bangs and aquiline nose, he could have been a togaed Roman bust. "It's about time," he grinned. "I wouldn't feel as if I'd done my job if I didn't hear a complaint."

"No complaints from this quarter," said Ben. "Everything happened so fast and so smoothly, I had no job at all."

"Your job has just begun." The nurse held up John Henry Emery, whose eyes had been cleared, skin swabbed, belly button stapled, now wrapped in a bright blue blanket, with a small, yellow knitted cap on his head. "Here's your bundle of joy," she said. She put him into Ben's arms.

Ben held his child aloft. "Lee?"

"You first."

Ben reached for the baby's hand. The baby wrapped its rosy, starfish fingers around Ben's thumb. Ben cupped the baby's head against his chest. "My son. My son," he said.

Lee was sure that she had never witnessed a more delicate, more tender scene. Was there, she wondered, a male equivalent of the word Madonna? She would have to ask somebody in Italian studies or Renaissance history. Ben sang to the baby in tones so dulcet that it wasn't until seven bars had passed that she realized he was crooning the Hannibal Hamlin College marching song.

Later that night, holding Johnny at her breast, with a beaming Ben at her side, she knew that this was a moment of perfect happiness. She wanted to freeze it into the still frame of a photograph. She wanted to trap the three of them under a bell jar so that, like Ben's surgical uniform, nothing from the outside world could contaminate them. Birth without death; love without compromise, untainted by *what if.* Only this green pasture and no others. Only here and now.

She touched the baby's silly yellow hat. What had Marguerite's nurse—Greta—said? *Something's lost and something's found.*

At last, after so much loss, she had found—had *founded*— a family. She looked across Ben's shoulder and out the window at the clear black sky. She knew there were stars up there, whole constellations visible on a night like tonight. A night in Maine. If she were outside, she could point out Orion, Cassiopeia. If she were outside, she could smell pine, tilled earth, new flowers. She was home.

At home Lee flips through the *Homestead Herald.* The city council is battling a proposed budget cut. A missing child has turned up at his grandmother's. The funeral for a former police chief will be held at noon today. She puts the paper down. Funerals, she thinks. Marguerite's. Her parents'. Now that she and Ben are middle-aged—middle age! How did it happen?—she can see funerals piling on funerals. She can see people disappear like Alice down the rabbit hole. She considers Simon's hole in the heart. His vanishing. She pictures Marguerite at the center of Violet and Henry's funeral and nearly offstage at her own. Amazing how someone larger than life can be reduced to a fistful of ashes; these toted around in a bag you'd use to cart home your half dozen pairs of on-sale pantyhose. She thinks of scattered ashes. Of scattered children.

Yesterday she'd finally reached Timmy after a phone tag marathon of calls and messages left with friends and friends of friends.

"I'm already late for a lecture, Mom," Timmy said sounding out of breath. His digs at Oxford, Lee knew, were under the sloping mansard roof at the top of five steep flights. Not that you could usually find him there.

"I won't keep you," she said, "just want to tell you the good news. We'll be in England June tenth. We'll come to Oxford of course. Take you and your friends out. You can give us the tour. It'll be so great . . ."

"Mom." Timmy's voice was cautious and gentle, her voice when she had to deliver bad news, the same modulated voice she had used, in those last years, with Marguerite. "Mom, I'm so sorry. But I've already made plans to go to New Zealand with a couple of kids from the college here."

At dinner, when she told Ben, he'd reached across the table and took her hand. "They're out in the world, Lee. At home in the world."

"Which leaves just you and me, kid," she said, "sailing together into old age. Just the two of us."

Ben squeezed her fingers. "And Nathaniel. Nathaniel makes three."

Now Lee thinks about her three children. Once, in the library with Maggie, who as a toddler claimed an unruly crop of red curls, a freckled nose, green eyes, and Marguerite's thick lashes, a woman leaned over and tousled Maggie's hair. She was checking out a series of books whose covers bore blondes with heaving bosoms and jutting-jawed men with beards and poet's shirts. "Isn't she just precious," the woman said. She put her books on the counter. Her knees creaked as she scooched down to meet Maggie's gaze. "Stay the way you are," she ordered. "Don't you dare grow up."

If only, Lee wishes now. All those good-byes. All those losses. From the minute the bundle of joy is placed in its parents' arms, the separations start. Scenes come to her like slides jerking through a recalcitrant projector, clicking out of focus, blurred, upside down, cut off, not fully settled into their frames: Johnny at cooperative nursery school and she, volunteering so often at the water table, the easel, the swing set, that the teacher had to suggest—gently—that perhaps another parent might have a turn. The howling child in the baby-sitter's arms; the mother frozen to the threshold of the door. The tears on both sides over the four nights in Portland learning basketball skills.

Even when they took Johnny to Freshman Week at Hannibal Hamlin College—where she and Ben had offices, where he could walk the few blocks home to do his laundry, raid the family refrigerator, use his father's toolbox and his mother's microwave—they might as well have been abandoning him to a dormitory room on the opposite coast. When the last CD had been put in its rack, when the last pair of socks were matched and balled inside the drawer, when the new extra-long sheets had been tucked into the mattress and the Red Sox poster tacked up, Johnny had flung his arms around both of them. He stood on the fire escape outside his room while they drove off. Crestfallen, Lee had watched him in the rearview mirror, her continually waving boy, diminishing into an anguished speck as his parents headed for the home he'd just left.

Yet, she marvels, Johnny, the child most attached to home, is the one farthest away. She remembers his shyness, the way he hated to stand out. When he confessed, years later, how embarrassed he was about the sandwiches Ben made for his junior high lunch, she had felt awful for both of them. Ben's sandwiches were as much labor-intensive works of art as works of love; he used to cut them like jigsaw puzzle pieces that fit together with notches and triangles and odd loops and curves. "No other kid will have a sandwich like this," Ben would boast.

"Why didn't you say something?" Lee had asked her mortified son.

"And hurt Dad's feelings?"

With such a history, who would ever have predicted that he'd love Japan? His letters are full of food she wouldn't eat, communal baths she'd never unwrap her towel for. He's learning Japanese, studying kendo and karate. Isn't it funny, he writes, that nowhere is a Westerner more foreign, and nowhere do I feel more at home. Lee suspects that his happiness, his ease in the world, has much to do with Noriko. Love knocks down barriers—of emotions, of language, of geography.

The letting go had been easier with Timmy. But only just. She still has the letters he'd written from summer camp. Short sentences about swimming and archery and canoes. Letters she knew were required to earn the dangling carrots of swimming and archery and canoes. Yet the way he had signed them—with as many words for love as the Eskimos had for snow: I cherish you. I bestow my affections. I offer my heart. I press my suit. I bear warm feelings. I send my caresses—raised alarms. Incipient glossolalia? Normal separation anxiety turning pathological? She and Ben had been puzzled and worried. Until they'd realized that they'd packed the thesaurus they'd given him for his tenth birthday into his brand-new camper's trunk.

After Timmy, Maggie had arrived with a vengeance. In the car, Lee had held her legs together. Without a single push from her mother, Maggie had propelled herself out into the world and onto the gurney in the corridor outside the delivery room. The little girl Marguerite was sure Lee'd have. At last. The child most like her namesake. Independent. Feisty. Who from the start was dressing up her footed pajamas with rhinestones and bits of lace. Who preferred waving good-bye to nodding hello. Who, even if she was here, was not.

Still, who her children are now, where they are now, is what she wants for them. What any parent wants for his or her child. All the milestones, the baby steps, the temporary good-byes are rites of passage on the way to the giant step of independence. If a child is at home in the world, Japan, New Zealand, Maine, the front yard, the next street, then the parent has done a good job. With her own parents, she hadn't said good-bye. The separation did not evolve in the natural order of things but sliced her world apart. Perhaps this is why she now clings, why she hangs on to Ben, finds it so hard to let go. To let go of children, husband, parents, grandparents.

To let go of old loves . . .

Her ticket to England lies in the bowl on the dining table. When she passes it, she feels compelled to reach in and touch it. How many times has she read her flight information, her seat number, her name? She, who once mocked Ben's obsessions about losing his life's work, can now, in the light of her own compulsive neurosis, accept this as a reasonable anxiety.

She opens the ticket. She's still sitting on the aisle in Seat 26C; the plane still departs on June 9 at 7:15 P.M. and is nonsmoking. For mad cow reasons and hoof-and-mouth reasons, she's specified vegetarian. She winces at the memory of all the Wimpys they ate in England fifteen years ago. Can good behavior in the present ever make up for lapses in the past? Will a former bad choice spoil a present-day compromise?

Lee grabs her pocketbook. She pulls out her keys. Because it's been fifteen years since she's been abroad, she needs a new passport. Not for her the Jiffy Photos While U Wait next to the Awash And Adry Laundromat, the building which also houses the tattoo parlor, Hiram Cross Watch-maker, and alas, the Pine Tree Press, generator of literary and dog-related humiliations. It's not that she's avoiding Beatrice. Who at any rate is avoiding her, refusing to answer her requests to reschedule a reading, neglecting to respond to her casual *By the way, what about the Friday literary event at Charlene's Golden Comb?*

No, she's not giving a wide berth to the Pine Tree Press because her book has commercially tanked. After all, she's far too mature to boycott a piece of geography, let alone the building that sits on it. She's simply choosing a real photographer who will take a contact sheet's worth of prints, who can touch up the sunbursts surrounding her eyes, and who knows how to adjust a light to sharpen the line of a chin.

But it's a passport photo, she can almost hear Ben say, *with a raised seal warping your face. They're supposed to be terrible.* In her middle age she's developing the vanity of Marguerite. Not that she could aspire to the face that launched a thousand suitors, that inspired Max Reinhardt, that drew out an elderly gentleman in a fur-collared coat on a cold winter's day, that set the Alistair Abernathys of this world to scribbling *darlings* and *beloveds* and *dearly adored.* Soon enough, Simon will confront the real Lee Emery. Minus the cosmetic enhancements and good lighting of Daniel Dussault and Son's Photographic Studio.

She went to school with the son. Marty Dussault. Has she gone to school with everyone in Homestead? Every policeman and florist and waitress? Lately, it seems that way. Marty has run the studio since his father died driving into a

moose on Route 201. In high school Marty took their senior photographs. Last year, he mounted a Lobstermen of
Maine exhibit at the library. He'd spent a week living on the
coast with a fishing family, going out on lobster boats, haul-
ing in traps. These faces, raw, weather-ravaged, life-ravaged,
are haunting. Nevertheless, such brutal honesty and naked-
ness are not what she wants. "Can you make me beautiful?
Gorgeous?" she'd asked when she called to set up the appointment.

"Piece of cake," Marty had replied.

She parks in the A&P lot, which borders the Dussault studio on one side and the city jail on the other. The high-
barred windows of the jail are just big enough to allow the
incarcerated a view of rolling shopping carts stuffed with a
month's supply of toilet paper and Frosted Flakes. Nailed
onto the side of the jail is a sign that students have tried to
steal—without success—since the founding of Homestead
High. *Please Don't Talk to the Inmates*, it warns.

The first thing Lee sees when she steps out of her car is
Beatrice talking to the inmates. One inmate in particular—
and she's pretty sure who that is. At the same time Beatrice's
holding a pad of paper and taking notes.

Should Lee duck behind the car? Weave through Chevys
and Fords in the alternate, circuitous path, inefficient but
inconspicuous, to Marty's studio?

Too late.

"Lee!" Beatrice screams. "Lee Emery!"

A woman holding a grocery bag and a toddler turns in

Beatrice's direction. A man with a six-pack of Budweiser hanging off each hand stares pointedly at the *Please Don't Talk to the Inmates* sign.

"Just the person I want to see," Beatrice says. "The *second* person," she amends. She grabs Lee's freshly pressed, photo-ready linen lapel. She tugs at it. She leans closer. She whispers in Lee's ear. "Will you stand guard?" she asks.

That Lee is more concerned with her memoir than the possibility that she might be doing something illegal is not to her credit, she realizes. "Can we discuss my book?" she suggests anyway. "Fair exchange?"

"In a second," agrees Beatrice. "Just watch out while I talk to Kenny. Please?"

Lee checks the time. "I've only got five minutes. I'm due at Marty Dussault's for a photograph." Lee doesn't add *passport*. Perhaps Beatrice will conclude she's posing for another book jacket. Lee Emery's not a one-book kind of gal, Beatrice will see, who took a single detour from her "real" career as Junior Year Abroad coordinator. She searches Beatrice's face for a flicker of newfound respect.

She doesn't find it. Beatrice squashes herself against the prison wall. Lee hears whispers, a pen flying across paper, pages flipping over fast like the calendar dates in old movies.

Lee stands feet apart, arms across her chest, rotating her head in the manner of Secret Service men guarding the president. Nobody seems the least interested in the illegal goings-on outside the A&P. People rattle carts; they carry bundles that they load into trunks and back seats. One driver opens his car door and shatters the mirror of the Jeep parked next to him. A couple of passersby nod approval as he tucks a note under the windshield. Nice law-abiding Maine citizens.

Except for Beatrice.

Except for her.

"Coast is clear," Lee whispers.

Beatrice and Kenny talk to each other in rushed snippets that Lee diplomatically tries to ignore: *Daddy, bail, awesome, original, lobsters, meter, husband, wife.* Finally, "Love you" rises into the air like the clash of cymbals that ends a symphony. Lee relaxes her vigilance. Beatrice scrambles to her side. "Thanks buckets," she says.

"It was nothing," Lee modestly disclaims. Should she take advantage of Beatrice's gratitude to ask about her book? "About—" she begins.

"About your book," Beatrice finishes.

"Just what I—"

Beatrice interrupts. "Now don't take this the wrong way. Don't expect the worst."

Lee expects the worst.

And gets it. "I've decided to change the focus of Pine Tree Press," Beatrice informs. "To go in a new direction." She clutches the pad of paper to her chest like both a shield and a baby who needs shielding. "I've decided to publish solely prison poetry."

Lee's mouth falls open.

Beatrice plows ahead. "Kenny let me see the light. He is so gifted. Brilliant. Publishing him—and his colleagues—will be an honor."

"*Colleagues?*" Lee stares at her. "*Ben* has colleagues, Beatrice. Kenny has—what? Fellow felons? A brotherhood of assault and batterers?"

Beatrice ignores her. She holds out her pad. "Shall I read you a sample? This is going to knock your socks off."

"I bet."

All sarcasm is lost on Beatrice. She smooths a page. She brushes a strand of hair out of her eyes. She clears her throat. "'Gas Station Blues,'" she intones. "'I pump the gas. I fill the tank. I'm in the tank. Filled with you. Point-blank. Bars on the window. Cap on the gas. Maine shits. The big house shits. It's little. You're little. Here's the riddle. Crime pays for my bread and water. For my gas. My ass. On, the fucking state. Too late.'" She holds the pad up like the flag that is hoisted over an Olympic athlete. "Yes!" she exclaims and thrusts her fist into the air.

"Well . . ." Lee starts.

"I knew you wouldn't appreciate it."

"Thanks a lot. This *poem*"—Lee draws quote marks into the air with her fingertips.—"is what's supplanting *me?*"

Beatrice turns the knife. "It's a generation thing." She pauses. "But I'm certain my decision is the right one. The socially responsible one." She looks at Lee.

Lee looks at the asphalt. She sees ground-out cigarette butts, a crumpled grocery list, something that glints like a ring but turns out to be a metal pull tab from a soda can.

"So, let's not beat around the bush," Beatrice goes on. "Your print run was seventy-five copies. We sold five."

Three kids and a husband, Lee thinks. And Simon. Simon makes five.

"So I'll sell you the remaining copies. At a discount. At ten dollars a book."

"Ten dollars a book? That's seven hundred dollars!" Lee exclaims. "Sounds like highway robbery." She stops. "Do highway robbers write poetry?" she asks.

"Or we can pulp them," Beatrice says.

"Pulp them?" A term that sounds lifted right out of Nathaniel Tarbell's labor relations along the Allagash.

Beatrice's face takes on the same beatific look of excitement as when she recited Kenny's "poem." "You should see how they do it," she exults. "It's the most amazing thing. There's this enormous sort of window fan with a conveyor belt. Stacks of books slide along it. The noise is phenomenal—whirring, munching. Then, ta da! Out the other end come bales of paper. Which we can sell to recycling companies."

"Someone should write a poem about this. Some death-row murderer," says Lee.

"Very funny. Be serious."

"I am serious." She considers. "So what do the recycling companies do with the books? Make toilet paper?"

Beatrice nods. "That. And other things," she says. "The lowest grade of paper . . ."

"Pine Tree Press paper?"

A question Beatrice neither acknowledges nor disputes. "The lowest grade," she continues, "is used for shipping material. Cardboard peanuts and the like. All ecological."

"So long as it's ecological." As far as Lee can see, she has two choices: her unselfish one is to save the planet; her selfish one, to clutter the cellar at the cost of seven hundred bucks. "I have to hurry," says Lee. "I'll let you know. Don't do anything," she cautions, taking the coward's nonfeminist way out, "until I've discussed it with Ben."

Marty is setting up when she arrives. "Come on in," he calls from the back. Nobody's in the waiting room. She casts a wistful glance at the neat stacks of *People*, of *Vogue*, of *GQ*. Not the usual fare strewing the tables in the waiting rooms of Homestead's offices. Where you expect to see tattered copies of *Down East*, *The Maine Times*, *Yankee*, *Family Circle* with the recipes torn out. On the cover of one magazine, she spots the portrait of a young Princess Margaret. The caption reads, *The Damages of Unfulfilled Love*.

Though she hardly needs to expand this particular horizon, she's tempted to spring for a copy herself. Not quite the companion piece to Ben's erudite journals of American history. She buys *The New York Review of Books*, which piles up like neglected homework while she devours the *People* of those lucky multitudes—neighbors, nonacademics, gossip mongers—who bravely subscribe.

She parts the chains of beads that separate the reception area from Marty's studio. Marty strikes a Charles Atlas pose in front of the blackout screen. He's wearing a Hawaiian shirt and parrot green shorts. "Wow! You look great," she exclaims. He's been to a tanning salon; he's been to the gym. "A regular Arnold Schwarzenegger."

He gives her a hug. She smells spicy cologne, feels the bulk of his muscles. In high school he was a slip of a thing, collar buttoned to the chin, pants hoisted up under his arms with the kind of city-best suspenders Aroostook County potato farmers clipped on for monthly trips to town.

He settles her onto a stool. He adjusts lights and lenses. He lowers and raises a tripod.

"It's been a long time," she says. It always amazes her that in such a small community, years can pass without your bumping into someone who lives a mile away from you. "I haven't seen you for an age. Since that exhibit at the library."

"I know," he says. He peers through a lens. "I suppose you haven't heard my news."

"What news?"

"Turn to the left," he instructs.

She turns to the left.

"Tilt your chin."

She tilts her chin.

"I've come out," he says.

For a minute she's puzzled. She who works at a college where memos about sensitivity to alternative lifestyles and personal choices appear with the regularity of February snow. Then she gets it. "Ahh," she says. And because such a response seems inadequate, adds, "How wonderful."

"Smile," he says.

"Do I have lipstick on my teeth?" she asks.

"You look fabulous. Say cheese. Say Velveeta."

"Cheese." The camera flashes. She blinks. "Was it hard?" she asks.

"Not compared to staying in," he says. "Sometimes what you think may be hard, making a big decision, making a huge move, dealing with your issues, turns out to be easier than being trapped in the old ways."

Under his brilliant choreography—"Here. Higher. Yes! Slow now. That's it!"—she tosses her head, bends her shoulders, smiles, pouts, faces the camera head-on, and from the side. "This is a little silly for a passport," she feels compelled to admit.

"Not at all. Nothing is more important than putting yourself in the best light. How you look, how you see yourself, how you present yourself has a lot to do with self-acceptance and self-esteem," he explains in the tone of the newly therapized. He tinkers with levers; he moves around silver reflectors and white panels. "In fact . . ." He stops. He holds each wrist. He flexes his fingers. "I've developed repetitive motion syndrome in my hands. From doing the same thing for so long. In the same old way." He bends a light. Then tips it to the side. "Talk about your wake-up call. You and I may be smack in the middle of middle age, but it's not over till it's over. We've still got plenty of time to change our life. To self-actualize."

"Do you have . . ."—she casts about for the right words—". . . a partner?" she asks.

He grins. "Not exactly. Not officially. But I have the hopes of one. Which is why I'm leaving. Leaving Maine."

"You're kidding," she says. "Where are you going?"

"Where else?" he says. "New York. The Big Apple. Gotham City. I've got a couple of contacts in fashion photography."

She looks around the walls. At the brides and grooms, graduates, babies, grandparents, soldiers and sailors, many of whose portraits she recognizes, many of whom she knows. There's her English teacher. Below him, her friend Sarah's Uncle Abe. Over there her parents' insurance agent, and the contractor who worked on the house. One whole wall is devoted to Marty's lobstermen. They pose eye to eye with their photographer. If they're not exactly a jury of his peers, they're expert witnesses as to where he belongs. "But Daniel Dussault and Son has been here from time immemorial," she protests.

"And wouldn't my father turn over in his grave, wouldn't he have a kitten if he knew?" He hesitates. "If he knew about me. About the business. Which, by the way, I'm selling. After all this time, it's time to move on."

Lee wants to lean back, to absorb this blow. Not so easy when you're perched on a stool. She swallows hard. "That's a lot to take in," she says.

"This town is just too boring, too small-minded. *So* not now. Even with the college right in the middle of it, it is utterly fifties. Just look at those people we went to high school with. Stuck in their boring, married lives."

"Like me?" she asks.

Lee heads for home. She turns on the radio, which is broadcasting a weekly program called *For the Birds*. It had been the orchestral accompaniment to her childhood; week after week her mother and father had tuned in, dumbfounded at the sightings of common grackles in the cemetery, white-winged crossbills ringing the standpipe. And what about those northern harriers in the vicinity of the dairy farm? A lot of heavy breathing over pileated woodpeckers and thick-billed murres. Normally, because of its association with her parents and because she prefers the twenty-four-hour news, she switches the station.

This time, something stops her.

The program's host is talking about wild parrots that have appeared in Brooklyn. In the Bronx. "Even in Chicago's Hyde Park," he says.

Hyde Park. A sign. Lee turns up the volume. She slows down the car.

From the announcer's professionally pedantic description, she learns that such birds, recognized by their bright green plumage and blue wing primary feathers, come from a species of tropical parrots originating in South America. Though Chicago boasts the harshest winter a tropical parrot could face, these birds have not only survived but thrived. They've developed city smarts. Considered pests at home, abroad they are extremely popular. "Which goes to show you," the announcer chuckles, "how birds—and *humans*—can act one way under certain circumstances, and completely differently under others."

After two minutes of fund-raising—*Pledge now and receive a* For the Birds *mug and a Sibley's guide*—comes an interview with Marilyn Koshland, a student at Brooklyn College, who has been studying a group of feral parrots living on a high wire—a Con Ed high wire—in the Bronx. "A spot of color in our bleak world," she exclaims. "These birds have family values," she emphasizes. "But, as you birders all know, birds are monogamous because of their commitment to their nest, not each other. Their nests are whole apartment buildings, condominiums. Probably more spacious than my own bathtub-in-the-kitchen Flatbush studio." She laughs.

The announcer laughs.

Lee smiles.

"I haven't figured it out yet," Marilyn Koshland goes on,

"but sometimes the breeding pairs are attended by a third parrot. What this means is going to form the basis for my next research."

"Sounds like best-seller material," says the announcer. He waits a beat. "What's smarter than a talking parrot?" the announcer asks.

"I haven't the slightest idea."

"A spelling bee."

"Ouch," says Marilyn Koshland. "But I have one for you. What figure is like a lost parrot?"

"A polygon," he supplies. "No bird joke can get by me." He stops. "Though seriously, folks." His voice fills with awe. "These are birds that stand out, that do not blend gently into their environment."

"High fliers," adds Marilyn Koshland. "It should be a lesson for all of us. We are more adaptable, have more options than we think. These are some birds."

Lee turns off the radio. She thinks of Marty. Of Marguerite. These are some birds, she marvels.

Marguerite was one of a kind. She walked the high wire. She performed the perfect balancing act. And never fell.

Until she had the nerve to die.

Lee stops at a light. On the corner is the Abraham Lincoln school. Across from it, All Souls' Church. Next to that, the Moose Lake Bank and Trust.

But Marguerite had a safety net. She had Sam. She had a husband. A husband she kept for all of his life.

Lee's own husband is sitting at the kitchen table when she opens the back door. He's reading the paper. He's drinking a Coke from the can. He's sticking his fist into a box of Lucky Charms. Neither of which she kept in her kitchen cupboard when the kids lived at home. "Caught in the act," Ben says. Two grocery bags crowd the countertop. Lee looks in them: Hershey's Kisses; Coke; Doritos. A can of salted peanuts. A jar of sweet pickles. A bag of pretzels. "I stopped at the store on my way home," he explains.

Lee puts the sweet pickles in the refrigerator next to two identical, unopened jars of them. "We're out of milk."

"I just realized that," he concedes, "when I went to fill the cereal bowl. I guess I should have checked." He crunches more Lucky Charms. He studies the sports section. From where she's standing, Lee can make out a photograph of the high school's baseball team. Striped uniforms and bats held like crossed swords. And the innocent faces of the young.

"Did you know that Marty's selling Dussault and Son's? That he's moving to New York?"

Ben doesn't look up. "So I've heard."

"You've heard this?"

He nods.

"Did you also hear that he's come out?"

Ben rustled the newspaper. "Heard that, too," he says.

"So"—she puts her hands on her hips—"am I the last to know?"

"I assumed . . ."

"You *assumed*!" Lee bangs the refrigerator closed. She pulls out the chair across from him; its legs scrape the floorboards. She rests her elbows on the crumb-strewn cloth.

Ben looks up. His face is pleasant. His expression, mildly

inquisitive. "Did you just run into Marty?" he asks with an infuriating reasonableness.

"I had an appointment with him to take my passport photograph."

"Marty?" he asks. "For a passport?"

"Yes," she says. "I want to look beautiful."

He turns the page. His eyes are fixed on a column of league standings and box scores. "You are beautiful," he says.

Automatically. With about as much conviction, with *less*, she decides, than he would use to state we're out of milk.

"Shut your eyes," she orders.

He seems surprised. "What is this?" He sounds anxious. "It's not a birthday? An anniversary?"

"Just shut your eyes."

He shuts his eyes.

"And don't you open them."

He taps two fingers against his forehead. "Scout's honor," he salutes.

"Here goes." She clears her throat. "What am I wearing?" she asks.

Panicked apprehension takes over his features. Followed by a mask of bravado. "Jeans? A shirt?"

"Not jeans. What color shirt?"

"Blue?"

"No."

"Yellow?"

"No." She bangs her hand on the table. "Keep those eyes shut."

"I hardly dare to open them."

"Do I have earrings on?"

He tries a diversionary tactic. "You're wearing Marguerite's emerald."

"You know I always wear her ring."

"Okay. Okay. Those silver ones. Those silver fish."

"No."

He opens his eyes. "Ah, the pearls," he says. His smile turns sheepish.

"Which only goes to prove . . ."

"Prove what?" His voice is defensive.

"How little you see me. How little you know me."

"You think whether or not I notice what earrings you're wearing proves that?" His expression is indignant, then incredulous. "I see you, Lee. I know you in all the ways that count. We know each other."

"Do we?" she asks.

He folds the paper on a chair. He closes the box of cereal. He finishes the Coke. With a backhand, overhead pass he lobs the can across the room and into the recycling bin. "Slam dunk," he cries. Then he crosses his arms on the table. He leans toward her. *You've got my complete attention now*, his body language says. His eyes search out hers with the intensity of a professor interrogating a student on the oral portion of his doctorate. "Besides the passport photograph, how has your day gone so far?"

She tells him about Beatrice, about her talking to Kenny in the parking lot of the A&P, about Beatrice's decision to use the Pine Tree Press as a vehicle to publish only prison poetry.

Ben laughs.

Then stops when he sees her face. He forms his mouth into a solemn line.

Do I appear that stricken? she wonders. That needy?

"So where does that leave you?" he asks.

"Between a rock and a hard place. Between Scylla and Charybdis. Do I buy back my book to the tune of seven hundred bucks?" She waits. "Or do I let it be pulped?"

She's said the magic word.

"Pulp?" Ben repeats lovingly. "Nathaniel was an expert on pulp. The best wood, of course, went into building ships. In Maine it was white pine. The lowest grade was saved for pulp. You know of course how paper was made . . ."

Is there an analogy here? Lee wonders. The highest grade designated for the hull of a fine ship. The lowest grade for shipping *material?* Worth only the paper that Pine Tree Press is printed on, the paper to be turned into pulp. Once, in the drugstore, she'd picked up a ribald best-seller. "Who'd want to pay good money for such pulp," her mother had sneered.

". . . and the pulp forms this kind of gray soup," Ben continues, "and then—"

"Ben!" Lee exclaims.

"But of course you should buy back your books," Ben says. Out of guilt.

"You think?" she asks. Out of guilt. "All that money?"

"No money at all." He smiles. "For *your* book."

And because she's opened the gate, the Nathaniel gate, with talk of pulp, he rushes right back in. He can't help himself.

But she can't either. When he talks about the lumber

camps' provisions of pork and beans and molasses, and hard cider, she imagines Marguerite's sweetbreads, and oysters, and *crème caramel*.

When he evokes the omnipresent odor of pitch pine, and sawdust and fried fish in the camps along the Allagash, she can smell the roses and lemon verbena and lavender-scented linens in hotel rooms overlooking the Grand Canal.

When he discusses the arrival of the logs in the spring bringing with it red-shirted lumberjacks heading for the river taverns, she thinks of April in Paris, of Marguerite in a new hat sipping a glass of Beaujolais Nouveau at an outdoor café overlooking the banks of the Seine.

Compared to Marguerite, Nathaniel couldn't be more boring. In all honesty, she asks herself, who would you rather read about? A dour, reticent, puritanical captain of industry obsessed by forests and trees, who liked to commune with nature in the pouring rain? Or the flamboyant, exuberant Marguerite who adored restaurants and nightclubs and a luxuriously feathered bower? Even if Nathaniel's heart stirred once for someone not his wife, those feelings had to be excavated by a scholar, the shards sifted with suspect psychohistory into a middle-aged romance. Which might never have existed. Whereas Marguerite . . . Where would you even begin? Lee shakes her head. If Nathaniel is all earth and root and shade, Marguerite is all air and light. And life. Wouldn't you rather read about someone's travels than someone's landlocked insularity?

It's not fair, she thinks, that Nathaniel will probably win a Pulitzer.

While Marguerite will be pulverized into pulp.

She sits at the table feeling guilty. These are hardly thoughts befitting a wife, she scolds herself. Thoughts about a husband who wants only to save his wife's book.

If she is having unwifely thoughts, Ben, however, seems to be entertaining husbandly ones. He reaches across the table. He holds her wrist. There's a certain come-hither look in the eye, a certain lusty slant to the mouth. She recognizes the signs: Nathaniel talk translating into pillow talk. Ben wants her even if he doesn't notice what she wears.

"How about it?" he says. He checks his watch. "I've got almost an hour before my next class."

Outside the kitchen window, sparrows flit around the bird feeder. She spots a pair of cardinals nuzzling in the maple tree. The top cabinet shelf displays her grandmother's plates: the German Meissen; the French Limoges. Crowded underneath, on the lower deck, sits their own humble, everyday Maine pottery. Thick brown dishes with no piag. The bowl on the dining room table holds her ticket to England.

Ben's ticket is in his briefcase. He leaves a few days after her though they're booked on the same plane back. "Maybe it's not a good idea for us both to be away at a time that overlaps," she'd said to him.

"I can't see why not. We don't have young children at home anymore." He shook his head. "You're not going to believe this," his voice filled with wonder, "but I'm rather looking forward to visiting England again."

England.

So far away.

Another life.
Another Lee.

In the bedroom, they draw the shades out of habit. Out of habit, they take their usual sides of the bed. Out of habit, Ben turns to her. He touches her the way he always does.

When they were first married, *before* they were married, they'd gone through all the positions in *The Joy of Sex*. So systematically, in fact, that she'd complained to Ben. "It feels like a manual, like we're studying auto mechanics or checking off each step of an assembly-required piece of furniture."

"It *is* a manual," Ben had pointed out.

Nevertheless, they'd arrived at an accommodation that suited them. And hardly varied from its path.

Her mind reels backwards. To England.

To the pull-out sofa in their crummy flat.

Now Lee wraps her arms around Ben's neck. Does all love, all passion, turn into an accommodation? she wonders. Is every relationship a kind of compromise? Do you stick to the old manual regardless of new inventions, new designs? She thinks of Simon; it's a fleeting thought, easily dismissed given the here and now, given the sighs of her husband and the lovely warm liquid feeling that is starting in her toes. There is something to be said for repetitive motion, she allows. Its soothing lack of surprise.

Ben leaves at quarter of three. "Are you going to stay in bed?" he asks. He leans over to kiss her, he strokes her breast. His hair is wet from his shower. He smells of mentholated toothpaste and almond soap.

"I might just lie about all afternoon, a wanton woman," Lee says. "After all, I've got to recuperate from a tough morning at the photographer's. From my high-stress stint as a prison guard."

"You've earned it," he says. "I'll bring home Chinese."

When he's gone, she slides over to his side of the bed. The sheets are damp and twisted. His pillow has been knocked to the floor. She shuts her eyes. She opens them. Too bad she's not like her grandmother, who in the middle of the afternoon would set cucumber slices on her eyelids, slip a white satin mask over them, fluff up her half dozen pillows in every size and shape, and slide between imported Egyptian sheets. "There's nothing wrong with an afternoon nap," Marguerite would say. "Beauty sleep is necessary— especially when you're going to make a night of it."

General Gau's Chicken and *This Old House* isn't exactly the night of it her grandmother meant, Lee realizes. She sits up against the headboard. She looks over to Ben's night table, which is cluttered with papers and books. A section of *The New York Review* announces "John Updike on the Rabbit Novels." She fishes out one of Ben's history journals. She checks the contents: *Impact of the Bicycle in China; Roman Toilets, Sewer Systems, and Latrines; Uncuratorial Objects in Lost and Found Departments in Tokyo Railroad Stations.* She puts the journal back. She picks up the book it was lying on.

It's called *Aging Well*, a title, unlike *Roman Toilets*, which surprises her to find on Ben's side of the bed. She opens to a random page.

She starts to read: *When we are old, our lives become the sum of all whom we have loved.*

Nine

❧ ❧

*I*n Seat 26C of British Airways, Flight 219, Lee requests a Bloody Mary and leans back against the headrest. The plane is packed. She's on the aisle of a three-abreast row. An elderly Indian woman in a gold sari with Nikes on her feet like two white porcelain bathtubs claims the window, then falls asleep. Between them a pudgy, fortyish man with a thin mustache and newscaster hair turns the pages in a loose-leaf binder; columns and tables and charts whip by so fast they seem animated. He slaps the covers shut. On the spine Lee can make out a logo embossed with a jagged lightning bolt inside a triangle. "A G and T. Tank-eree, no rotgut, and a slice of lemon not lime," he instructs the stewardess.

Since takeoff Lee's been aware of throat-clearing noises and darting glances in her direction. So far she's made two mistakes: she let him lift her carry-on into the overhead bin. And she didn't stick her headphones on her ears and bury her nose in a book the second she sank into her seat.

Timmy had warned her. He'd become an expert in defensive traveling after serving a prolonged apprenticeship in buses, trains, planes, held captive by the life stories of perfect strangers. "I don't understand it," he'd lamented, "but the minute I sit down, little old ladies tell me all about their gallbladder operations and their good-for-nothing kids."

"I understand it perfectly," Lee said. "Your face is an open invitation for anyone to pour out his heart. You'd be the ideal therapist," she'd added. "Or priest."

"Oh, Ma," Timmy sighed. Then told her how to set up barriers to make herself unreachable.

Her neglect in this department is reinforced when the man in the center seat nudges her elbow off the shared armrest and points to her plastic cup. "So what's your poison?" he asks.

Before she can indicate the obvious clue of Bloody Mary mix, he announces, "Mitch Fontina. Like the cheese." He holds out his hand.

She shakes it. Circling both little fingers are gold pinkie rings.

"Where you from?" he continues.

"Maine."

"Nice state," he grants. "Cold."

"Yep."

"Not that I've been there. I'm from Jersey," he confides.

"Oh." She stirs her drink with the celery stalk. If she sticks to monosyllables, maybe he'll take the hint.

He doesn't. "Business or pleasure?" he asks.

"Pardon?"

"Are you traveling for business or pleasure?" he repeats. He inserts spaces between the words as if he's talking to an idiot.

She feels like an idiot. Business or pleasure? Now that's a question to fan a Jesuitical debate. She weighs the possibilities. "Business," she says.

"Me, too."

She sips her drink. She extracts the in-flight magazine from the seat pocket crunched against her knees. She opens it.

"What's your destiny?" he asks.

"Excuse me?" She supposes he means destination. A rhetorical question since the plane's British Air nonstop to Heathrow. Yet the question gives her pause. What is her destiny? "England. In the west," she replies.

"Whattya know. Talk about coincidence."

Her heart sinks.

"I'm heading for Swindon."

"Wyechester," she concedes with relief.

"Too bad. Not the same route." His eyes move from her lap to her breasts.

She rustles the magazine. She snaps some pages. She studies a list of perfumes on sale, duty-free, in the forward cabin: Shalimar. My Sin. Arpège, which remind her of her grandmother. Oh, for the days of plane travel when the drinks came in a real glass, when the napkins were linen, when you got dressed up, and when no Mitch Fontina would be wedged between you and a sleeping, sari-clad Indian.

"What's your line of work?" Mitch Fontina now asks.

She holds still. She could be anything. An atomic scientist. A welder. An opera singer. Not to mention, doctor, lawyer, Indian chief. She's by herself. Defined only by her passport which he doesn't need to see. By her age and body type which he seems to be seeing all too well. She's suspended between two parts of her life: what she's left; what she's going to.

Her destiny.

"I'm a writer," she says.

"Fancy that." Marveling, he shakes his head. "Me, too," he exclaims. "I do this newsletter for the company. I try to make it real personal-like. Always stick in a few jokes, my own opinion about the product. I got to admit the feedback just blows my mind." He gnaws open his bag of peanuts. "What's *your* topic, writing-wise?"

Writing-wise. She considers. "Life and death. Love and loss . . ."

"Sounds heavy. I like a good thriller myself. A bit of sci-fi. Are you on one of those book tours?"

"As a matter of fact," she says, "I've got interviews scheduled. Readings. A little TV, some radio." This is fun, she starts to realize. Like acting. In junior high she played Jane Eyre. In high school she was president of the drama club. Her best role was Kim, the fan who got to kiss Elvis in *Bye Bye Birdie.* "Incandescent," declared the school drama critic whom she was dating at the time.

Mitch Fontina zooms in on her face with enough eye contact to make Dale Carnegie proud. "What's your name? I bet I've heard of you."

"Probably not. It's my first book." She ducks her chin. "Magnolia Lee."

He blinks. "Sounds like a writer. You know," he says, "your name rings a bell. Could I have read about you in *People*? The *Post*?"

She fakes a humble shrug. She flashes him a false-modesty smile.

"So what did you write?"

"A novel," she confesses.

"I thought as much. You're pretty famous. I'm sure of it." He twirls the ends of his mustache like the villain in a melodrama. "Can I ask you a question?"

Can I stop you? she wonders.

"Is your novel fiction or nonfiction?"

Serves her right. She gulps down the rest of her drink. She studies a photograph of The Macallan being poured out by a kilted host against a wall crammed with a taxidermist's antlered wares. "Well, a novel is always fiction," she instructs.

He looks surprised. "Oh, yeah? You learn something every day, I guess." He squeezes his lemon slice. "As for my own writing . . ." he begins. He's off at the starting gate, heading into the marathon. His newsletter—he thought up the title himself—is called *Nuts and Bolts on Nuts and Bolts*. He sells nuts and bolts which are not your ordinary run-of-the-mill. The bolts have a triangular head, made out of titanium, which is quite revolutionary. "State of the art." He laughs. "State of the part. Get it?"

"Got it."

In fact, Triangular Bolts, the company, his company,

where he's been since he got his associate's degree, is known for . . .

Lee settles into the comforting white noise of Mitch Fontina's sales pitch, history of the firm, invention of the triangular-headed bolt. Her mind wanders to country houses and single malt scotch. To triangles. To all the forms they might take.

Right now she concentrates on Ben and Nathaniel. In two days Ben leaves Maine for London. He has appointments with potential publishers. They're putting him up in a suite at the Connaught; taking him to dinner at the Savoy Grill, popular with the royal family, Arab sheiks, stars in West End musicals. He's already planning to order the oysters and the Dover sole. Should he have the trifle or a simple Stilton for dessert? He's careful not to lord his stately digs over her dormitory cell, his corner banquette and towering seafood medley over her high-table fish and chips in the college dining hall. Ever since he missed her reading-that-wasn't while gathering his own accolades at the Organization of American Historians, he's been infuriatingly sensitive when it comes to her self-esteem. He talks of Iris Kidney in the same reverent tones with which he drops the name of the international agent who sought him out and signed him on. He talks of her memoir (which he credits himself with saving from the pulping machine like the hero rescuing the damsel tied to the railroad tracks) as if it bears the Nathaniel Tarbell weight of a hundred pages of endnotes and indices. "When I'm done in London," he said, "I'll come to Wyechester."

"You're kidding," she'd exclaimed, barely keeping the horror out of her voice. "I mean," she amended, "there's no need. I don't want you to cut short any meetings for my sake. It was all decided. We'd meet at Heathrow after our respective business was finished and fly home together."

"I don't think my end of things will take as long as I thought. I gather, from our dealings so far, the publishers will be quite willing to accede to my every wish. How much rich food and drink can I take? In addition to the loneliness of a fancy, big, fat hotel bed without my wife. Besides, I'm eager to meet Iris and Nigel. Let's grab a last weekend somewhere in the countryside. You pick the place. Just the two of us."

"If that's what you really want," she'd replied. Not telling him exactly what part of the countryside she had in mind. Not mentioning that "the two of us" hadn't meant the two of *them*.

How was she to know, when she set up this trip, this *business* trip, that Ben's business would take him to London? Even more, that he'd find time to drive down to Wyechester. What to do is a far harder choice than between the trifle and the Stilton. Should she invite him to come with her to Netherend? Ask Simon if she can bring Ben? Or abandon him to the hospitality of Nigel and Iris Kidney? It's a Florence Nightingale mission of mercy, she'll explain, to account for her speeding off alone.

Maybe she needs to reevaluate this whole cockeyed idea.

Mitch Fontina is talking about Cyril at Airsprung Beds and Viv at Rover Technologies, both believers from the start in triangular-headed bolts. After they close the deal, they'll live it up. A bit of pub crawling. A spot of nightlife. Cyril's divorced; Viv's a bachelor. Two good old boys who could just as well come from the good old U S of A. And let's face it, there's the humongous, freezing Atlantic between him in Swindon and the wife and kids back in Jersey. What they don't know won't hurt them. Out of sight, out of mind, as the wise men say. Would Mag-noy-ya (rhymes with annoyya) like to see a pitcha?

He whips out the photo of the wife and kids. "Dee Dee," he explains, "and Tony and Nicole."

Lee puts down the magazine. She picks up the photo. Dee Dee and the kids flank a backyard barbecue. Dee Dee is pretty with a lot of dark hair arranged in an architectural spire. She's wearing shorts under a bibbed apron which proclaims in red letters stretched across her impressive breasts, *Proud to Be a Mom and a Wife*. The kids, puddingishly preteen, resemble their father. They're sporting matching Triangular Bolts T-shirts. They squint at the camera; the sun glints off their braces.

"Nice," Lee says.

"Aren't they," says Mitch Fontina. "I'm way, *way* proud of them."

By the time his so-called chicken marsala and string beans amandine and her own hyperbolically touted lasagna aubergine and broccoli hollandaise arrive in their segmented plastic trays, Lee knows all about Mitch Fontina. About his two adulteries—"no, three, but that one hardly counts"—about Dee Dee's fibroids, Tony's ADD, and Nicole's seesawing weight. About their marriage counseling and kitchen remodeling and IRS audit. He introduces each snippet of his autobiography with "You're the novel writer, maybe you'll want to put this in your book."

Her punishment for a lie.

Her punishment for impure thoughts.

Her punishment for planning this trip under false pretenses.

Her punishment for one tiny, fifteen-years-ago adultery.

She imagines Ben taking this same flight—219—two days from now. What further punishment lies in store for her?

Finally, she pleads exhaustion. She needs sleep. She has a full schedule in the morning. She pulls the blanket up under her chin.

"Before you hit the hay," he says. He yanks out a pad of paper printed at the top with Triangular Bolts and stamped at the bottom with the triangle containing its jagged lightning slash. He writes something on it. He rips off the page. He hands it to her. "Can you jot down the title of your book?" he asks.

She sees that he has scribbled, in big, bold, Palmer-method letters, *Book Author—Lee.*

She hesitates.

Then writes: *To Kill a Mockingbird.*

Iris Kidney picks her up at the Wyechester train station. Though Lee's never met her, she spots her immediately among a crowd of matinee-going matrons and briefcase-toting middle managers. Iris is tall and handsome with a bony intellectual face, strong nose, graying hair cut short in a bowl haircut, no makeup and no jewelry except for a man's watch worn outside the cuff of her crisp white shirt, and a thin gold wedding ring. She exudes efficiency and good humor.

And warmth, Lee realizes, surprised and pleased when, instead of the brisk handshake she's expecting, Iris plants a noisy kiss on each cheek. "At long last," she says.

After five minutes, Lee feels she's found a soul sister. If they lived near each other, they'd schedule breakfast at the local pancake house, tea at their kitchen tables, cocktails on front porches displaying bowls of skewered Gulf-of-Maine shrimp. They'd swap clothes and books. And program each other's numbers into the first speed-dial button on their telephones.

Now Iris guides her car through narrow country roads. On both sides, hedges scrape the windows. At every turn, she honks the horn but doesn't slow down. Sheep scatter in her path. Bicyclists steer into trees. Hikers squash themselves against stone walls. A collie chases her spinning tires for half a mile and then gives up. "If you hesitate," Iris explains, "you won't get anywhere."

They dispense with business fast. Iris explains the setup: all the Junior Year Abroad representatives will be housed in single rooms in the same dormitory with baths "shared but better than most." There's a fairly loose schedule of panels and lunches and smaller, breakaway discussion groups. Lee's panel will be called *Expanding Horizons for Students from Small Rural Colleges*. Iris will act as moderator. In addition to Judy Teagarten, her fellow participants will include an administrator from a small school in Montana and an agricultural major from Iowa who spent a term at Beijing University.

When these details are settled, they move from things abroad to things at home. In the way of women who are used to sealing their friendships with intimate revelations, in the way of women who sense that, at the core, the true self is not professional but domestic, they talk about marriage, about parents, about children. Would Ben ever speak like this with someone he's just met? Lee wonders. Would he even talk like this with a friend he's known forever? With a member of his family?

Or with his own wife?

Iris tells Lee about her father and mother's silent but contented marriage, their recent, equally silent, no-fuss deaths, a brother who was sent down from Oxford, Nigel's high cholesterol.

Lee tells Iris about her parents' airplane crash into the Amazon, their bird books, the blue-faced, crested hoatzin. She describes Marguerite.

Iris beeps her horn at an oncoming truck. The driver pulls into a ditch to let her pass. He shakes his fist. A gesture Iris either doesn't notice or chooses to ignore. "Marguerite sounds like quite a character," Iris offers. "Did you ever think of writing some of these stories down?"

Lee, who only a few hours ago awarded herself the Pulitzer Prize for Literature under Mitch Fontina's questioning, now, faced with Iris's scrutiny, feels shy and apologetic. "Actually, I did write about her," she confesses.

"Splendid."

"A very small publisher. Local. Tiny sales. Five books for the family. And close friends."

Friend.

"Nonsense," says Iris. "You're far too self-deprecating. The flaw of our sex. I hope you've brought me a copy."

"It never occurred to me . . ."

"Then you must put it in the post as soon as you get home. If you've got an extra, that is."

An extra? How about seventy extra? "I can send you one for every room of your house."

Iris laughs. She swerves to avoid a fallen branch. Lee feels her body flip sideways like a test-car dummy. Iris reaches out a hand to steady her. "Sorry. Nigel complains I'm a menace on wheels." Her voice turns serious. "Is it the kind of book you were able to write only after your grandmother died?" she asks. "Would it have bothered her if she were alive?"

"Not Marguerite. She would have adored each and every word. Even the harshest criticism—not that there is much of it—she would have construed as flattery."

"Lucky for her. And for you."

They are entering the village of Wyechester; not exactly the picture postcard the brochures in Lee's office would have led her to believe. Petrol stations and boarded-up shops blight the landscape. Small front yards, asphalted over, have weeds poking through their cracks and crumbling cement garden gnomes dotting their walkways. Streets and paths are deserted. A huge complex identified by a battered sign-post as Nirvana Estates seems anything but.

"It gets better closer to the college," Iris explains, reading her thoughts. Then, without a transition, adds, "My daughter Amanda has written a novel about Nigel and me."

Lee sits up. Something in Iris's tone stops her from exclaiming *How wonderful.* She waits.

"Comes out in August. She got a huge advance. Her editor

is talking about a Booker nomination. Nigel and I read the manuscript. And haven't had a good night's sleep since."

"Oh, no," says Lee.

Iris stops at a zebra crossing. A woman pushing a double-wide stroller passes. Four small hands twist and wave like chubby little birds. Twins. From the look of the stomach preceding her, the woman is expecting another set. Iris points. She wags her finger. "Just wait till they grow up," she mutters. "Blessed event, bundle of joy. Rubbish!" Iris drops her head onto the steering wheel. "I might as well have been stabbed," she says. "Nigel and I might as well have been hung out naked in the town square."

Lee turns. "That bad?"

Iris shifts into gear and proceeds through the town square empty of everyone, not just humiliated naked citizens. Lee looks out at a statue of a soldier on horseback. A plaque commemorating the Wyechester war dead. A doll-size post office. A fish and chips; a Boots; a secondhand bookstore; the Cackling Crow Pub; A. Morris, Drapers and Decorative Interiors; Pippa's Plumage, High Fashion Slightly Used. A few straggly geraniums droop from terra-cotta pots.

"That bad," Iris groans. "I feel used and abused. Not that I'd ever say anything to Amanda. Who is so excited. So terribly talented . . ." Iris turns right at a sign indicating Wyechester University. The street widens. The trees look older and thicker. The houses more stately, set back on lush lawns behind elaborately curlicued iron gates. Just like Homestead, Lee notes, where the best real estate surrounds the college and disintegrates into shacks the farther away you go from it.

"Amanda's fame, her success," Iris continues, "will rise from the picked-over carcasses of her parents."

Lee keeps silent. She doesn't move.

"Who as far as she can see deserve what they get."

Lee waits. She knows that there's no rushing this kind of story, that it will unfold in its own time. She could imagine—so easily—her own daughter writing a tell-all if only Maggie knew what to tell. Ben, she's certain, would consider it his biographer's duty to reveal everything his research might expose. While Lee herself, discovering Marguerite's secrets, refused to betray them on the pages of her memoir. Even after Marguerite's death. Even realizing that the inclusion of such love affairs would sell more books.

"Does any marriage exist that isn't complicated?" Iris asks. Then answers her own question by adding, "Except for my parents.'"

"Mine, too," Lee agrees. "But not the marriage of my grandparents. Of Marguerite." She conjures up Alistair Abernathy's letter to her grandmother. She knows its lines by heart: *Leaving wrecked lives behind in the wake of our selfishness would be beyond comprehension to either of us. In the ordinary scheme of things such actions would be unthinkable. But our love is not ordinary and thus compels extraordinary measures.* She pictures Hermione Abernathy in her twinset, an elbow laced through her husband's pin-striped arm. She supposes Simon, too, would view his parents' marriage as uncomplicated. How would he know otherwise?

Iris pulls into the parking lot behind St. Stephen's Hall, a Gothic building with stained glass medallions and two stone steeples that don't match. "Inspired by Chartres," Iris explains. "Pretentious for a relatively new red-brick, though I love having my office in the tower." She tugs at her hair. "Who can ever know what goes on between a husband and wife?"

She and Lee slide their seats back. They stretch out their legs. Students call to each other across the car park. A white van with blacked-out windows waits for their space, turn signal blinking. Iris waves it on.

Iris tells her story in a flat, clear voice with no inflection, as if all emotion has been wrung out of it like a sopping washcloth suddenly spun dry. She married her college sweetheart and had Amanda. Nigel married his college sweetheart and had two boys. And when she and Nigel met, her first year of teaching, his fifth—he was already an academic star—they knew that to be together was their destiny.

But such things are messy. The timing's off. You can't always know your destiny before you've taken your first wrong turn.

"A *coup de foudre*," Iris calls it. "We were young; everything was possible. You never see yourself, then, with thinning hair and a paunch and a mortgage and high cholesterol; you never see the fallout, the bodies strewn in your path. Love conquers all, you are sure. Your passion will surmount all obstacles. You don't think of the pain you can cause, only the pain of being apart."

They left their spouses. Amanda was three. Nigel's boys, eight and ten. They had their own two boys together. Their happiness was sublime.

Soon enough the bubble burst. Her first husband killed himself. Dooming her to feel forever that her joy was built on the foundation of somebody's misery; her life, on somebody's death. Add to this, Nigel's ex-wife drinks. She needs to be fetched from pubs, taken to small, private drying-out hospitals for which Nigel pays huge fees he can ill afford. For years the boys of Nigel's first marriage, resentful of the boys of their father's second one, turned Christmas dinner into a wake. In their thirties now, they rarely see their father. There's a granddaughter Nigel's not once set eyes upon. They've never forgiven him. Amanda has never forgiven her. Or Nigel. Even though he adopted her soon after her father died. And loves her like his own.

Which hardly prevents her, come August, from humiliating both of them.

"After all these years," Iris beseeches Lee, "wouldn't you think the statute of limitations might apply?"

Tears leak from the corners of Iris's eyes. She doesn't bother to wipe them away. "You expect that when the children are grown, they'll understand. That by the time they've had their own inevitable ending-in-tragedy love affairs, their parents' behavior wouldn't touch them so much. They'd learn to forgive."

Iris blows her nose into an immaculate man-size handkerchief. "Amanda's brothers are championing her book," she continues. "They're convinced that airing laundry, letting it all hang out—as you Americans call it—is therapeutic. But of course they find it impossible to believe that their staid, middle-aged, dull parents could not only have felt lust and love, but also acted on it. The audacity. That we've been married for twenty-five faithful, good-citizen years doesn't seem to warrant a pardon. Not even an acknowledgment of mitigating circumstances."

"Kids," Lee sighs.

"Kids," Iris echoes.

For a while they sit silently. They watch cars wind in and out of the parking lot. Clouds gather, gray and swollen with English weather like ominous responses to shameful disclosures. Pigeons waddle from puddle to puddle. Another car pulls up. A man rolls down his window. He's sucking on a pipe. His eyes are watery behind smudged glasses in wire frames. "So?" he asks. He raises a professorial brow in the manner of someone whose every human interaction emerges formally framed in the Socratic method. "Are you staying or are you leaving?"

"Staying," Iris says.

"Knowing what you know now," Lee asks Iris, "would you still have done what you did?"

"I can't answer that," Iris says. "Yet the idea of leaving Nigel, the idea of losing him . . ." She stops. She turns to Lee. "In my position, what would you have done?"

"You're asking *me?*" says Lee. "If you only knew."

"Knew what?"

Lee tells her. She starts with Hyde Park. The pledges of eternal love. The funeral and the wedding. The blanket on the floor at Netherend. The purple underpants. One-time extraordinary extramarital sex. Full-time ordinary matrimonial sex.

Lee sinks lower into the seat. With Iris she doesn't feel the need to cast herself in a good light.

Though she could use some kind of absolution. She

confesses her faults; the Ten Commandment ones: dishon-
esty, adultery, envy; coveting another woman's husband,
neglecting her own, the yes-I-married-him lie to her dying
grandmother. The smaller ones: pretending to be Harper
Lee, losing Marguerite's ashes, mailing her memoir to
Simon. She discloses her reasons for getting herself to
Wyechester. For asking Iris to invite her. "I have some gall,"
she says.

"You do," Iris agrees. "Real cheek." Her voice grows solemn. "Regardless of the reason, I'm so glad you came. I
firmly believe that once you start something, you need to
get to the end of it."

"But what if you yourself don't start it. Circumstances set
it into motion. Or a grandmother with an opaque motive of
her own . . . ?"

"Yes, but you've helped the process along. By looking up
Simon's name in the library, making a call, sending a
book . . ."

"You're right. I feel so guilty . . ."

"Guilt has nothing to do with it." Iris thumps her chest.
"To repeat a cliché, you must follow your heart."

"If you know your own heart." Lee pauses. She mulls
over Amanda. She contemplates her own grown children.
Now on their own. Or are they? Will they ever be? What
is that adage crackerjack mothers quote with a wag of the
finger and a superior smile?—*Small children, small problems; big children, big problems.* Could it be more important
to stay together for the grown children's sake, rather than
for the toddlers you had only to keep out of the path of
electrical cords? As far as the children were concerned,

once they were away from home, she would have sworn she was home free.

She's surprised—and relieved—to find that the four-day Junior Year Abroad colloquium is a distraction and a delight. She loves being housed in a dormitory with others equally delirious to be let loose from their moorings of family and jobs. She's back in college again, bed unmade, clothes thrown on the floor, staying up late and drinking wine with instant friends from places she's never been, towns whose names she's never heard. Add in the novelty of coed floors. Knute Olafsson is down the hall; Rich Dubois's next door. Up above, Bob Golden's sneakers squeak across the planked oak boards. The delectable gossip of close quarters abounds: infatuations and unclosetings. Hanky-panky in the corner room between a woman from New Hampshire and a man from D.C.

Each night, after hours, the "boys" bring the beer; the "girls" supply the pretzels and the crisps. It's easy to play hooky, to skip the college meals and head for the pub; to break away from breakaway committees to take long strolls on wooded paths.

To talk and talk and talk.

She learns different ways to solve funding problems, how others deal with lost passports and lost students, crazy parents and crazy politics, food allergies and parasites. She discovers techniques to transform what goes wrong beyond your wildest worst-case-scenario dreams into a model of hands-across-the-sea.

Lee feels invigorated; ready to go back to work; full of

new ideas, new opportunities for Hannibal Hamlin students.

That is, if she weren't so beset by—

So sidelined by—

Pick one: Regret. Nostalgia.

Love.

She's made arrangements with Simon. A rushed conversation surrounded by the raised voices and high spirits from the Junior Year Abroad's nightly sherry hour. "Yes, of course, bring Ben," added Simon in a tone whose timbre, because of the noise, she could barely gauge.

She's made arrangements with Ben. "Simon wants us to come for the weekend," she'd said, hearing in the background the laughter of his publishers. He'd agreed with surprising alacrity. "Sure," he'd said. No questions asked, as if he'd never proposed their private holiday. She remembers his exact words: *Let's grab a last weekend somewhere in the countryside. You pick the place. Just the two of us.*

Her panel is scheduled for Thursday afternoon right after lunch. It's the final meal of the conference, and the dining hall is putting on the dog. Or rather, the pigeon. For two days, the menu's been tacked to the St. Stephen's bulletin board. A parchment scroll with singed edges and a calligraphied list of the kind of dishes Tom Jones might have made mincemeat of. Mincemeat's included. Along with enough savories and sweets to pique the palette, to cleanse it, and to require a forklift truck to get the postprandial you out of your chair. The entrée is pigeon in a ("famed local") Wyechester sauce.

At one P.M. sharp, the diners sit down at long tables. On either side of the plate, the utensils and stemmed glasses take up half a foot. Somebody in a long scholar's robe bangs a gong. Frock-coated waiters parade between tables bobbing platters humped with silver domes. When they remove the domes—with the flourish and clang of the percussion section of an orchestra—each course is revealed, ringed with a bright necklace of kumquats and crab apples and candied fruit. In its center, however, the food congeals into the same muddy grayish brown.

And tastes like mud.

Iris leans over. Something drops from her fork with a ping. "Be careful," she warns. "Watch out for buckshot in the pigeon."

Lee tries one spoonful of the stringy, gelatinous bird. No lead pellets tap against her teeth. She tastes Worcestershire in the Wyechester sauce, lumped with flour. She looks down at her plate. Headlining the morning paper had been an article about the pigeons in Trafalgar Square, how they were ruining Nelson's Column, contaminating benches, spreading disease. There was a campaign to cull them. The man who had been selling bird feed for fifty years was losing his job. There was a campaign to save them. *Keep the Pigeons, Keep the Pigeon Man* was the rallying cry. Lee studies the mess in front of her. She feels provincial: a rube from Maine. In her long career of culinary adventure, Marguerite would have devoured pigeons the way Lee might plow through a bag of potato chips.

Lee gazes at a stained glass window of a phoenix and a unicorn. Mythical beasts. She herself feels mythical, not quite real, as if she's acting something out, part of a *tableau vivant* in which present-day figures freeze into the stylized poses of characters from the past. What would Marguerite think of Lee now? Is she re-creating, in some way, her grandmother's history? By returning to Netherend will she be fulfilling a wish? Changing a destiny?

She reaches for the wine, both plentiful and surprisingly good. A perk her fellow conferees have also discovered; the level of hilarity rises. Across from her, Knute Olafsson sticks out an elbow and knocks over a glass of white which, in turn, falls against a glass of red. Two waiters rush over to sweep up the shards. Knute stanches a bubble of blood with a napkin the size of a pillowcase. Lee remembers another glass shattered into slivers, a thin dark line of blood . . . Now laughter bounces off the walls, rises to the arched ceiling with its modern copy of Gothic buttresses. Goblets empty and refill.

Not a good sign for the panel.

She is right. When the panel assembles, people are already nodding off in their straight-backed, hard wooden chairs.

"Where's Judy Teagarten?" she asks Iris. Jim Smith—from Montana Central College—and Susie Porter—Beijing U 1997—have already taken their seats at the draped table with its pitchers of water and floral centerpiece.

Iris checks the watch strapped outside her cuff. "We've got seven minutes. She's coming from London in Mohammed's father's car." She points to the front row, roped off with a slender cord of yellow braid. "Judy promised she wouldn't be late; says she's looking forward to extolling the merits of foreign study offered in your college catalogue.

Yesterday she phoned to request we reserve five seats for Hilda and Phil, Mohammed and the in-laws. One big happy family. Who would have thought."

A minute later, the big happy family arrives in a pack. Lee is surprised. None of them looks the way she expected them to.

What did she expect? Hilda and Phil in those shiny warm-up suits with elastic at the ankles and the wrists? Outfits which squeak and swish every time you walk. And Mohammed's parents? A black-tented mother, a chador hiding her face except for a flashing pair of eyes? And the father? A flowing white robe and red-checked Yasir Arafat kaffiyeh?

She should have known better. She, of all people—an employee of a politically correct college, an expert on international study abroad—should have been sufficiently enlightened never to form preconceptions of foreigners.

She learns her lesson. The Teagartens et al. stick out from the homogeneous flock of rumpled academic navy and gray and beige. But not in the way that she'd assumed. Judy and Hilda and mother-in-law sparkle in flowered silk and flying saucer hats fit for a queen, fit for *the* Queen. The men wear pale suits of shantung with pastel shirts and glowing ties. Lee remembers Judy—now so pretty in pink, her hair swept into a French knot—walking the campus in ripped jeans and stained sweatshirts, unwashed and uncombed like—she shivers—Lee's own Maggie Emery. Marriage becomes Judy. Mohammed, a hunk, becomes her, too. What's more, all this youth and beauty and prosperity rubbing off on Hilda and Phil certainly upgrades Lee's first (by-telephone) impression of them.

Hilda now approaches, scarlet-tipped fingers outstretched. "I'm afraid I owe you an apology, Mrs. Emery."

"Lee."

"Lee. I was hoping you'd say that." Bracelets slide up and down each arm in the manner of Marguerite. "The last time we talked, I fear I was a little rude."

"Don't mention it," says Lee. "Completely understandable. When it comes to our kids . . ."

"Motherhood can make you crazy." Hilda nods in the direction of the object of her maternal affection. "We *were* rather upset. But look how it all turned out." She beams. "Thanks to you, of course."

"It was nothing," says Lee. It *was* nothing. She did nothing. Handed Judy an application once Judy decided she preferred a place where the natives spoke English, sold cashmere, served decent beer; a city where showers weren't the exception to the rule. It had taken Lee only minutes to adapt the generic recommendation stored in her computer's hard drive.

"You're much too modest," Hilda grants. She casts a soulful glance at the reserved front row. "We adore our son-in-law. Whom Judy wouldn't have met if it weren't for you. His parents are charming and so refined. Phil and I are taking a course on the Koran at Open University. We're all going to Kuwait next month. Your program has opened our horizons enormously, let alone Judy's. In spite of our differences, we've discovered more in common than we ever would have believed."

Iris introduces the panel. Lee explains her program; Jim Smith, his; Susie Porter describes how a girl from the farm feels after she's seen Beijing—"awesome"; and how once she's seen it, she can't go home again. She's returning to teach English and follow in the footsteps of Buddha on her holidays.

Judy talks of finding her one true love, along with more cross-cultural stimulation than she's ever bargained for. She owes it all to her fine liberal arts education plus the benefits of small-town Maine, which, because of its lack of distractions, generates the desire to leave it. "Frankly," she confides, "without Hannibal Hamlin, there would be no Mohammed."

The questions from the audience are easy and predictable: funding, inoculations, crises domestic and political. Until Mohammed's father, Fuad Al Farid, stands up.

"Miss Lee Emery," his voice booms. Those slouching in the lassitude of three different kinds of lunchtime wine turn suddenly alert.

"Yes," Lee says. Her own voice shakes.

"Does Hannibal Hamlin College have Department of Islamic Studies?" he asks.

Here it is. She can see the protestors now. Placards. Sit-ins. Ben denounced as a monster of white male Eurocentrism. Proceed with caution, she warns herself. "Not a separate department, alas," she begins, "but courses offered under the aegis of art, of music, of history . . ."

"Does Hannibal Hamlin College have mosque?" he asks. He puts a hand in his pocket.

Lee feels a moment of terror. Underneath the table, skirted in striped taffeta to hide drooping socks, scuffed shoes, trembling knees, Iris nudges her toe. Is Iris anxious, too?

314 • Mameve Medwed

"A mosque?" Lee repeats. "I'm afraid . . ."

Fuad Al Farid pulls from his pocket a rectangle of burnished red calf. He reaches into his jacket; he produces a gleaming gold pen. He grins a huge smile. "Then, in honor of my son Mohammed's lovely bride, I write for Hannibal Hamlin College a great, big check."

They sit in Iris and Nigel's kitchen. Ben has just arrived from London, sleep-deprived, yet heady with forty-eight hours of basking in toasts to Nathaniel Tarbell's assured success. Iris is pleased with the panel, relieved the event has come to an end. Lee is thrilled with Fuad Al Farid's generous check. "And more where that comes from," he'd added with a wink.

She's already phoned the Hannibal Hamlin College Office of Development. "My only hesitation," she confided, "is the incongruity of a mosque rising from our pine-needle-strewn lawn. Will alumni object?"

The director of development's voice sounded rapturous. Delight crackled over the line. "Don't worry," he advised. "Why not a mosque with squash courts in the basement and visual aids in the dome? You've done a fabulous job, Lee. What a magician you are. No small feat to turn that sow's ear of a Judy Teagarten into a Hamlin cash cow."

Ben, too, is excited about Lee's financial coup. He's sure the administration will look more kindly at funding some of his own projects in light of the contributions of Professor Emery's wife. "To think, I might be riding on the coattails—the wedding train—of my own bride," he exults.

Nigel Kidney heats up soup. He slices bread. He's a dapper man with a deep belly laugh. He shoots adoring glances at Iris. As he moves around the kitchen, he reaches out to touch her shoulder, to stroke her cheek. Lee's sure she has never met a better-suited pair. A combination, she can't help noting, that took them a couple of tries to get right. Nigel lifts the ladle. "More, darling?" he asks.

"Perfect. Thank you, darling," Iris nods.

Lee sighs. It seems impossible that Amanda's novel, a mere piece of writing, could ever dislodge the rock of harmony, of love, supporting the two of them.

The two of *them*—the Emerys—are spending the night in Nigel and Iris's spare room, and are leaving tomorrow for Netherend. Though the triumph of the conference (and its plentiful wine) has distracted Lee from her anxieties about the weekend, they're rising now in all their teenage tongue-tied and knock-kneed horribleness. She touches her hair, her waist. If only she had a girdle—do they still make them?—to disguise her middle-aged mother-of-three actuality.

Oh, God. What will she wear?

What will she say?

Will he recognize her?

Will she recognize him?

And if he is really ill, what will she do?

Perhaps her memoir, like Amanda's novel, is stirring up trouble where once there was none. She'll blame the Simon chapter and the poetic license that may have turned it fictional. Does she really believe that a kiss in the park, an hour on a blanket in front of a fire is a memory strong enough to connect the present with the past? And if not, if the visit ends up awkward and sad and empty, will she be relieved, finally, to know the truth along with its consequence: seeing Ben in a new light, and Simon no longer through the eyes of Marguerite. So much for the cautionary words *you can't go home again*. She *has* gone home again. Her dilemma is this other place she's going to.

With Ben.

She opens her hand. The bread she was holding is now pulverized into a pellet fit for a pigeon in the park. She puts it in her mouth. She can't even begin to tally her worries over the inclusion of Ben. She's dreading the minute they get alone and they start to discuss the trip. The rented car, an upgrade with racy lines and leather bucket seats in a take-no-prisoners red, sits in the Kidneys' garage. "A last hurrah for a man of middle age," Ben apologized. "A midlife moment-of-madness for a Volvo-driving solid citizen."

Now Ben chats about Nathaniel's middle age, about Nathaniel's middle-aged love affair. Nigel and Iris lean forward in their chairs.

As does Lee, surprising herself that, oversaturated with Nathaniel, she's still interested to hear more about his moment of madness, *his* last hurrah. After all, the Tarbell canon is hardly *Goodnight Moon*, a book her children demanded she read again and again, the sort of story so enchanting you can never get enough of it.

"Mrs. Tarbell, Nathaniel's wife, found a cache of letters," Ben explains. "But she had her suspicions long before. She notes in her own diary that Nathaniel had seemed remote. Could be found not writing at his desk but moping in dark corners of seldom used rooms."

"Did she know whom the letters were intended for?" Iris asks.

"I can't tell. Even on paper, she's very discreet."

"Would that everyone were," sighs Iris.

"Darling," Nigel consoles.

"Nathaniel himself writes very little about this woman," Ben continues. "He mentions an unnamed friend of the family. Somebody he liked to take walks with. Someone who had—in his words—'a gentle smile and haunting eyes,' whose sleeve brushed his along a wooded path." Nigel passes the wine. Ben holds up his glass. "There's not much I've been able to find out. I think this dark lady might be the daughter of family friends who lived in London, summered in the Forest of Dean, and emigrated sometime after Nathaniel went to Maine." Ben dips his spoon in the soup. "It's hard to tell whether the knickers actually came off or whether the affair consisted solely of yearning looks across a crowded room. Although, it doesn't matter really. It's the feelings that count."

"What information do the letters give you?" Iris asks.

"That's just the problem. Mrs. Tarbell tossed them into the fire. Without even reading them."

"Imagine!" Iris exclaims. "What an extremely moral being. Faced with such a find, who could bear not ripping them open. Devouring them?"

Lee focuses on her grandmother's letters. Like Mrs. Tarbell, Lee, too, could have been an extremely moral being and thrown Alistair's letter into the fire unread along with the rest. All things considered, it might have been better not to have known.

"She didn't want to know," Ben goes on. "She loved her husband. Her marriage meant the world to her. Maybe she assumed the letters were like that sports car out there in the garage. An instance of temporary insanity. In her diary she writes, 'I shall forbear.' She was an admirable woman. Remarkable." He leans back. He sips wine. He tears off a piece of bread.

Lee is sure that he has never looked so content. He taps her elbow. He turns his head toward her. His voice is casual. He's tossing off sentences like so many peanut shells discarded into a bowl. "I must have forgotten to tell you this, Lee," he says. "But in Chicago, at the OAH, I met a young woman, a promising scholar, who is contemplating a book on Nathaniel Tarbell's wife."

On the walls of the Kidneys' spare room, old maps of the area around Wyechester stretch from ceiling to floor. Ben's eye zeroes in immediately on the Forest of Dean. "This is a beauty," he says. "Eighteenth century. Exquisite and rare."

Lee pulls off her clothes, throws them on the floor, and falls onto the flowered duvet. She feels half dead. Under the influence, she figures, of two days of dormitory life, and too much of Nigel's wine. But before she can go to sleep, there's something she has to get off her chest. She's guilty of manipulating herself to Wyechester when her secret directional signals were all blinking in the direction of Netherend. She's guilty of acting in the interest of the Junior Year Abroad when her true interest lay in recapturing her first innocence abroad—and the loss of it on a carpet in a fire-warmed, rain-lashed sitting room. She can't go on this way, blindsiding her innocent husband who thinks only the best of her. For the sake of full disclosure, she needs to confess. "Ben," she begins.

Ben's nose is so close to the map of the Forest of Dean that he's fogging up the glass. "Yes?" he says.

"I have to tell you something. Before we go to Simon's . . ."

Ben doesn't move. From the back he looks frozen, a statue of a tall, well-built founding father in the center of a geranium-ringed town square.

It comes out in a rush. "About Caroline. Simon's alone. Living by himself at Netherend. She left him."

Ben's shoulders loosen. His whole body seems to relax. He doesn't turn around. His words are muffled. "Yes, I know," he says, "she wrote me."

Lee sits up. Eyes open. All effects of food and wine vanish in a *poof.* She's wide awake. "She wrote you?" she shouts. Though she's aware of Nigel and Iris on the other side of the wall, she can't keep her voice down; she can't keep the high screech of incredulity out of it.

"Yes." Ben spins around. His eyes fix on a spot on the floor. "From time to time, I've heard from her."

"I don't believe it!" She tries to take this in. She searches for the right response. Her throat is dry. Her tongue tastes cottony. "She wrote you!" she repeats. "Impossible. I'm sure I would have noticed letters from Netherend." Boy, would she have, like a heat-seeking missile, like a Geiger counter above a lode of uranium.

"She writes me at the office."

Lee stares.

Ben's voice takes on an irritating and excessive righteousness. "Why should this surprise you? She *is*, let me remind you, an expert on the Forest of Dean."

Vanquished, Lee falls back against the pillows. There's still one arrow in her quiver, however, still a little fight, a little *flight* left in this broken-winged bird. "You might have told me," she sputters.

"On the relative scale of things, it was so unimportant it never even crossed my mind."

Ten

❦

The first thing Lee sees, as the blaring red Jaguar pulls up in front of Simon's house, is the wreck of a former hutch where the rabbits used to live. There are no rabbits. No goats; no pony; no Cheshire cat sunning itself on stone steps. There are no stone steps, or at least they're so buried in brambles you can't make them out. The rotted window boxes, which once bloomed with pansies, now sprout weeds. Dead branches hang from a tree scarred and split by lightning. Rusty rakes and hoes, a bald rubber tire, half a wheelbarrow are piled around it like cairns. Near the front door, three mottled pigeons poke at a crust of bread.

"Jesus," Ben whistles through his teeth.

It's a sunny day. This morning, when they drove off from Iris and Nigel's, the sky was such a brilliant blue not a single pair of sunglasses remained in the Wyechester Boots. On the campus lawns, students lay stripped to the tiniest bits of cloth. Even the faculty shed their academic gowns to bare an elbow or a knee.

Now, given the desolate scene before them, such glorious weather seems a mockery.

"Cold Comfort Farm," pronounces Ben. "Bleak House. The Fall of the House of Usher. Simon's let everything go." He twists his neck to take in the whole view. "No wonder Caroline left," he adds. He catches Lee's eye. This is the first time Caroline's name's come up since Ben's pen-pal revelation last night, since they set out this morning from Wyechester with Iris's thermos of coffee and Nigel's home-made sausages.

Lee turns defensive. "He's been sick. It can't be his fault." She remembers Caroline's organic chickens, her free-range disdain. It's a classic chicken or egg problem. What came first? Is this state of disrepair the result of Caroline's leaving? Or the cause?

"Whatever the reason, it's too bad," Ben declares with admirable diplomacy.

They're both on their best behavior, careful with each other. She thinks back to this same ride so long ago: the kids fighting in the back seat, the confusing gears, the unfamiliar roads, her anxiety.

How astonishing, fifteen years later, to recognize the same anxiety, which has been rising with every mile ticked off on the sleek odometer. She's much too adult for such teenage fluttering over a trip doomed to end up as a fool's errand for fool's gold. Unless she can discover, and bring to a close, whatever it is she needs to know.

What does Ben expect?

What does Ben suspect?

The whole way here, they made neutral conversation about foreign study panels and British publishers; discussed the children and the monarchy and England's green and pleasant land as viewed through the polished windows of their polished rental car. All sideways glances at her husband revealed only a pleasant obliviousness.

"In Chicago, I saw a street person holding a sign," Ben chuckled, "which read: *Arguments: One Dollar for Five Minutes*."

Lee laughed. "Did you give him a dollar?"

Ben shook his head. "You know me. No arguments."

No arguments is the unspoken pact between them. Safeguarding this treaty means tiptoeing around the mention of Simon; the mention of Caroline. They're taking things at face value: Ben's been consulting Caroline in her capacity as an expert on the Forest of Dean. He and Lee are visiting Netherend because they're in the neighborhood of an old friend. To listen to them, they might have been setting out for a holiday in Brighton or two days hiking the paths of Windermere. Ben drove as if he'd been driving in England all his life, Lee noted. No sign of the trouble he'd had with the Morris Mini when they lived on Prince of Wales Terrace, the windshield wipers they couldn't figure how to turn off, the car's warbly, alarming veerings across the center lane. Now Ben was negotiating roundabouts and right-hand turns from the left-hand side like the Fred Astaire of steering wheels. "You've become quite the traveler," she approved.

He was pleased. "The things I do for Nathaniel," he said, "things I'd never do for myself."

Is he doing this for Nathaniel? she wonders. Driving her here; spending two nights. Or for her? For their marriage? For himself? She must stop thinking like this. Why try to uncover motives when there are none. She has an accommodating husband who's accommodating her. She's complicating simple truths: she's married; they're a pair; they've been apart for a few days and are now having a little vacation before they set out for home.

Some vacation spot.

She and Ben climb out of the front seat. No wonder aging beauties like Marguerite demanded dimmers on their lights, threw scarves over lamps, kept candles low on the tables and high on the shelves. The bright sun picks out every flaw. What might, in the dark, look like one of those paintings of a romantic ruin so popular in the nineteenth century is, in the glare of day, a ruin stripped of all romance. Before their eyes stretches a landscape detailed with such decay as to make one leap back into the buttery leather, gleaming chrome, every-mod-con womb of their luxury car and speed away into the fabled, anywhere-but-here English countryside.

Except that, unlike most tourists, she hasn't come for the scenery.

Except that, she isn't a tourist.

She's revisiting a scene from her youth.

Revisiting the scene of the crime.

The scene has changed, however.

The youth has turned middle-aged, however.

"What a dump," Ben states. "Where's Simon?" he asks. He opens the trunk but doesn't touch the luggage. He kicks a rock out of his path. He brushes dust from the car's hood, which leaves a grimy streak in the shape of a thunderbolt.

Nuts and bolts, Lee thinks. *Triangular.* She feels bound together by nuts and bolts, shinbone connected to knee-bone. Will the joints hold? Where *is* Simon? The last time they were here, the whole Abernathy family had tumbled out of the front door the minute the Emerys' car turned into the drive. First came Caroline. Followed by the children. Then there was Simon. She pictures the plump white rabbits. The storybook pony. The luscious fields.

"Maybe he didn't hear us pull up," she says. "I'll ring the bell."

The bell is broken. Its brass surround hangs off a frayed wire like a flower dying on its drooping stem. The curtains are drawn.

"Is there anyone there?" calls Ben from his stance by the car. He's primed to shut the trunk and rev the engine, she knows the symptoms. Let's find a B and B near the river, he'll say, with good views and a real garden and thick clotted cream to spread on just-baked scones.

She tries a few tentative raps on the door. She puts her ear to the heavy wood. She hears nothing.

"Knock harder," Ben instructs.

She bangs with the flat of her hand. She starts to pound with her fist. "Hello! Hello!" she calls through a curtained window frame. Has she tripped herself up in her eagerness and given Simon the wrong date? If no good deed goes unpunished, she's the living proof.

At last, she can make out a faint shuffling. The knob turns; the door creaks open.

And then there is Simon.

Lee holds her breath. Mr. Rochester, blind and crippled, stands in the ruins of his house. She shuts her eyes to make the image disappear. And opens them on Simon, pale and thin. Dark hollows crater his cheekbones. Which, though alarmingly ridged, are nevertheless still remarkable. Along his jaw, bits of paper are stuck to two small razor cuts. Her gaze shifts to the whorl of black hair that peeks through his gray shirt. In the seam near the shoulder, she notices a small frayed hole.

This is what she focuses on. The hole. The hole fills her with sorrow. She can't move her eye from it. Could there be a more telling symbol of neglect? Of the gaping, ever-widening maw of emptiness? He's uncared for. He needs taking care of. Is there a woman on earth who isn't ready to dip into her bag of tricks—needle and thread, Band-Aid, chicken soup, empathetic heart, people skills—to mend a gash, to heal a hurt?

She stares at the hole.

"Lee," Simon says. He steps on a small square of glass that's fallen out of the front window. It crunches. "The crows eat the putty," he explains.

What to do next? Where's the instruction manual for lost loves found in tattered condition? She considers the merchandising terms: *worn; damaged; seconds; irregulars.*

As is.

She steps forward. A platonic kiss? A collegial hug? A fraternal or sororal shake of the hand?

A quandary solved by Ben, who crosses in front of her. He claps Simon's shoulder. "Good to see you again. We thought for a minute you'd forgotten about us. That there wasn't anybody home."

"To the contrary. I've been looking forward to your visit with enormous delight. No. I've been in my darkroom. My apologies. It's at the back of the house. Once I'm shut in there I hear hardly anything."

"Photography?" asks Lee. "I didn't know . . ."

"A new hobby. It passes the time." He tugs an earlobe. "There's quite a lot of it these days."

Lee looks at his hands. The nails are clean but ragged; the knuckles, raw. A blister tips one thumb. The long, slender fingers seem translucent, like the ghostly images of bones on an X-ray. Yet even now, she can conjure up the unghostly, thrilling touch of them.

"What do you photograph?" Ben asks.

Simon picks at the blister. "This is going to sound extremely strange." He hesitates. "Tumors, actually. Ones I've studied. Sectioned. Reported on. Odd, really, but they have a kind of beauty in their awfulness. Not that I'd inflict them, the photographs, on anyone else." He frowns. "Though I do have a few pinned up around the house. To fill some space. I should have thought to take them down."

Lee supposes that this is the opening for her or Ben to jump in with *Oh, no, but we'd love to see them. Really, we would.*

Neither of them does. Ben goes to get their suitcases out of the car. Lee stands there feeling stupid, feeling sad. This trip is already a mistake.

Why did she come?

Once again, she looks at Simon's fingers.

How could she not have?

Simon moves toward her. "You haven't changed, Lee. You're exactly the same." His smile is wistful; his eyes have a far-off, *à la recherche* . . . cast to them.

"You, also," she lies. "In spite of—well—all you've been through."

"You're being kind," he says and turns to lead them into the house.

If he appears worn, damaged, irregular, so does the inside of his house. She remembers big chintz sofas and armchairs. Rugs and paintings. She remembers comfort.

Now cold comfort.

Cold Comfort Farm—Ben is right. The rooms, shades drawn against the sun, are dark. The chintz sofas have disappeared. The floorboards are bare. Gone is the rug on which Lee tossed her purple underpants. Did Caroline take everything warm and soft and light and leave Simon with everything cold and hard and dark? Yet she can see he's made an effort. Daisies fill a chipped vase. A bunch of violets cram a mottled jug. A paisley shawl, carefully folded, drapes the back of a settee; its single pillow, centered and fluffed. But still . . . Lee surveys the wooden chairs pulled up to the black hole of a fireplace, the tables covered with papers and books. More papers and books lie on the floor. She stops. She freezes. Between a sheaf of old sheet music and fanned-out *Lancets*, she spies Marguerite's photograph. It's her memoir. Has it been here since she sent it months ago? Since he read it? *I was touched*, he had said. Touched enough to drop it to the floor and leave it there? Her work, her grandmother's life, treated like this.

She shivers. Despite the warm June day, the room is chilly. Mildew marks one wall; across the ceiling float clouds of water stains. A moth-eaten stuffed bird under a dusty dome of cracked glass graces the mantel. A teacup holds a tangle of rubber bands. Scotch-taped to the wall, where once hung framed prints of flowers and vegetables, are photographs, edges curled and cracked, of gloomy geological formations, hills, ravines, oddly striated and lumped landscapes which, Lee realizes, must be the tumors that comprise Simon's profession and now make up his hobby, too. She has never seen rooms that cry out so desperately for a woman's touch.

They eat in the kitchen. The centerpiece is a tower of Simon's Inland Revenue forms which he moves to the side. The salt shaker is empty. There's a sticky spot next to Lee's plate where something spilled—honey? juice?—and was never wiped up. Simon has bought cold cuts and cheeses. He pours wine into plastic tumblers. He passes one to Lee. "Sorry," he says.

Lee remembers the fragile antique glasses, how Caroline had ordered Simon to take good care of them, the angry whispers over the goblet that Lee had crushed in her hand. She finishes her wine. She holds out the tumbler for more. She scans the kitchen, the pale squares empty of the still lifes, the pegboard stamped with the rusty circles of long gone saucepans and cooking implements. Has Caroline taken everything?

Simon seems to be reading her thoughts. "Caroline took

nearly everything," he offers. "I wanted her to. It was mostly hers anyway. She had upholstered the furniture, framed the prints, found odd bits of china at jumble sales. She was the person who'd made the house a home. I don't have the slightest idea how one would begin to go about it."

"Because you're a scientist. Because you have other things on your mind, more important things," Lee says.

"You're very kind," Simon says, "but I am basically incompetent. In the workings of the world. In everyday life." He pauses. "At least I've become that way."

"It's not fair that she took so much," Lee complains.

"If it was hers in the first place, if she did all the work herself . . ." Ben reasons.

Lee scowls at him.

"I didn't need it. I inherited a ton of stuff, you see," Simon goes on. "My parents died last year, within a month of each other."

"I'm so sorry," Lee says. She pictures Hermione and Alistair. Twinset and tweed. Tweedledum and Tweedledee. Inseparable, like her own parents, she had thought then.

"So sorry," echoes Ben.

"I had all their things stored in my shed. Antiques, silver, pictures, photos, books, letters. My sister and I had planned to go through them at some time in the future when she could get away—she's a barrister in Edinburgh—at a point when we felt up to viewing the photographs, reading the letters . . ." His voice trails off. He turns his head.

Letters, Lee thinks. Drawers filled with them. Tied with ribbons. Dried roses pressed between translucent pages. Letters from Marguerite to Alistair?

Simon fills his glass again. He drains it in three swift gulps. He wipes his mouth with the back of his hand. His fingers tremble. "Then I came home from work one day and found the shed door ripped open. Everything gone."

"How horrible," Lee exclaims.

"What happened?" Ben asks.

"Thieves with a big truck. Professionals. The padlock was flimsy. I had assumed—misguidedly I know now—that since Netherend is not London, since this is the country, here one's belongings are safe." He cracks his knuckles. "I gather gangs of robbers have been striking in the area. They ship the goods to the Continent. The police tell me it's virtually impossible to recover anything."

"Oh, Simon," Lee says. She wants to reach over. To touch his elbow. To stroke his shoulder under the small frayed hole.

"They're just things," he says. "What I have of my parents can't be taken away. Like you, Lee, with yours, with Marguerite. My happy childhood. Their happy marriage. Until the very end they were so devoted to each other, so much a complementary pair, a unit unto themselves. Frankly if I hadn't witnessed such a marriage, seen how love can endure and mature, how two people can exist only for each other, I would never have believed such a flawed institution could work." His face grows sheepish. "I have my own skewed view," he apologizes. "I'm sure your marriage, yours and Ben's, is a very happy one."

"Very happy," confirms Ben.

Lee keeps her mouth shut. Maine people don't boast. Yankees don't lord their luck over another's misery. She holds out her glass to be refilled. She's matching Simon drink for drink.

Ben nudges her rib. "Haven't you had enough?" he asks. One eyebrow rises in disapproval as if she's a student acting up.

"The glasses are small," excuses Simon.

"I'm sober as a judge," adds Lee. In fact she's never felt more alert. She's hyperaware—of every movement, every sound, every dish and glass and speck of dust, the holes in the sliced Swiss cheese, the circles of fat and the peppercorns in the slabs of processed meat, the drip from the kitchen faucet, the whir and chug of the refrigerator. An attention *surplus* disorder, she diagnoses, undulled, *undullable*, by alcohol. *Indelible.* How fortunate, she judges—judges soberly—that the elder Abernathys' possessions were stolen. Simon can hold on to his illusion. She thinks of her parents' comfortable, *comforting* marriage. She pictures their bird books, their binoculars, her mother's crisp aprons hanging on the back of the kitchen door, her father's battered tweed coat flung over the bench in the hall. She sees herself going through Marguerite's things after her death. Each dress, hair clip, pen, book, shopping list, a further opening of an already gaping wound.

Followed by the shock of discovery. The chasm left in its wake.

Simon will be spared the truth. He'll never learn that his parents' marriage was not what it seemed. Simon will never find a letter, a lock of hair, a perfumed handkerchief. He'll never know that if Marguerite had nodded her dimpled chin, crooked her dainty finger, said yes, *mais oui*, Alistair would have flown out of the nest, and the perfect marriage would have been shown to be as full of holes as this slice of cheese, as Simon's frayed gray shirt.

Now Simon traces his finger along the table's edge. "Except for my children," he says, "I've lost everything that meant so much to me."

They sit in silence. Lee considers another glass. She looks at Ben. His eyebrow stays arched as if it's thumbtacked to his forehead. His shoulders are broad; his shirtsleeves are rolled up on forearms brown, muscular, and sinewy from chopping wood in their backyard, patching the roof, shoveling snow, mowing grass, plastering walls. Keeping up their home. Their Homestead home. A man who lets nothing go, Ben's a wide shoulder to grasp; a big hand to clutch. A hard solid center to hold on to through all the shifting losses: her parents, Marguerite; the empty nest, the end of youth. His hair, though graying, is thick and shiny. Lush. His open-as-the-plains face is ruddy and smooth; no secrets there. Compared to Simon, he's so large, so healthy, so solid. So confident.

And so rude, she realizes with a start, when he leans toward Simon and says, "If you don't mind my asking, why did Caroline leave?"

"Ben!"

Simon holds up his hand. "It's all right," he replies. His voice is puzzled. "She said she was unhappy. She said she wanted someone like . . ." He stops. He shrugs. "She said she was unhappy is all."

After the cottony cake from a tin, after the granulated instant coffee, Lee sends Ben and Simon into the drawing room. She washes the dishes. She puts them on the drying rack. She sponges the counters; she wipes the crumbs and sticky spots off the table. She sweeps the floor. She pulls open the kitchen curtains; she polishes the rattling, putty-less panes behind them. It's dark outside now, and she can see nothing but a bleak stretch of fields and the humps of trees. Outdoors, beyond these gloomy rooms, these crumbling uncared-for walls, the air will smell fresh; stars will fill the sky the way they do at home.

Home.

The day after tomorrow she and Ben will be going home. She opens a jar of Marmite, sniffs it, then throws it out.

In the drawing room Simon has put on a tape. She hears the mournful strains of a bagpipe. A fiddle wails to the stately, somber tempo of a dirge. Poor Ben, she thinks, whom she's dragged to this place. Poor Simon, she thinks, who has to stay in this place.

Who stays in place.

She scrubs the soapstone sink; she scours the grout between the tiles. There's a dark red spot that won't come off. Her blood from fifteen years ago? Like Lady Macbeth, she rubs and rubs. She wants to clean and wax and polish until everything shines. She wants to make a house a home. To make an unforgiving place a welcoming bower.

She wants to make a broken heart whole.

Before they go to bed, they map out the next day. "I've been trying to think of something to amuse you," Simon says.

"You don't have to amuse us," Lee says. "It's lovely just being here. Just seeing you."

He picks up a brochure from the table. He holds it out to her. Gracing the cover is a photograph of a hawk perched on a stone. The four corners are anchored by an owl, a vulture, a condor, and a kestrel. Scary eyes and terrifying beaks. *Birds of Prey Centre*, Lee reads. Then, underneath: *Man and Rapture.*

Man and Rapture?

Rapture?

She looks closer. No. Man and *Raptors.*

"This has just opened up a few miles from here," Simon explains. "I thought that perhaps we'd go after breakfast. I've heard they have quite a decent tearoom. And exhibits which might be interesting . . ."

"Just up Lee's alley," Ben pronounces. "Her parents . . ."

Simon nods. For an instant, a flash of something familiar—wet grass, a paper airplane, a dimpled knee, the song of a nightingale—marks his dark eyes, edges his soft mouth.

"It sounds wonderful," Lee says.

"Indeed it does," Ben says. "Nevertheless . . ." He waits. "If you don't mind . . ." He coughs. He picks his words. "While the two of you set out on this particular expedition, I might just drive over to the Forest of Dean. For old times' sake."

"Whatever you want," says Lee.

"Of course," Simon agrees.

They're put in the same guest room they occupied fifteen years ago. This room, like the rest of the house, has fallen on hard times: peeling paint, mismatched sheets, a ragged quilt. No guidebooks, no thin volumes of Milton grace the nightstand. No landscapes of neighboring villages hang on the walls. Clean towels and a jam jar of black-eyed Susans aren't enough to offset the musty smell of unused, unloved space.

As soon as they've shut the door, as soon as they hear Simon's footsteps retreat down the hall and down the stairs, Ben flops on the bed. He starts to laugh. "Can you believe it?" he says.

"Ben," Lee cautions.

"This is something out of Dickens. If I'd read it in a book, I'd accuse the author of melodrama, of overkill."

"Shhh," Lee warns. "He can hear you."

"I thoroughly doubt it. I've never seen such a sad sack. He's probably lost his hearing along with everything else."

"It's not funny."

"I know that. But still. You've got to admit the guy's disaster-prone. What a catalogue of horrors." He holds up his fingers and starts clicking them off. "The poor bloke loses his wife. The house falls apart. He gets sick. Has surgery. His parents die. All their stuff is stolen. His hobby is photographing tumors, for God's sake."

"If you say it like that, of course it sounds bad."

"You couldn't make it sound *good*." He shakes his head. His eyes widen in disbelief. "And this is the big romantic hero you wrote about in your memoir? With such feeling. With such tenderness. That portrait really got me where it hurt." He points to his stomach. "I'm so glad I drove here with you. If only to see how the real thing turned out. This Simon is a shadow of the person you created. No resemblance to *your* character living or dead. You must be, too."

"What do you mean?"

"Be glad to see the real thing. Now you can put an old ghost to rest. Isn't it a relief to know the end of the story? That you made the right choice, averted a certain misery?"

"It wasn't his fault. He had bad luck. Things might have been different . . ."

"Women always think they can save someone. Baloney. You can't save anyone. You can't step into the path of a downward spiral and reverse gravity. The only solution is to behave like Nathaniel's wife, accept things, make the best of it. But of course *you* don't have to, personally, because . . ." He stops.

"Because?" she repeats.

"Because, you've got me!" Ben gets up from the bed. He moves to the window. "Jesus, this house is freezing. The window's shut and cold air's pouring right in. Along with everything else the wretched soul's probably got chilblains from the damp and these drafts."

"Simon can't help it. The crows eat the putty."

"Then he should repoint the windows. The place is a disaster. The whole kit and caboodle's a disaster. You need to fix things. Keep up with repairs. With relationships. Why, if I let my life, my work, my house go like this . . ."

"You're blessed, Ben."

"We all make our own beds. Look at you, Lee. Your parents died so young. You didn't let everything go. You didn't fall apart."

"I didn't?" She sees Marguerite's basket of funeral baked

meats that supplied their town hall wedding feast. When her parents died, she couldn't get married soon enough. Would it have made a difference whether it was Ben or any other Barkus-is-willing groom?

Ben considers. "Of course you had me. You married me."

"True."

"The best thing you did."

"The best thing *you* did," corrects Lee. "Compared to Simon, you've lucked out. Hearth and home and health. Parents playing golf in Florida and driving you crazy from a distance. Can't you cut him a little slack?" She smooths the pillowcase. "Besides, you've got a wife. And a book that's going to be a wild success."

"You think?"

Lee nods. "I know."

Ben holds out his arms. "Come here."

"Not here," Lee says. She points to the floor. To the bedroom below theirs. "It'd be much too cruel. A slap in the face."

"I guess you're right." He yawns. He stretches. He pulls his pajamas from his suitcase. "This has been quite the week. For both of us." He yanks off his shirt. "Busy day tomorrow," he says. Then adds, "For the both of us."

Simon drives Lee to the Birds of Prey Centre. The car is tiny, like the Deux-Chevaux French movie stars are always smoking their postcoital Gauloises inside. She doesn't know the make, but it feels like a circus car for midgets. And makes their old Morris Mini rental seem as big as a limousine. "Sorry," Simon says. "It's practical for one. Rarely do I have a passenger." Cassette cases crowd the dashboard. Duct tape patches one seat. She compares it to the Volvo station wagon of her carpooling days; kids sardined into the cargo area, lunchboxes spilling out, backpacks piled, the cages of gerbils and guinea pigs lugged home from the classrooms on weekends to the delight of the kids and the reluctant good sportsmanship of their parents.

"Sorry," Simon says again. The interior is so narrow that every time he shifts, his hand brushes her thigh.

And burns her flesh.

A response she chalks up to old feelings, out-of-date reactions. For the person he was. Not who he is now. Like clinging to your bell-bottoms when everyone's wearing Capris. A temporary holdover.

Isn't it?

Simon comes to a hill. He shifts again. His fingers slide along her jeans. Fingers that once unsnapped her garters. That once rolled her stockings down. Her skin tingles. A *frisson*, her grandmother would trill with a rapturous quiver. "Middle-age spread," Lee excuses.

"Not you," he says. His grin accentuates the lapidary cheekbones and off-center features that used to charm her. And now? Just an odd face, she tells herself, eyes, nose, mouth staking their separate territories.

And yet . . . If she stares at him long enough, she can make out, underneath the mask of tragedy, underneath the built-up hard clay of a hard life, the fine, pure armature. Fragments of his former self—a depth of feeling, a glint of humor—are still visible in this ghost of his former self that he's become. Tarnish collects only on the surface; the essential metal can be polished to a shine. You don't completely lose the person you were, she supposes. Take as an example, her grandmother: on her deathbed, blind, frail, unrecognizable, she had, nonetheless, squeezed out the words: *Dying's so boring. Frankly, I've never been so bored in my whole, entire life*—a phrase completely, ineluctably Marguerite.

Could she have saved Simon? If she had waited? If she hadn't rushed to marry Ben? If her parents hadn't died?

If she had known her own heart?

"Tell me about your heart," she asks him now.

"I might have died. For a while, when things were horrible, I wanted to."

"Don't say that."

He turns to her. His eyes are dark. His face ravaged. From the tiny side window, the sun frames his head like the halo on a suffering saint. She moves her own head away. She stares at some fat sheep in a field. Beyond them she can see the black outline of cows. This surprises her. The papers are full of foot-and-mouth disease; across their front pages range photographs of funeral pyres all over the English countryside heaped with the carcasses of sheep and cows and hogs. She's assumed that all the farm animals had disappeared like the rabbits in Netherend. *You wanted to die because of me?* she yearns to ask. And is appalled at her own self-centeredness.

"It's hard to live without love. The heart shrivels. Or empties out until there's nothing left but a hole."

"Simon . . ."

"I'm speaking metaphorically. And with inexcusable self-pity in the land of the stiff upper lip." His hand skims her shoulder, a gesture so fleeting she thinks she may have imagined it. "Oh, Lee. It's not your fault, of course. And the human body is amazing. The minute I got sick, the life force returned in full throbbing glory. Despite myself. Surprising me. Though not my doctors to whom the will to live is completely natural. As a pathologist, I seldom see the life force swimming under my microscope. It turns out the hole was congenital. Something they might never have discovered, never even have known about . . ."

"If . . . ?" she supplies.

"No ifs." He stops the car. A farmer crosses the road leading a flock of sheep, a barking dog. At the end of the procession a lamb falls over on gawky legs, then sits right down. The dog loops back, pokes at it, circles it, barks some more. The lamb refuses to move. The Gandhi of ovines, Lee notes with admiration. "There's a creature who knows its own mind," she says, "dances to its own drummer."

"The classic loner. The one who doesn't fit in" is Simon's glass-half-empty reply.

Finally, the farmer marches back into the road. He gives an apologetic wave. He scoops the lamb into his arms and, carrying it like a newborn, returns it to the rest of the flock. "Back to where it belongs," Lee finishes. She scoots closer to the side door to leave an inch between the gearshift and her thigh.

Simon depresses the clutch. "Maybe. Maybe not."

"We were talking about . . ."

"I'm fine now," Simon says. "They patched me up with

some extraordinary synthetic fiber they use for parachutes. For the clothing of scientists visiting Antarctica."

"So you're as good as new."

"Through the miracle of science, even better, I'm told." His laugh comes out as a harsh bark. "Though can any of us be quite what we were?"

The staff at the Birds of Prey Centre seem to outnumber the visitors. At first, Lee's afraid she and Simon are the only ticket buyers there. But once inside the gates, she spies a family of four—redheaded and sturdy, graduated in height like a short flight of stairs. Grouped under a tree slouch three denim-clad teens. "The flying demonstration is at two," announces a woman in a khaki uniform with an eagle embroidered over her left breast. "And the raptor lecture is held on the hour in the auditorium."

"Shall we just wander?" Simon suggests.

Lee nods. They study the map and set off down a path. "What are raptors anyway?" she asks.

"I looked the word up. One who seizes by force. A predatory bird."

"My parents would have known." She stops. "Can you believe I read it first as rapture," she confesses.

Simon smiles. "You're not far off. The root's the same. Meaning transported. Carried away. In the sense of being abducted, it's related to rape. Amazing isn't it how two words which at first seem so opposite can be connected at the core."

They reach the row of vultures. Cages extend the length of a city block. She reads the captions: Turkey Vulture—

Cathartes aura; Black Vulture—*Coragyps atratus;* King Vulture—*Sarcoramphus papa;* there are Lappet-Faced Vultures; Hooded Vultures; Palm Nut Vultures; a long list of different names for hideous birds that look the same. Birds of bad dreams, of horror films, carrion-eating birds, the birds of death. She shudders. What does it mean, this stroll among vultures and condors and kestrels with someone who takes pictures of tumors, who examines diseased tissue under a microscope? She forces her eyes to the birds, first one, then another. She studies a vulture with yellow talons, a ragged beak, molting wings; a flinty evil eye. *Milvus migrans parasitus.* She imagines her peacock of a grandmother, her *swan* of a grandmother, who would never have set a well-heeled foot in such a place. If Simon had hauled Lee to the Birds of Prey Centre when she was eighteen instead of—the name hits her with a jolt—the Birds of a Feather Pub, would Marguerite have still favored him? Provided, of course, she'd had Lee's welfare in mind and not her own prospects with Alistair. Perhaps such questions are moot. If Simon hadn't shriveled from lack of love, suffered a damaged heart, skirted death, he'd now be wandering amid rabbits and ponies and hosts of golden daffodils, not these carrion-seeking, carcass-eating, ugly birds.

Unless ugliness, like beauty, is in the eye of the beholder.

"What a beauty," croons a man in back of them. Lee recognizes the flat vowels of mid-America.

She spins around. Aha! No *rara avis* here. A birder. It's one species whose traits she can identify: the binoculars hanging from the neck; the spiral-bound notebooks, the guides sticking out of the pockets of the multipocketed safari shirt. The sunburned nose and freckled scalp. In his hand he holds a cap; its brim boasts white letters spelling National Ornithological Society.

"Magnificent," he sighs.

With a huge fanning whoosh, the vulture spreads its wings, an enormous black span the breadth of the cage. The three of them jump back even though they're separated by thick latticed wire. The vulture flies to a higher perch. Then glares down, scorning their paucity of rotting flesh.

"Will you look at that," the man exclaims. "What a beauty," he repeats.

"I wouldn't choose that particular word," Lee says.

"Ah, you're an American." The man's voice holds both delight at finding a compatriot in such a spot and disdain for that compatriot's lack of appreciation for such a spot. "The beauty's there," he insists, "if you only know where to search for it."

His name is Earl; he's from Ohio, in "sales," and nothing would suit him more than if Lee and Simon would join him for a cuppa though he's a coffee man himself.

"We've only just started," Simon says.

"We haven't even visited the eagles yet," Lee adds, hoisting the red, white, and blue.

Earl from Ohio won't take no for an answer. "How often do I come across another raptor fancier from my own backyard?"

"But I'm from Maine," Lee protests.

"Maine. Ohio. What's the diff. We both crossed the same old ocean. I insist that you and your husband join me." He pokes a thumb at his chest. "*On* me. And I'll even throw in one of them scuns—the lady at my B and B told me how to say it right."

Lee raises an eyebrow at Simon, who returns an amused nod. Neither of them corrects old pal Earl. Years ago, a concierge had told Marguerite that her *daughter's* room wasn't ready while holding both of their passports open in front of him.

The red-haired family sit at the next table; they share a plate of sandwiches. They pass around a bag of chips. They chat and laugh with the kind of easy familiarity that in a family breeds not contempt but content. Lee longs for the family trips they took when her kids were the age of these kids. Expeditions to museums, national parks, historic burial grounds. Though she realizes she's looking back through the rose-colored glasses of time passed, she can still feel a pang for time past.

All three, including Earl the coffee drinker, drink tea. They've rejected the scones—scuns—which, behind fly-specked glass, reveal a slightly greenish cast. Gracing the walls, like the city fathers in the Homestead town hall, hang portraits of the local dignitaries—falcons, eagles, vultures, buzzards. A whole community. When you consider what *they* eat, the tea cakes and biscuits and salmon mousse here can make you lose your appetite.

Earl pours sugar into his mug. He rummages around his pockets; he pulls out a photograph. Lee expects the wife and kids; a backyard barbecue. She wouldn't be surprised to hear he sells, if not nuts and bolts, then screws and nails, staples and brads. She glances at Simon. Her life is a movie rolling over and over in a continual reel; its film, used, old, damaged, worn; its scenes, *as is* images that lack the sharp-edged clarity of when they were new.

"Take a gander at these," Earl says.

Lee and Simon bend forward. No wife and kids; no back-yard fence. Only photos of a small brown bird.

He holds one out. "Nice, huh?"

Since the rather sweet, ordinary bird is clearly not a raptor, Lee has no trouble nodding yes. "Adorable," she agrees.

Earl rattles off three Latin names she can't quite catch. "An accidental bird," he explains.

"Accidental bird?" Lee repeats.

"One found out of its habitat. One who managed to fly beyond its range. I notified the Audubon. Sent in all my observations. They posted them right up there on the Web." He smirks. He nudges her shoulder. "This baby's a Yank. Like you."

"Imagine that."

"A New Englander to the core. Flew in from the Colonies and landed here in Ye Olde."

"That's quite a bit beyond its range. An ocean's worth," Simon observes.

"You're telling me! When the news went out, so many birders—they call them twichers here, that Brit sense of humor, got to give 'em—*you*—credit." He winks at Simon. "Anyway, so many twichers showed up they created a traffic jam for thirty miles. Not to mention how they emptied the beer in all the pubs." He laughs. "They drank the town dry! There wasn't a pint left."

"What happened to the bird?" Lee asks.

"No happily-ever-after. A tragedy. Most birds that end up out of range perish. They can't find their way home. They may try to seek a mate. But unless they can hook up with one of their own—unlikely—they're pretty much doomed. If they do mate with a local bird, their offspring are infertile." He shoves the photo back in his pocket. "The lesson, I figure, is stick with your own kind."

"Which doesn't necessarily denote geography," Simon points out.

"Not for human beings, *Homo sapiens*," grants Earl. "It sure seems to work for you. A chick—don't mind my French—from Maine, and a limey bloke. One thing I can recognize when I see it is a good match."

Earl checks his watch. "Well, gotta go. Signed up for a hawk walk. Unless you . . . ?"

In concert, they demur.

Earl sticks out his hand. He shakes first Simon's. Then Lee's. Crunching her bones. If she hadn't spent the last hour staring at hawks and understanding the need for verisimilitude, she might have complimented him on his hawk-like grasp. "You keep all your ducks in a row now," Earl warns. He tips his cap.

On the ride back to Netherend, the strain between them seems to have lessened. Perhaps their encounter with vultures has put their own encounter into perspective. Perhaps Earl's assumption that they're husband and wife makes them feel more relaxed as a couple. Especially since they know their present state of affairs is temporary. Their past affair

is past. Simon was ill and has grown better. She was crazy
and has become sane. Tomorrow this accidental bird is flying from out of its range to home on the range. At this time
tomorrow, she'll be sleeping in her own bed in Maine.
When Simon shifts, she keeps her thigh in place; her defiant flesh neither flinches nor burns at his touch. The fever
has broken. *I'm cured*, she wants to shout.

Not so fast.

"I've been hoping to talk to you about your memoir,"
Simon begins.

Lee's hand tightens on the *Man and Raptors* brochure.
She hasn't realized she's been holding it. She looks down at
the hawk. A crease in the paper ribbons its breast. She looks
up at Simon. His eyes are so hooded, she can't decipher his
thoughts.

"I've read it two, three times. I treasure it."

She forces her attention back to the photograph of Marguerite dolloped with dust kitties and peeking out between
*Lancets. That's how you treat a treasure, by dumping it on the
floor?* she's ready to ask with her had-it-up-to-here, mother-
of-messy-kids annoyance. Instead, she waits a beat. "My
grandmother was quite a woman" is all she says.

"It's not your grandmother I mean. *You're* quite a woman,
Lee." Signaling left, he veers right. Lee bounces against the
flimsy seat. "Actually. As a matter of fact. Well," he warms
up. "Well, I don't think I've ever recovered from Hyde
Park. And that other . . . our afternoon together, that afternoon on the blanket in the drawing room."

Lee catches her breath. *Slowly. Slowly*, she warns herself.
She struggles to hold back a rush of emotion: its source, the

ardor of an eighteen-year-old pulled out, like Russian dolls from Russian dolls, by the Hyde Park chapter of her memoir. Did she actually believe they would never speak of this? Did she hope that for two full days they could ignore this elephant in the room? She wraps her arms around her breasts. She presses her knuckles into her ribs. *Recover.* As from an illness?

He reads her mind. " 'Recover' isn't quite the word. It's a memory, a moment etched in my soul, in my heart." He pauses. "Not that you duplicated the scene in your memoir. Not that you described it in specific terms. But *I* knew. *I* could read between the lines. What wasn't put into words contained as much meaning—*more*—than what you wrote."

"Simon," she says. She has no more words. Poor Simon. She stops.

Poor *Ben. It was hard*, Ben had admitted. *So much feeling*, Ben had sighed. For all her delicacy, for all her worry about causing harm, she has spared no one's feelings. Not Ben's. Not Simon's. Not even her own. She summons up her book. Its sixteen-point Times Roman title, the slightly smaller *Lee Emery.* For an instant, she wonders if she'd written a tell-all, bare-all bodice-ripper, whether Beatrice would have switched to typesetting house-of-correction couplets. Not that Lee would ever have done such a thing to Ben. She stumbles for the apt verbs and the precise nouns. Like a student of English-as-a-second-language, she speaks haltingly. "I know you told me that Caroline left because she was unhappy," she begins. "But . . ." She folds *Man and Raptors* into a neat square. She crumples it in her fist. ". . . do you suppose one of the reasons she left might be because she found out about us, about our—that interlude?"

He steers close to a privet hedge to let a cement mixer pass. "She left because she felt I was unsatisfactory. She said she wanted someone like Ben."

All at once traffic bunches up; more trucks are barreling toward them on this winding single-lane road. Simon has to stop and start; wait and go. He needs to concentrate. Lee holds this hot potato in her lap, this astounding remark in her head. Simon has now pulled so far to the side that branches are sticking through the open window of the car. Leaves tangle in her hair. She plucks at them.

Lee is aware that she's hanging on to this bit of news like a cat with a bird, a bird with a worm. She works it over.

What does Simon mean?

What had Caroline meant?

Where does Ben fit in all of this?

She forms a hypothesis. Just suppose . . .

For instance: Ben and Caroline are in touch for reasons professional; in the course of their dealings, the fact that Caroline had left Simon would naturally crop up but would have nothing to do with Ben.

Except that: Caroline might use Ben for reasons antimatrimonial. A way of getting a rise out of your domestic partner, your domesticated partner, if you're mad at him. To Caroline, Ben would be unattainable and thus safe. Under such circumstances, why not throw out the name of a big, competent, handsome man to puff yourself up and deflate your spouse.

Besides: How could Caroline express a desire for someone like Ben when—despite Forest of Dean e-mails, despite Forest of Dean letters—she doesn't even know him, has never spent a consecutive week with him. (That Lee herself has never spent a consecutive week with Simon is another story altogether and thus irrelevant.)

In conclusion: Caroline's excuse for leaving Simon must be a subterfuge.

Which shows you the kind of person Caroline is. The kind of person to make a husband's life a misery.

Which is only what you might expect from a second-choice wife.

"What do you think she meant?" she asks Simon at last.

"Nothing," he says. "A figure of speech."

"I'm sure you're right," she agrees even though these words, *She wanted someone like Ben*, are starting to seem less like a hot potato and more like an undetonated bomb buried in both of their laps. From the corner of her eye, she takes in a clenched jaw and hands fisted over the steering wheel. They've come too close to speaking of dangerous things, she knows. Before the bomb explodes, they'd better clear the field. Before lightning strikes, they'd better make their escape. What a respite to rush toward the safety of the mundane; what a relief to move from man to beast: vultures and buzzards and hawks. From affairs of the heart to affairs of the hearth: children, weather, scones.

Until they arrive at Netherend.

Look!

There's Ben at the edge of the driveway, sitting on the stump of a trunk and studying a map.

The rest of their stay passes in a whirl. They eat dinner at an Indian place in the center of town. Ben reports on his outing: the trees and moss, the sylvan paths and sparkling brooks, his sense of peace. Lee and Simon take their turn: the birds of prey, the huge wingspan, the knife-sharp beaks, their sense of terror. They all go to bed early. Lee falls into a deep and dreamless sleep.

In the morning, it's time to leave Netherend. Time to drive to Heathrow.

Time to go home.

Ben drags their bags outside to load up the car. He prides himself on arranging things. He's a whiz at all kids' games labeled "educational"—those puzzles and cubes designed to test and raise your IQ. Long after she and the children had given up in frustration, long after Maggie had turned to her Barbie dolls, Johnny and Timmy to their Tonka trucks, Ben would be sitting there, patient, curious, successfully fitting square pegs into round holes. At home, he signs up for dishwasher duty. He wastes a good half hour moving around glasses and bowls and silverware. "This appliance is sold as a time-saver," she'd pointed out.

"One needs to take the time to get it right," he preached. "You have to treat things carefully, Lee, to prevent them from being hurt."

Now Lee looks at Simon: the man she hasn't treated carefully enough, the man she has hurt. She has left Ben to his packing and gone back inside the house. It's time to tell Simon good-bye. For the last time, perhaps. He'll be fifty soon. Not old if you consider the normal span of life. Yet he's frail; he almost died; he lives without love. For a short afternoon at the Birds of Prey Centre, she'd glimpsed his old self. A smile, a glance, a flash of longing. The face of the boy she'd known, the man who'd made love to her. Brought out by the fresh air. The breath of fresh air she brought: conversation, companionship. She studies him. Once again, he's back in the shambles of his house; the shambles of his life. This morning he wears the shirt with the frayed hole.

"I guess it's time to say good-bye," he says. His eyes glint. With fever? With tears? Or simply the blinding shaft of light slanting from the open door?

She feels tears start behind her own eyes. She blinks them back. "I hate good-byes."

He takes her hand. His skin is cool and dry. The knuckles rise in a sharp ridge. "Wait," he says. He reaches into his pocket. And brings out a rabbit's foot.

Her rabbit's foot.

The white fur has yellowed; its sheen dulled, the little nails broken; the metal top that clamps it is now a circle of rust.

"You've still got it," she marvels.

"Didn't I promise you I'd keep it forever?"

She feels chastened. *Don't some of us keep our promises? Don't some of us mean it when we pledge eternal love?* hovers between them. What had her mother said about the length of eternity when you're young?

"We were so young," she says. She reaches out. She scoops the rabbit's foot from his hand. She rolls it between her fingers. The little nails prick her flesh. "Somewhat the worse for wear," she notes.

"Which makes me value it even more," he says. Then adds, "As witnessed by my having carried it around all these years."

"It doesn't seem to have brought you much luck."

"It's my own fault." He dips his head. He lowers his eyes. "When you wrote me you were marrying Ben, I should have come to you. I should have flown right over to Maine. Perhaps if I had been there . . ."

"All those *shoulds*. All those *ifs*." She runs her thumb along the patchy matted fur. Imagine keeping such a silly thing for thirty years. Her throat constricts.

"Even so, I can't help playing the same tape. Over and over. What if I'd come after you? What if you hadn't married Ben? What if your parents hadn't died? What if we'd met when we were older? What if I'd managed to get your grandmother to plead my case?"

"Believe me, Simon, she pled your case." She laughs. In her ears, the sound rings hollow and false.

"Then . . ." He slides the rabbit's foot out from between her fingers. He stuffs it back into his pocket. "Then, what if you'd listened to her?"

"Oh, Simon. This does no good." Her voice cracks. "It's too late."

"You don't think I know that, Lee? You don't think I remind myself of this every minute of every day?" He rubs an eye. "Yet I can't stop believing I'd be a different person if I'd come to you."

"You can't be sure, Simon. You could have traveled all that distance only to have it end in disaster. Remember what Earl said about the bird out of its range? It perishes."

"You're my range, Lee. It's here in my own backyard that I'm . . ." He stops. He shuts his mouth.

She's glad. She doesn't want him to fill in the blank. She doesn't want to hear him say the word *perish*, to hear him say that he's perishing.

Because she knows it's all her fault.

He speaks again. His voice softens. "It's not your fault, Lee. I should never have brought this up. Especially now, when you're leaving." From outside comes the sound of Ben loading suitcases, slamming car doors. Simon moves closer. "Dearest Lee," he whispers, "I've loved you all my life."

Her breath turns ragged. Her mouth falls open.

"I don't know what to say."

"There's nothing to say. Only this." He pulls her to him. His cheek lies against hers; his heart beats against her breast, his lips brush her ear. She sees Hyde Park. She sees a blanket rolled out on a carpet. She sees a black sky filled with dazzling stars. And a boy who once, long ago, held her head to his heart and opened his soul to her.

In a second, he lets her go. "So lovely," he murmurs. "It was. You are." He steps back. "My darling," he says.

My darling, he had said in the damp grass. A nightingale sang. Thunder rumbled; lightning crackled. And then he'd kissed her. This is it, she had known. This is love. She moves toward him. "Simon . . ." she begins.

"Ben's waiting." Resigned, he shakes his head. He squares his shoulders. He manages the brave smile of a boy. She thinks of Johnny's smile when they left him at college. Of his waving hand receding in the car mirror, then vanishing. She stares for the last time at the frayed hole in Simon's shirt. She's comforted that in these final, sad moments with

Simon, her feelings are maternal ones. Yes, *clearly* maternal, she tells herself.

He stands in the doorway and waves. As they turn off his road, as they drive away from Cold Comfort Farm, she sticks her head out the window and sees that he is still standing there and waving still.

In the car on the way to Heathrow, Ben slides a CD into the CD player. A group called the Forest People pump a hurdy-gurdy and wail about caves and mines and birds and sheep and man at one with nature. Or at least that's what she figures from the odd words she can distinguish in a dialect she knows to be English but which might as well be Hungarian. Ben drums an accompaniment on the steering wheel. "La la la," he hums in the tuneless voice of one appointed chorus manager. For no reason she can explain, he's been getting more and more on her nerves with every mile they've put between this garish embarrassment of a chariot and the house at Netherend. "It's music of the area," he instructs. "You can hear the Welsh influence from the proximity to the border."

How can a tin ear claim such a field of expertise? "Does the CD come with the car?" she asks him. She wouldn't be surprised that, along with the state-of-the-art bells and whistles, geographically correct compact discs are supplied to sound-surround the territory you're driving in. The Chieftains for Ireland, for example. Robert Burns songs for Scotland, the Beatles for Liverpool. Just one more amenity added to a vehicle they wouldn't be caught dead in steering Homestead's rutted roads.

"Don't be silly. No, I just got it. It's new." *La la la. Da dee dum*, he croaks.

Lee raises her hands to cover her ears. She leans her head against the window. Through the side mirror—*objects in the mirror are closer than they appear*—the road narrows to a point. She pictures Simon receding until he's just a slight black speck. Will he recede from her heart the way he's vanished from her view?

Her thoughts shift to Marguerite and Alistair. She hadn't told Simon about his father and her grandmother. They're both dead; why open up that Pandora's box? As for the letters . . . *World enough and time*, Alistair had written. They hadn't had either. Without time together could they ever have known what their life together might have been?

The CD ends. Ben reaches over. He presses *play*. Did Marguerite marry Sam for the reasons Lee married Ben? A solid rock to cling to in the shifting plates of a confusing universe. A contradiction in terms for a woman who never shrank from the world, its adventures, its challenges.

Or so Lee had assumed. Maybe there's a whole layer missing from her memoir. Maybe she's more like her grandmother than she had ever dreamed.

They stop at a restaurant on the side of the highway. It's an English version of the orange and aqua Howard Johnsons of her youth, now replaced all along the Maine turnpike by Burger Kings. This particular Old World interpretation seems to have grabbed the New World prototype and run with it. Larger and more elaborate, its exterior is half-timbered, faux Tudor but painted in Caribbean colors hardly native to Ye Olde. Flowers ring the car park where two shiny tour buses sparkle in the sun. A wishing well stands beside the front door. Lee peers into the shallow water at the twinkling silver coins, the bright copper pence. She digs for her wallet.

Ben takes her elbow. He steers her inside. "Don't be ridiculous," he says. "When the restaurant closes, how much do you want to bet the staff fishes out that money and blows it at the track. Besides . . ."—he accepts two menus the size of an atlas from a woman with a gingham bow in her hair— ". . . you know that Oriental curse: 'May you get what you wish for.'" They squeeze into a booth covered with purple vinyl that makes whoopee-cushion noises as they bounce along it.

If only she knew what to wish for.

If only she knew what she wants.

She looks around her. Three large rooms open into each other. Each room swarms with ladies of a certain age in sensible shoes and sturdy suits whose lapels sport badges secured by lily of the valley pins. The whole space is abuzz with chattering. "Must be a convention of the garden club," Ben says.

A lady in Black Watch plaid passes them. *Busby Grove Garden Club Tour*, Lee reads. *Bus number one*. "You're right."

They each order the soup du jour and an egg mayonnaise sandwich, then settle back in convivial, matrimonial silence.

Or so Lee assumes.

Ben clears his throat. "About Simon . . ." he begins.

Lee sits up.

Ben gets right to the point. "It's over then? You've closed the book on him?"

Lee feels her cheeks smart. Her throat tighten. She fights to hide her surprise. What did Ben notice? What did he see? Close the book? What is he getting at? "I have no idea how to answer this, Ben, since I have no idea what you mean."

Her words have no effect. Ben is too wise for the *dog ate my homework, my grandmother died, it was so long ago* excuse. "Caroline knows," he informs his wife.

Lee grabs the table edge. "Knows what?"

"About you and Simon." Ben's lips purse with sucking-lemons distaste. "Your thing."

Thing? "What is a thing?"

"Don't play dumb."

"I'm not. You read my memoir. We've been over this."

"Not quite. Haven't you left something out?"

"You're the professor. You're the expert on history. *Past* history. You tell me."

He takes his pedagogical stance. His shoulders rise. His chin juts out. "Let's review the vocabulary: Tryst. Episode. Love. Copulation. Fucking. This is a multiple-choice test, Lee. Pick one of the above. Or . . ." He hits his spoon against his water glass. "Adultery."

"Ben!"

"Caroline told me."

Lee leans back. The vinyl pops. At another time, under other circumstances, the slow gassy sound would make them laugh. Nothing's funny now. She's not so much stunned as confused. Her fears circle like hovering crows. She remembers her worries over having, in her moment of abandon, abandoned her purple underpants. Her terror of Caroline's finding them. But she hadn't forgotten the underpants. Had she left behind some other Hansel and Gretel trail of crumbs?

She pins her eyes to the bottle of Worcestershire. *Focus on an object*, a yoga teacher once instructed. An object closer than it appears? She tries to sort her thoughts. When Caroline admitted she wanted a man like Ben, did Simon leap to the equal-opportunity challenge and confess he'd had Ben's wife? No, he would never, ever . . .

Ben taps his spoon again. As if he's signaling the end of a round. "She found letters," he supplies.

Letters. Letters from when she was eighteen? Letters, which along with the rabbit's foot, he kept for thirty years? She's in the middle of a nineteenth-century melodrama while sitting in a twentieth-century vinyl booth. Are letters a strand of Marguerite's DNA not simply passed on to her but genetically programmed to trip her up?

"They must have been letters I wrote when I was eighteen. Before I met you."

"Yes. But he kept them. And Caroline's no dummy. She can put two and two together. I gather she managed to worm your little secret out of him."

Yet there's a hole in the logic. There's a problem with the sequencing. "When did Caroline tell you this?" she demands.

"Yesterday afternoon."

"Yesterday?"

"I saw her. She lives near the Forest of Dean." He shrugs. "She gave me the CD," he adds conversationally.

The waitress brings their lunch. Her gingham bow has come untied and swings over her left ear. Lee looks at the chicken soup skimmed with fat; at the sandwiches oozing globs of mayonnaise. Her stomach turns. She pushes her plate away.

Ben picks up his sandwich. He stuffs half into his mouth. Egg flakes his chin. Normally Lee would offer a napkin, point a wifely finger at the offending spot. She keeps her mouth shut. Her hands clutched in her lap.

"Caroline is remarkable," says Ben. "She runs this organic chicken farm. She started it all herself. Now it's a huge operation. Her chickens are famous. She's the Perdue of England. Though hers are of a higher, purer quality. Nutritionally sound. Free range. She just won the royal warrant of approval. It will be part of the packaging. She supplies all the best restaurants in London. Can you believe this? Un-beknownst to me, it was her chicken I ate at the Savoy Grill when I was taken there by my publishers."

Screw the chickens, Lee wants to say. Or let plump, perfect Caroline take care of that. She examines her husband. What is his wide-as-the-plains face but ideal camouflage? Can you ever know anyone? Even those you're sure you know best? "So you saw Caroline," she states.

"*You* saw Simon."

"What is this? Tit for tat? Cookies parceled out among the children in equal numbers, of an equal size?"

"You've had your fling." He slurps his soup. Even open and flecked with yolk, his mouth is smug. "And I've had mine."

She starts. "You had a fling?"

"That time in England. It was raining. You stayed with Simon. Caroline and I took the children to the Forest of Dean."

"You were with the children! *Our* children!" she exclaims. Indignant on their behalf fifteen years in retrospect.

"Don't worry. We were very discreet. We—"

Lee holds up her hand. "Spare me the details."

"Believe me, I wouldn't give you them." His voice turns kinder. Soup glistens in the corners of his lips. "Or ask for yours. It's over now. A bit of midsummer madness."

"Madness with consequences."

"Who are you to call the kettle black?"

She ignores this remark. She continues. "Simon told me Caroline left him because—I quote here—she wanted a husband like Ben."

His eyes widen. He struggles not to appear as pleased as he patently feels. "He said that? She said that?"

Lee looks away.

He shoots his arm across the table. He pushes aside the Worcestershire. "Let's make a pact. Let's swear never to discuss this again." He taps her fingers. "I love you, Lee. We're here. Together. We've got a history." His eyes hold hers. She sees the boy he was. The boy who scraped gum off her hem. The boy she married. The eyes she gazed up into and pledged her troth.

The same eyes fall to her uneaten sandwich. "Do you mind?"

"Be my guest."

Unpleasant business completed, unfinished business finished, he starts to talk about Nathaniel. The cover; the galleys; who'll give blurbs. How easily, his easy smile implies, they've disposed of one topic and have moved on to the next.

His words wash over her.

Ben did what she did.

Did he feel what she felt?

The question is: what does she still feel?

She excuses herself. She gets up. She staggers toward the ladies' room. Her feet are lead. Her body feels jet-lagged— as if she's crossed two time zones in the one hour they've been traveling.

The ladies' room door bears a swan on the front. She looks across the hall to the men's, which sports a generic bird wearing a top hat and tie. Raptors. Birds of prey. Men— all peas in their higher-up pod. Can opposite sexes ever inhabit the same range? Can they ever successfully share one nest? She runs water over her hands. Next to her, a garden club lady leans into the mirror. She draws on a rosebud mouth. She gazes down at the basin. "If you keep your hands in water so long, dear, you'll pucker the skin."

Lee turns off the spigot.

The woman nods approval. She's somebody's mother, Lee is sure. By the look of the white curls, the owl-shaped bifocals, somebody's grandmother, too. And as soon as Lee thinks this, she feels such a sudden sharp sting at the loss of her grandmother—of *a* grandmother—that she bumps back a step.

The woman reaches for her. "Are you all right, dear? You seem a little peaked." The woman pats her arm. She smells of rose petals, of lilacs. "Was it something you ate?"

Lee is so grateful for her concern, her sweet Granny face, the old-fashioned rickrack trimming her blouse, her bright green suit, her flowery perfume, the lily of the valley clipped to her lapel, her thick ankles in their lace-up shoes, her un-Marguerite grandmotherhood, she wants to fling her arms around her. To lay her head on that maternal breast.

"I'm fine," she says.

The woman notices her ring. She bends closer. Lee can feel the heat of her breath. "What a beautiful emerald. The color of new leaves; the depth of old moss."

"It was my grandmother's."

"She must have loved you very much to give you this."

"I suppose she did."

The woman smiles. Interest and concern crinkle her brow. Her blue eyes—robin's egg blue—are expectant. Encouraging. Go on, they say.

Lee goes on. "Her name was Marguerite."

The woman giggles. A sound like wind chimes. "Imagine that! Marguerite, you must know, is the Italian word for Daisy."

It is? she marvels. "I never knew," she says.

"I do, because that's my name. Daisy. Daisy Maguire." She shakes her head in wonder. "Marguerite," she repeats. "As president of the garden club . . ." She points to her badge.

Lee looks. She reads *Busby Grove Garden Club*, and underneath, the word *President*.

". . . I confess to being a bit flower-obsessed." She adjusts a perfect curl. "My three daughters are called Violet, Lily, and Rose."

Lee laughs. "My mother was Violet Rose. My name is Magnolia."

The woman claps. The charms on her bracelet—spade, hoe, shears—jingle. "Magnolia. Lovely. I adore magnolias. I have the most exquisite tree in my garden. Though not native to England, it does particularly well here. Funny isn't it, how plants often grow better in foreign landscapes. In soil not native to them."

"They do?" Lee stares at her.

Daisy nods. "Because they escape the pests and problems at home. Magnolias bloom profusely in these parts. Some absolutely thrive. Then there's your Virginia creeper, for example; it's all over the walls at Oxford. It's extremely popular there, though in your country it's often disdained as a weed." She puts her lipstick back into her bag, which is made of straw and embroidered with tulips. "The things one finds out in the ladies' loo." She chuckles. "We're going on a little trip to the Forest of Dean. The roses are at their prime." She checks her watch. "Our bus leaves in about fifteen minutes."

Lee wipes her hands. She clears her throat. As if from a long distance, as if from a stranger's mouth, she hears herself ask, "Is there room on your bus?"

Daisy tilts her head. She considers. "Actually, yes. Perrin Ireland and Claire Cook couldn't make it at the last minute. Both husbands under the weather. Husbands can be so demanding. Though not, of course, for you young people.

Things are different now." She hesitates. She searches Lee's face. "Do you want . . . ?"

"I left something behind in Netherend. It's only a few miles from the Forest of Dean."

"It'll be no trouble at all to drop you off, dear. In fact, I'll make sure you sit next to me. I'll insist on hearing every detail about your delightful grandmother. Bus number two. The iris decal on the side. Let's meet in fifteen minutes in the car park."

"I'm going back," Lee tells Ben.

Ben rises from his seat. He drops his spoon. It clatters to the floor. He leaves it there. "You're what?" he exclaims.

"Going back," she repeats.

"Not funny," he says.

"It isn't a joke."

"You could've fooled me. I've never heard anything more absurd, more ridiculous."

"I can see how you'd take it that way. And I understand. But I've made up my mind."

He stares at her. "May I ask why?" His words are measured.

"Unfinished business, I guess."

"For Pete's sake, Lee," he cries, exasperation poking up like weeds through the just-mowed surface of his tone, "didn't we just agree to bring this chapter to a close? Come on, we've got tickets. Plans. Our plane—"

"I realize that."

"Then?"

"I have to do this, Ben. I have to. I don't know what's going to happen. But I need to spend some time to find out." She puts her hands on his shoulders. "I'm hitching a ride with the ladies of the garden club."

She takes her hands away. Ben sinks back down. The upholstery wheezes and pops. Slumped in the seat, Ben appears smaller, deflated as if all the air's been sucked out of him.

Guilt rises.

She tamps it down.

"I'm sorry," she says.

He bestows the sort of disdainful tsk he'd give a failing student. "You're not making sense," he states.

"Not to you, perhaps."

"Lee," he pleads. "It's been so long. *Us.* So much water over the dam."

Her jaw tightens. "Don't you suppose I know that?" She forces herself to smile. To speak with the brisk false cheer of a nurse. "You'll be fine. You *are* fine. What's more . . ."—she grabs a lifeline—". . . Nathaniel's going to win the Pulitzer."

It works. He brightens. "You think?"

"I'm sure."

"In that case . . ." His eyes shine; visions of history prize sugarplums dance in front of him. He blinks. ". . . even if not the Pulitzer, there'll be testimonials. Celebrations. You'll be missing out. You're my wife. I want you by my side, to share in my success. You've lived so long with me and with Nathaniel, you've earned the right to reap the rewards of my life's work. Besides," he pauses and Lee can see the lightbulb spark, "all my publicity couldn't help but have a spillover effect on your own book."

"I wouldn't want to steal your thunder, Ben."

"How could you? You're my wife."

She looks at him. Then drops her head into her hands.

For a few moments, they both fall silent. They study the tabletop as if underneath its laminate lie answers to questions they've barely formed. Ben grows solemn. He frowns. "But why, Lee?" he asks again. "Because of me? Because of Caroline? Because—"

"No. Not Caroline. Not you. Not even Simon. It's me, Ben. I can't even begin to explain. All I can say is something's lost and must be found." Her voice breaks.

His own voice shatters. "Lee," he whispers. "Lee," he entreats.

She leans forward. She pulls back.

He shakes his head. "I don't believe this. I don't believe this is happening to me." His hair falls over his brow. He brushes it away. "You've got three children. A house. A husband." He pauses. "Besides," his mouth twists, "you're no spring chicken, dare I add."

Lee starts to slide to the end of the booth. "I'd better get my suitcases. The bus is waiting. I have to leave."

"Stay there. I wouldn't want anyone—especially any of these old ladies here—to think I'd allow my own wife to carry her own bags."

"It's hardly necessary . . . under the circumstances."

"Permit me," he orders. "I insist."

Ben gets up. He goes to the car.

Lee sits back. She stares at a crumpled napkin, the crust of his sandwich. A fly bounces on the rim of his soup bowl. She brushes salt from her lap.

When he returns, he's gripping the handles of her bags so tightly the tendons of his hands pop up. He bangs the suitcases against his side. "Do you really intend to set off with these? What could be sillier?"

She reaches out.

He swings the bags behind his legs. His chin tilts up with the catch-me-if-you-can defiance of a child. But she's been married to him much too long not to recognize the flickers of sadness and fear underneath the bold front.

For a second, she hesitates. *You've got three children. A house. A husband*, rattles inside her head. Then she hunches forward to grab a welted canvas edge. "Let go, Ben," she demands. "Let go."

"You've made your point."

"Please."

"I don't want to let go," he says. "I categorically refuse." He doesn't move.

They watch each other.

Until his mixed emotions funnel into a single bolt of pure rage. He slams her bags onto the floor.

A luggage tag falls off. It rolls against her foot.

The ladies are now filing through the door. Lee can pick out Daisy's green suit, the tulips on her pocketbook. A yellow scarf flaps over one woman's shoulder like a wing.

"How can you? Have you lost your mind? We have the perfect life together. A perfect marriage." Ben is nearly shouting. A busboy, moving toward them, swivels his tray in the direction of another booth.

Lee bends down. She scoops up the luggage tag: *Lee Emery, 58 Evergreen Road, Homestead, Maine, USA.*

"It won't work out," she hears.

Lee says nothing.

"You'll be back."

She turns away.

"He's a loser, Lee," Ben calls after her.

She crunches the tag in her fist. She throws it in the trash. She heads for the door. Outside now, the garden club ladies circle the white-pebbled paths, a resplendent flock of them swooping and bobbing toward the car park. Somewhere, not far away, an airplane takes off. In a shaft of sunlight, Lee can see the gleaming silver bus. "Wait for me," she cries and starts to run.

Acknowledgments

My heartfelt thanks to:

My fab-u-lous agent, Lisa Bankoff, who, among her many extraordinary talents, can pull rabbits out of hats.

Lucia Macro, whose enthusiastic commitment to publishing this paperback has made all the difference.

Jamie Raab, Tina Andreadis, Esi Sogah, Tina Wexler, and Dee Dee DeBartlo for their considerable contributions of time and effort on behalf of these pages and my other books.

Darling John Aherne, this novel's guardian angel and guiding light.

My first reader and exceptional friend, Elinor Lipman, for her perfect eye, ear, and heart.

My boys and their girls, Daniel Medwed and Sharissa

Jones, Jono Medwed and Marnie Davidoff for unconditional and unwavering support.

My husband Howard, who had the good sense to make the phone call and to take the trip. That was the start. Yet again, kid, and with my love.

A+

AUTHOR
INSIGHTS,
EXTRAS, &
MORE...

FROM

**MAMEVE
MEDWED**

AND

AVON A

Following is an excerpt from
Of Men and Their Mothers
By Mameve Medwed
Coming in May from William Morrow

One

If you look inside my refrigerator, here's what you'll see: one shriveled lemon, one kiwi banana yogurt a week past its sell-by date, a bottle of Don Popov vodka, a five-year-old bag of coffee beans from Brazil. If you pull open the freezer compartment, you'll find two All-White Deluxe Pollock's Potpies so old they qualify for archeological excavation, three ice-encrusted popsicles, and breast milk in a mayonnaise jar, the Hellmann's label still intact.

No, it's not my breast milk. It's Jack's, or, rather, the property of Jack's client at Legal Aid. Jack is my on-the-way-out boyfriend. The milk belongs to Darlene Lattanzio, whose mother-in-law has custody of Baby Anthony Vincent Lattanzio while the courts and the Department of Social Services decide whether Darlene's an unfit parent. Darlene hates her mother-in-law.

I can empathize. Mine was worse, I told her when she telephoned a few months ago about sending Jack to make a deposit in my breast milk bank.

"No way," she said.

"You'd better believe it," I said.

"Not so," she said.

"Yes, so," I said.

On and on we went like toddlers in the sandbox until I declared a truce. "We'll agree that we *both* have horrible mothers-in-law," I mediated.

Actually, mine is an ex mother-in-law. Mother of the unlamented ex, Rex Pollock, heir to those freezer-burned Pollock Pot Pies still in my fridge. I don't get it, all those women friendly with their former spouses, yakking to them on the telephone, meeting for an old-times'-sake dinner. The previous and current husbands and wives even vacation together, their babies siblinged up with halves and steps. One big happy blended family, all the lumps and odd ingredients filtered through a sieve and smashed smooth.

Not my situation. To take a page from the tree falling in the forest book—can you count a mother alone in her kitchen as part of a family if you can't see anyone else there? My son is at his father's for his court-mandated summer visit. He's one hour away, though he might as well be on another continent.

I guess I should introduce myself. Maisie, birth certificate Margaret, Grey, formerly Maisie Grey-Pollock. Though I usually reply "Cambridge" when people ask me where I live, my official residence is actually Somerville, Massachusetts, on Forest Street. Outside my window, I can see the green signpost that announces *Cambridge Somerville Line*. Half of my toilet seat and all of my washbasin are in Cambridge; the rest of my apartment is in Somerville. My parking sticker bears the Somerville city seal and I'm registered to vote in the firehouse on Lowell Avenue. When I get up to flush, I sometimes have one foot in each city, a symbol of my divided, sliced-down-the-middle life. This worries me.

I've got a lot to worry about. In due course you'll hear the complete catalogue. My immediate focus, however, is the breast milk. It's been there longer than the glaciered popsicles. At first, Jack swore that Darlene Lattanzio's landlord was supposed to fetch it. He didn't. Next there was talk that a boyfriend might show up with an insulated tote bag. No one rang my bell. This really annoyed me as I waited out the eight a.m. to six p.m. sentence of household imprisonment customarily set by deliverymen. Meanwhile, things went bad between Jack and me, and in the process of deciding whether we were going to survive as a couple, the breast milk got forgotten. I didn't accuse Jack of not giving his pro bono client (his law firm insists on a certain number of hours of public service) the same attention he would have allotted one of his corporate bigwigs. But I certainly thought about it.

Now I wonder how long I can freeze the breast milk. I take out the jar; the milk is the color that the stationer who engraved my wedding invitations called ecru. I wanted to make my own invitations—my own silk screens on hand-made 100 percent recycled paper—but Mrs. Pollock, the MIL in-waiting, wouldn't hear of it. No class, she said, a phrase she repeated almost as often as the words *the* and *it*. Once, from the other side of the room, I heard her stage-whisper to her son, "I must say I have doubts about your fiancée's" . . . ominous pause . . . "background. Her taste. And intelligence."

She was wrong. My family—the Greys, my father's Episcopalian side—had the background. Or at least what passes for class among certain near-extinct American dinosaurs—good lineage, good bones, good if shabby antiques, good schools, fish forks and dessert spoons. My mother, the daughter of CCNY college professors descended from Talmudic scholars, provided the intelligence. We just had no money. The life of the mind doesn't fill the pocketbook; trust funds depleted by black sheep heirs don't pass through the generations to cushion earnest but clueless businessmen like my dad.

But my mother-in-law will require a whole separate section, if not a doctoral dissertation, all her own. For the moment, let's keep to the subject at hand: this jar of milk *in* my hand.

I shake the jar. It's frozen solid. What did I expect? The slurping liquid of a Magic 8 Ball? I suppose Darlene Lattanzio was in love with the father of her baby, too. But when things go sour and the milk of marital kindness curdles (if you will), look where love gets you. The fallout can flatten hearts and minds like a category five hurricane. Until nothing is left in its wake except for the baby, the prize in the crackerjack box of a cracking marriage.

I know it's a cliché but still. . . . can there ever be a greater love than that between a mother and her child? All you have to do is sign up for an introductory art history course and study all those Madonnas. The blissful look on the faces of the mothers. The adoration passing between her and her child, the way she clutches him to her breast. As if she'll never let go.

When your child is a newborn, you can't begin to imagine the letting go. During the first halcyon years of marriage, could you predict your husband would ever be other than your heart's desire? Cradling your infant, can you conceive of never again cuddling a sweet-smelling soft-cheeked baby? No matter what comes latter— overactive sweat glands, a scratchy jaw—the maternal, if not the marital, bond remains. And even though, these days, there seems to be a war zone in the hall between Tommy's room and my own, such a tie is a consolation.

I look at the photo stuck to the refrigerator. Tommy scowls from the back row of his soccer team. How can Darlene not feel about Anthony Vincent the way I feel about Tommy? It's in the blood. It's in the hormones. It's an artifact of the umbilical cord.

I'm not naïve. I understand some crazy rotten people abuse children, neglect them or worse. But I'm pretty sure Darlene isn't one of them. Did she really leave Anthony Vincent alone to go to a bar? Jack didn't think so. He confided that, contrary to most of his pro bono clients, this particular accused was innocent of the accusation. He swears that the father was at home slumped down in front of the TV. His sleep apnea caused him to snore so loudly one of the neighbors offered to testify as to those thunderous stops and starts. Then the neighbor moved away with no forwarding address. As a result, it's the baby's father's word against the baby's mother. And it's the baby's father's mother—the MIL—swooping in and laying a claim on what's not hers.

If you ask me, I know Darlene's innocent the way I knew OJ was guilty. When you experience such visceral certainty, gloves that don't fit, snores that rattle walls hardly matter. Only a loving mother would go to the trouble of pumping her breasts and messengering jars of breast milk over to a neutral party's refrigerator.

Now I scrape some ice off the Hellmann's glass and slide the jar into two doubled-up Ziploc bags. I throw away the popsicles. I dump the Pollock's Potpies in the trash. And even though I need to rid my life of emotionally charged artifacts, I stick the milk back in the freezer. How can I toss it out knowing I might be depriving a child?

It's been sixteen years since I had breast milk. I never had to pump it or freeze it or refrigerate it. For all those months until Tommy's serious teeth came in, I was an endless on site, on the spot, on demand fount of nourishment. "I'm here. I'm right here," I used to call to him. "I'm at your beck and call."

"You're not here for me," was Rex's parting salute.

"And I suppose your mother is?"

"I won't even grace that with a reply." Rex opened his car trunk and hoisted into it his suitcase, his box of books, and the basket of dirty underwear his mother was dying to export to her own Tide-and-Clorox-stocked laundry room to wash. *And* iron. Do I dare mention she ironed his shorts?

These days Tommy's the one who's hardly ever here, either hanging out in the Square with his friends or tethered to his iPod, so inaccessible he might as well be at that boarding school for children from broken homes his grandmother wanted to send him to.

I sigh a few mother-of-a-teenager sighs. There are some things I can't do anything about. And others I can. I find Darlene Lattanzio's telephone number stuck to the refrigerator with a grinning chicken magnet. I dial.

"Yeah? Who is it?" a man answers.

"Mister . . . Mister Lattanzio?"

"You jokin' or what?"

"Whom am I speaking to?"

"Not that nutcase of a husband, that's for sure. Lady, I'm not buying anything. What do you want?"

"Are you the . . ." I pause. ". . . the *gentleman* who was supposed to pick up . . ." I pause again. Somehow the words *breast milk* seem too sexually charged to voice to a perfect stranger—and a hostile one at that—over the phone. ". . . a package in Somerville?"

"What the hell do you take me for? The UPS guy? Who is this? Some kind of hoity toity anchor woman?"

"Could I speak to Darlene, please?"

"Why?"

"I have a question for her."

"Yeah? Well, get in line. Like where did she put the keys to my car? Like when will she get her ass home? Like why there's nothing in the fucking fridge. Like . . ." he stops. I hear a bottle cap pop off, then the slam of the phone.

Well, it's pretty obvious that Darlene is still making bad choices in men. We've got more in common than we thought: not just lousy mothers-in-law, but boyfriends as iffy as the husbands that preceded them, and nothing in our fucking fridge.

What does it mean that the only nourishing item in my refrigerator is the property—close personal property—of somebody else? What does it mean that I'm only incubating it? I might as well be the holding tank for chickens waiting to be baked into a Pollock's Potpie. Or the rented womb of a surrogate mother. This dilemma is all Jack's fault.

Jack. In spite of our mutually-agreed-to cooling-off period, in spite of our planned meeting two weeks hence to hash things out in the demilitarized war zone of Redbone's bar, I think about breaking our pact and calling him. Jack's been my boyfriend for nearly a year; that is, if an on-the-cusp of forty woman can have a "boyfriend." A boyfriend is what Tommy is to those girls who leave the vampirish red marks all over his adorable neck and who instant-message him half the night keeping him from history papers and algebra. What's Jack to me? You'd need a Shakespeare to come up with the right term and a Freud to deconstruct the emotional symbols behind the word.

Well, whatever he is, I dial the number of his Boston law firm—the chances that he'll be occupying his cubicle at Somerville Legal Services are slim.

"Maisie," exhales his secretary, Judy Pareti, the second she picks up the phone.

Oh, how I hate caller ID. "Hi, Judy," I answer. I hold off from my once habitual *how's the husband, the kids, seen any good movies lately?* attempt to bond with the (platonic) women in Jack's life. "Is he in?" I ask. "This is a business call," I clarify, as if I'm a client needing an estate plan.

"Haven't heard from you in a while," she says. "Let me check."

I wonder what women she *has* heard from. Perhaps a whole catalogue of female names were lining up on the caller ID waiting to be put through to Jack. At least with my ex-husband there was only his mother and me. Not much of a comfort. Jack, on the other hand, is what one of Tommy's Jessicas or Sophies or Zoes or Chloes or the current (though one hopes equally temporary) September Silva would call a babe magnet. Like Tommy. "I can't help it," my son would say with his bad-boy grin. "Women just fall all over me."

"They're *girls*," I said. "At your age, they're *girls*."

"Maisie," Judy says now, "I can put you through. But just for a minute. He's up to his *ears*."

"Maisie," Jack snaps. "I thought we called a moratorium." He taps a pencil against the receiver, a Morse code whose dots and dashes signal *don't waste my time*.

"I'm fine, thank you. How are you?"

"Do you have a *legal* problem?" He sighs. "I assume if there were a problem I'd hear about it." He hesitates. "Right. I guess I *am* hearing about it. What's up?"

"It's Darlene Lattanzio's breast milk. I want to get rid of it."

"That's why you called me at work?"

"Is that a crime?" I ask. Maybe it is a crime to call an on-the-outs boyfriend at work, a boyfriend who never was that much in, a boyfriend who never placed his running shoes under your bed, stuck his toenail clippers in your bureau drawer, a man who never left an extra set of clean underwear behind.

But he is a man who left his client's breast milk in my refrigerator. Which when you look at it—the way I see it—does connote a kind of intimacy.

"If I remember correctly, your refrigerator was never so full that storing a client's property meant an encroachment on your space," he points out.

"Not my *physical* space." I wait. "But certainly my personal space, my psychic space. Besides, Darlene Lattanzio isn't my client; she's yours." I stop. "And you do have a freezer compartment of your own." A fact that, for some reason, has never before occurred to me.

Nor to Jack either, obviously, since he shuts up. Maybe he feels that storing a client's breast milk in your bachelor flat is like keeping somebody's box of Tampax on your night table. Maybe the utilitarian purpose of breasts threatens a guy for whom milky mounds connate only all things erotic. I shake my head. I don't want to get into this.

Neither does Jack. "Look, I'll call Darlene and ask. Maybe the milk's no longer any good—hasn't it been a few weeks?"

"Indeed. *Longer*. Besides, when Tommy comes home from his father's I'm going to have to fill my fridge with all the healthy food a growing boy needs."

"I understand." In the background, I hear Judy's voice pose a question. "Overnight it," Jack orders. "Actually, Maisie, I'm glad you called."

"You are?"

"Yes, I was meaning to telephone you. In fact I put a notation in my daily planner for this afternoon."

I could just picture it: *file Supreme Court appeal, meet with Presidential committee, set up multinational corporation, sign trust documents for Saudi royalty, call Maisie*. I am not thrilled. "In spite of our moratorium?"

"This is business. I have an idea. It's about Darlene."

"Oh." I try not to sound too disappointed. "A new batch of breast milk traveling on the Underground Railroad to Somerville?" I ask.

"She needs a job, some stability. But she's not trained for much of anything, though she picks up a little money off the books cleaning houses. It's not enough. Plus she'll have to have flexible hours when she gets Anthony Vincent back from Mrs. Lattanzio."

"Are you suggesting I hire her to clean my house?"

"Of course not." Somehow his tone of voice does not imply my apartment is so spic and span I don't need extra cleaning help. "I thought you might take her on in your business. Let her work for you at . . . oh, what's it called? . . . yes, Factotum, Inc."

What's it called? The nerve, I fume, Factotum, Inc. being not only part of our pillow talk for almost one solid year but also the topic sentence in the contracts he helped draw up for me.

Oblivious, he goes on. "I think it would be great for both of you if you hire her."

I am too proud to say I can barely scrape by myself, let alone hire a second person; besides, if I were to hire a second person, Darlene Lattanzio would not be the person I'd have in mind. "As you know, my company is a company of one," I lecture.

He reads my mind. "You don't have to *pay* her. That was not my intention. I thought she might work out as an intern. I thought she could learn" . . . he pauses . . . "a trade?"

I ignore the question mark on the end of *trade*. "Really?"

"I figured she could start with you."

"You're kidding."

"Come on. You could use some help. Let's face it, your life is a bit of a mess."

"There's nothing wrong with my life that getting rid of Darlene Lattanzio's breast milk won't cure."

"Think about it. It will be good training for her. It'll be a help to you."

"Will it?"

"And you'll be making a contribution to closing the gap between the haves and the have-nots. Look at it as your own pro bono work." In the background a buzzer goes off. Voices rise. Someone calls, *Jack*. "Gotta run," he says.

"I'll think about it," I reply, but he has already hung up the phone.

Q&A with Mameve Medwed,
Author of END OF AN ERROR

Q: How did you get the idea for the book?

I always wanted to write about my grandmother, a larger-than-life, Auntie Mame kind of figure who took me to Europe when I was eighteen. Though I had written essays and short stories about her, I needed a larger canvas. She was a force of nature I hadn't exhausted yet. I also hoped to do something more ambitious than my other two novels—to cover a larger amount of time and spread myself over a greater geographical area. And though I always write with humor, I also planned to dig deeper into the sadness and the losses in my characters' lives.

And of course, like everyone, I've always been intrigued by the *what if* of first love. What if you'd picked that person instead of this one, how would your life have turned out? I happened to meet an English boy on that trip to Europe with my grandmother. As a naïve, small town girl from Maine, I was bowled over by the accent, by the fish and chips, by what I saw as exotic and sophisticated, and all those *what ifs* started flooding in. Though the book's scenarios weren't mine, I did manage to find my inner Marmite (as a novelist friend pointed out).

Let's face it, the power of first love lasts forever. I read somewhere that in all those high school searches on the internet—the ones advertising *find your lost classmates*—people ten, thirty, forty years out of high school are surfing those sites primarily to reconnect with old loves.

So the questions that came to me were not only what if you married your first love, but also what would it be like to revisit that teenage boyfriend at different stages of your life: as a young mother, as a contentedly long married woman in your forties. And notwithstanding how we all pledge eternal love at the first blush of first love, what if you can't quite let go of those promises? What if something happens to make you feel that not keeping a promise when you're young might have terrible consequences later on? Might things have been different if you kept your word?

Q: Do you have certain themes?

What I am dealing with in this novel are the many kinds of love—the love of a small town girl for a worldly, glamorous grandmother, the elation of first love, the secure love of a woman for a husband who's her rock, the love of a mother for her children, and the pain of not only the losses in life that we all have to bear but also the changes that occur both between people and inside ourselves.

Another thread I weave through the book is the safety of the known: husbands, parents, home, hearth, familiar food, the side of the bed you sleep on, etc., as opposed to the excitement and adventure of the unknown: an exotic grandmother, foreign cities, a boyfriend you knew when you were eighteen and no longer know, the terror and thrill of leaving what's comfortable, of leaving the nest. Not to mention the difference between being eighteen yourself and having children that age.

People always wonder what they might have missed. In life we don't usually have a chance to find out, but my character does. It's a gift for a writer to play God that way.

Q: Is this autobiographical?

It's the same issue of the known and unknown. I start with what I know: my grandmother, first love, Maine where I was born and grew up, marriage, family. But then the story and the characters take on a life of their own and grow and develop and do such surprising things that they are no longer your grandmother, your kids, your husband (and thank goodness for that!), but their own people who might or might not bear a faint family resemblance to their actual ancestors. That's the art, I suppose—creating a world more real than the one it's based upon. It's like dialogue. If I were to transpose a conversation word for word, you'd be bored; the writing would feel awkward and stiff—but when dialogue works well enough that your readers praise its authenticity and laud your perfect ear, you've touched both the artifice and the art in writing. The writer struggles for the same transformation the painter attempts: those few lines that can magically reveal an essence, a soul, that an exact replica can't.

Thus, the fiction writer has the best of both worlds, the real and the imagined. In real life, I married my childhood sweetheart and now I am writing about the one that got away (and creating what might have happened if he hadn't). So I can have my cake and eat it too. I can change history. Pimples can turn to smooth skin, stammering to articulateness, being dumped to being pursued.

Q: Did you ever see your English boyfriend again?

I did, after many years. And I was so relieved that I hadn't ended up with him. I couldn't picture myself with the person he'd become. And I was horrified by the place—a farm in the muddy English countryside with not a neighbor (let alone a Starbucks or a movie theater or bookstore) in sight.

Q: How would you feel if he read this novel?

Just terrible. And I hope there's no chance of that—he's a Luddite, no computers, no answering machine. (Don't ask how I know this!)

Q: Since this novel is your third, was it easier to write than the first? And if a first novel is like first love, is the writing (and the publication) also less exciting?

No, with each new book you start all over again. A whole new set of characters, a new story, new problems, and always the fear and doubt over whether you can pull it off. Were the first two just flukes? Can you do this once more? Who was that person who managed to write two novels? You're astonished it was you!

Your first novel is like your first child. You can't believe you will ever be so enthralled again. But then comes the second, the third child. Let me quote my character, Lee Emery, on the birth of her children in this:

"She remembers holding Johnny, then two years later, Timmy, then three years after that, Maggie. Her first baby in her arms for the first time had the power of first love. She had worried about the second child. And the third. What could ever match that moment when Johnny wrapped his translucent fingers around hers? Wouldn't the strength of those initial feelings be diluted over time, by repetition? She knew the second-child syndrome: hand-me-down clothes and nary a photograph. But it hadn't been the case. Each new baby thrilled her as much as the one that preceded it."

Q: How do you find so much humor in situations potentially so serious and even sad?

This is a question that goes to the heart of what and how I write, of what and how I think. I've come to realize that among a lot of readers there's a built-in conviction that something funny has to be light (or lite), that dealing with universal issues of love, of family relationships, requires solemnity and a dirge to accompany it. Many people assume you don't joke about serious subjects. Maybe it's the Puritan (or the Maine) in us that requires any pain to be painted in the gray tones of suffering. But because so much of life is ridiculous, I trust my readers to see (and they always do) that underneath the jokes lies the real stuff. Stories are more poignant if they aren't underscored by heavy-duty orchestration. Humor can deal with profound themes. Easy reading takes hard writing, says Trollope. It's a sentence that always comforts me.

Photo by Debi Milligan

MAMEVE MEDWED is the author of *Mail*, *Host Family*, *How Elizabeth Barrett Browning Saved My Life*, and the forthcoming *Of Men and Their Mothers*. Her stories, essays, and reviews have appeared in many publications including the *Missouri Review*, *Redbook*, the *Boston Globe*, *Yankee*, *Playgirl*, the *Washington Post*, and *Newsday*. Born in Maine, she and her husband have two sons and live in Cambridge, Massachusetts.

Mameve Medwed